# WOLFE'S LAIR

## Club Twist Book One

**Alice Raine**

Published by Accent Press 2018

The right of Alice Raine to be identified as the Author of
the Work has been asserted by her in accordance with the
Copyright, Designs and Patents Act, 1988

ISBNS :

Print: 9781786152572

eBook  9781786152565

# Other titles by Alice Raine

**The Untwisted Series:**

The Darkness Within Him

Out of the Darkness

Into The Light

Enlightened

The Final Twist

**The Revealed Series**

Unmasked

Unravelled

Unveiled

Undone

**Short Stories:**

Christmas with Nicolas

Christmas with Nathan

Sinful Seduction

# Acknowledgements

The first book in a new series is always an exciting and nerve-racking time, so I just want to take a moment to dedicate this book to my lovely readers, which seeing as you are reading this, presumably means *you*. Thank you! Your support and encouragement really do mean the world to me.

A huge thanks must go to my fabulous editor, Liz – how you put up with my rambling and typos is beyond me, but thank you, you are my very own grammar goddess!

I must also extend massive thanks to my publisher, Accent Press, for their continued support of my writing. In particular, Hazel and Nia for the time and effort you put into working with me.

Huge shout out to the beta readers who contributed to this book – I love you all for the constructive feedback and encouragement you always give me. So now for the name drop: Leah Wetherall, Sam Berwitz, Grace Lowrie, Melinda Knight, Beth Jones, and Heather Roadknight – massive hugs to each and every one of you!

My besties, Helen Lowrie and Karen Wilmot, for your never-ending support, book chats, and filthy gossiping sessions. (OK, so that last one is mostly Karen's fault ...) You are both such incredible women, and never fail to inspire me. Love ya!

Technical help with this book came from Sarah-Jayne McIntosh – again – thank you! You are now officially my go-to criminologist and law adviser!

Huge apologies if I have missed anyone out ...

Thanks again for reading,

Alice xx

# Prologue

I'd had dreams about him before.

A stranger with dark eyes, and a penetrating stare so intense that I *felt* his gaze upon me, way before I actually turned and found him watching me. At least I think I had. I work as a writer, so my dreams often blur with things I've read, or written, and sometimes it can be difficult to distinguish between them. I'd certainly had dreams about what my ideal man might look like, so perhaps that was what kept niggling at me tonight.

The feeling of being watched was definitely swirling around me, but as it fluttered across my skin again I dismissed the smoky images of the perfect man from my dreams, and put it down to nothing more than my overactive imagination playing tricks on me.

There was a very good reason why my brain was in overdrive tonight, and that was because I was in a place called Club Twist for the first time. This was not just a bar, or nightclub, as the name might outwardly indicate; oh no, it was London's most exclusive sex club, a place with an A-list clientele, and one where the members were encouraged to "explore their twisted side".

And I was now perched on a stool at the heart of it.

I read a quote once that said, "Life is found in the dance between your deepest desire and your greatest fear." I hadn't placed much importance on it at the time, but now, finding myself in the warm confines of this club, the quote came floating back into my mind, feeling particularly appropriate. Just a brief glance around had given me a deep feeling of resonance that I couldn't even begin to understand, but for some reason, I felt oddly at home here.

Even as my pulse rose with curiosity, there was no denying that these four walls also represented my greatest fears. I was Robyn Amber Scott, a relatively reclusive writer, with no sex life to speak of; there was no way I could want what these people had. Was there? And even if I did, I couldn't see myself managing to lower my inhibitions like the carefree souls who surrounded me.

Taking a sip of my drink, I gazed around, trying to loosen off the tension in my body. The deep bass of the music was helping me relax, but also soaking right into my core, throbbing in a way that was undeniably heightening my arousal. There was already a potent sexual energy saturating the air of the club around me, but I had to shift on my stool to ease the sudden ache between my legs.

My cheeks flushed with embarrassment at how easily my neglected sex drive had been ignited, and as I tried to suppress the jittery feeling in my stomach I became aware of something moving across my skin; not an actual touch, but a tingling awareness, like the gentle caress of fingers moving just millimetres above my skin and brushing the hairs there.

No one was touching me, but as I felt the sensation again, I became convinced that someone *was* watching me. Instead of being scared by the thought, exciting visions flashed in my mind again of a stranger with a stare so intense that it could reach across the packed room and affect me to this extent.

I let out a dry laugh at my vivid imagination. What was more likely was that I was allowing the heady experience of my surroundings to influence my thoughts. I'd reached the age of twenty-seven without ever experiencing an initial connection with anyone like that, so tonight was hardly likely to be my first.

The strange electricity zinged across my skin again just seconds later, warming me throughout, increasing my already amped arousal. Then, as if on cue, the hairs on the back of my neck all stood up in unison. It was so unusual that I scanned my eyes over the club goers to see if my earlier suspicions had been right.

Everyone seemed caught up in their own particular pleasures, be that drinking, dancing, or kissing. Even the girls I'd come with – my flatmates, Chloe and Sasha – were just dancing and enjoying themselves.

Shaking off my earlier sensation of being watched, I turned my gaze back to the bar, and that's when I saw *him*. Someone *was* watching me. And he was exactly as my dreams of the perfect man had conjured: dark hair, dark eyes, and with a dangerous air about him that made me shiver with anticipation. His eyes were intently focused on me from the far end of the bar; eyes so dark that they looked like smouldering coal across the space between us. The distance did nothing to reduce the impact of his gaze, because my skin went wild with chills, and my heart accelerated so rapidly that I could hear it thundering in my ears.

Try as I might, I just couldn't drag my eyes away. His gaze locked with mine, somehow freezing me on the spot. He appeared to be rather handsome, but he was partly in the shadows, which made it tricky to tell. Thinking about it, his place in the darkness almost seemed menacing, but I was also intrigued by the thread of electricity that seemed to be connecting us. Just as I was mulling this over, he shifted slightly, his whole body coming into view as he leaned sideways against the bar, his gaze still fixed with mine.

It was now confirmed – he was definitely a very handsome man. In fact, it would be no exaggeration to say he was quite possibly the best-looking man I'd ever laid eyes on in all my years on this planet. With his chiselled cheekbones and unruly hair, he was the perfect mixture. Drop-dead gorgeous meets dark and dangerous – because this man was dangerous. Just one short glance at his come-to-bed eyes, sexy smirk, and overtly confident posture convinced me of that fact.

There was something emanating from him that screamed "run", but even sensing this, I couldn't persuade my head to turn away. He was utterly compelling, and his eyes continued to hold mine captive. He didn't seem to care that he was staring, either. In fact, as his gaze flitted briefly across my body and returned to my eyes, he looked rather smug about it. With his half smile, and the way his eyes were possessively burning into me, it felt like he assumed every right to watch me. Like he already considered me to be his, somehow.

That last thought caused shivers to run up my spine, and finally kick-started my brain into dropping my gaze from his. Instead of turning away as I had planned, I found myself looking over his tall, broad body, which was wrapped up to perfection in a dark three-piece suit and crisp white shirt.

**Looks, dress sense, and a stare that sent my hormones crazy. Good lord. He was over ten metres away,** but somehow this stranger had brought my dreams to life and, in the process, sent my mind and body wild. Giving a dry, nervous laugh, I ripped my gaze from his body and forced myself to turn away. I was here to research my novel, not find a man. Dreams were fine when they happened in the darkness of your bedroom, but stepping beyond that safety was a whole other level, and not one I could contemplate. I downed the last of my drink, turned back to my phone, and saved the notes that I'd made so far. Perhaps it was time I left.

# Chapter One

## Robyn

*Four hours earlier*

Grinding my teeth in annoyance, I listened as Sasha huffed out a breathy moan for what must have been the fifth time in two minutes. I rotated my neck, trying to loosen the stiff muscles, and leaned back from my laptop, too distracted by Sasha's agitation to keep typing.

'What the heck is wrong with you?' I finally demanded, glaring over at the sofa where I knew she was reclining with a book and a cup of tea. I couldn't see the book, or the tea for that matter, because my view was blocked by the back of the sofa, but she was there all right, in all her huffy-puffy glory. In fact, the only part of Sasha I *could* see were her stripy-sock-clad feet which were dangling over the arm rest and swinging perilously close to a vase of week-old flowers.

'This book is totally hot! I can't believe I waited so long to read it!' she exclaimed, her mass of wild blonde curls appearing as she sat up to look at me over the sofa cushions. 'I think I might need fifteen minutes in my room with the contents of my vibrator drawer,' she added with a cackle and a cheeky wiggle of her well-plucked eyebrows.

Since she was momentarily distracted from whatever she was reading, I swung to face her. 'You have an entire drawer for vibrators?' I'd known Sasha since we were teenagers. How did I not know this about her? 'No ... no ... actually, don't answer that, I don't want to know!' I held up my hand to stop her with a wince and an amused grimace. Blimey, I only owned one vibrator, which barely ever got used. How many did she have to justify allocating a specific space in her living quarters for such things?

Wow, sex toy storage, what a thought. Maybe that

5

could be a new range for Ikea to consider.

Rolling my eyes, I looked at Sasha and saw her unashamed look. Her cheeks were flushed and there was a smile as wide as the River Thames on her face as she raised up the book she was reading. 'Have you read it? It's called *Fifty Shades of ...*'

I cut her off by raising my hand again.

'Stop,' I said firmly, 'Sasha, you may not know the code of etiquette when it comes to authors, but to spout the name of an international best seller to me when I am struggling to get one or two damn copies of my latest book sold is not what I need right now.'

Writing romance was what I wanted to do full time, but my books weren't exactly flying off the shelves at the moment, so I also worked part time as an editor for a local newspaper. It was perfect – I got to work from home, but it paid enough to cover my bills and rent.

'Oh. Sorry.' She flushed further and hid the book below my line of sight but not before I'd glimpsed its now infamous black and grey cover. 'I bought a copy of your book, too,' she added supportively with a perky smile.

'Yeah?' I gave her a weak nod. 'Have you read it?'

If possible, Sasha's flush got even deeper. 'Well ... I was sort of halfway through it when I found this in my bedside drawer still unread ...' She wiggled the goddamn best seller at me again. 'Yours was really good and everything but I kinda got distracted and started reading this instead ...'

A huge sigh escaped my lips, 'Exactly!' I exclaimed, jumping up from my seat at the dining room table – also known as my work desk – before hoisting Sasha's legs off the sofa and plonking myself next to her dejectedly to snatch *the book* from her hand.

'How the hell can my crappy chintzy romances compare to this stuff?' I flicked miserably through the pages and could instantly tell where the naughty bits were because Sasha had turned the corners of the pages over.

There were a lot of turned corners.

My lips tightened as I examined the pages. I might not like to admit it, but I'd read a couple of the most recent "erotic" novels on the market, including this one, which had started the whole craze a few years ago, and they even got me pretty hot under the collar, which seeing as I'm not really into sex is saying something.

'Don't shoot me for saying this but you have a point, babe,' Sasha said, retrieving her book protectively and sticking a bookmark in to keep her all-important page, 'These types of books are still selling like hot cakes,' she admitted with a nod. 'People thought it was going to be a fad, but it's continued. Apparently, a nice bit of hanky-spanky soft porn is exactly what ladies want these days.' Her smirk caused me to let out a deflated sigh.

Hanky-spanky soft porn? I really was doomed. There was no way I could write that type of stuff; I had no clue about any of it.

'You're a really good writer, Robyn, and you already write loads of different genres ... why don't you just expand your horizons a bit and write one of these?' she suggested helpfully.

I practically choked on my own near-hysterical laughter. 'Yeah right, because I know *sooo* much about erotic kinky sex!' I said, rolling my eyes at her. 'You've known me my entire adult life, Sash. Exactly which of my ex-boyfriends do you think could act as fodder for a kinky book?'

I was currently single, and my five exes were all that way for very good reasons: Xbox fanatic, immature student, *Star Trek* geek, pot head, and workaholic, in that order. They might have been funny and considerate enough to attract my initial attention, but none of them could ever be labelled as "exciting in the sack", hence my general lack of interest in sex. All my friends said it was great, but I'd never found that when I'd been between the sheets.

'Okay, point taken …' Sasha conceded, 'Didn't the *Star Trek* guy have a toe fetish?' Her lip curled up in amusement as she spoke, but I grimaced, remembering only too well Brian's excessive lust towards my feet. *Freak.* '*Ugh*, yes, not discussing that again – *ever.*' I shuddered. 'Besides, I'm not writing a kinky novel about a guy with a toe fetish. It's hardly going to appeal to the reading masses, is it?'

Giggling loudly, Sasha shook her head, causing her blonde curls to swirl around her face. 'No … probably not,' she agreed when she could finally suppress her grin. 'Well, I could help with ideas for some of the sex scenes … Although I've not done much kinky stuff either,' she admitted with a grimace which looked more disappointed than disgusted.

'You've just done most of the men in London with a pulse,' I joked, not altogether untruthfully.

'Yeah, yeah.' Sasha dismissed my friendly insult with a casual flick of her wrist. 'Least I'm not celibate like you.' She gave a teasing bump to my shoulder.

Yes, that's right. Not the most exciting status to have. But after five failed attempts at relationships I decided late last year to have a man-free period in my life and concentrate on my writing.

Celibate, however, is not a real word for Sasha. She would probably consider it more of a blasphemous term and has gone out of her way to do the exact opposite of me, by shagging anything as long as it's male and breathing. I know this because we have adjoining walls in our bedrooms. Yeah, lucky me. But it's fine because Sasha is my best friend, so I put up with it – plus I have a *really* good pair of earplugs.

It makes me cringe to think of the number of men that Sasha must have totted up since we've shared our flat together for the last three years, but sex is her coping mechanism. Her story is a really sad one, and the reason for her casual "bang 'em and leave" lifestyle. Her father died unexpectedly when she was just seven, and she lost her mother to cancer at seventeen. They both died way before their time, and after she moved in with her aunt she developed a motto of "live each day as if it is your last", and boy, has she stuck to it.

She's worked her arse off to get her dream job with an interior design magazine, and now lives a pretty decadent lifestyle: nights out, luxurious holidays, fancy food, and, of course, a long string of different men to warm her bed. The only reason I can afford to live in Central London is because Sasha pays the lion's share of the rent on the apartment we share.

The five guys I've dated are also the only men that I've slept with – no one-night stands for me, Little Miss Goody Two-Shoes – and all of them I dated for a few weeks before allowing things to progress to the bedroom.

Breaking me from my reverie, Sasha adjusted herself on the sofa. 'I suppose we could probably find some stuff on the internet to help you out,' she suggested, which I had to grant her was actually quite a good idea if I really was going to attempt to write an erotic book of some sort. Me, an erotic novelist? I nearly snorted at how ridiculous it sounded.

'Or ...' She had a sudden gleam in her eye which I didn't like the look of *at all*. It was her *I have a cunning plan* look, which usually ended with alcohol, dancing, trouble, or all three combined.

'Let's think about it from a different perspective ... We could go out and do some research first hand.'

Research first hand? She couldn't possibly be thinking what I thought she was. Even Sasha wasn't *that* crazy.

Was she?

## Chapter Two

## Robyn

It turned out that yes, Sasha really was that crazy, because several hours later, after being plied with multiple beers to persuade me, I found myself dressed up ready to go out on an erotic research mission to the local bars in Soho.

Heaven help me.

More to the point, heaven help my poor readers.

We nearly made it out of the front door, but just as I was reaching for the latch it swung open to reveal intense disapproval in human form – also known as Chloe – who gave my attire one long, sweeping look and placed both her hands on her hips in instant admonishment.

Ah yes, dearest Chloe.

As well as sharing my flat with Sasha I also have another roommate. She's a little … how can I put it politely? Stuck up? Boring? Prissy? She's lovely, but she's definitely a bit more of a prude than Sasha and myself. She works in risk management, and the caution she implements into her work has transferred into the rest of her life. Considering that she is mid-twenties like Sasha and me, her behaviour is sometimes more akin to that of a sensible old lady.

'Jesus Christ, you look like a couple of hookers. Where the hell are you two going dressed like that?' she sighed, stepping inside the apartment and slamming the door behind her. Flicking the lock, she then turned and gave us both a raised eyebrowed look. Perhaps we weren't going out, after all. Not in the immediate future anyway.

Her words regarding our outfits might have sounded a bit harsh, but to be fair Chloe was probably right. The alcoholic buzz from my earlier beers and shots had begun to wear off and as I glanced down at the clothing that I had allowed Sasha to dress me in, I winced. Luminous pink

10

boob tube, leather miniskirt and knee-high boots. It was a *long* way off from my usual attire, and I suppose Chloe wasn't far from the mark with her "hooker" label.

Needless to say, after we'd explained our plans for the evening, Chloe was firmly against it. 'Oh, come on, Chloe,' I started, putting on my most persuasive tone. 'It's just for research. I need to get something published soon, and to hit the right market Sasha thinks I need to see this stuff first hand.'

'Why am I not surprised that this was your idea?' Chloe muttered, glaring at Sasha who was still grinning away happily.

'I'm only going to help Robyn with her research. I'll behave, I promise. Pinkie swear?' she said solemnly, holding out her little finger towards Chloe. Both Sash and I knew this promise would never be adhered to – Sasha was not the most honest of girls at times – but Chloe, being the newest addition to our flat, was luckily oblivious of this and narrowed her eyes before linking her little finger with Sasha's and shaking it to bind the agreement.

'Okay fine. Research. Perhaps a quick drink, and then we leave,' Chloe stated and crossed her arms firmly over her chest.

Sasha and I exchanged shocked glances. 'We?' Sasha asked carefully.

'Of course, I'm hardly going to let you go on your own, am I? So what exactly does one wear to visit a sex club?' she asked sourly, making a huffy gesture and putting her hands onto her hips again.

'As little as possible!' Sasha giggled gleefully.

'Don't think for one second that we're going out with you two dressed like that. Go and change your bloody clothes and then we'll go,' Chloe ordered. She might be a bit prudish, but Chloe was definitely the stand-in mother figure around our place, and so, with grins splitting our faces, Sasha and I dutifully headed to our rooms to change.

The knee-high boots stayed, but I exchanged the micro miniskirt for one that fell to just above the knee and peeled off the boob tube in exchange for a nice silk blouse. A look in the mirror showed the result. I looked sexy, but not whorish. In other words, much better.

Sasha had taken charge of our night out, and after popping into one of the bars in Soho to get recommendations of local venues we now stood staring up at a disused theatre. It certainly didn't look like the hottest sex club in town. The exterior looked bland, as if the place was vacant, but the guy who had given Sasha the address said that behind the plain frontage was a wild night ready to be enjoyed by all who ventured in.

The plaque on the door stated that this place was called Club Twist, and below the name was a tag line – "Explore your twisted side". Pointing at the words, Sasha grinned. 'This sounds just like the type of place we need, doesn't it?'

Explore your twisted side? My stomach squirmed with nerves. What the heck was I doing here? I tried to tell myself that I was young, free, and single, there was absolutely nothing wrong with what I was doing, but only ended up exhaling harshly and shaking my head at my stupidity, I was going into a sex club – of course there was something wrong with what I was doing!

Wiggling her eyebrows at me in glee, Sasha grabbed the large brass door handle and pulled it open, allowing a rush of warm air and the deep, throbbing bass of dance music to escape.

*Here we go then.*

Our nervous laughter and wobbly footsteps were abruptly stopped by a burly man standing just inside the door, who informed us that this club was so exclusive that you could only gain entry as either a member, or a listed guest. We opted for guest status, and he took some details from us and stamped our hands with a red, coiled logo. We were each given a booklet of ten guest passes and ushered towards a dark corridor. After the ten passes were used up (although I doubt I'd ever be making use of the other nine), we either had to become members, or never come back.

He gave us a definite smirk as we entered, but with our attire and shocked faces we must have screamed "never been to a sex club before" and he was clearly wondering what we were doing here, too. My heart was galloping painfully, and I started to find it hard to breathe. Yep, I was on the verge of a major panic attack.

I calmed down surprisingly quickly, because inside was nowhere near as shocking as I'd been imagining. It wasn't sleazy, sticky, or coated in plastic. In fact, the interior was the complete opposite: tasteful, relaxed, and spotless. There was a bar along one wall, a large, bustling dance floor, and a few pedestals with some erotic dancing taking place on them. I'd had visions of huge orgies, or stages with where full-on sex occurred, but from my first few glances I couldn't see either of those.

Yes, there was more skin on display than in other nightclubs I'd been to, and yes, there was some rather provocative dancing, but apart from that, it had a chilled vibe, and looked like any other London venue for a night out.

No sooner had we entered the club then Sasha had downed a vodka shot and shimmied her way onto the dance floor. Watching her progress, I couldn't decide if I should be impressed, or terrified by her ability to instantly attract the opposite sex. She'd been on the dance floor for no longer than five seconds and she was already surrounded by a circle of men and somehow managing to practically dry hump every single one of them.

'She made me a pinkie promise that she'd behave

herself!' Chloe spluttered, before staring at me aghast, then striding off towards Sasha murmuring something about "going to rein her in".

Looking down at my gorgeous, but hugely uncomfortable new boots with a wince, I chose to grab a stool at the bar, instead of following her. The short walk here had nearly finished me off; dancing would just about cripple me.

Making myself comfortable on the stool, I started to mentally list all the interesting things around me that would make good fodder for my book. There was plenty. What with all the Spandex, leather, exotic dancing and other more intimate things going on, I wasn't short on things to look at. Next time I'd have to bring a notepad. There was way too much stuff here to remember it all.

Suddenly, the most bizarre feeling tingled through my body. Electricity seemed to zing across my skin, warming me throughout. Then, as if on cue, the hairs on the back of my neck all stood up in unison. It was unnerving, just like the sensation of someone watching me, so I began to pass my eyes over the club goers to see if I was right.

Everyone seemed caught up in their own particular pleasures, be that drinking, dancing, or kissing. Watching as Sasha attracted the attention of yet more men on the dance floor, I rolled my eyes at her flirtatious moves, then giggled as Chloe tried and failed to control her.

Shaking off my earlier sensation of being watched, I turned my gaze back to the bar, and that's when I saw *him*.

He was exactly as my dreams had conjured, and as I registered that his steely eyes were focused solely on me from the other end of the room, a surprised gasp leaped from my throat.

# Chapter Three

## Oliver

Who was that girl? I'd certainly have remembered her beautiful face if I'd ever met her before. She'd entered about five minutes ago with two friends, and they were now sat at the bar ordering some drinks. Her looks and posture were drawing me to her, and I felt an immediate urge to speak to her, but I didn't fraternise with the customers – it was one of my personal rules – so I tried to distract myself from her addictive features by glancing around the bar.

It was still relatively early, so it was good to see it so busy in the club tonight. As well as lots of familiar faces, there were quite a few groups of newbies, too. Potential new members, hopefully. Business fluctuated, but times had been tougher ever since Westminster Council had decided it needed to "clean up" Soho a few years ago and rid it of all the sleaze. As far as I was concerned, as long as things were done of their own bidding, I didn't care what shops people went into, where they drank, or if they liked to indulge in an hour of mindless fucking in our club to de-stress after a long week at work.

Against my will, I found my eyes straying again to the brunette at the bar. I could quite happily entertain the idea of some mindless fucking with her. She was one of the newbies, I'd place money on that, because she had the slightly dazed look that a person got when they first arrived here and took in everything going on around them. She had an air of innocence about her, too, which appealed to me, and made her stand out like some sort of fragile angel when compared to the rest of the clientele.

She was on her own now, both of her friends choosing to dance, not drink. Looking down into her lap, she started to root through her handbag, causing her long brown hair to cascade around her face. It looked so soft and shiny that I was practically itching to go over and tuck it behind her ears for her, just so I could get a feel. The shifting of her arm caused her top to slip down her shoulder, exposing a triangle of pale skin and a cerise pink bra strap. The sight was instantly arousing, causing my cock to give an interested twitch, and made me wonder if perhaps I was wrong about her innocence – could I be wrong? I was usually such a good judge of character, but was she perhaps as wild in bed as her choice in underwear colours?

Suddenly, she tensed and looked up. As she rubbed at the back of her neck she ran her gaze over the crowd and caught me staring at her.

*Mierda!* I didn't usually focus on the new talent like this, so God knows why this girl had caught my attention. I inwardly chuckled to myself about how I still resorted to Spanish when swearing, but as my eyes locked with the brunette's I forgot all other thoughts. Instead of looking away as I should have, I found myself cockily stepping from the shadows and leaning on the bar so she could clearly see me watching her.

Her eyes widened at my blatant observation, but to give her credit, she didn't break our gaze. My body felt alive, my mind churning with sudden possibilities. What was this peculiar reaction streaming through me? It was like a current or magnetic force trying to pull me closer to her. She was naturally beautiful, yes, and wearing hardly any make-up, which appealed to me, but still, this was getting stupid. I was staring at her like a stalker.

Assessing her features again, I changed my earlier assessment; she couldn't really be labelled a "girl", she looked at least mid-twenties, but her open naivety in these surroundings was clear on her face, making her look far more innocent than those who shared the bar with her.

Before I could decide if I should break my own non-fraternisation rule, the girl looked away, busying herself with her handbag again, and the moment we'd shared was broken.

Drawing in a long breath through my nose, I tried to suppress the urge to go and speak to her. I hadn't socialised with, or fucked, any of the customers for years. It was far better to keep business and pleasure separate. But *dios,* she made it so tempting.

I ripped my gaze away and held my glass up to David for a refill, hoping the burn of the liquor might help. As the first sip of the thick, oaky liquid coated my throat I caught sight of a large silhouette making its way around the perimeter of the club.

When I saw who it was, my lip curled in distaste. Dominic. A dominant, sadist, and all-round moody bastard. As another of the part-owners of this place he might be my business partner, but that was where our relationship ended. I couldn't stand him, or his approach to sex. My lips thinned as I watched him stalking in the darker corners of the club, no doubt selecting his next target from the women here tonight.

My hackles began to rise as I saw him pause, his expression turning interested as he seemed to focus on someone. Zeroing in on his target for the evening, no doubt. Following his gaze to see who he'd selected, I saw him staring at a girl at the bar.

*My* girl at the bar, the brunette I'd been watching since she'd arrived.

*Mierda.* No.

Surely even Dominic had enough decency to realise that she was a newbie and steer clear of her? His tastes were far too extreme for someone unacquainted with this lifestyle, as I would bet this girl was. I stood up from my stool and watched him walk towards the reception area, craning my neck to see what he was doing. He spoke briefly to the guy on the desk and pointed towards the girl at the bar before both of their heads dropped to the entry log. Was he trying to find out her name? Fuck. He was. There was not a chance in hell that she would ever be ready to experience the things that Dominic liked to do. But would she be brave enough to knock him back?

I felt my back straighten out vertebrae by vertebrae until I was stood rod straight and was surprised I hadn't heard my bones cracking from the tension now in my body. I had no idea why I felt so protective over a girl I'd only laid eyes on just over twenty minutes ago, but I did, and there was not a chance in hell that I was letting Dominic get his paws on her.

Expelling a breath, I adjusted my shirt collars until they felt perfect, flattened down my suit jacket, and began to make my way through the crowds. Looked like my no-fraternisation rule was about to go up in smoke, because if anyone was going to be talking to her tonight it was going to be me, not Dominic.

# Chapter Four

## Robyn

I hardly dared to look up again. Not after that weird staring moment I'd just shared with the intense man across the bar. Holy smokes he was handsome, though. The temptation to look back, perhaps even have a little flirt with him, was crawling through my system, but after reminding myself that I was in a sex club I refrained. He might want far more than just a drink and a flirtatious chat, and that was something I most certainly was *not* planning on researching within the club. Not even with someone as stunningly good-looking as him.

Thinking of my research, I decided that if I kept my gaze away from his side of the bar I could still make this evening a productive visit.

After spending a few minutes gawking at my surroundings and dreaming wistfully of my notepad and pen sitting at home beside my laptop, I dug into my handbag and retrieved my phone so I could write some ideas in the notepad app.

I was so completely engrossed in describing the juicy details of the club that when I felt a warm breath feather over the skin near my left ear I let out a startled yelp.

'First time visitor?' a deep, accented voice close behind me enquired, and I'm not kidding, I think my arse actually leaped a full foot off the leather seat before I crashed back down and wobbled precariously until a firm hand gripped my arm to steady me.

Tingles were exploding on my bare arm where I was being supported, but instead of dragging it away I settled myself on my stool again and took a breath to try to calm myself. God, I was wound so tight from nerves that just a few whispered words had me practically running from the club screaming like a lunatic. To be honest, the only thing that had stopped me doing exactly that were my painful boots. It would hardly have been a speedy exit with the blisters I had.

I took several shallow breaths that did nothing to help my equilibrium, and finally turned to my left in trepidation to see who had addressed me – and who was still gripping me.

Oh good God. It was *him*. The man I'd dreamed about. Mr Handsome from across the bar. Except he wasn't across the bar any more. He was right beside me, in all his suited, booted gorgeousness, well and truly invading my personal space and making all the hairs on my body fly up with awareness again.

Funnily enough, the first thing that sprung to my mind was *phew*, because out of all the outfits here tonight – leather catsuits, PVC shorts, bikinis made from wire – Mr Handsome did at least look normal. No corset, whip, or rubber suit in sight.

As I turned to fully face him, I realised that he was a particularly lovely example of normal as well. On closer inspection, it was also obvious that he was way more attractive than any man I could have dreamed up. He was superbly well dressed, his gorgeous navy suit was obviously high quality, and his outfit was completed with a waistcoat and a white cotton shirt that was open at the neck revealing just a touch of chest hair and tanned skin which I couldn't help but stare at for a few seconds.

Above his collar things just got better. I'd thought he was good-looking from across the bar, but wow, now he was this near, he kinda took my breath away. He was a seriously attractive guy – well, to my tastes anyway. His hair was dark, cut short on the sides, but left to be a little spiky and unruly on top, which didn't really match his super smart attire, but looked utterly gorgeous.

His face was really striking, too. Like a perfect incarnation of the exact type of man I was attracted to. A square jaw and dark eyes that looked black in the dim light of the bar, and older than me by a good ten years. The only minor imperfection was his slightly crooked nose, but the fact that he wasn't quite perfect made him more accessible somehow, and just seemed to add to his overall appeal.

The feel of him uncurling his fingers from my elbow snapped me out of my ogling, and I cleared my throat in embarrassment. Recalling his earlier question, I finally found my voice. 'Um, yeah, it's my first time. Am I that obvious?' I replied with a small grimace and an awkward smile as I tried to stop gawking at him like a total idiot.

'Not particularly,' he replied with a shrug, placing his drink down on the bar. 'You just seemed a little jumpy and wide-eyed and I don't recall having seen you in here before.' From the twitch I saw at the corner of his mouth, it seemed that he was attempting to suppress a smile at my expense.

Wide-eyed? It was hardly surprising considering the things that were going on in front of my eyes, was it? Given all the erotic outfits around me, and blatant displays of almost-but-not-quite-sex on the dance floor, I was about as far from my comfort zone as I'd ever been.

Ignoring my skittering heartbeat and clammy palms, I reeled in my nerves and tried to appear unfazed and calm. 'So, do you come here often?' As soon as the words were out of my mouth I realised that it had sounded exactly like a cheesy chat-up line, and my already wide eyes boggled even more. Unfazed and calm? Ha, hardly! *Stupid, stupid, stupid girl!* A furious blush rose on my cheeks and I started to blurt out an attempt at covering my blunder.

'I ... I didn't mean, you know ... I meant ...' The stranger next to me merely continued to suppress his amusement and took a sip of his drink, remaining cool and calm whilst I sank deeper and deeper into a pit of fidgety awkwardness.

Bloody Sasha! I was going to kill her later for

persuading me to come here. Seeing my continued panic, Mr Cool and Calm proceeded to roll his eyes at me and gave a strangely alluring tight-lipped smile that immediately transformed his face into something even more appealing. It made me want to see what a real, full-blown grin would look like. I bet it would be pretty phenomenal.

He must have taken my silence as continued panic because he shook his head and began to try to reassure me. 'Breathe. Calm down, I know what you meant.' He definitely had an exotic lilt to his voice that I couldn't quite identify; Portuguese or Spanish, perhaps. But whatever it was, I liked it, and it merely seemed to add to his mysterious appeal. 'And in answer to your very poorly worded question, yes, I come here quite often.'

'Why?' I seemed to have no control over my mouth tonight, because the word had escaped my lips before I'd even processed it. What a ridiculous thing to say. Why the hell did most guys go to sex clubs? For sex, obviously. Although why a guy as handsome as this needed to come to a club to get sex I had no idea. He must have women falling at his feet on a daily basis.

'Actually, not for the reason you're thinking,' he replied with a dark smile, apparently reading my mind. 'I'm one of the owners.'

One of the owners? 'Oh.' *Oh*. Even though he'd basically just said he didn't come here for sex, if he was one of the owners then surely he must be into some of the … *stuff*… going on around us? 'Does that mean you …?' But my words failed me and I merely waved a hand around in the air instead. I mean, coming out with a question like, 'Are you a sexual deviant?' is hardly polite conversation, is it?

'One of my friends offered me part ownership a few years back. It was a good deal, plenty of prospect for profits, so I took it.'

My eyebrows rose. He took another slow sip of his drink, and as he did so my eyes became almost fixated on his lips. They were sinfully kissable. As he lowered the glass, my gaze shifted to the column of his throat and I watched him swallow, his Adam's apple bobbing up and down behind a thin layer of dark stubble and tempting me to reach out and run a finger down it. My hand even twitched in my lap but, thankfully, my sanity prevailed and I resisted the urge.

If this place were an investment for him then maybe he didn't make use of the club in the way I had been thinking, and *maybe* I could consider a little flirtation with him after all.

'I'm not really active in the scene any more, but if I partake I do so as a dominant,' he said smoothly, making me gulp and do a U-turn on my previous thought. Drawing in a deep breath, I tried to look unaffected by his declaration, but I was actually quite shocked. He looked so ... so normal, and yet he'd just confessed that he *was* into the kinky stuff, and from his relaxed demeanour he was completely at ease with this fact.

From the intensity of his stare he seemed to be watching my reaction with interest, so I gave a casual shrug and nodded. 'Right. I see,' I said automatically. Although I didn't really see. How could I? This was the exact reason I was here in the first place, to learn about people just like him because I knew nothing.

'What about you?' he enquired smoothly.

'I'm not a dominant!' I squawked immediately, my eyes opening even wider than before, as I swallowed far too loudly to ever be considered normal or ladylike.

'No? Really? I would never have guessed,' he remarked sardonically, clearly teasing me because of my high-strung state. God help me, I'd never behaved more like a prattling baboon in all of my life. 'You're not a dominant.' He paused, giving me another ironic twitch of his lip which almost but not quite passed as a smile. 'So what are you? A submissive? A voyeur? Or just a girl in the wrong bar?'

Glancing down at my phone, I saw the notes I'd been making and angled the screen towards him with a small raise of my shoulders. 'None of the above. I'm a writer.' I hadn't thought my words were particularly shocking, but no sooner had he looked at my phone then Mr Cool and Calm didn't look anywhere near as composed. His expression blackened as his entire frame tensed, his back straightening even further than before, and his eyes narrowing.

He slid from his stool and guided me down from my seat with a firm hand around my elbow. The grip instantly made me wince, not from pain, but from the searing heat that it sent coursing through my skin again. What was that reaction about?

Jerking my head up, I saw that he was momentarily staring at where we were connected, his nostrils flaring as if he perhaps felt the burning sparks, too, but then, noticing my attention, he blinked, and the shared moment was lost as his face iced up again.

'We don't allow journalists in here. I'm going to have to ask you to leave.' His tone had lost all of its earlier warmth, and sounded so cold and distant that it felt like someone had run an ice cube down my spine. Goose pimples flooded my skin, but I barely had time to even shiver before he indicated towards the exit with a sharp jerk of his chin.

# Chapter Five

## Robyn

Quickly trying to engage my brain before I found myself skidding across the wet pavement outside, I frantically shook my head. 'I'm not a journalist!' I squeaked, feeling slightly intimidated by both his threatening demeanour, and size. God, he was so tall! Or perhaps that was just because he was standing, and I was sagging on wobbly knees, only being held upright by his grip on my elbow.

'I ... I ... I write romance novels ... I'm just here to learn a bit about the scene, I'm not writing about your club ... I promise.' And believe me, this promise held way more truth to it than all of Sasha's "pinkie swears" added together.

'You're an author?' he hissed through gritted teeth, even though his expression still burned with intensity. Gosh, I could really see the whole "dominant" side of him coming out now. This guy was so intense, and I was unable to think of doing anything but replying to him immediately.

'Yes. Um ... I don't suppose a man, um, like you would read many women's romances, but in the last few years there's been a huge turn in the genre. All the publishers seem to want erotic novels with bondage and spanking and ...' I paused to grab a breath, realising that in my panic I had just stuttered the sentence without so much as one inhale. 'And I don't know anything about that, so I thought I might be able to get some ideas so I can write about it.'

One of his dark eyebrows was raised as he studied me, apparently assessing if I was being genuine or not, and even though he was obviously irritated, I felt a stirring of lust unfurl in my belly. He quite literally embodied everything I found attractive in a man: tall, broad, older,

25

dark hair, strong jaw, and a confidence that bordered on arrogance. 'So, you're writing a book on the BDSM scene?'

All thoughts of desire fled my mind at his words, and I felt my cheeks blanch of colour. *BDSM scene?* I wasn't entirely clear what that meant, but I was fairly sure it was the path I was aiming for with my book. 'Umm ... sort of. I just want to write a romance book that's a bit kinkier than the stuff I used to write,' I admitted, realising what a ridiculous idea this had all been. I was *definitely* going to kill Sasha later.

'I see.' Mr Cool and Calm still seemed to be weighing up whether to have me chucked out or not, so I gave him my best attempt at a smile and hoped he could see that I was telling the truth.

Tilting his head to the side, he watched me closely, and finally nodded before leading me back to our stools at the bar. 'I apologise for my overreaction. As I'm sure you can imagine, the press doesn't always write about us in the most favourable of lights.' As he continued to assess me, the grip on my elbow softened, his thumb now caressing me instead of ensnaring me. It was as if he were somehow backing up his apology with his touch, and as much as I knew I should tug my arm away, I didn't. The contact warmed me, sending a shudder of desire flying through my body and causing my breath to hitch.

Our eyes met, and there was a second or two where I felt certain that I was transparent to him and that he could see exactly how much I was lusting after him. The problem was, he was affecting me so violently that I didn't even know how to hide my feelings from him.

'I hope you can forgive me?' His words were low and velvety smooth, and his touch was making me feel so good that I would probably have forgiven anything at that point, but truthfully there wasn't really anything to pardon, so I nodded jerkily.

'And this little research mission has been prompted by other books on the market?'

Swallowing hard, I tried to ignore the distracting sensation of his warm palm on my arm and nodded jerkily. 'Yeah. I think they're targeted at women, so you probably haven't read them, but you must at least have heard of *Fifty Shades of ...*'

Before I could finish, Mr Cool and Calm smiled and laughed, the grip disappearing from my arm as he suddenly relaxed back into his stool with an amused look and took a sip of his drink.

Luckily, my legs had regained most of their composure by that point, so I took a step sideways and slid back up onto my chair, glad of the reprieve it gave my wobbly knees.

'I've read it,' he said with a smirk that made me widen my eyes in surprise. 'Why do you look so surprised? It's a book written about a man with supposedly similar sexual interests as me. Of course I read it,' he explained with a shrug. 'I discovered one main thing: I prefer doing kinky things rather than reading about them.'

*Wow.* I didn't expect that response at all. His mood had swung quicker than a pendulum, and his mention of "doing kinky things" caused my cheeks to flare with colour as I imagined exactly what it might be that he liked to do.

Now that I was fairly sure he wasn't going to throw me out, I decided to see if I could learn anything from him for my book. 'So you know the type of stuff I'm trying to research, then.' I exhaled in relief before deciding to act whilst the iron was hot. 'Can I ask why you like the things you do?'

He placed his tumbler back on the bar, then turned to me and finally put me out of my misery by laying me low with a real genuine grin. It was ten times more stunning than I had imagined, and seemed to cause my brain to short-circuit. Holy smokes, his eyes were burning with warmth now, and as the spotlights from the dance floor shined across us I realised his irises were dark blue, not black, or brown as I'd thought earlier. They were like soft denim, but I didn't get to lose myself in them for long because I suddenly realised he was holding out his hand to me.

'Perhaps we should do some introductions before you start your interrogation?' he enquired lightly, his tone full of amusement.

Oops. Perhaps I'd been a bit too keen to get my story. Looking down at his outstretched palm, I knew I should take it, but I hesitated. Shaking hands was the polite thing to do, but I couldn't help thinking that touching him wasn't the best of ideas; he'd already sent my senses wild with his last touch to my arm, and witnessing his grin had nearly had me salivating all over him.

Adding further skin on skin contact to the mix wouldn't ease my peculiar attraction to him at all, I was sure of that.

It would be outright rude to ignore his gesture, though, so finally, I tentatively placed my palm in his. The same tingly heat instantly spread through my body, and a small gasp escaped my lips as his fingers closed around mine, warm and strong and so large that they completely dwarfed my tiny digits. I couldn't help but lower my eyes and stare at our joined hands as my body seemed to come alive.

His touch felt so good.

Secure, and … right somehow.

Still shocked by my reactions to this man, I jerkily raised my head, praying that my expression didn't give away the tumble of emotions I was currently feeling.

Looking back to his face, I saw one of his eyes twitch slightly, as if he was also trying to diagnose what was occurring between us, but also drawing a blank. Then he cleared his throat and nodded his head once in greeting.

'I'm Oliver Wolfe.'

I digested his name with a small smile. Wolfe. It actually suited him perfectly, because he seemed just as predatory and strong as his animal namesake. 'I'd be more than happy to help you get acquainted with our world.'

Get "acquainted" with his world? Did he mean physically? Like treat me to some kinky sex? Because as tempting as sex with a man as captivating as him might be, I wasn't sure I was really in his sexual league. Seeing me blanch at his suggestion, he chuckled again, giving a mild shake of his head. 'As appealing as that idea in your head might be, I can assure you I meant purely in terms of assisting you with your research. You can ask me questions and I'll answer them as best I can.'

*Phew.* Relief flooded through me, coloured also by a blush of embarrassment, because he'd just confirmed that he really could read what was on my mind.

A tiny tinge of regret chased away my embarrassment as I looked him up and down again. I was pretty sure that Mr Big Bad Wolfe here would put my previous five lovers to shame with his skills in the sack; his confidence seemed to scream of sexual experience and competence.

'That would be great,' I responded with a keen nod, trying not to look down at where our hands were still joined. Surely this was overly long for a handshake? Why hadn't he let go of my hand yet?

'So, your name?' he enquired softly, giving my hand a gentle squeeze as a prompt.

Oh! I hadn't introduced myself yet. That must be why he was still holding on. 'I'm Robyn. With a y,' I added, feeling a shy smile spread on my lips, and wondering why I suddenly felt the need to duck my head and try to break the magnetic bond between our eyes. 'As in it's spelt with a y. Not like the bird,' I babbled to cover my growing embarrassment.

'It's a pleasure to meet you, Robyn with a y,' he

murmured in amusement, before giving my hand one last squeeze and finally letting it go with a low chuckle.

My skin immediately felt chilled from the loss of his touch, but I consoled myself by absorbing the lovely sound of his laughter. It was deep and raspy, like perhaps he smoked, or used to smoke, although he certainly didn't smell of cigarettes. So far, the only aromas I'd detected coming from his direction were that of crisp linen and soap, both of which had appealed to me and made me want to lean in closer.

'How about starting with a tour?' he offered, gesturing around the club with his hand. 'We could walk and talk?'

'Oh, OK, thanks.'

I slid from my stool and walked with Oliver as he made his way towards one side of the club. 'So, you wanted to know why I'm a dominant?' he asked, glancing down at me and clearly loving how much I was squirming from embarrassment again, but I stayed brave, bit down on my lower lip, and nodded.

His eyes strayed to my trapped lip and darkened, and for some reason I got the distinct impression that he was imagining biting it himself. Would I enjoy that? My core clenched as my mind was instantly flooded with erotic visions of him pouncing forwards and snagging my lower lip with his teeth before sucking it into his mouth and capturing me in a kiss. From the way my heart rate had rocketed I'd say that, yes, I would definitely enjoy that. There was an audible "pop" as I hastily released my lip, causing me to wince with embarrassment at my sensual daydream, at the same time that Oliver let out another of those delicious chuckles.

I'd place money on the fact that he'd read my mind again, but thankfully he didn't comment this time. 'I'll answer your question, but first let me ask you this, what is your favourite food?'

Was he planning on asking me out for dinner? I was

slightly thrown by the change of topic but with a shrug I decided to go along with it. 'Uh … Chinese, I guess.'

'OK, why do you like it?'

I jerked my shoulders again, unable to quite voice my reasons. 'I don't know, it's just nice. I like the spicy flavours.'

'It's exactly the same for sex,' he explained simply. 'People might not openly admit it, but just like favourite foods, drinks, or sports, everyone will have favoured sexual positions or activities.'

Oh, as simple as that. I'd never really considered it that way, but I suppose that made sense.

'For me that involves being in control.' He leaned in closer, and as I imagined him kissing me again, my body froze. His face was just a few centimetres away now. I could feel the warmth of his breath on my cheek, see the darker flecks in his denim blue eyes, and even though I knew it was dangerous, *he* was dangerous, I couldn't summon up the effort to move away. 'And like you, I also like it spicy,' he added in a low, wicked tone, giving a suggestive jerk of his eyebrows.

If it were possible for words to suck the air from my lungs, then that statement would have done it, because I could barely breathe. I'd never met someone so fascinating. His looks were obviously appealing, and confidence oozed from his very being, but it went way beyond that. His expressions, the tiny movements of his eyebrows, the way his lip tweaked when he was suppressing a grin, the movement of his hands as he spoke … He was so compelling I couldn't look away. Plus, he had sex appeal by the truckload, which helped, too, I guess.

I cleared my throat, hoping that perhaps I could distract myself from the overwhelming stimulation that was Mr Oliver Wolfe, and finally managed to shift backwards slightly and create a little breathing space between us to reflect on what was occurring.

It didn't look like I was getting a dinner invite, as I'd first thought, either, and as stupid as it was, I once again felt a little pang of disappointment.

He distracted me from my pondering thoughts by holding up his hands in a dismissive gesture. 'I'm a bit of a let-down, aren't I?' he said, sliding his hands into his pockets and drawing my attention to his long legs which seemed to go on forever.

*A let-down? I wouldn't say that*, I thought dryly, running my eyes back up his strong thighs and over his impeccable suit until I was looking at that incredible grin again. His teeth were so straight that he simply must have worn braces as a kid.

'It's nowhere near as exciting as the tortured characters in the books you've read, I'm afraid. I think it's just the way I'm built. I like control. Especially in the bedroom,' he added, throwing a sly smile my way that sent a pulse of desire to my groin and made me gulp and shift my legs to try and ease my arousal.

'Uhh ...right,' I said, just for something to fill the awkward silence. 'That's not a let-down,' I remarked softly. 'I wouldn't want to try and write about a tortured soul on my first attempt, anyway.'

'Quite right,' Oliver agreed with a nod, before a devious twinkle sparkled in his eye. 'Perhaps you would rather be the one being tortured?'

My eyes widened so quickly that my top lids briefly ached. 'What? No! I ... er... *no*.' What a gigantic swing in the conversation! He was certainly keeping me on my toes. 'I ... er ... I ... just wanted to soak up a bit of atmosphere, really,' I stammered, not entirely sure if he was coming on to me, or simply playing with me. Probably the latter, if the wicked glint in his eye was anything to go by.

Oliver lifted a hand and rubbed at his jaw, and I could have sworn he said "shame" as he did so, which caused

32

my heart to skitter wildly in my chest.

How did I respond to that?

Outwardly this man was dreamy to look at, but that feeling of danger was never far from my mind. Not in a threatening way, but I had a feeling he would be distinctly hazardous for my heart's health if I let him close.

I didn't reply to his whispered remark, so in the end we both just stood there in silence staring out at the dance floor for a few minutes. The reprieve from his intense stare was definitely needed, and I managed to take my first proper breath since meeting him.

'So, the tour,' Oliver announced. 'You've already seen the dance floor and performance pedestals. What do you think of the place?'

'It's nice. Not what I expected at all, really.'

Tilting his head, he smiled. 'What did you expect?'

Shrugging, I rolled my eyes. 'I dunno. Sex, I suppose,' I blurted, embarrassed by my naivety. 'But there's nothing like that at all.'

Oliver hummed, as if considering my words, and then swept back a curtain behind himself with a flourish. 'Like this, you mean?'

Oh good God and holy hell balls.

Behind the curtain was a side stage, illuminated from above with spotlights and containing … well … containing two people shagging rather vigorously. Except they weren't *just* having sex. The man was banging into her and tugging on her breasts, but the woman was spread-eagled on some type of bench, each of her limbs tied down so she was unable to move, and in her mouth was a black rubber ball, presumably to stop her speaking.

Jeepers. I blinked, then blinked again, and my mouth dropped open as I watched in muted fascination. Her skin was slick, as if covered with oil, and her nipples were bright red from the attention they were getting. The scene aroused me far more than I would have expected it to.

33

After allowing me to watch for a few moments, Oliver dropped the curtain and turned back to me. He rolled his shoulders back to straighten his already perfect posture, and grinned wickedly as he raised a hand and used a thumb to gently assist me in closing my gaping mouth. 'I am assuming, from your delightful blushes, that your sex life thus far has been vanilla?'

God. This was all a bit much. Talk about straight to the point! I'd only met him ten minutes ago and now he was asking me about my sex life!

I had been desperately hoping to steer the conversation back to more mundane topics, but all this talk of torture, punishment, and now "vanilla sex" was seriously making me question why I was spending my Friday night here. I had no clue about half the things he was talking about, or half the things I'd just witnessed.

'V-vanilla?' I stuttered, my throat raspy and dry. 'Like normal? Boring?' I was fairly sure I'd read that term before.

Oliver barked out a short laugh, and ran a hand through his hair, his dark eyes twinkling with mirth. God, he was so attractive it made my stomach clench with need.

'Boring?' he questioned, clearly amused. 'Poor little Robyn with her boring sex life. It's no wonder you've ended up wandering through our door.'

I tried for an outraged expression, but instead my mouth merely hung open again, causing Oliver to laugh at me yet again as he held his hands up in surrender. 'Don't look like that. You said it, not me.' His smile was pure wickedness. 'But yes, I meant normal, as in not kinky.'

My head bobbed around uselessly, and my tongue felt like a piece of dry carpet as I tried to answer. 'Um. Yeah.'

'Interesting.' His eyes swept over my features again, and he briefly bit down on his lower lip, as if imagining something utterly filthy and wicked. Something like the forbidden fantasies I occasionally had, but would never dream of telling anyone about. His lust-filled expression made me quiver between my legs, and I had to fist my hands to try to control the sudden trembling in my fingers.

Finally breaking the eye contact, Oliver drew in a deep breath and placed a hand on my lower back, his touch making me jerk briefly, before I managed to control myself. 'Come, this way.'

We navigated the edge of the room to the other side, passing several small candlelit booths as we did so. 'These are the watcher holes. Small and cosy if you fancy a private drink, but also positioned with a perfect view of the second stage.' He pointed to another curtain, and I could just see beyond it to where a woman in a black catsuit was strutting around a naked man bound to a cross. Holy smokes, this place was insane! Although I had to give it credit for its discretion, because until Oliver's enlightening tour, I had been completely unaware of the naughtiness occurring in here.

'And, finally, this corridor leads to the private rooms.'

That caught my attention, and I ripped my eyes away from the stage and back towards Oliver. 'Private rooms? Like a hotel?'

Oliver smirked at me, and nodded. 'If you mean hotels which rent their rooms by the hour, then yes.'

Oh. My cheeks were burning with heat by now and I found myself averting my eyes as Oliver continued to stare at me.

'Would you like to see inside one of them?'

His husky words brought my head snapping up again and I rapidly shook my head. 'No!'

It seemed that Oliver could no longer contain his amusement, and he threw his head back and laughed at me, before leading me back to the bar where our stools were still vacant. His timing couldn't have been better, because after all his flirtatious remarks, lust-filled looks, and teasing comments, my legs were just about ready to

# Chapter Six

## Robyn

Now his intense gaze had shifted away from me, I felt a wave of relaxation in my muscles but, confusingly, it was tinged with a pang of disappointment at the loss of his attention.

Shaking off the sensation, I shifted on my stool, rotating it towards him and resting one arm on the bar so I mirrored his posture. I sat facing more towards Oliver so we could talk, but also see the room around us.

Before I even had the chance to ask any of the hundreds of questions brewing in my mind, we were approached by a huge man who came to stand right before me, far too close for my comfort. He must have been near to seven feet tall and was built so broadly that he completely blocked my view of the dance floor.

'Good evening, Oliver.' The new man had a voice so deep and rough that it rumbled through my chest, and perfectly matched his rugged appearance. He may have been speaking to Oliver, but I noticed his dark eyes were well and truly latched on to me as they raked unselfconsciously over my body, making me feel an almost instant revulsion towards him. Talk about intrusive.

'Dominic,' Oliver replied curtly, his voice noticeably cooler than before. Glancing across in surprise at his chilly tone, I saw that Oliver now sat bolt upright, the front of his shirt straining as some seriously decent muscles seemed to stretch the fabric almost to its limit. Oliver didn't introduce me formally to his acquaintance, but that didn't stop Dominic from swooping forwards, grabbing my hand, and lifting my knuckles to his lips for a kiss. The sensation of his dry lips skating over my skin made me shudder. There was something innately unsettling about him that set my nerves on edge and had me tugging my hand free and snatching it back into my lap.

'And you are?' he asked, as he looked at my clenched hand with a flicker of a frown. I only just managed to avoid the urge to wipe my knuckles on my dress, then rested it back on the bar, well out of his reach.

Before I could reply, Oliver did the job for me, his tone still frosty. 'This is Robyn.'

Although I barely knew Oliver, I felt the sudden need to shift closer to him. He seemed to offer so much more safety than this unsettling newcomer, and I leaned sideways on my stool to close the distance between us. As if sensing my discomfort, Oliver released his glass and shifted his hand next to my arm, so his index finger was brushing the skin of my wrist. Oddly enough, even this minimal contact from him, a virtual stranger, somehow reassured me.

My guardian's movement may have been small, but Dominic's gaze immediately shifted from my face to look at where Oliver's hand was now touching mine. His eyes narrowed as Oliver wrapped his fingers more firmly around my hand, an intimate gesture that I would usually have pulled away from with a new acquaintance, but in the presence of this unnerving man I found myself instinctively turning my hand and linking my fingers with Oliver's.

Oliver dipped his head to look at our handhold, and briefly we made eye contact, his gaze searing into me as I gave a small smile. He returned my smile, and nodded his head, as if approving of my action.

'And as you can see, Robyn is with me.'

I wasn't with him, not really, but there seemed to be some strange power play occurring between the two men, so I chose to remain quiet. This was his home territory, he knew how things worked around here, so I was happy to let him take the lead.

Dominic gave an indecipherable grunt of apparent

irritation. 'Finally back in the game, are you, Oliver?' he asked in a decidedly scornful tone as he pushed his meaty hands into the pockets of his trousers, to which Oliver shrugged and nodded.

Oliver was now rhythmically stroking the side of my hand with his thumb, and I couldn't deny that the sensation was rather lovely, so much so that I began to return the gesture to his hand with my own thumb, which caused his grip to increase around mine. 'It would appear so.'

After giving us both a hard stare, Dominic looked again at our linked hands with a narrow-eyed look of irritation. 'Then I shan't disturb your evening further.' Tearing his gaze away from our hands, Dominic stared intently at me again, making me shrink back a fraction in my seat. 'Enjoy Club Twist. If there is anything I can assist you with, Robyn … anything at all, don't hesitate to find me.' His disturbingly suggestive tone made my skin crawl. His gaze roved over me one more time before he shot an intense look at Oliver and stalked away.

As soon as he was gone I felt my shoulders sag in relief. That had been one seriously weird encounter.

A few seconds of silence passed after our unplanned guest had departed, and neither Oliver nor I immediately moved to separate our hands. I'd only just met him, so it felt strange to be holding on to him, but equally, he made me feel safe, so I wasn't quite ready to give up the contact while Dominic was still circling the bar area like a shark.

In the end it was Oliver who instigated the separation– albeit somewhat reluctantly – by pulling his hand away slowly and dragging his fingertips across my palm in the process. Excited shivers ran up my arm and I shuddered with pleasure before averting my eyes and shifting awkwardly on my stool. He'd have to have been blind not to see my response to him, and I inwardly kicked myself for being so transparent. This man made me feel like an open book.

'My apologies for his behaviour,' Oliver murmured, picking up his drink and taking a large swig, as if he, too, were trying to avoid eye contact with me. 'Dominic is another of the owners of Club Twist.' He placed his tumbler back down and finally raised his gaze to mine again, but this time his face was twisted in distaste. 'Between you and me, he's a *cabrón*. Watch yourself around him if you meet him again.'

'What does that mean?'

Oliver gave a thin smile. 'My apologies. For some reason, even though I've lived over here for years, I still swear in Spanish. *Cabrón* is not a polite term ... it's similar to arsehole.'

So my sixth sense had been correct about Dominic being bad news, but more interestingly, Oliver had hinted that his native language was Spanish, which would certainly explain his accent and dark good looks.

'You're Spanish?'

He quirked an eyebrow at me, and then nodded slowly. '*Sí, señorita.*'

The sound of the familiar foreign words purring from his lips made my stomach lurch and a wave of pure lust washed through me as I had visions of him whispering sweet nothings in my ear in his low Spanish accent.

My response to him was so unexpected that I was really floundering; and just taking in a normal, non-wheezing breath suddenly felt like the most complex task on earth. 'So, is Dominic, you know ... is he like you?' I asked hesitantly.

Meeting my gaze straight on, Oliver shook his head. 'No, he and I are nothing alike.' His statement was almost spat out, showing exactly how much he disliked Dominic. 'But if you meant with regards to sexual outlook, then yes, he's a dominant, too.' The grim expression on his features suddenly lightened, 'I don't like the guy but you gotta love the irony of his parents' name choice. Dominic, as in

40

"Dominic the Dom".' He chuckled, and I found myself grinning, too, until Oliver's face sobered again, 'Seriously. though, he's bad news, Robyn. If you choose to come here more often to do your research, stay away from him, please.'

'OK.' For whatever reason I felt like I could trust Oliver, so I agreed immediately, 'He was pretty intimidating.'

Rubbing his chin, Oliver nodded, his gaze hooded. 'He is. He's into some very extreme stuff,' he confided, his voice lower now and causing me to lean closer so I could hear him over the music. 'Actually, he's probably a bit more like the characters in the books you read. He definitely had a troubled upbringing. God knows what went on in the children's home where he lived but he likes dishing out some serious pain while he's having sex.' A shudder ran though me at Oliver's blunt words and I suddenly felt cold despite the oppressive heat inside the club.

'Dominic can be …' Oliver paused, frowning as he seemed to be deciding what to say, 'Predatory,' he decided upon finally. 'When he sees something he wants, he goes all out to claim it. I thought I saw a gleam in his eye when he looked at you, which is why I took your hand.'

'Staking your own claim, were you?' I asked in what I hoped was a jokey, light-hearted response, but my wobbly voice probably gave away my nerves.

*Please say yes. Please say yes.*

The thought caught me off guard, surprising me with how instantly I had been attracted to this man, and how thrilled I would have been if he showed a real interest in me. Thrilled, that was, until I really gave it some thought, considered his bedroom tastes, and ran for the hills.

Who was I kidding? I might find the guy attractive, but he was a self-confessed control freak in the bedroom, and I was as *vanilla* as they came. If he actually made a move on me, I'd be utterly terrified.

'You're joking, Robyn. But yes, I was,' Oliver murmured, his words causing my heart to flutter wildly and my breath to catch. His eyes gleamed wickedly as he looked back up at me, but then he softened his expression into a smile. 'If Dominic thinks you're with me he should leave you alone.'

Suddenly, Oliver leaned towards me purposefully and I got another hit of that clean linen and soap smell. It was almost homely, and comforting somehow, and a total contradiction to where I was currently sitting.

'Promise me you won't try to get close to him just for character research.' He was repeating his warning from just a few seconds ago, but suddenly Oliver's tone was more demanding, and I raised my eyes to his to find him staring at me intently.

I nodded, but Oliver frowned and shook his head. 'Let me hear you say it. Promise me,' he demanded, his low, commanding tone seeming to reach inside me and make me desperate to bow to his will.

'Sorry. Yes, I promise,' I vowed, and I meant it. I might want to get some ideas for my book but there was no way I wanted to get sucked into the sex life of some kinky sadist like Dominic.

Oliver nodded, apparently satisfied by my response, but he stayed close, close enough that just a small dip of his head would bring our lips together. His gaze fluttered down towards my mouth, but before either of us could decide to make that final move, Chloe and Sasha tumbled into my side, knocking me away from Oliver as they fell against the bar in a tangled heap of giggling limbs. Well, Sasha was giggling, Chloe was scowling and gripping Sash by the elbow in an apparent attempt to stop her running back to the dance floor.

I flicked a look at Oliver, and saw him still staring at me, but now with a look of reluctant acceptance on his face at our untimely interruption. Had he been about to kiss me? I guessed now I'd never know.

Chloe grabbed my handbag and held it out to me. 'Some clever idiot on the dance floor was handing out vodka shots. Sasha's totally off her tits. Time to go, Robyn.' Looking at Sasha, I found her grinning back at me like a buffoon, but that was nothing unusual, seeing as she'd just been surrounded by men vying for her attention. Chloe must be exaggerating like usual. Sash couldn't be that drunk yet, we'd only been here an hour.

'Ooooh … hellllo … who are *you,* handsome?' Sasha slurred, suddenly looking incredibly interested in my drinking companion as she swayed back and forth and staggered in her heels towards Oliver.

God. OK, so maybe Chloe hadn't been exaggerating about Sasha's drunken state. Flashing an apologetic glance at Oliver, I found him ignoring my embarrassing mates and instead staring at me intently, his blue eyes effortlessly snaring me once again. He really was so full on. Maybe Chloe's interruption had been a timely one, because who knew what I'd have agreed to if I'd had a few more moments alone with him and his teasing smiles.

'I'm sure I recognise you from somewhere,' Chloe murmured, giving Oliver an intent look.

He briefly returned her gaze, then shook his head. 'I don't think we've met.'

Chloe narrowed her eyes, and shrugged. 'Nah, I think you're right. You probably just have one of those faces.'

One of those faces? A ridiculously handsome one, is that what she meant?

Sasha staggered again, and Cloe grabbed her and cursed, giving me a pointed "hurry up" look.

'Looks like we're leaving,' I said quietly. 'Thanks for the uh … the chat.'

'It was a pleasure, Robyn with a y,' Oliver murmured, his eyes twinkling in that teasing way that I'd already become accustomed to. Standing to move away from us, he dipped his head close to my face and whispered his parting words, his lips brushing across the shell of my ear as he did so. 'I'm here most Fridays, so you know where to find me if you want more.' And with that he was gone, leaving me spluttering and speechless in his wake.

If I wanted more?

More what?

Information? Questions answered? Or more, as in the implied *more* ... A sexual, dark, deviant kind of more where we picked up from the near kiss of a few moments ago?

Swallowing loudly, I watched his broad back as he strode away from me. Good grief. I was feeling ridiculously flustered as I slid from my stool to leave, tottering around on my high-heeled boots almost as badly as Sasha. But even above the noise of the music I could have sworn I heard Oliver's deep, wicked chuckle behind me as we left.

## Chapter Seven

## Oliver

As mischievous as it was, I couldn't help the wicked laugh that escaped me as I saw Robyn's flustered stumble upon leaving. My ego would like to credit her state to my effect on her, but realistically it could easily have been down to the stupidly high-heeled boots she was wearing tonight.

Stupidly high, but so fucking sexy that an image of them clinging to the tight muscles in her legs would forever be burned into my brain. *¡Dios!* Getting to see her wearing those boots and nothing else was now firmly embedded at the top of my fantasy list.

Returning to my usual seat at the far end of the bar, I ordered another whiskey and swirled the amber liquid in the glass as I pondered the events of the evening. Robyn with a y. My lips pursed as I created an image of her in my mind again; those wide, beautiful eyes of hers had drawn me in all evening. The colour was fascinating: a mix of grey, blue, and green which seemed to swirl and change with her mood. Her infinitely tempting lips were almost as perfect, as were her arousing blushes and that long, slightly curling brown hair that would no doubt feel incredible wrapped around my wrist as I thrust into her from behind. The vision made my cock jerk and I shook my head in amusement. Yes, her hair was quite the temptation. I'd done well not to reach out and touch it as I'd so wanted to.

Her presence here tonight had certainly cheered up an otherwise drab evening, that was for sure. My nights here were mostly spent on my own, or talking to David about business. Occasionally some of the old-school regulars – who I now classed as friends – would make an appearance and we'd share a few drinks, but as a rule I didn't really socialise while at the club. It was a personal choice, my way to keep business and pleasure separate, but after years of politely dismissing the people who had tried to start up conversations with me – mostly women – the regulars had quickly picked up on it and now left me alone.

But Robyn had had me ditching my rules and making a first move. As I'd sat with her I'd seen a few regulars casting curious looks our way, and I couldn't blame them, really. I never started up conversations with the new customers, and in the last eight years it had been unheard of for me to hold someone's hand or start a romantic liaison within the walls of the club.

Recalling Dominic's blatant move towards Robyn made my teeth grind together in irritation, but then when I remembered how shocked he'd looked to see me with a woman, *and* holding her hand, I couldn't help but smirk.

She'd made the move to link her fingers with mine, though, which had been an interesting play on her part. A show of her hidden bravery, and one I could only assume meant that even though we had only just met, she trusted me more than Dominic. Or perhaps she felt the binding connection between us, too.

Why had I felt the need to protect her from Dominic? This wasn't just an easy lay sex club; the rules here at Twist were rigid when it came to non-members. If by some miracle he had persuaded her to go to one of the private rooms with him she would have first been interviewed by David, or myself, to check for compatibility and ensure the safety of all involved. She wasn't at risk, not really. He might have made her feel uncomfortable with some heavy chat-up lines, but really, was that any worse than me? I'd definitely seen her squirming under my attention a few times, too.

The urge to pass her my business card as she left, or try to get her number had been incredibly strong, but the strange look that her friend had been giving me had distracted me – I'd thought she was going to vomit on me, and that was not something I could look away from. I was normally far more focused than that, so I was kicking myself for my slip. I could have been holding Robyn's number in my hand right now, but instead I sat here alone, hoping that perhaps she would come back in at some point to continue her research. The lack of control over the situation was incredibly irritating.

Now Robyn was gone, the club around me seemed dull and uninspiring. The sight of men trying to charm women, or women draping themselves across potential partners, left me cold. Throwing back the last of my whisky, I stood and buttoned my jacket. It was time to head home, and perhaps if I were lucky, I'd see Robyn waiting in the taxi queue and could pass her my business card, or even offer to see her home safely. With that thought in my mind, I bid David goodnight and strode from the club with a grin on my face.

# Chapter Eight

## Robyn

Six in the morning felt like it came around in the blink of an eye. We hadn't been particularly late back from the club, stumbling in just before midnight in the end, but with my creative juices flowing from all the new book ideas careening around my head, sleep had been almost impossible.

Book ideas hadn't been the only thing keeping me awake. Oliver Wolfe, Mr Cool and Calm, had been on my mind, too. He'd also got my juices flowing, but in a rather different way. He'd managed to flick all my switches at once; in some ways he terrified me, or rather, his bedroom tastes did, but on the flip side he attracted and aroused me like no one I'd ever met.

Once the darkness of my room had settled around me last night, I'd remembered how his deep, rough voice had made me quiver, and how his intense gaze had sent shivers of lust running across my skin. I'd tried and failed to get him out of my head until the clock on my bedside table read 2:00 a.m. and I was still tossing and turning. In the end, I had resorted to easing the throbbing between my legs with my one and only vibrator. It had done the job, but it hadn't felt as good as his touch no doubt would have. Perhaps I should invest in a vibrator collection like Sasha's to give me some variety.

Thinking of the idea of Oliver touching me caused my skin to flush with heat all over again, and I threw off the covers with an impatient grumble. I fanned my face and tried to calm my raised breathing. Sleep clearly wasn't going to happen, so I may as well try to get some of my ideas down on my laptop while they were fresh in my mind.

I rolled out of bed and stretched, my muscles

complaining that I hadn't had nearly enough time below the duvet yet. There was no point trying for more, though. My brain was way too active for sleep.

As I stepped from the rug onto the hard, wooden floor I realised my feet were sore, too, and after examining the blisters on my heels I grimaced. My gorgeous but hideously painful new boots sat in the corner of my room looking all sexy and innocent, but I threw them a disgusted glance and hobbled towards the kitchen in search of coffee.

As I got the milk from the fridge, my gaze passed across a photograph stuck to the door with a magnet. It was of me and my family, taken recently at a gathering for my brother Tom's thirtieth birthday; my parents were smiling at me from the image, and my brother stood by my side with his characteristic grin spreading on his face and a ridiculous birthday hat on his head. The sheer normality of the image made me pause, then blush as I wondered what they would make of where I'd spent last night. God. My parents were so *normal*; living in their semi in Pinner with their cat, Ginge, a big garden, and an occasional night spent down the local pub.

I was pretty sure my mum would pass out if I told her I'd visited a sex club and been chatted up by an older man who liked to dominate women in bed.

A nervous giggle rose in my throat, and so, trying to push thoughts of my family aside, I grabbed the milk and turned away from the fridge ready to refocus on what I wanted to write today.

The stimulus of Club Twist had certainly given me plenty to get started on with my book, that was for sure, but as I stood waiting for my coffee to brew it was visions of Oliver that once again filled my mind. My fingers tightened around the mug in my hands as I recalled his confidence and intense demeanour. It had been a little intimidating to start with, but something about the way

49

he'd so effortlessly taken control of the evening was definitely attractive.

Luckily, creativity and caffeine went hand in hand for me, so I filled my cup and padded into the lounge to fire up my shiny new laptop.

I moved around the apartment as quietly as possible, knowing that Chloe would be sleeping for a few more hours, and that Sasha probably wouldn't be emerging from her bed – and hangover – until well into the afternoon.

Sitting at my computer, I took a deep breath, and began to type.

Three hours later, I sat back from my laptop and chewed on a fingernail as I let out an aggravated grunt. My ideas had been flowing brilliantly, but this part was getting decidedly tricky.

'What's up?' croaked Sasha from her prone position in an armchair across the room. She had appeared from her bedroom about an hour ago, and after mumbling a groggy "good morning" and vowing never to drink vodka again, she had retrieved an ice pack from the fridge, clapped it to her forehead, and plonked down into the armchair.

She hadn't moved since.

This was Sasha's trademarked hangover recovery procedure. That plus a Chinese takeaway, which she'd probably ask me to order in another hour or so. Chloe was up, too, but currently in the shower, so I felt able to talk to Sasha about my current quandary.

'I'm trying to write my first proper sex scene. I'm loosely using some of the stuff we saw last night for inspiration, but I'm stuck,' I admitted, a blush blooming on my cheeks as I reread the text I'd written.

'Stuck with what?' she murmured, still concealed firmly behind her ice pack. At least with her eyes hidden it was less embarrassing for me to explain what I was struggling with.

'Well, I don't want to use the words "penis" or "vagina", they sound so clinical, but I don't know what words to use instead,' I explained, feeling my blush deepen.

'Hmmm … gotcha. Depends on the context, I think. Read me what you've written, and I'll help out.' There was a slight shift as Sasha made herself more comfortable, but I still couldn't see her face, so, feeling brave, I cleared my throat and began to read out what I'd written so far.

*The heavy beat of the music in the club only seemed to add to her excitement as sweat trickled down between her breasts and mingled deliciously with the remaining oil from her earlier massage. Taking advantage of her slick skin, the stranger wasted no time in sliding his fingers across her nipples, massaging them into needy peaks before trailing his hands to her exposed back and pulling her towards him so their naked hips clashed together, making her buck against him wildly.*

*'Fingers of onlookers stretched to join in, tugging on her nipples and fondling her until they were red and sensitive, and she was writhing below them, desperate for more. The stranger growled possessively, and pushed the intruding hands away before he captured one of her nipples in his mouth, sucking hard, making her whimper from the beautiful mix of pleasure and pain that darted across her skin. Using his palm on her stomach, he pressed her willing body back against the hard, wooden podium so she was spread before him, laid out like an offering. Kicking her legs apart he exposed her slick …*

'Bleep!' I made a comedy buzzer noise to indicate that I didn't know what word to use to describe my character's anatomy, then continued reading.

*His throbbing … bleep! … pressed against her pliant flesh before driving forcefully into her in one hard thrust, causing them both to cry out and gasp in a pleasure that was shared by all those who were watching from the sidelines ... '*

Sitting back with a huff, I shrugged. 'It carries on, but I'm stuck on words for their anatomy. Any ideas?' I looked across at Sasha, and was surprised to see that she was now sitting up, staring at me with her mouth hanging open, the ice pack discarded on the floor by her feet.

Wincing at her gawking expression, I looked away from her as another blush rushed to my cheeks and my shoulders slumped. 'Oh God, it's utter crap, isn't it?' I groaned. 'It's only my first attempt, though, so maybe I can improve it?' I mumbled awkwardly, embarrassed by how stupid I was for ever thinking I was capable of writing something sexy.

I barely ever had sex; how the hell did I think I'd be capable of writing it?

'What are you talking about?' Sasha exclaimed, her voice sounding painfully raspy from all the shouting last night.

'Yeah, I guess that's the problem, I don't have a clue what I'm talking about,' I agreed glumly, my shoulders slumping as I leaned forwards and rested my forehead on the dining table in defeat.

The sound of Sasha's chair scraping the floor made me look up again. She jumped up, waving her arms around as if she was attempting to waft away a swarm of wasps at the same time as making a loud spluttering noise. Wow, hungover Sasha jumping around was *not* a usual occurrence. 'No! That's not what I meant. That was bloody brilliant, Robyn. Holy shit, it was hot! Talk about voyeuristic. Let me see the rest.'

Before I knew it, Sasha had crossed the room, shouldering me out of the way so she could lean down and avidly read the rest of the paragraph.

I blinked several times as I watched her greedily soaking up my words. Really? She liked it? I reread the paragraph myself, and have to say it was slightly arousing as the text conjured up erotic images in my mind. I hadn't actually witnessed this exact thing last night, but it was loosely based on the couple having sex that I'd seen during the tour Oliver had given me. Obviously, as well as arousing me, the scene had also inspired me. Apparently, I was a voyeur. Who knew it? That would surprise Oliver.

Hmm. Oliver. So I was thinking about him *yet again*. It was slightly disconcerting that my mind kept replaying the moment when I'd felt his hot breath flutter across my lips and thought he was going to kiss me. I bet he would have, too, if Chloe and Sasha hadn't interrupted us. The look in his eyes had been one of pure and utter determination.

Now that image *really* was arousing for me, but with Sasha right here next to me it was hardly the time to linger on it. Blinking several times, I shut Oliver out of my mind – for now, anyway – and tried to focus back on my writing.

'I think in this instance you should go with "cock" and "folds",' Sasha decided with a firm nod, before pointing to the gaps in my work then pinching my coffee cup and leaning back on the wall to enjoy it.

'His throbbing cock,' I said out loud, testing it. 'Yeah, that's probably the best option,' I agreed, typing it into my text. I definitely wasn't using "penis", and when books used words like "rod" or "phallus" I always cringed, so they were a big no-no for me, too. Once you got down to the nitty-gritty of it there really were only so many nouns for a good ol' cock, and sometimes the tried and tested names were the best.

'And you think "folds" for her vag?' I said with a frown. I wasn't quite as convinced by her choice this time.

'Yeah, *her slick folds*,' Sasha announced breathily, making speech mark actions with her fingers as she said it.

Seeing my sceptical look, she wagged my coffee cup at me, and gave me a determined glare. 'It's better than vagina, and I hate it when erotic books use the "c" word to

53

describe a woman's area. It's just such a horrible word.' I had to agree with Sasha there; it wasn't one of my favourites, either. 'Trust me on this, Robyn, I've read a lot of erotica and they always use words like lips, folds or slit, never an actual name.'

'Right. Use describing words for the vagina rather than an actual name for it. I can do that,' I said decisively before adding "folds" into my text and pressing the save icon.

'But if you ever describe it as her "moist valley" or her "dark love cavern" I will unfriend you in real life *and* on Facebook,' Sasha told me haughtily before flashing me a wink.

'Love cavern?' I asked on a giggle.

'Yup. Seriously, I've read both of those in books before! Can you believe it?'

I actually couldn't, but seeing as Sasha was the in-house expert on erotica I'd have to take her word for it, and we both promptly collapsed into creases of laughter.

'God. What a way to start the day! I can't believe we're discussing this. I think I need a bucket load more coffee.'

'I'll stick the coffee maker on again,' Sasha announced, 'and I'll get the takeaway menu. I need Chinese for lunch.'

It wasn't exactly a run of the mill start to the weekend, was it? Writing explicit sex before the sun had even risen, then casually chatting about vocabulary for sexual body parts with my best friend.

Maybe if I could get this book written and published this would become a typical Saturday morning around here.

'So, are we going to go back to Club Twist again? You know ... to help your research?' Sasha asked hopefully from the kitchen area, just as Chloe joined us once more.

The idea of going back to the club made my stomach quiver as I imagined seeing Oliver again. He'd said he was there most Fridays, so I'd know when to find him. He'd

54

also offered me more … which was still playing on my mind. The unanswered question of "more what?" was still looping in my brain, closely followed up with the more important question of whether I wanted more with a man like him?

Maybe we could venture to the club again, just so I could ogle him a little more. He'd managed to kick start my libido for the first time in ages, so it couldn't be all bad. 'Um … I dunno. Maybe?'

'I think we should. The guest passes we got allow us ten entries before we have to decide on membership or not, so we might as well use a few of them,' Sasha said, before fanning her face dramatically. 'It would be worth it just to see that guy again. My God, he was just so hot.' Wiggling her eyebrows for effect, she giggled. 'Bagsy first shot at him! Girl code!'

'Which guy?' Chloe asked in confusion, taking the words out of my mouth.

'The hot one! You couldn't exactly have missed him. He was at the bar a lot, and the best-looking bloke there. A bit older than us. He knew the staff really well, so he might have worked there, I'm not sure. I didn't manage to speak to him for long.'

Was she talking about Oliver? Damn. He was hot, *and* older, *and* had been at the bar. And Sasha had spoken to him, albeit briefly, and in a very drunken state. Not that I would have been brave enough to do anything with him, but she'd shouted "girl code" which in our house meant one thing – he was now strictly off limits because she wanted first try at pulling him.

My lips drew tight as I tried to erase the image of my confident mate pouring herself all over Oliver. He'd probably love it. For some completely irrational reason, the thought made me feel sick to my stomach.

# Chapter Nine

## Robyn

Against my better judgement, the following Friday I found myself at the large entrance doors to Club Twist again. I had been reluctant to go at first, because the idea of Sasha hitting on Oliver right before my eyes hadn't sat well in my stomach, but after much persuasion I had agreed to come, just to stop her whinging at me.

Surprisingly, Chloe had been up for it, too, with no arguments at all, and so at just gone nine-thirty the three of us handed over our second guest pass, got our visitor stamps, and stepped into the dark, warm interior of the club.

Like some sort of magnet, my eyes were immediately drawn to the area of the bar where I'd first seen Oliver last week, and my stomach gave a huge lurch as I saw his broad-shouldered profile. He sat on a stool and was leaning forward as he spoke to the guy behind the bar.

He was here. Just as he'd said he would be.

Knowing Sasha had her eye on him, I decided not to approach him. Instead, I made my way through the crowd to the same stool I'd occupied last week, which was at the opposite end of the bar from him. I'd expected Sasha to make her move right away, that was usually her style, but she ordered us a round of shots, downed hers, and dragged Chloe off towards the dance floor, leaving me to make some more notes for my research.

I'd remembered my notepad this week, and was soon so engrossed in my scribbling that I didn't pay any attention to the customers directly around me. I didn't even notice when someone took the stool next to mine. I did, however, notice when a very recognisable voice ordered a double single malt with a touch of water.

*Fuck*. Oliver was now right next to me. He'd moved to sit beside me. My stomach flip-flopped wildly with nervous excitement, and I allowed myself a moment of calm before the storm and closed my eyes, drawing in slow, steady breaths and trying in desperation to slow my pounding heart. His clean scent washed over me, and I felt my skin heat, just from his proximity. This man really did do crazy things to my body.

Eventually, after several seconds of silence, I slid my notepad and pen into my handbag and plucked up the courage to turn towards him. I raised my gaze up his gorgeously suited body. He looked just as perfect as he had last week, with a ramrod-straight back and one foot propped on the rung of my stool. I continued to raise my eyes until they met his deep denim blues, and then gulped nervously when I found an intense, purposeful expression on his face.

'Hi, Oliver,' I mumbled awkwardly.

'Good evening, Robyn.' Oliver smiled at me, and lifted his glass to his lips, pausing to tilt his head and examine me before he took a small and somehow sensual sip of the amber liquid. 'It's a pleasure to see you here again tonight. You'd looked quite nervous last week, so I wasn't sure if I'd see you again.'

Clearing my throat, I shrugged self-consciously, wishing that my shot glass was full so I could down it all over again to boost my confidence. 'It was a bit shocking, but, you know, the more research I do the better the book will be.'

'Absolutely,' he agreed, sounding like he meant more than his simple word conveyed. 'Can I buy you a drink?'

Uh. This was awkward. Sasha had claimed girl code over him, so I really shouldn't, but how did I refuse without sounding rude?

'Um, I'm fine, thank you.'

Frowning, he looked to the empty glass on the bar

beside me, then gave me a curious look. 'Just one?'

Huffing out an irritated breath, I looked away and my eyes immediately landed on Sasha who was giving me a thumbs-up from the dance floor. Did she want me to get her an introduction with Oliver? God. This was a really weird situation. I was attracted to him, but friends came before guys, so feeling bound to Sasha I instead decided to give her the opening she'd wanted.

'Look, if you must know, my friend likes you, so, you know, I'm respecting the girl code,' I muttered, feeling ridiculous.

'Girl code?' Oliver repeated, a smile breaking on his lips. Instead of waiting for me to explain, he continued. 'Which friend? One of the ones you arrived with?'

Avoiding eye contact, I picked up my empty shot glass and twirled it in my fingertips as a distraction. 'Yeah, the blonde one.'

'The blonde, huh?' The curious tone to his voice made me feel sick. Of course he would be curious; she was gorgeous. He would no doubt be attracted to her; all men were. 'She has a funny way of showing it, seeing as she's currently staring at my friend like she wants to eat him alive.'

My head snapped up, and I looked to the dance floor to see that Oliver was in fact correct. Sasha was no longer looking my way. She now stood a few feet away from us, staring at a blond guy at the bar with lust-filled eyes. Jeez. Had she moved on already? I could barely keep up with her. Just as I was thinking this, she turned and saw me watching her, before darting in my direction.

'Excuse me for a second,' I said to Oliver, quickly moving away from him to meet Sasha. 'I was only talking to him. His name's Oliver.'

'Who?' she asked with a frown.

Jerking a thumb over my shoulder I leaned closer and lowered my voice. 'The hot guy you liked. He's one of the owners of this place, and his name is Oliver.'

Frowning, she peered over my shoulder and, to my mortification waved, presumably at Oliver. The back of my neck prickled and, somehow, I just knew he was now standing behind me. One brief glance confirmed my theory. He was indeed beside us, right inside my personal space again, and giving me and Sasha an amused smile.

'As handsome as you are … Hi, I'm Sasha, by the way,' she announced before looking at me again. 'That's not the guy I was talking about.' Turning her head, she pointed through the crowd at the blond guy at the other end of the bar. '*That's* the guy.'

Oh. A different hot older guy. Oops. I'd been so infatuated with Oliver that I'd just assumed she'd been talking about him, and hadn't bothered to ask her to describe her crush to me. A simple "what colour hair did he have?" would have saved all these issues, because these two were like chalk and cheese.

'I'm going to dance. Feel free to chat up Robyn, she's young, free and single,' Sasha declared with glee, giving Oliver another eyebrow wiggle.

'Shut up Sasha, you're drunk,' I chided playfully, watching her knock back yet another vodka shot then slam the glass down.

'So? It's Friday night! Besides, alcohol makes you tell the truth, doesn't it? And you *are* young, free and single. And desperately in need of a good fuck.'

Oh, Jesus Christ, she hadn't actually said that, had she? My stomach just about dropped from my body in horror as her words hung in the air between us all. Judging from Oliver's raised eyebrows and the wicked smirk playing at the corners of his lips, she had.

'Good to know,' he murmured dryly, as Sasha waved and swayed her way back to the dance floor. I was going to kill her later. 'Blunt, isn't she?'

Forget a simple blush on my cheeks, my whole body

now felt overheated with mortification. 'You have no idea,' I groaned, desperately wishing for a sinkhole to swallow me up.

'Now we've cleared up that misunderstanding, can I buy you that drink?'

I paused, staring at the floor and biting my lower lip as I tried to decide. I was so tempted; I was really attracted to Oliver and, under different circumstances, would have ripped his arm off for a drink, or a date, but he was the owner of a sex club. He liked to control women in the bedroom. I had no idea what else it might entail, but I knew I was way out of my depth with him.

The feel of a gentle finger on my chin broke me from my thoughts as Oliver tipped my face up towards his. 'I won't bite,' he murmured, his voice low and teasing. 'Not unless you want me to,' he added, the playful expression from last week returning to his face.

He was joking about the biting. Wasn't he? Before I could really think it all through and persuade myself out of it, I found myself nodding and depositing the vodka glass on the bar. Fuck it, why not? 'No to the biting, but yes to the drink. I'll have a white wine, please.'

Oliver grinned at my joke and we took our seats once more as he ordered me a drink.

As he spoke to the barman, I fiddled with the clasp on my bag, making sure it was closed, but looked up when he spoke again. 'She's not my type, by the way.'

My eyebrows rose in surprise at both his statement, and the force of his gaze as he stared at me from under slightly hooded eyes.

Not sure how to respond to the way he gave me so much of his attention, I glanced out to the dance floor and located Sasha. She was grinding against one guy, while another danced closely behind her, pressing his groin to her buttocks in a move so innately sexual that it made me cringe. It was about usual for Sasha, though. With her confidence and seduction skills she could usually be most men's type if she put her mind to it.

'Why?'

Oliver held out a glass of wine to me, effectively drawing my gaze away from Sasha's antics and back to him. 'I don't mean any offence, but she's very … loud. And I suspect she's flighty, too. I saw her last week dancing with practically every man in here. I bet she's never with the same guy twice, that sort of thing?'

Wow, he'd described my bestie to perfection and I momentarily gawked at him in surprise. If he could tell that much about Sasha from just a few observations, then God only knows what he had read in me.

'I'm a good people reader,' he murmured in answer to my questioning look. Great, so he probably knew exactly how affected by him I was.

Ignoring the pang of embarrassment, I shrugged, glancing at Sasha again. 'Guys seem to love Sasha. I'm surprised she's not your type.'

In response to my words, Oliver leaned back on his stool and gave me a very thorough look up and down, his gaze causing goose bumps to appear across my skin. His eyes travelled right from the tips of my stupidly painful boots to the top of my head, before he licked his bloody divine lips and grinned at me.

'My type falls more to gorgeous brunettes, about five foot seven, with the most unique coloured eyes I've ever seen, a very attractive blush, and a stubborn streak that will no doubt drive me insane.'

I blinked in surprise at how blatant his words were, then I blinked again, not quite sure how to respond. Finally, I managed to swallow and answer. 'Oh.' It wasn't much of a response, but it was all I could manage.

'Yes, "oh" indeed,' Oliver agreed. He clicked his glass against mine in some sort of toast, then took a sip. I was too stunned to sip my drink, though. To be honest, I was too stunned to move.

Was he really hitting on me? I paused, wondering if this were another of his teasing jokes, and not wanting to make a fool of myself if it was. One thing was certain – joke or not, I was definitely feeling rather giddy from all the attention I was getting from this gorgeous man.

Apparently picking up on my hesitant confusion, Oliver smiled at me and nodded once. 'I apologise if I have made you uncomfortable with my words, but I won't take them back. It's the Spanish blood in me, it makes me say what I think. I can't help it. You're rather lovely, and I would very much enjoy getting to know you.'

He thought I was rather lovely? None of my past boyfriends had been particularly flowery in the words department, and although I might have had the odd "you look nice tonight" comment, I'd never received compliments like this before. It was all quite overwhelming, really. The way he'd said it with his slight Spanish accent had sent a jolt of desire curling into my belly and I tried to get a grip of myself before I swooned at his feet.

'Your silence is particularly telling. I think perhaps you are more curious about our lifestyles than you want to admit,' he speculated casually as he sipped his drink. 'Perhaps it is also me? Are you curious about me, Robyn with a y?'

Yes. Yes, I was. I swallowed hard enough to make an audible noise and blushed as I saw the corner of his mouth lift in an answering smile. He'd hit the nail right on the head. I was curious about the club ... about the sex ... about him. He really was a good reader of people if he'd managed to get all of that from my expressions.

I didn't want to admit it out loud, but just as I was fumbling for what to say, he suddenly laughed, a lovely warm sound that vibrated through me and chased away the chill of nervousness from my skin. 'I'm teasing you. I'm sorry, please forgive me. It is another trait of my culture, we are merciless jokers.' Giving me an apologetic smile he wiggled his eyebrows hopefully. 'I do like you, that part wasn't a joke, but look, don't put so much pressure on yourself. Why don't I just help you with your research and we can get to know each other a little in the process. You'll have to put up with my teasing, but I promise there are no strings attached. I will expect nothing in return except your company.'

Reaching up, he ran the pad of his thumb across my cheek and smiled fondly. 'And your blushes,' he murmured. 'You blush so beautifully when you're embarrassed.' Pausing, he briefly bit on his lower lip then his smile darkened. 'I wonder if you also blush like that when you're aroused?'

My face now felt like it was on fire. His touch sparked some crazy chemical reaction within me that sent my hormones wild, and his teasing statements were almost too much for me to handle. This was all getting really intense really quickly, and as much as I was enjoying it on some level, I was also quite terrified of my reaction to him.

Ignoring his last question, I focused on the part of his statement that I could deal with. 'No strings?' I rasped, my voice rough from nerves.

'None, I promise,' he replied, removing his hand from my cheek and placing it over his heart as he graced me with another of his breath-stopping grins.

I knew what the sensible response would be. Thank him for his time and leave. Walk away and not look back. I was too affected by him to linger, and he was way too charming and handsome for me to resist, so I was bound to get burned by any type of relationship with him, even if we were supposedly just friends. But even knowing that, it's not what I ended up saying. 'OK, then. Deal.'

Oliver's eyes twinkled with happiness at my acceptance and he raised his glass towards mine. 'To new acquaintances,' he murmured. Once again, his tone seemed to say so much more than he vocalised, and as I lifted my glass to gently chink it against his I decided that I was definitely in dangerous territory with this man.

New acquaintances. Hmm. I could think of so many levels that I'd like to be "acquainted" with Mr Oliver Wolfe, but none were really within my sphere of bravery. He was a self-confessed sexual dominant, not to mention older than me, and therefore presumably far more experienced, and I was ... well, I was Robyn, the girl who'd never achieved a climax through penetrative sex because all my boyfriends had been dreadful in the sack.

Or perhaps it was me who was awful in bed?

God. What was I getting myself into?

# Chapter Ten

## Robyn

Surprisingly, after my initial nerves, I found that sitting with Oliver and chatting wasn't half as scary as I'd expected. He behaved himself impeccably, he didn't tease me – well, not too much anyway – and was in fact turning out to be amazingly helpful for my research. He was like an encyclopaedia on the subject of this club, and had so far answered all of my questions without hesitation.

We'd been speaking for a while about the varying reasons that drove the customers to the club, when we were approached by two men – one being the man Sasha had expressed her interest in earlier – and I craned my head back to look at them. Crikey, were all the men in here mutants or something? Because these two were almost as large as Dominic and were carrying some serious muscle, too.

'Good evening, Oliver,' the taller of the two men – Sasha's crush – said, and I wondered if I could detect just a hint of an American accent in his tone.

'Marcus, Nathan, good to see you again,' Oliver replied with a smile, and I noticed that although these new arrivals looked a little intimidating in their stature, Oliver sounded genuine with his greeting and didn't seem to bristle with tension as he had last week when Dominic had approached.

He also didn't take hold of my hand again, which sensibly should have been a relief, but wasn't, and I actually found myself wishing he would reach out for me and stake his claim again.

I was in so much trouble here. I'd only met the guy twice and already I was infatuated with him. Damn. I was usually so much better with my self-control, but his proximity seemed to remove all my usual restraint.

Oliver's manners seemed to insist that he did a full greeting, and he held out a hand and gestured at the men. 'Robyn, this is Marcus Price,' he said, referring to the one Sasha fancied. I stored the name away, so I could tell her later. Marcus gave me a dazzling smile in return, complete with a set of perfectly straight teeth and dimples in his cheeks. He was at least as tall as Dominic had been, but with his relaxed posture, floppy blond hair, and warm expression I didn't feel any of the fear I had last week, so I tentatively nodded my head and found myself smiling back. I could see why Sasha liked him. He was a good-looking guy, and his grin was actually quite infectious.

'And this is Nathanial Jackson.' My gaze travelled to the other man and I felt my smile becoming a little strained. He wasn't threatening like Dominic had seemed, but he radiated some sort of shuttered tension. He was tall, blond, and had the iciest blue eyes I'd ever seen. He was nowhere near as friendly as Marcus, his posture was stiff and defensive, and overall, he made me feel uneasy.

'Call me Nathan,' he corrected immediately, with a vague nod of greeting, all the while keeping his eyes fixed on my cheeks, which made me worry that I had something smeared on my face.

Giving my cheek a quick wipe with my hand, I tried to shrug off my worry, then took a calming sip of my drink. It suddenly occurred to me how stupid I was being – I was sitting in a sex club as a compete newbie, and was now surrounded by three attractive – not to mention huge – guys. They must put growth hormones in the drinks here, because I couldn't see how any of these men would be below six foot five, and that included Oliver. What if they suddenly expected me to partake in something with them all? Three men and me? Crikey, I wasn't even sure I was imaginative enough to envision *how* the biology of that would work ... but even though I found the idea quite intriguing, it also terrified me, so I quickly slid from my seat and grabbed my bag.

'I should find my friends, I'll leave you guys to it.'

All three sets of eyes turned to me, but it was Marcus who spoke first. 'Don't leave on our account,' He smiled again, and I felt some of my anxiousness releasing. He really did seem like a genuinely nice guy. 'We're just grabbing the drinks for our group.' With a jerk of his chin he seemed to be indicating to a table against the wall where two women sat with a dark-haired man. I watched with interest as Nathan caught the eye of one of the women and winked at her, which in turn caused her to grin back at him, his entire body seeming to relax from their eye contact. Interesting. For a few seconds he transformed into a completely different man, so presumably she was his girlfriend, or partner.

Turning back to us, Nathan immediately stiffened again. He picked up the drinks from the bar and, with a swift nod at myself and Oliver, he departed towards his friends.

I was already playing with fire by sitting with Oliver, so maybe this had given me the perfect opportunity to leave. Judging by the way Oliver's stare was now intently fixed upon mine again, though, he wanted me to stay.

Marcus broke the connection between Oliver and me by leaning in between us to get to the bar. 'Don't mind Nathan, he's just a bit of a quiet one,' he remarked with a smile as he picked up the remaining drinks. 'It was a pleasure to meet you, Robyn. Enjoy your evening.'

'Thanks.' I mumbled, because I had no idea what else to say.

'Still on for squash on Thursday?' Marcus asked Oliver with a raise of his eyebrows.

Nodding, Oliver shared one of his own smiles. 'Of course. I believe it will be four-nil to me if I win again this week?'

Laughing, Marcus nodded. 'Indeed it will, but that's

only because I'm rusty. Give me a few more weeks to get back into my game and I'll be wiping the floor with you, old man.'

There was no way Oliver could be termed an old man, but he took the banter with a grin and nodded. 'It'll be fun watching you try.'

With a wink and a cocky grin Marcus then left us. I hesitated, still unsure whether to retake my seat or try to take my leave and go in search of Chloe and Sasha. I knew what the sensible option would be, but the prospect of spending more time in Oliver's charismatic company was making me pause. As if sensing my uncertainty, Oliver gave my stool a brief pat and raised his eyebrows hopefully. 'Sit a little longer with me?'

At his invitation my tummy gave a little leap of excitement, which was ridiculous, because I was far too boring to embark on some wild fling with a self-professed sexual dominant, and yet I still climbed back into my seat.

'Marcus is the man your friend liked, yes?'

Nodding, I took a sip of my drink to try to calm my hammering heartbeat.

'I don't know what she'd be looking for, but he just got out of a relationship, so I suspect casual would be all he'd be up for at the moment.'

Casual was all Sasha did, she was a specialist at fucking without commitments, but I decided not to enlighten Oliver with that lovely fact. 'He seemed nice.'

'He is. He's a good friend of mine, very decent guy, too. He's a chef, only recently got back from a stint working in New York. Unfortunately, he's found himself single again, because his girlfriend decided she preferred America over him.'

Frowning, I glanced across at Marcus, then turned my attention back to Oliver. 'Poor guy, that's horrible.'

Oliver gave a shrug. 'She was a money-grabbing bitch. He's better off without her.'

My eyebrows rose at the chill in Oliver's tone, so, sensing it was a sensitive topic, I changed the subject slightly. 'Nathan seemed almost as intimidating as Dominic,' I remarked, watching as Nathan and Marcus joined their friends. Marcus was on his own, happy at the head of the table, but as soon as Nathan sat down he wrapped an arm around the shoulder of the petite blonde woman and tugged her firmly against his side.

Oliver laughed and glanced towards the group. 'He might look it, but I've known him a long time, and believe me, he's quite a soft touch underneath that prickly exterior. He's got a permanent partner, Stella, the blonde he's with now. They've got a young child, too, so we rarely see him in here nowadays. Guess someone's babysitting to give them a night off.'

Wow. Parents choosing to go to a place like this on their night off. What a peculiar thought. 'Did they meet here?' I asked, finding myself incredibly curious about the relationship the two of them must have. It would probably make a fascinating book.

'Actually, they did. David Halton – he's another of the owners here – set them up, and he's very proud of that fact, too,' Oliver commented dryly. 'You've no doubt already seen him around. He's the tattooed guy that works behind the bar.'

I did recall seeing him, but was surprised by Oliver's mention of yet another owner. 'How many owners are there?' I asked, thinking that already there was Oliver, Dominic, and now this David guy.

'Four. David is the majority shareholder and the only one with an upfront role in the business. Myself, Dominic, and a woman named Alexandra loaned him the money he needed to start it all up, and in return we get a percentage of the takings. The three of us all have jobs outside of the club, so we're silent partners, really, but I also do the accounts as a side job.'

'What do you do for a day job?' I asked, hoping that I wasn't pushing our arrangement too far into personal waters for his liking.

'I'm a financial advisor. I own my own company now, so I can be choosy about my clients.' Which I took to mean that he only represented filthy rich people, and was rather successful at what he did.

After that, we sat in silence for a few moments as I watched all the goings-on around us. 'So, did you have any more questions you wanted to ask me for your research?' Oliver asked with a curious tilt to his head. 'Or perhaps we could find a more practical way to kill some time? There's plenty of things here within Club Twist that we could entertain ourselves with.'

Gulping at his suggestion I felt my cheeks burn, and proceeded to open and close my mouth three times, each time not managing to actually speak. He looked so serious. Was he actually suggesting what I thought he was?

Tipping his head back, Oliver laughed so loudly that several people turned in our direction to look at him.

'I'm joking, Robyn!' He wiped a tear from his eye and grinned at me. 'You are such fun.'

I wasn't sure I liked being teased like this, but his grin was so beautiful that I found myself relaxing with a wry smile of my own as I shook my head in mock chastisement.

'I'm sorry, I couldn't resist.' He didn't sound repentant at all, but I had a feeling that with his twinkling blue eyes he could persuade me to forgive pretty much any misdemeanour.

'Maybe you should try harder then,' I replied, trying for a chiding tone, but giggling at the end of my sentence as I felt myself getting more and more flustered.

There was something between us, I was sure of it. Something potent. A pull, or attraction, that I suspected would only get stronger the more time I spent with him, and I was hardly helping matters by joining in with his banter.

'So, questions?'

Clearing my throat, I nodded. 'Oh … uh … yes, please.'

He slid from his stool, straightened his jacket, and buttoned it, drawing my eyes down to his impossibly trim torso. 'Let's go somewhere a little quieter.'

Somewhere quieter? That sounded decidedly dodgy, so I gave him a tentative look and shook my head. I might be a little infatuated, but I hadn't completely lost my mind.

Seeing my stubborn expression, he laughed again. 'I'm not going to drag you off to a bedroom, Robyn. I have never needed to trick or force a woman in my life, and I don't intend to start now.'

His comment was supposed to reassure me, but it gave me a sour taste in my mouth, and as hard as I tried to dismiss the wave of jealousy that swept over me, I couldn't. How many women had fallen at his feet over the years? Given his charm, looks, and build, it was probably countless amounts.

A sudden pain in my hands made me realise that I had clenched my fists so hard that my nails were biting into the skin of my palms. I'd never been one for jealousy before, which made this even more laughable, because Oliver wasn't even mine to be protective over. Taking a deep breath, I relaxed my hands and shoved my irrational thoughts aside.

As I looked back at his face I found him watching me curiously, as if he'd read my mind and knew exactly what I'd been stewing over. Damn it. I really needed to work on hiding my emotions from his all-seeing eyes.

'Trust me?' he asked softly, holding a hand out for me.

# Chapter Eleven

## Robyn

'Trust me?'

As stupid as it might be, I did trust Oliver. I'd only met him twice, but in that time he'd protected me from the predatory advances of Dominic, and apart from his flirtatious teasing – which was actually rather appealing – he'd done nothing but be a complete gentleman.

I braced myself for the jolt of reaction when our skin touched, and placed my hand in his. Just as expected, my skin instantly tingled, but because I'd been expecting it I managed not to gasp out loud like the last two times, which was a least a minor improvement.

As I took his hand I noticed several other people in the bar halt their conversations and look over in curiosity. Oliver didn't seem bothered at all, but from the interest that his simple gesture had gained, I could only assume that leaving hand-in-hand with the boss probably meant a good deal more than simple contact.

I'm not sure if I was imagining it, but a lull seemed to have fallen over the club, too; the music was still blaring, but to me it felt as though conversations had practically stopped as the staff and other customers watched us leave. Oliver seemed just as relaxed as before, though, so maybe I was just being paranoid.

Holding my hand tightly, he led me through a set of silver-framed doors to a quieter side of the club, and then through another door marked as "staff only". It let us into a bar area that had a large name emblazoned on the wall. *Twist*.

'This is the adjoining bar and coffee shop. David owns it, too. It's quieter here, much better for talking.' Which, in fairness, it was. So Oliver had once again kept his word – he hadn't tried anything funny, and he hadn't taken me somewhere dark so he could push his luck. I had been right to trust him.

Oliver led me to a booth and only let go of my hand after he'd got me seated. 'I'll get us some fresh drinks. Why don't you message your friends and tell them where you are, so they don't worry?'

Nodding, I pulled out my phone, opting to message Chloe, because Sasha would no doubt be too busy dancing – or too drunk by now – to check her phone.

I received an immediate reply telling me to have fun, but be careful, which was pretty standard for our overprotective Chloe.

Just as I was popping my phone back in my bag, Oliver returned with our drinks and joined me, making it obvious that he intended to sit beside me in the booth, rather than opposite. The booth wasn't that large, and a small tinge of panic ran through me at just how close he was going to be.

A waft of his clean scent filled my nostrils as he sat down, and his thigh brushed mine as he made himself more comfortable. A small shudder of desire ran up my spine as the heat from his leg felt like it was burning through my jeans, but he made no effort to move it.

This man had such an effect on me it was almost beyond the realms of my comprehension. Once again, his close proximity sent my senses into overdrive, and it took me several seconds to settle myself enough to brave looking across at him. When I did, I found a bottle of wine in a cooler before us, and Oliver looking at me intently.

Before I could express my thanks for the drinks, I noticed a tall blonde woman standing several steps behind him, glaring at me with a hate-filled look. There was simply no other way to describe her expression. The expression on her face gave me instant chills down my spine and I found myself sitting up and raising my chin defensively. Who the heck was she?

Oliver must have noticed my prickly demeanour,

73

because he glanced over his shoulder, tensed, then turned to face her, inadvertently moving himself even closer to me in the process. God. Now his entire side was pressed against mine, and the heat from his frame was making my skin burn with an excited blush.

'Good evening, Alexandra.'

Presumably this was the other owner that Oliver had mentioned earlier. She didn't return his greeting. Instead, she strutted closer, running her gaze over the two of us. Apparently, she didn't like the fact that we sat so closely, if the twitch in her left eye was anything to go by.

'I didn't realise you were dating again,' she sniped. Oliver's features remained neutral, but as I was sitting so close to him I saw the marginal narrowing of his eyes at her comment. Just because we were sitting together didn't make it a date, but she had assumed so anyway. Her words were also similar to Dominic's comment last week when he'd asked Oliver if he was back in the game. Why hadn't he been dating? And why was it such a big deal to everyone?

Suddenly, I was filled with a desperate need to fill the tense silence that hung around us. 'Oh, this isn't a ...'

My sentence was cut short as Oliver took hold of my hand and gave it a sharp squeeze, causing me to stall in my speech and look at him in surprise. This hand holding was becoming almost commonplace now, not that I really minded.

His eyes darted to mine, and even though it was the briefest of glances he flashed me a wink and gave me a look that I took to mean "don't finish that sentence", so I didn't, snapping my mouth closed instead.

When she saw our joined hands, Alexandra's face stiffened, making me wonder if there a history between the two owners, but she chose not to say anything, and I certainly wasn't going to.

'Was there something you needed, Alex?' Oliver asked

in an icy tone that I was glad wasn't directed at me, but the gentle rub of his thumb across the back of my hand was far from icy. In fact, it was lovely, and I felt warmth seeping through my veins regardless of the glacial stare that was still being directed at me from Alex.

There was another lengthy pause where I almost thought Alex was going to challenge me to a duel of ownership over Oliver, but finally she shifted, her social mask seeming to drop back into place as she ignored me, and flashed Oliver a seductive smile. 'No. I need to go and find Joshua. I'll see you in the club later.' As a parting gesture another glare was directed at me, then she turned on her heel and strode in the direction of the club.

She was certainly intense, which is my polite way of saying she was a raving bitch. Oliver turned to me with an apologetic wince. 'Sorry about that. Alex can be a little ... peculiar sometimes,' he said by way of explanation.

He lowered his gaze as he examined our joined hands and, after giving one more soothing rub with his thumb, he released me.

'That's OK.' My hand was still tingling from his touch, and I was almost tempted to reach out and reinstate it, but instead I tucked it into my lap.

'Who's Joshua?'

'Her partner. How he puts up with her attitude I have no idea.'

She had a partner? So why had just been shooting daggers at me because I was sitting with Oliver? I sensed there was something else going on, but decided not to bring it up.

Curious about what both Alex and Dominic had said, I decided to brave my other question. 'I know this isn't a date ...' I began, suddenly worried that I was being too personal with someone I barely knew. 'But what did she mean when she said that you were dating again? Don't you date?'

Oliver gave me a long scrutinising look, but didn't answer.

'And last week Dominic had said something similar about you being back in the game,' I added, hoping he didn't think I was prying, which I clearly was.

'He did,' Oliver finally agreed, with a shrug. 'I don't date, no. Or should I say, I haven't, not for many years now.'

My eyes widened at his response and he gave a short laugh. 'Please don't misunderstand me. I'm not an angel. I might not have dated romantically for a few years, but I've spent time with plenty of women in that time.' Which I took to mean "I've screwed plenty of women in that time". How lovely, and once again I felt the sharp bite of jealousy in my chest.

'Through choice I've been single for several years. I also haven't fraternised with anyone within the club for a very long time. It's probably been a bit of a shock for people to see me with you, so I assume both Alex and Dominic were asking if I was getting back on the horse, so to speak.'

Oliver smiled, but he seemed to have relaxed now, because once again it was the expression that came with narrowed eyes and a teasing twinkle in those blue depths. It was a decidedly wicked smile, that somehow made my stomach tremble and my heart rate accelerate.

He'd been single for several years? Now that *was* an interesting nugget of information. And he didn't usually interact with the customers? Why had he approached me, then? Instead of asking that question, though, I blurted out something completely stupid. 'And are you?' Holy smokes! Why the heck was I asking that? He made me lose all control of my tongue. I didn't need to know the answer; what this man did in his private time was no business of mine. Although I couldn't deny that the thought of him naked was certainly a tantalizing prospect.

Tilting his head to the side, Oliver propped his chin on his hand and ran his forefinger briefly over his lips. I tried not to follow the action, but of course I did, and ended up staring at his mouth for way longer than was socially acceptable.

'Perhaps,' he murmured cryptically. He lowered his hand then crooked the very same forefinger that had just been at his lips and stroked it from my knuckle to my fingernail before retracting his hand. 'Why, are you volunteering for the position?'

That, surely, was either the most teasing line ever, or an out-and-out come-on. God. He'd warned me he was a tease, but I couldn't tell when he was joking and when he was being serious. A guy like Oliver wouldn't seriously be interested in me; he'd surely want an experienced submissive to have his fun with. No doubt he was just playing with me like a cat plays with a mouse. Perhaps given our names it would be more appropriate to say the Big Bad Wolf targeting a floundering Robin …

'I … eh … No … I was just curious,' I stammered.

'There's that blush again,' he commented with a smile. He leaned in towards me and my breath caught in my throat, but even though I saw his hand flex on his thigh, he didn't stroke my cheek like he had the last time. 'You're so perfect,' he murmured. 'Your responses to me, you feel the connection between us, don't you?'

Shit, shit, shit. This conversation was all my fault for being stupid enough to ask whether he was dating again. I really needed to learn when to hold my tongue around him.

As for his question – did I feel the connection between us? – I did. I definitely did, but I couldn't admit it to him. Could I? Surely if I did, it would lead towards me doing something with a guy I'd met in a sex club, which seemed so wrong, so I shrugged jerkily and remained silent.

'I would very much like to help you expand your

77

research parameters into some physical exploration.' My already wide eyes expanded even further at Oliver's words. Oh my gosh. 'Would you allow me to help you do that?'

Throw my "oh-my-gosh" in the trash, and up it to a "holy fuck". Did he really just ask me that? Forget panting – I was now full-on hyperventilating and seriously concerned that I might have a heart attack at any second. The stupid thing was, above all my racing heartbeats and panicked sweating, I was actually tempted to say yes, because this club, and this man, were opening my eyes to things that had secretly fascinated me for years. It was only because my sanity made me clamp my teeth together that I stopped the word from escaping.

'I ... uh ... I ...' I couldn't speak, which was hardly surprising given the circumstances. 'You said no strings ...' I muttered desperately.

Oliver sat back and folded his arms, looking cool as a cucumber while I was melting beside him like a panicky, sweaty mess. 'There are no strings,' he replied coolly. 'I haven't said I would kiss you, or bend you over and fuck you, have I?' I winced at his bluntness, but it was true; he'd said he wanted me to expand my physical understanding, so perhaps I was overreacting. 'I merely said I wanted you to experiment a little, broaden your understanding of our lifestyle. Perhaps if you've seen inside one of the private rooms, run a flogger through your fingers, and sat in a ready position you will have a deeper understanding and be able to convey it to your readers.'

It all made perfect sense when he said it like that. But no. There was no way I could do something so sexually charged with Oliver.

'I'm not denying the fact that I would get quite a thrill from it, too, though,' Oliver added, reaching across the gap between us and briefly trailing his fingers over my forearm. The hairs on my arm stood up, and as I gasped at my crazy response I heard Oliver release a small, satisfied chuckle. 'Your blushes would no doubt drive me wild.' His voice was now low, and seductive, and the word "wild" had practically purred from his tongue.

The combination of exhilaration, fear, confusion and arousal were making normal bodily functions almost impossible, but I pressed to my feet, determined to do what any sensible person in my position would do – run like hell.

I swayed, standing there on wobbly legs for a second or two, but Oliver remained seated, his eyes raised and assessing me with that bloody unaffected look again. 'I need to go,' I finally managed in a thick voice, causing Oliver to raise an eyebrow in amusement. Yeah, I was a complete coward.

I'm glad he found all of this amusing, because I certainly didn't. But just as I went to turn and leave he was up, moving so fluidly I'd barely registered it. Gripping my wrist, he leaned in close to my ear, his touch igniting a series of sparks under my skin that felt blissfully sinful. 'Think of me when you touch yourself tonight,' he murmured, his breath warming my cheek. 'Because trust me, Robyn, you will touch yourself,' he added with certainty before turning and walking away from me.

Even though I had been the one to say I was leaving, I had to physically restrain myself from calling him back as I watched his powerful frame disappear elegantly into a group near the bar.

I couldn't move. My face was burning, my legs shaky, and my core was clenching with the need to do exactly as he'd said – touch myself. Or perhaps beg him to touch me. God, I was so aroused that the briefest of touches would be enough to send me over the edge.

Gaping at where he had been sitting just a few seconds ago, I finally shook myself and took a step towards the exit. I couldn't take the short cut again, because the way we'd entered the bar was clearly marked "staff only", so I'd have to hope I could find my way back along the street to the club entrance so I could tell Chloe and Sasha that I was leaving.

Staggering out into the cool night air, I took a breath and ran through everything that had occurred. Oliver was quite an enigma. With his smart suits and perfect manners, he came across as a professional gentleman, but then he could completely floor me with a few whispered words of filth. "Think of me when you touch yourself." I still couldn't believe he'd said that as his parting comment. Running a hand across my brow, I felt how hot I was again, and rolled my eyes – I was definitely blushing, which had no doubt been Oliver's intention all along.

# Chapter Twelve

## Robyn

'Sooooo …'

I winced, knowing exactly what Sasha was going to say, and feeling slightly amazed that it had taken her this long to mention it. Neither Chloe nor Sasha had said much on the short trip home from Club Twist, but now we were in our PJs and slouching on the sofa and I saw the inquisitive twinkle in my best mate's eye.

'Before we start the gossip, I remembered where I recognised your guy from,' Chloe stated.

'He's not my guy.' I didn't add that from the way things tonight had ended, I'd be surprised if he ever spoke to me again.

'Whatever. Is he married?'

Chloe's question completely threw me, and I turned to her with a frown. 'No. He said he doesn't date. Why on earth would you think he's married?'

She frowned and shrugged. 'He was in my offices a few weeks ago with a blonde woman. I remembered him because … well … he's quite memorable.' She looked embarrassed by her admission that she'd been checking him out.

I couldn't blame her, because Oliver Wolfe certainly was check-out-able, not to mention memorable.

'Just because he was with a woman doesn't mean they're together,' Sasha pointed out, stating exactly what I had been about to say. 'It could have been a work colleague, a relative, or just a mate.'

Chloe nodded. 'Yeah, it could. They looked pretty close, though. He definitely had his arm around her as they left.'

Now that brought me up short. Had he lied to me earlier when he'd said he didn't date? Did he have a girlfriend? Or a wife? 'Maybe it was a relative, a sister or something, and he was accompanying them to give advice?'

'Maybe.' Chloe sounded distinctly unconvinced. 'I only saw them for a minute or so, so you're probably right.' She stood up and yawned. 'Anyway, I'm knackered from all that dancing, I'm off to bed.'

I barely knew Oliver, so he didn't exactly have to explain himself to me. Having said that, he hadn't appeared deceitful at all, so once Chloe had left us to it I pushed her comments aside, and turned back to Sasha, who was still grinning at me expectantly.

'Now, where were we …? Oh yeah … so, we'd only been in the club ten minutes when you disappeared with the gorgeous Mr Wolfe. I need details!'

It had been far longer than ten minutes, but I didn't bother to try to explain that. Kicking off my slippers, I flexed out my toes then wandered to the booze fridge and grabbed a bottle of wine – if we were to have this conversation then I needed another drink.

'Did you shag him?' she asked, unembarrassed by her bluntness.

'No!' But I think I probably could have. Although it was difficult to tell, really, because he seemed to give out so many mixed messages. 'Not everyone gives it out as easily as you, Sash,' I joked as I made my way to the couch, hoping to deflect the attention away from me.

'Yeah, yeah. I'm a slut. I get it,' she said with a grin. 'You both looked awfully cosy if you ask me. I saw hand-holding and everything. Do you fancy him?' Her tone was just a little bit too interested for my liking. From the corner of my eye I could see Sasha watching my reaction carefully, and I tried to focus on the TV as a distraction from the blush that I knew was going to explode on my face any minute now.

And there it was. My cheeks felt so hot I was surprised

that steam wasn't rising from them.

'Oh my God! You do like him. The plot thickens,' she exclaimed with glee, turning to face me and snatching the TV remote from my hand. She switched it off, then chucked the remote away and poked my leg. 'Or did something happen tonight?' She leaned forwards on her knees and dumped her glass onto the coffee table with a thump. 'There has to be a reason for that blush! Come on, spill the beans, what happened?'

'Nothing happened,' I lied weakly. Apart from some hand-holding, strange encounters with icy-stared women, his whispered dirty words, and oh yes, not forgetting how I abruptly declared I was leaving, only to have him up and walk out on me. Talk about complex.

Sasha, of course, was having none of it, and with a few more probing stares and encouraging arm flaps had managed to wheedle the full story from me.

'So yeah, basically that's it. He asked if I wanted to extend my research to physical stuff and I said no and left.'

As soon as I had finished my explanation she burst from her seat in excitement, clapping her hands and looking quite a lot like a performing seal as she jigged from foot to foot. 'I knew he liked you!' she exclaimed excitedly.

I took a swig of my wine and flopped back onto the sofa with a dejected sigh. 'He doesn't *like* me, Sash,' I said, emphasising the word "like". 'He just wanted to show me some more stuff for my research.'

'But he said he would get a thrill from helping you do it. I think that definitely hints that he likes you and wants more.'

'Even if he did want sex with me, which I'm not saying he does, but even if he did, he's a dominant, so it would only be because he likes the idea of me submitting to him. That's very different from *liking* me. You know I don't do casual sex.'

'I know. But I have no idea why, it's fucking brilliant,' Sasha cooed with a grin. 'Besides, he must fancy you, otherwise he wouldn't have suggested it. He probably feels that crazy chemistry you mentioned just as strongly as you do. And you said all your conversations have been interesting so there must be something more than just wanting you for sex ...'

Sasha leant in closer, and fanned her face. 'I can't believe he told you to think of him when you touch yourself. Holy shit, Robyn, that's so fricking hot! He's like the best of both worlds.'

His dirty words had been petty arousing, but I had no clue what Sasha meant. 'What do you mean?'

'I mean, he's like a complete gentleman, but with a filthy mouth and dirty mind. He'll treat you like a princess, but shag you until you can't walk straight.'

'Oh my God, Sasha! Shut up!' My cheeks were now bright red, and so hot that I felt like sticking my face in the freezer for half an hour. Mind you, the thought of Oliver treating me like a princess then shagging me senseless definitely had an appeal.

'So anyway, I was chatting to this guy tonight, Samuel, one of the club members – well, I say chatting ...' Sasha wiggled her eyebrows and flashed me the filthiest grin. 'Really it was mostly kissing ...'

Closing my eyes, I shook my head in disbelief. 'I thought Chloe was looking after you. How the hell did you still manage to hook up?' I squeaked.

'I didn't "hook up", we just had a snog. The blond guy I liked didn't seem interested, and when Chloe went off with someone I had free rein,' Sasha said with a happy sigh. 'After Blondie, Samuel was the best looking, and made it very clear he was interested in me.'

It didn't surprise me that Sasha had pulled, it was a pretty regular occurrence, but something else she said had really shocked me. 'Wait! *Stop. The. Press,*' I said, holding up my hands to halt any further talk. 'Chloe went off with a guy? *Our Chloe?* Chloe, who doesn't even talk to men, went off with a guy?' My eyes were boggling out of my head by this point. This was like the news of the century.

'Kind of. I think they just talked.'

That was still fairly major progress for Chloe. 'Who was it?'

'Some cute Japanese guy. He was giving a demonstration of some bondage thing, wrapping this woman up in ribbon and rope.' Sasha paused and looked thoughtful, 'It had a name, Kina... something. I can't remember.' She dismissed the name with a floaty wave of her hand. 'Apparently, it appealed to her arty side. Chloe thought it looked beautiful, so she wandered off to have a closer look. They chatted for a bit and he asked her to come back next week. That was when Samuel approached me, so I didn't see her for a bit after that,' she finished with a dreamy sigh.

Bloody hell, I could hardly get my mind around all of this. Not only had I spent the night chatting to a dominant who wanted me to explore more physical things with him – whatever the hell that meant – Sasha had hooked up with a guy, and Chloe, the prude of our house, had found interest in some random rope guy. How we'd all changed! Well, not Sasha; her behaviour was pretty much run of the mill.

'Anyway ... what I was trying to say, was that Samuel was really shocked when he saw Oliver leading you off by the hand.'

Now that sounded interesting. 'Why?'

Sasha retook her seat and gave me a smug smile. 'He said Oliver never mixes with the customers, and never ever makes public displays of affection like that. Reckoned it was the first time he'd seen him with a woman in years.'

OK, so she definitely had my attention now.

'Oliver hinted that he didn't date, but he didn't say why. Did Samuel give you any more details?'

Sasha shook her head. 'It was loud, so difficult to hear, but no, I don't think so. He just seemed really surprised to see Oliver approaching you.'

Hmm. And he'd held my hand three times now, which if he didn't do public displays of affection was probably quite symbolic.

Sasha's eyes narrowed, then she turned to me and grinned broad and wide. 'Fuck it, you should totally do it, Robyn. Do some "physical research" with him, see where it leads.' She even used her fingers to make speech marks as she spoke, but I was already shaking my head.

'Are you totally insane?' I screeched, before clapping a hand over my mouth so I didn't wake Chloe.

'I am a bit insane,' she conceded with another smile, 'but he's hot and probably wants to show you a whole other world of pleasure. He'd be good in bed, I'm sure of it. He's older and he's got that competent look about him.' Well, if anyone would know, it would be Sasha and her vast bedroom experience. 'Actually, now I think about it Samuel said Oliver has a good rep in the sack.'

'What? How the hell would Samuel know about Oliver's capabilities? Is he … are they … have they slept together?' My voice was hoarse and dry, I totally couldn't imagine Oliver in bed with a guy.

'No!' Sasha laughed. 'Although Sam said sexual freedom is quite common amongst the members of the club, but no, he just told me that when Oliver used to partake in club stuff he was really well respected amongst the members. He hasn't had a sub for ages, but the rumours are that he was an amazing dominant and lover back when he used to play. Controlled and really strict, but always abiding by the rules of safe, sane, and consensual.'

Wow. Okay then. I suddenly felt warm. Too warm. I could totally imagine Oliver being controlled. He was

86

always so correct and dignified, and I had no problem whatsoever imagining that he'd be a good lover – something about his confidence and grace just implied it – but strict? He'd never appeared overly strict in our interactions. Although thinking about it, I had seen a colder, harder side to him when he'd talked to Dominic. He'd been pretty severe then, but at the time I hadn't minded because it wasn't directed at me.

I chewed on my lip, unsure as to whether the thought of him being masterful and commanding with me scared me or aroused me. From the way I suddenly had to fidget in my seat to calm the ache between my legs, I suspected the latter. Not that it mattered, I told myself firmly. I had enough research for my book now, I didn't need to go back to Club Twist any more.

'How long has it been since you got laid?' Sasha asked from beside me, breaking me from my reverie. 'Way *toooo* long. That's how long,' she answered with a grimace, not giving me the chance to give a more precise reply, but to be fair she was right. With my little period of celibacy, it had been an absolute age since I'd gone to bed with anything other than my right hand or battery-operated boyfriend.

'No,' I replied firmly, causing Sasha to flash me a devious look. 'No, Sasha, I mean it. I'm not going back there again.' But even as I spoke I wasn't entirely sure who I was trying to convince, Sasha or myself.

# Chapter Thirteen

## Robyn

It was the following Friday night, and I sat surrounded by notes, photographs, and sketches, attempting to work on a chapter of my book. Unfortunately, it involved writing about the charismatic bar owner that I was basing roughly around Oliver, and instead of thinking about my actual character, I couldn't get *him* out of my head, the real him. Oliver Wolfe, the man who had turned me on beyond all belief with just a few intimate gazes and whispered words, and who I had then walked away from.

After twenty very unproductive minutes of getting myself decidedly hot and bothered, I gave up writing and wandered to the bathroom to take a shower and get ready for bed.

It didn't really occur to me what I was putting on as I dressed after my shower, but it certainly wasn't my pyjamas. Then, dressed to impress, I found myself wandering to the lounge just in time to meet up with Sasha and Chloe, who were heading out to Club Twist.

'You changed your mind about meeting up with your hunky Dom, then?' Sasha enquired with a cheeky grin and a waggle of her eyebrows.

'He's not my Dom,' I corrected her snappily.

'Not yet, but I bet he could be if you wanted him to be,' she teased. She sashayed her way over to me and bumped her hips with mine, but I folded my arms defensively, too confused about my feelings for Oliver to be in the mood to play along.

'I don't want him to be,' I stated, wondering why the words felt a little less convincing than they should have been. 'It's Friday night, I'm just coming out for a drink with you guys.'

'Sure you are.' Sasha and Chloe exchanged an amused glance, then Sasha pulled open the front door and waved her arm to get us to leave. 'Have a chat with him if he's there, see how you feel. You said you were attracted to him, so you could give it a go. You never know, you might like it.'

*Hmm. Yes, I might.* I think that was what was worrying me.

So, after adamantly declaring that I wouldn't be coming back, here I was, using up guest pass three of ten, perching on my usual seat at the bar and completely and utterly shitting myself. I had hardly left things with Oliver on a good note last week, I'd been freaking out and it had ended up feeling horribly tense, but I couldn't deny the thing that had occupied my mind most of the week, and was currently dominating my thoughts – the simple fact that I wanted to see him again.

The only problem was, he wasn't here. According to David – the tattooed guy behind the bar tonight – Oliver wasn't even on the premises. So I sat feeling like a right lemon while Sasha and Chloe burned off some calories dancing. What the hell was I doing? Had I seriously been thinking about saying yes to him?

Taking a hearty swig of wine to try and calm my nerves, I looked around and watched with interest as a man and woman entered and sat in a booth opposite me. They spoke for several moments, the man's head bowed reverently, then he slipped to the floor and took up a kneeling position at her side.

The woman smiled appreciatively and stroked his head, almost like you would pat a dog, and in response he looked up at her with an adoring smile. Wow. I couldn't drag my eyes away as I frowned at the whole exchange. How very bizarre.

'Confused? That's the type of thing I would have

explained to you, if you had taken up my offer last week.'

Oliver's voice beside my ear was so unexpected that I yelped, and sloshed my wine over the rim of my glass, soaking the knee of my jeans in the process. Pulling in a steadying breath, I swivelled on my stool and found him standing close beside me, his proximity once again doing insane things to my insides and giving me a sharp reminder of why I had come back here again tonight. He affected me more than any man I'd ever met, and as much as that terrified me, it fascinated me, too.

'H –hi, Oliver.' My voice was scratchy from nerves, so I cleared my throat and swallowed, even though it probably wouldn't help.

Oliver, however, went a step further than my simple greeting, and picked up my free hand before dramatically pulling it to his lips and placing a lingering kiss on my knuckles. 'Good evening, Robyn with a y.'

The gesture might seem over the top coming from some people, but Oliver, with his sharp suits, suave manners, and slight Spanish accent, pulled it off to perfection, and instead of feeling embarrassed by it, I found myself swooning and ridiculously flattered by the attention.

'I didn't think you were here tonight,' I murmured quietly.

'I wasn't, but David messaged me and said that a beautiful brunette named Robyn was at the bar asking after me, so, seeing as I was just around the corner I decided to pop in.'

He'd come down just for me? 'I'm ... I'm glad you did,' I confessed quietly, really not sure what I was getting myself into, but somehow finding myself unable to resist this man.

At my words Oliver's expression visibly altered for a second or so. He looked thrilled by my admission, then he nodded with a soft smile. 'As am I,' he agreed, before turning to David and ordering us a round of drinks.

While he was busy at the bar I remembered my earlier fascination with the couple across from me, so turned to watch them again. The man was still on the floor, and the woman was still stroking his hair, but now she was also talking to a friend who had joined them.

Once Oliver had handed me a drink and taken the stool beside me, I indicated to the couple. 'So why is he kneeling for her then? Is that part of submission?'

Oliver took a sip of his drink and nodded. 'It can be, yes. The degree to which couples live the lifestyle is obviously very personal, but in general, kneeling at someone's feet is the ultimate show of respect and submission.'

'So she's in charge?'

'Indeed, in this relationship she's the Domme. And he is about to get in trouble, I believe,' Oliver added with a low chuckle.

Watching them again, I couldn't see anything different about their positions. Seeing the confusion on my face, Oliver leaned closer to me, to explain. 'Just a second ago when she was speaking to him, he rolled his eyes at something she said. That won't go down well.'

'Why?'

'Because in here, Robyn, we have certain rules, a certain …' Oliver waved a hand in the air as he searched for the correct word. 'Etiquette. If he has agreed to be with her as her submissive, then when they are inside Club Twist he should act that role accordingly, or expect a punishment.'

Aware of Oliver watching me intently, I eventually managed to drag my eyes away from the couple and turn to him.

'It goes both ways,' he continued. 'As his Domme, she must care for and protect him in here, and if she didn't, then a member of the management team would step in.'

'It's really that strict?'

'Absolutely. It's one of the reasons that David runs such a successful club.' Oliver took a sip of his drink, but just like last week, his eyes never left mine. The concentration he focused on me was quite overwhelming. 'What they do in private is their own business, but here, they should respect the lifestyle.'

As he finished speaking, a loud slapping noise rang out to my left, and I jerked my head back in time to see the man receiving a firm spank on his leather-clad arse. Then another, and finally a third. Once done, the woman retook her seat, and the man folded back to his knees beside her looking remorseful.

Wow. This was just a whole other world, wasn't it?

As I continued to watch them, I couldn't imagine it appealing to me. Then an image of Oliver standing over me flashed in my mind, and the possessive look in his eye began to make me change my mind. Perhaps it wasn't just about the position, but about who you shared it with, because the idea of kneeling at Oliver's feet was nowhere near as scary as it probably should have been.

'This is where that hands-on practice I offered would have helped you understand better. To truly understand what he is feeling as he kneels at her feet, you need to experience it.'

I took a sip of my drink and nodded jerkily. My throat felt parched, but I knew that I was already damp between my legs just from discussing this with Oliver.

'You look curious. Have you changed your mind, Robyn? Would you like to see the positions? Try them out?'

As insane as it seemed, I was tempted, but there was one thing holding me back – Chloe's comment from last weekend was still playing on my mind. 'Are you married?' I blurted awkwardly. I'd been wondering all week if perhaps that was how things worked here – people used the club for sex, but still maintained a normal life beyond the doors. Did Oliver have an unaware family waiting in at home for him?

His eyebrows rose considerably, then he tilted his head to observe me. 'No. I told you last week that I hadn't dated for a significant time, but perhaps I should have clarified that also means I haven't married anyone in that time either, hmm?' He was using that teasing tone again, and from his relaxed demeanour I decided on the spot that Chloe's concerns had been unfounded.

'Sorry, my housemate Chloe said she remembered seeing you in Williams Risk Management – she works there – and she saw you with a blonde woman, and I just jumped to conclusions, I guess.'

'No wife. No girlfriend,' he confirmed mildly. 'Just a flaring interest in the beautiful brunette sitting opposite me.'

I was so crappy at accepting compliments that my cheeks flooded with heat, and I found myself biting down on my lower lip and dropping my gaze away from his.

'So, back to our earlier conversation … You're tempted with a little exploration, yes?'

I gave a slight shrug, which was almost a nod, and saw Oliver smile in response. 'You're hesitant, which is completely understandable,' he soothed, resting a hand on my shoulder. I think his touch was supposed to be calming, but the heat from his skin did its usual and jacked my heart rate up, causing my hot flush to spread from my face and envelop my entire body. 'You can remain fully clothed, if you wish. Think of it as another level of research …'

'Just for research?' I asked weakly, knowing that I was close to giving in to his persuasion, and also knowing that regardless of what I said, this had chuff all to do with my research. I wanted to see Oliver in that more domineering role, end of. The idea of it was turning me on immensely. *He* was turning me on immensely.

'If that's all you want, then yes,' he replied with a nod.

Which surely implied that he wanted more, didn't it?

'And you'll behave yourself?'

I had been completely serious in my question, but in response Oliver laughed, the sound vibrating through my body and sending a shiver straight to my core. 'Spoilsport. But if I must, then yes, of course.'

Oh hell, you only live once, don't you?

'OK then.' My voice was no more than a tiny squeak, but Oliver looked genuinely thrilled by my acceptance. After knocking back his remaining whisky, he stood, smoothed down his suit, and held out a hand for me again.

'Let's go somewhere private.'

## Chapter Fourteen

## Robyn

The connection fizzed and rolled between us as he guided me through the club in the direction of the entrance. Just before the corridor that led to the main doors, Oliver paused by a thick velvet curtain, and pulled it back to reveal a second corridor. I remembered this from my tour – this was where the private rooms were located, and my stomach clenched with nerves.

As anxious as I was feeling, I managed to follow him in silence, keeping a tight grip on his hand as we walked past door after door, all of which were closed. Each one had a small bronze number upon it, much like a hotel would – one that rents rooms by the hour – but we didn't stop at any of them. Instead, Oliver led me through a door marked "private" and up a small staircase before coming to a halt.

'This is my office,' he remarked as he typed in a code on a small keypad then pushed open the door for me. 'I thought you might feel more comfortable in here.'

I was touched by his thoughtfulness, and felt myself relax as I looked around. It was larger than I'd expected, furnished with a huge wooden desk, a thick rug below our feet, and several antique bookcases which lined the walls. Despite its size, it had a cosy feel about it. 'Sorry about the mess, I wasn't expecting company,' he murmured, as he swapped the main light for several lamps dotted about. I let out a dry chuckle at his comment, because apart from some paperwork on the desk, there didn't seem to be any mess at all. It was neat, organised, clean, and fitted perfectly with the control freak personality that he'd told me about.

Once I had finished looking around his room, I glanced back at Oliver and found that he had removed his jacket and was now in the process of rolling up his shirt sleeves.

My throat dried, and my eyes were magnetically drawn to the way he folded his sleeves, creating perfect rolls effortlessly, and making the task seem so much more sexual than I'd ever considered it before.

My pulse rose with each smooth action of his hands, until it was roaring in my ears and almost deafening me. I'd never had a particular attraction to forearms, but God, Oliver's were something else. There was a dusting of dark hair over his beautifully warm tan, and I could see the muscles rippling below the surface as he worked on his sleeves hinting at just how in shape he was below his clothing.

I let out a shaky breath, and drew my gaze back to his face, finding that his eyes hadn't left mine. He was now staring at me with such intensity that it made me shudder, as I desperately wondered again what the heck I was doing up here with him.

Apparently seeing my concern, he gave me a reassuring smile, but somehow, on his devilishly handsome face it just seemed sinful and darkly dangerous. 'Don't look so worried, Robyn. You can trust me. You may keep your clothes on. I was just warm, so decided to remove my jacket, that's all.'

Now he'd mentioned it, it was warm in here, but whether that was down to the central heating or the heat we were producing between us, I had no idea. Seeing how incredibly sexy he looked standing there in his shirt and waistcoat – with his hands in his trouser pockets and a heavily lidded expression – I was inclined to think the latter.

I shrugged off my own jacket, placed it on a chair along with my bag, and turned back to him. Was this really just going to be something to help my research? Or had Oliver just used that as a ruse to get me alone? Did I care either way? I guess I'd find out soon enough.

'So, let us begin.' Oliver drew in a deep breath and

walked to one of the bookcases behind him. He pulled something from a shelf and turned to me. My eyes dropped to the item in his hands and my blood immediately turned ice cold.

It was a riding crop. 'Uh ... I don't think so,' I replied, immediately taking a step back and ready to make my exit.

Oliver rolled his eyes. 'Give me a little credit, I'm not going to hit you, Robyn.' He gave a dry chuckle. 'This was actually meant to put you more at ease, but perhaps I should have explained first, before picking it up.' Walking towards me, Oliver held the crop in one hand. He used his thumb to tip my chin back, so I had to drag my eyes away from the leather shaft and make eye contact with him.

My heart was racing so hard I felt light-headed, and my legs were trembling, but the sight of his steely, confident gaze somehow grounded me. 'You asked for me to be on my best behaviour, but seeing as touching you seems to spark some sort of reaction between us, I thought perhaps you would prefer it if I minimalised the amount of physical contact.' He was admitting that he felt the chemistry, too, which thrilled me, but I still couldn't quite shake my attention from the shaft in his hand.

'I was simply going to use this –' he held the crop up and waggled it '– to give you directions instead of touching you with my hands.'

Oh. OK. I had asked for him to be on his best behaviour, but the idea of him not touching me made me feel a little bereft.

'May I start?' he enquired, looking genuinely interested in whether I was going to see this through or bolt for the door. It was a close-run thing, but eventually I nodded. 'Yes. Sorry.'

As soon as I had spoken, Oliver seemed to transform right before my eyes; his posture became even more perfect, his shoulders pulling back, making him impossibly taller and broader somehow. His face took on a calm but stern expression and he pulled his hand from his pocket and folded his arms across his chest. He screamed power, and I suddenly realised that he was showing me his dominant self.

It was an incredibly impressive sight, not to mention seriously hot, and one that took my breath away.

'During a play session you would usually be expected to call your Dom Sir or Master. Perhaps you should do that while we are in here, just to give you an idea of how it changes the dynamics of your feelings. My preference is Sir.' Even his voice had changed, dipping slightly lower than usual, and oozing authority to such a degree that a shiver ran down my spine.

Sir. I knew about the title from some brief reading I'd done this week, but I couldn't quite decide how I felt about using it. Dropping my gaze, I shrugged. 'Um, OK.'

'OK, *Sir*,' Oliver immediately corrected me, and my head snapped up to look at him again. I'd been expecting to see a smug smirk, showing how much he was enjoying winding me up like this, but Oliver simply stood observing me with the same look of cool interest on his features.

Hmm. Maybe he really was just trying to give me a full experience for my research. Clearing my throat, I nodded once and licked my lips. 'OK, *Sir*.'

'Better.' He nodded his acceptance of my adjustment and took one step back from me. 'There are no truly fixed rules between a Dom and Sub, because each couple, and each Master, will have their own preferences, but there are some things which are fairly standard that we can work through to give you an idea.

'Trust is vital in a Dom/sub relationship. Without it, the experience simply is not the same for either party. If this were the start of a real relationship we would ideally do some training first to develop a bond of trust between us, but for the purpose of tonight's session, let us assume we already have that trust.'

Oliver didn't know about my usual caution with men, otherwise he'd have realised how much I already did trust him. I couldn't quite understand it myself, but I did. I wouldn't be in a private room with him, about to do God knows what, if I didn't.

'I'll start by addressing your question downstairs about the man kneeling. It is a fairly standard ready position used in the lifestyle to show your submission to your master. Some people call it the kneeling position, but if you were mine, and my submissive, you would know it as ready position one.'

If I were his. As crazy as it sounded, the phrase definitely held some deeper, carnal appeal to me.

'Kneel.' It was barely a sentence, and he didn't say please, but something within me had me complying instantly as my legs crumpled of their own accord and I found myself kneeling at his feet before I'd barely even thought about it.

He let out a raspy hum, which sounded approving, and made me smile. 'Very swift, good girl.' His compliment was accompanied by a brief stroke to the top of my head, which caused me to gasp, partly from surprise, but partly because of the tingles that ran across my scalp, skittered over my skin, and settled somewhere deep in my core. Almost as soon as the gasp feathered across my lips, the contact was removed, and he stepped back. 'My apologies, I forgot myself. I shall attempt to limit my physical contact from here on.'

That hadn't been why I'd gasped, but seeing how aroused I already was, keeping our physical interactions to a minimum might be the only way I would survive this without blurting out something ridiculous, or begging him to fuck me, which, right now, was exactly what my body was craving.

'Now, head held high, please ... Good ... and eyes towards the floor. Perfect.' The crop suddenly came into my vision and I watched as the leather tab moved between my knees and gave a gentle tap. 'Knees spread a little wider.' I complied, and immediately heard another hum of approval. The tab of the crop was then trailed up my body, teasingly touching across my leg, belly, and chest. He took his time, and I couldn't help but wonder if Oliver were imagining that it was his fingers touching me instead of the leather. I certainly was. Finally, he slid it over my arm and gave a small tap to my shoulder. 'Shoulders back. Hands on your thighs.'

Once I was positioned to his exact specifications Oliver walked a slow lap around my body, before pausing in front of me again.

'Feel how it opens you up to me?' he asked, his voice low and silky, and only adding to the bubbling desire within my stomach. I did feel it. I felt like I was displaying myself to him, just for his pleasure, and it was an undeniably potent sensation. 'If you were naked, your breasts would be thrust forward, and I'd have a perfect view between your legs.' With these words, his voice dropped, the tone now seeming to vibrate right through me. More specifically, it vibrated right between my legs, and I swallowed so loudly that it seemed to echo around the room.

Oliver walked another slow trail around me, then crouched behind me. He wasn't touching me, but I could feel the heat of his body radiating against the thin cotton of my top, and I had to close my eyes for a second or two to try to get a grip on myself.

When he next spoke, his breath whispered across the skin on my jaw, telling me that he was leaning right in beside me, and must only be maintaining his "no touching" promise by a mere hairsbreadth. 'If you were mine, Robyn, my preference would be that you only open your legs if you were before me, because I can be extremely possessive, and the idea of others seeing your pussy ...' He paused, letting the word hang in the air, before drawing in a shuddering breath. 'Well, quite frankly, it makes me feel murderous.'

Good God. This was all too much. I was sweating, throbbing between my legs, and aroused beyond anything I'd ever known before, and for some crazy reason, his proprietary talk was only enhancing that feeling. I should be running a mile from a guy who talked about me like I was a possession, but with the way my core was twitching and my heart pounding, there was no denying how turned on I was.

How turned on Oliver was making me.

On some deeper level, I *wanted* to be his. The problem was, I was totally out of my depth here. I'd only ever had standard relationships, "vanilla" as Oliver had termed them, and while the thought of venturing down this path with him might be thrilling, it was utterly terrifying, too.

It was that fear that had me lurching to my feet and turning towards the door. 'I need to go.' I was so overstimulated that my body felt leaden, and I staggered, crying out as my legs buckled and I began to tumble towards the floor.

Oliver slid his strong arms around my waist, preventing me from hitting the ground, and dragged me back against the security of his firm chest. I was suddenly surrounded by his strength and scent as he lowered his face close to my ear, and in my over-sensitised state it felt like he was completely blanketing me with his warmth.

'Wait. Breathe, Robyn,' he instructed me softly. 'Breathe.' His voice was almost hypnotic. 'Breathe.' As he began to rhythmically murmur the word I followed his instructions, drawing in air over and over until I gradually felt myself calm in his arms.

'That's it. Good girl. Nice and steady.' His whispered praise warmed the skin of my neck, and made me quiver in his tight embrace. It also filled me with the urge to turn in his grasp and bury my face within his chest, but I didn't.

'OK, now?'

'Y–yes, Sir.' After I had spoken, it occurred to me that I had added the title without even thinking about it.

'Good. Let's move to ready position two. Stay standing and widen your legs.'

Just thirty seconds ago I had been intent on leaving, fleeing from here as quickly as my wobbly legs could manage, but there was something in Oliver's tone that was so persuasive, so alluring, that I found myself complying and widening my stance.

The supporting arm around my waist shifted, and after making sure I was steady, Oliver left me standing on my own and moved before me. Our eyes met and that now familiar jolt of connection flared through me, causing me to suck in a small, shocked breath. Oliver's eyes widened briefly, as if noting my response, before a small smile flickered briefly at the corners of his lips.

'As before; back straight, eyes down.' My body was now obeying Oliver on autopilot, and I responded before I'd even decided if I wanted to or not.

I heard another hum of approval, presumably at just how quick my reaction had been, then he used the tab of the crop to tap lightly on the insides of my thighs. 'Wider, please.' I shifted my feet a little more until I saw Oliver nod from my peripheral vision. 'Perfect.'

He stood right at the edge of touching distance, the crop being used as an extension to his arm, but still his presence was like an overwhelming cloak around me. It was utterly intoxicating.

Just when I started to think that I was now coping quite well with all of this, he trailed the crop up the inside of my thigh, following the seam of my jeans and making my insides clench. That light touch from the leather had my legs wobbling again, and I dropped my head, my eyes closing as I tried to pull in a full breath.

A sharp sting on my right breast had my eyes opening again, and I yelped, whipping my head around to find that Oliver was now standing to my right with a small frown on his face and the crop floating just inches from my stinging breast.

'You dropped your shoulders,' he informed me calmly, presumably explaining why I'd received the harder snap to my nipple. It had worked, though, because I'd straightened my back out again pretty quickly.

'Better. Eyes down.'

I dropped my gaze, trying desperately to control my erratic breathing, but rather than moving the crop, Oliver gently laid it on my breast again and lightly circled it over my nipple. My already strained breathing hitched another notch, until my quick, aroused pants puffed from my lips and around us. Oliver repeated his teasing circle, and even though I was wearing clothes, the sensation caused heat to rush to my cheeks and a wave of dizziness flooded my overworked brain.

This had surely gone beyond the line of research now, hadn't it? He was basically caressing my breast, albeit with a crop, and not his hand. And yet I wasn't telling him to stop. I didn't want him to stop. I was so turned on that if I stayed any longer it wouldn't be surprising if laid myself out on the desk and begged him to take me.

A ragged moan rattled through the air, but it was only when Oliver moved behind me and once again slid an arm around my stomach to support me that I realised the desperate noise had come from me.

I was panting and moaning, very audibly. Not to mention so aroused that my knickers felt soaked through. I was trembling, too, so much so that I moved my hands up and gripped at Oliver's forearm to try to ground myself. I should probably have been trying to peel his arms off me and run away, but I didn't. I gripped tighter, soaking up the calming sensation of his strength. His skin was hot, and the hairs felt almost wiry to touch. Then, before I could stop myself, I found my hands tentatively exploring the way the muscles bunched and wrapped around his forearm.

'You're so affected by me.' It wasn't a question; Oliver murmured the words as a mere statement of fact, and, irritatingly, I couldn't deny it. I was affected by him. Impossibly so.

'I ... uh...' But my stuttering attempt at a reply was halted as he leaned down close to my ear.

'I think all of this is turning you on. It is, isn't it? The idea of letting yourself go? Of trying something new and unknown?' His hot breath shifted the hair by my ear and tickled my neck so deliciously that I shuddered slightly and leaned closer. 'Do I turn you on, Robyn?' But all his questions were obviously rhetorical, because he didn't bother to wait for an answer for any of them before continuing, or perhaps the keen responses in my body were all the answer he needed. 'I think I do, I think you're wet between your legs already, aren't you? Wet, and slippery, and wanting.'

*Oh – my – God.*

This was dirty talk on a whole new level. His words had me so aroused that I was practically quivering. No, wait ... I *was* quivering. My hands, arms, stomach, damn it, even my thighs were trembling with what I could only assume was intense physical arousal. I'd never felt anything like this in my life, and he'd barely touched me.

What with my panting, moaning, and trembling, I probably didn't make the most attractive sight, but there was nothing I could do about it. I was the living personification of desperate and needy, but oddly enough, I didn't care at the moment. My entire world was currently focused on Oliver and the things he was saying.

'Am I right?' he enquired silkily.

*Yes, yes, yes.* But I didn't say it. I couldn't bring myself to admit it out loud, not yet. I *was* wet because of him, and I was intrigued by the way that he lived his life. Well, his sex life, at least. In fact, I was slightly jealous of the way the people here approached their sexual desires with such careless abandon, but that didn't mean I would be joining them.

He ran his fingers slowly and distractingly across the light material of my blouse, almost but not quite touching me, until every hair on my body stood to attention and I wanted to scream for him to give me some proper contact.

'Let's find out, shall we?' Maintaining his hold on me with one arm, Oliver snaked his other hand around my waist and slowly trailed it down my body until it rested on the zipper of my jeans. I might still be fully clothed, but the heat of his fingers seemed to burn through the denim as he ran them down the zip and across my clit, and my head fell backwards onto his shoulder.

'*Dios.* You've soaked right through your jeans. Do you want more?'

I had no idea what "more" he was referring to, but I desperately wanted the climax that was burning just out of my reach and found myself answering breathily. 'Yes … Please, Sir.'

The seam of my jeans was so perfectly positioned over the sensitive bundle of nerves that, as he pressed again, my clit pulsed and my channel convulsed in response, greedily begging to be filled. Oliver had barely even touched me, but as he repeated his circling just a few more times I suddenly felt my muscles clench, and a wave of pleasure rush up on me, and I cried out as I found myself coming, my back arching and fingers clawing at his forearm as a climax rushed at me with such power that it turned my legs to rubber.

Oh. My. God.

That had been impossibly fast, and so potent that my

whole body was thrumming with pleasure. I felt drunk on the high, my channel clenching as I came down from my release, and a moan pushing up my throat as my head lolled uselessly on his shoulder.

I wasn't the only one affected by the moment. The evidence of Oliver's arousal was pressing persistently into my lower back, and the feel of his erection brought home to me what I'd just allowed him to do to me.

As I stood there stewing in a confused mess of thoughts, he continued to work me down from my peak with his fingers, all the while holding me firm against the strength of his body with his other arm. Neither of us spoke, or made any attempt to move, so, finally, I persuaded my slack muscles to reconnect.

Lifting my heavy head from his shoulder I stared forwards, trying to work out how that had all got so out of control so quickly. But I couldn't find any good reasons. Other than the obvious one – he'd asked me if I'd wanted more, and I'd said yes. I'd begged him. I never begged for anything, but ten minutes alone with this man had reduced me to a confused mess begging for a climax.

Oliver was seriously skilled with whatever the heck *this* was, not to mention dangerous for my heart to be around. The ease with which he'd made me explode in his arms showed me just how addictive he could be if I let him in, and I doubted I'd ever recover from something so potent once it ended.

'Submit to me, Robyn,' he demanded, his voice now low and compelling.

'Y-you said no strings,' I argued weakly, well aware just how late my pathetic statement was.

'I did, but I've changed my mind. You're too beautiful, and the connection between us is far too good to pass up.' With those complimentary words he lowered his head and placed a hot, open-mouthed kiss on my neck that had me groaning in his arms and almost begging for round two.

It was completely crazy, but I was actually considering saying yes. He made me feel incredible, and safe, and cared for. It helped that my climax had also been out of this world. Would it really be so bad to try a relationship with him? Just because I'd never stepped beyond vanilla before didn't mean I wouldn't enjoy it.

'Let me show you how good this lifestyle can be. Let me show you how good sex can be, when you really open yourself up to the possibilities.'

It was these words that finally brought a fragment of my sanity back, because he wasn't talking about a relationship at all. He didn't say, "we'd be incredible together", or, "what a great couple we'd make". He said, "let me show you how good sex can be".

Oliver wanted me for sex. Nothing else. And as tempting as this dark, domineering man might make that seem, I was still traditional in my views. I needed romance to let down my barriers with someone sexually. At least I'd thought I did until about ten minutes ago. Being this close to Oliver was making it impossible to think straight.

Coming to my senses, I started to wriggle in his embrace. 'No ... Oliver ... I can't. I'm sorry.'

'Can't, or won't?' he whispered, as his lips fell to my shoulder again and laid one single kiss on the skin.

It was tempting to give in.

My eyes fluttered shut as warmth danced across my skin, and even though I'd only just climaxed I felt my core clench again in invitation for more of his sinful touch.

God, it was *so* tempting.

But no. This was crazy. I knew nothing about this lifestyle, but I knew enough about myself to know that I would fall head over heels for this guy if I gave him a chance, and that was not something I could risk.

'I can't. I need to go,' I reiterated, pushing at his forearm again, which he finally removed, freeing me.

I missed his warmth immediately, and staggered

slightly as I made my way towards my jacket and bag. He didn't try to catch me this time, or help to steady me and ease my embarrassment, though. Instead, an awkward silence fell between us as I pulled my coat on, then I finally plucked up enough courage to turn and face him.

He was examining his arm, and to my horror, as I looked down I saw several dark red scratch marks on his skin from where I'd grasped at him in the height of my passion. 'It's not usually me who wears the marks after a scene,' he remarked in a low tone, and even though I knew I should apologise, I couldn't get my voice box to function.

Pulling in a deep breath, he began rolling his shirt sleeves down, but his eyes rose and fixed on me, his gaze intent, but oddly detached. He was utterly infuriating – his expressions gave absolutely nothing away.

Once he'd shrugged into his suit jacket, he straightened the sleeves then buttoned the front, seeming to make me wait while he settled his clothes to his satisfaction. Finally, he looked up again, impeccable and untouchable, his armour well and truly back in place. 'Will I see you again?' he murmured.

Embarrassed heat flooded my cheeks, and I squirmed on the spot, trying not to think about how he'd just reduced me to an orgasmic bundle in his arms, but I cleared my throat and shook my head. 'Umm, no. I think I've done quite enough "research" for now …'

Risking a glance at him I saw a flash of something cross his face before he smoothed his expression and gave one single tight nod. Had that been a trace of disappointment in his features?

Pah! Who was I kidding? He was so controlled that I seriously doubted he actually had one emotional bone in his entire body.

He walked briskly to the door and pulled it open, pausing to wave his arm at the gap and indicate that he wanted me gone. 'Goodbye then, Robyn with a y.'

Nodding jerkily, I managed to persuade my wobbly legs into action and made it past him, absorbing one final inhale of his scent as I went. Just as I turned to say something, anything, to make this less awkward, he closed the door in my face. I was left staring at the solid wood, feeling decidedly close to tears, although I couldn't for the life of me identify why.

# Chapter Fifteen

## Oliver

*Hijo de puta!* I couldn't believe I'd just pushed things with Robyn like that. Knowing she was completely new to this lifestyle, I should have taken my time, introduced her slowly, and allowed the allure of it all to seduce her. I could see her temptation; it would only have been a matter of time until she had given in to it.

But no. I'd allowed my attraction to her to overwhelm me and taken things to the next level, even though I'd promised her I wouldn't.

Throwing my hands up into the air, I let out a low growl of annoyance. She might only have known vanilla up to now, but she was a natural sub, I was sure of it. Her responses to me had been almost instinctual, and so powerful. The way she'd immediately dropped to her knees ... *Dios* ... she'd been perfect.

I could do with a drink. It was a tempting prospect, but I didn't head back down to the bar. Instead, I opted to raid the small fridge in my room and stay hidden in my office to give Robyn time to leave. I needed the space to cool off, and I didn't want her to see me again and notice how upset I was. I kept my emotional side in check at all times – club members rarely got to see me lose my cool – so I certainly wouldn't let Robyn know how much her refusal had aggravated me.

Having poured myself several fingers of whisky into a tumbler, I prowled around the room in agitated circles as I drank and dwelled on thoughts of Robyn.

I wanted her so badly that it burned in my system like a lit stick of dynamite, but she'd declined my offer. The irritating thing was, I was fairly certain that if I hadn't just overstepped the mark I could have had her. She shared the attraction between us, I'd place money on that fact, and I knew she felt the explosive bond, too, because I'd seen it in her eyes. I'd never had a reaction like it, and from the few shocked gasps she'd emitted when we touched, I was fairly sure that it was a new experience for her as well.

But I had gone too far, greedy in my need to make her come, scaring her off with the intensity of it all, and now she was probably running home desperate to never see my face again.

I turned towards the panel of switches on the wall and banged my palm into the on button for the air conditioner then flicked the light off so I could stew in the calming darkness. The cool air washed over my heated skin from the unit above the door, and I leaned back on the wall as my eyes fluttered shut.

The way she had come undone in my arms instantly filled my mind. *Dios*. She'd been so affected by me that it had only taken the barest of touches to tip her over into her climax. And what a climax it had been! Her response had been flawless; back arching, skin heating, and the cry that had escaped her throat had been so sexy I'd nearly joined her and come in my trousers like a teenager. One thing was for sure; it would forever be engrained in my memory.

She wasn't the only one affected by our connection, and as I adjusted the erection that was still tenting my trousers expectantly I grimaced. My dick obviously hadn't caught up with the fact that Robyn was gone, even though my mind could think of nothing else.

I might have the reputation of being composed and level-headed around here, but Robyn had certainly made me lose it. The first girl to really stir my interest in years, and I'd scared her off by going too far too fast. I really was such a hot-headed fool.

111

## Chapter Sixteen

### Robyn

I dashed down the stairs, sprinted along the corridor lined with doors, and burst into the club like a gang of murderers were on my tail. As the thick velvet curtain wafted around me like a cape, several people turned to look at me with wide eyes, and thankfully one of them was Sasha. Now if I could just spot Chloe we could get the hell out of here.

Frowning, Sasha immediately left the guy she was dancing with and dashed to my side. Gripping my arm in concern, she dragged me to a quieter area at the side of the dance floor. The wrong side for the exit.

'Other way, we need to go,' I pleaded, trying, and failing, to tug her back the way we'd come.

'Not until you tell me why you're as white as a sheet. What the hell happened, Rob?'

How the heck did I even begin to explain what had just happened? Closing my eyes, I drew in a deep breath to calm myself, but it didn't work. All my screwed-up emotions and feelings were still lying on my shoulders like a tonne weight. Talking it through might help, and seeing as it was Sasha standing before me, I decided to suck up my courage and just tell her the truth. 'I was upstairs with Oliver. He was showing me a few things to help me get a better understanding of what it was like to be a sub so I could use it for my book.'

'And?' Sasha made an impatient flapping gesture with her hand, clearly wanting me to speed up my tale. 'Did he hurt you? I'll fucking kill him if he did.' From the expression on her face, I believed her, too.

'No, no, nothing like that,' I quickly reassured her.

'So what is it, then? Didn't you like it?'

I winced, and slumped my shoulders, feeling

completely ashamed with what I was about to tell her. 'The opposite. I think I liked it a bit too much,' I confessed as a furious blush heated my cheeks.

Her eyes widened, and a filthy grin spread on her lips as she raised her hands and pumped a fist in the air in celebration. 'Oh, I'm going to need more deets than that, Rob!'

Grimacing, I ran a hand through my hair, not surprised in the least to see that I was still shaking like a leaf. 'He made me come,' I blurted, before turning my eyes down towards the floor.

'Holy fuck!'

'Yeah.' I sighed, trying to work out why I had reacted so potently to him, and coming up with nothing but the simple fact that it was him, pure and simple. Oliver Wolfe lit me up like an open flame to dynamite. 'He was showing me some ready positions, so I was kneeling on the floor, still fully clothed, but he was trailing this crop over my body and God, Sasha, it was the hottest thing I'd ever experienced.' Swallowing hard, I fanned my face as renewed heat surged around my body from the memory. 'Then I panicked and stood up, but because I was so turned on my legs were wobbly, and he had to catch me to stop me from falling over. That's when he ...' Clearing my throat, I tried to appear calm and cool as Sasha always did when discussing sex, but knew that I would probably fail miserably. 'Well, that's when he reached around me and touched between my legs. I was so turned on I climaxed almost instantly.'

'Through your jeans? And you still came that easily?'

'Yup.' Even I couldn't believe how quickly I'd come undone. It was like he had magic fingers or something.

'Wow. That sounds hot!'

It was. It had been so hot that my brain had apparently melted in the process. There was one final revelation I had to make. 'Then he asked me to submit to him.' My voice was a whisper, but judging by the way Sasha's eyes boggled, she'd heard me just fine.

'Fuck! Like a one-time thing? Or be his permanent sub?'

'I have no idea. We didn't discuss it, I just walked away.'

'You walked away?'

'Well, I kind of stumbled. But yeah, I said no and left.'

'Didn't you enjoy it?' She looked completely confused now.

Huffing out a breath, I struggled to comprehend my own feelings, let alone be able to explain them. 'I did, but this stuff is kinky as hell. It's hardly sensible to try and continue anything with him, is it?'

Sasha curled her lip in disgust at my words. 'Fuck sensible! And as long as you enjoy it, who gives a shit if it's kinky? As much as you might believe it, sex doesn't always have to be in the missionary position, Robyn.' She glared at me knowingly and then threw her hands up. 'Just have some fun for a change.' Which was exactly the response I'd expected from her.

Seeing my hesitation, she softened her expression and leaned in closer. 'Look, are you attracted to him?'

A snort of laughter ripped up my throat as I rolled my eyes. 'Um, yes. You've seen him, who wouldn't be?'

Grinning, she wiggled her eyebrows. 'He is hot, but I just had to check. And you like him, too?'

'Yeah. I think that's what's holding me back. I like him, Sash, and I'm worried I'm going to fall for him, when all he wants is sex.' I folded my arms and shrugged. 'I don't want to get hurt, and with the way he makes me feel I think Oliver could have the ability to well and truly break my heart.'

Sasha breathed out a long "wow" and nodded solemnly. 'I totally get that, but from what Sam said last week I'm honestly not sure that Oliver just wants you for sex. Why would he suddenly make so much effort after years of not seeing anyone from the club? There's got to be more to it.' Pausing, she chewed on her lower lip for a second then gave me an intent look. 'I see the look in your eye when you talk about him. Even if it is just sex, can you honestly walk away from him and have no regrets?'

Could I? Or would I forever be imagining what it would have been like to be with him, kneel for him, and share his bed? Fuck.

My silence must have spoken volumes, because Sasha made a sympathetic face and gave my shoulder a rub. 'Why don't you go back up there and ask him to be honest about what he wants. Then if it is just sex he's after you can walk away?'

# Chapter Seventeen

## Oliver

I had no idea how long I stood in the dark of my office stewing over my stupidity, but a quiet knock on the door startled me into jumping around and dragging the door open in irritation. No doubt it was one of the club workers here to get my help with something that they could deal with themselves if they actually bothered. 'What?'

But it wasn't. The vision beyond the door was like my dream come true – it was Robyn. But instead of smiling at me like she had earlier, she was looking at me with wide, concerned eyes, probably because of the way I'd just snapped at her. *Dios.*

'S-sorry ... I'll go ...'

'No!' I was so desperate to keep her near that I practically shouted the single word and saw her flinch again as I did so. Pulling in a calming breath, I made the effort to quiet my volume, and smiled as I gestured with my arm into the office. 'Come in. I'm sorry, I wasn't expecting it to be you.'

Robyn looked hesitant and, without moving, glanced past my shoulder and frowned. 'Why were you sitting in the dark?'

Reaching sideways, I flicked the switch that controlled the lamps and the room was once again filled with soft lighting. 'I was irritated with myself, and the dark helps me think.' Softening my voice, and my expression, I stood back and hoped she'd take the cue to enter. 'I'm so glad you came back. I need to apologise to you. Please come in?'

Robyn blinked several times, apparently surprised by my words, but finally nodded and stepped past me. 'I wanted to apologise, too. I shouldn't have just run away like that.'

'You have nothing to apologise for, Robyn, the fault was all mine.' Closing the door, I turned and saw Robyn wrapping her arms around herself with a shudder, and realised the air con was still running. It was a habit from when I visited Spain. I liked it cool indoors, so I'd had the unit fitted here, but I knew that most Brits found my preferred temperature too cold. I flicked the switch to turn off the cold air then walked to my coat rack and pulled down a soft cashmere jumper before holding it out to her. 'I can see you shivering. I had the a/c on. Here, you can wear this.'

Robyn accepted the jumper with a small thankful smile and tugged it on. The material completely swamped her, but there was no denying how adorable she looked when her messy head of hair popped out of the neck hole. As much as I knew she might want distance from me at the moment, I just couldn't help myself, and with a chuckle I moved to her side. Taking hold of one arm, I helped her roll the sleeves up, then brushed the wayward hairs back from her face.

My contact caused awareness to thicken the air, and once again our eyes met in shock at the crazy bond between us. I wanted to kiss her so badly that I had to clench my teeth to avoid the urge. Instead, I allowed my fingers to linger on her cheek for a second, rather enjoying both the feel of her soft skin, and the opportunity to look after her.

The need to care for and protect had always been an integral part of my dominant character, but usually the feelings were for my family members – being the eldest brother to five impetuous sisters could do that to a man. I was slightly taken aback by how strongly I felt it with Robyn, though, especially after knowing her for just a few weeks.

I hadn't felt this protective or possessive over a woman for … well, for a very long time, but my little Robyn had sparked something within me, and, crazily, it felt like she was bringing me back to life. I couldn't let that go. I couldn't let her go. Not without a fight.

We seemed to be sharing a moment of some kind, but her wide eyes reminded me of her nerves, and so, with reluctance, I removed my hand from her cheek and gently guided her towards a chair, where she sank down, looking thankful to be off her feet.

I was so relieved she had come back tonight that my body felt alight with sensation, but still my dominant streak demanded that I remained at least some semblance of self-control, so instead of dragging her into my arms and inhaling her scent as I wanted, I sank to my haunches beside her so our eyes were level.

'I can't apologise enough for my behaviour, Robyn. I overstepped my boundaries, and it was utterly inappropriate of me.' I was a proud man, but I had no issue with apologising when I knew I was in the wrong, and today, I had definitely been in the wrong, no matter how her responses had thrilled me at the time. 'You placed your trust in me, and I abused that trust. A good dominant should never do that.' Closing my eyes, I grimaced. 'I'm appalled with myself,' I admitted quietly, hoping she could hear the genuine remorse in my tone. 'I allowed my overwhelming response to you to overrule my common sense.' Feeling her come in my arms had been incredible, but not when I'd done it in such circumstances.

'I asked for it.'

Robyn's soft words broke me from my self-chastisement, and I snapped my eyes open to find her staring at me with flushed cheeks and a nervous smile on her lips. 'You asked if I wanted more, and I said yes. You didn't force me, Oliver.'

She was trying to console me? *Dios*. This whole situation was reversed to how it should be, but I couldn't deny that her words did ease my guilt a fraction.

Robyn dropped her eyes and began to fidget, twining her hands together in her lap. 'The reason I came back up here was to apologise as well. I should have spoken to you, not just run off. I ... well, you asked me to submit to you, and it freaked me out.'

Was she changing her mind? It was a wild thought, but certainly a tantalizing one. I pushed to my feet, and then leaned back against my desk so that I was still beside her, but not crowding her.

'Do you feel the connection between us?' I asked quietly, determined to get to the bottom of this once and for all. 'Did you feel it in the scene?'

Robyn's cheeks darkened with a further flush that sent a jolt of matching heat to my cock, and she nodded, but kept her eyes averted. 'I do, it's the most potent feeling. I can't seem to control it.'

I knew exactly what she meant, because I felt precisely the same way. The way my body reacted to hers was unprecedented. I'd never felt it with anyone before, and it was utterly addictive. I wanted more. So much more.

'And as for during the scene? I think my enjoyment was made pretty obvious by my reaction,' she murmured, clearly feeling embarrassed by her climax. The thought irritated me. She was perfect, and that climax had been like a beautifully wrapped gift just for me.

'You were so perfect, Robyn ... your responses to me were beautiful. It's nothing to be ashamed of, you know?'

'Maybe.' She shrugged, not convinced. 'What you were teaching me earlier ... it was ... interesting,' she acknowledged, and I had a feeling that we were finally going to get somewhere with this conversation. 'But more than that, I ... I liked it. I enjoyed the way you controlled my body, the way you made me feel ... and that terrified me. That's why I ran.'

'Why?' I needed to see her face to read what she was thinking, so I reached out, gently tipping her chin up so I could see her eyes. To my surprise I saw that they were shiny with unspent tears. The sight sent a jolt of pain through my chest.

'Because ... I like you, Oliver, but I'm so out of my depth here. You ... you do the things you do, and I've never even considered them until recently. I'm quite traditional, vanilla as you called it, and I'm not sure I'm brave enough to give you what you want.'

I understood her hesitation, but her words were like music to my ears. She was tempted. It was all I needed to work with.

Suddenly, she raised her head and looked me straight in the eye. 'In all honesty, I'm worried that I'm going to get hurt. Not physically. I mean emotionally. I'm worried I'll get too attached, and once you've had your fun you'll walk away. Tell me truthfully, is this just about sex for you?'

Her words brought me up short, and I straightened my shoulders out defensively. It had always just been about sex for me. I didn't do relationships with feelings, not since Abi, and that had been nearly twenty years ago now. *Mierda*. Just thinking about that whole messy incident brought a cold sweat to the back of my neck.

Huffing out a breath, I closed my eyes and shook my head in an attempt to clear the fog that had settled from my painful memories. As I opened my eyes again I found Robyn gazing up at me, innocence, worry, and hope all playing across her features in a constant swirl. *Dios*, this could get messy quickly.

As much as I didn't want to let her slip away, I couldn't lie to her, not when she was being so open and honest with me. 'Robyn, I don't date,' I reiterated. 'At least I haven't, not for a very long time.' A bitter taste passed across my tongue again at my reference to the past, and I hoped like hell that she wouldn't ask what my cryptic comment meant.

Thankfully she let it pass. Her eyes had cleared of tears now, and she looked resilient and set on her path, whatever that might be.

'And I don't do casual sex, Oliver, so either we walk away from this now, or we're both going to need to compromise a little if you want to take this thing between us forward.'

Raising an eyebrow at her determined declaration, I smiled briefly at her feisty side, before sobering my expression. Walking away wasn't an option for me, but could I really be considering the alternative? Could I do it? Go against the way I lived my life, for her?

I pushed away from the desk, turned away from Robyn, and ran my hands through my hair as old memories and pain scratched at me from the depths where I'd buried them long ago.

My delay was obviously stretching on too long for her liking, because I heard the scrape of the chair as Robyn stood up. 'So we're calling it a day now, then? I'll thank you for your help with my research and walk away?'

*No.* That was the overriding reaction in my gut when I heard her words, and I spun around again and shook my head. 'What you're asking is completely out of character for me,' I confessed. But then again, the way I felt about her was completely out of character as well. Not that I spoke those words out loud. I already felt off kilter enough, I didn't need Robyn to see my weakness as well. What it really came down to was one simple fact – I hadn't felt this attracted to a woman in years, and if I let her walk away I knew in my bones that I would regret it.

'I can't make any promises, Robyn.' I answered honestly, my tone sounding just as regretful as I felt. As much as I liked her, I didn't do relationships.

Robyn graced me with her first attempt at a smile since entering the room, and I just knew that I was following the right path by pursuing this. She was worth it.

'I'm not making any promises, either, but you want me to submit to you, and I'm tempted ... but I could only see myself doing that if I really got to know you first.'

My brow lowered, and I crossed my arms as I weighed up her words. 'OK, what are you suggesting, exactly?'

'Can we take it really slow, just get to know each other? No submitting, or kneeling, or pressure ... or sex. I trust you, Oliver, I do, but this lifestyle is so new to me, I just need a little longer to see if I think I'll be able to relax into any of that stuff.'

No submitting. No sex. Nothing. It wasn't exactly what I would have desired, but Robyn was at least considering the idea of submitting to me, so it was a start. A compromise, as she said. 'So, basically, you just want to build a friendship between us?' I clarified, wanting to make sure I had the facts straight from the outset.

Robyn winced as she nodded. 'Yeah, I would need that first before I could consider moving on to more. I know how boring that must sound to you, but it's just how I am.' She lowered her shoulders slightly, and began the worried twisting with her hands again. Her words reminded me of just how young she was compared to me, and I wondered how inexperienced she was.

'I totally understand if you would rather us just part now. I bet you could walk downstairs and pick any woman and she would willingly fall at your feet,' she finished glumly, a frown creasing her forehead.

I dropped to my knees, grabbed one of her hands, and held it within both of mine, my action causing her gaze to leap up and lock with mine. 'I don't want any other woman. I haven't for years.' I pulled her hand to my lips and placed a kiss on the back of her knuckles.

'But *you,* you I want.' I lifted one hand to sweep some stray hairs back behind her ear and gave a dry chuckle. 'So much so, that I'm willing to go against everything I've ever done, step back, and wait until you tell me if you're ready for more.'

Leaning up, I placed a kiss on her cheek, allowing my lips to linger for longer than was necessary, and getting a kick from her soft blush and the way her pupils had dilated when I leaned back. She wanted more with me, I was sure of it. She just needed time to accept that fact herself.

'You have yourself a deal. I accept your terms, Robyn with a y.'

# Chapter Eighteen

## Robyn

Despite his claims that "he didn't date", and the fact that we were supposed to be "just friends", over the next few weeks Oliver proved himself to be rather lavish with the attention that he showered upon me. We only saw each other on Fridays, when I dared venture to the club with Sasha and Chloe to use more of our free vouchers, but whenever I was there, it wasn't long until Oliver magically appeared by my side.

On each occasion he'd been a perfect companion, helping me with my research, keeping me entertained, and generally making my Friday evenings the absolute highlight of my week.

We hadn't stepped beyond my enforced friendship boundaries, but Oliver's flirtatious side was never far below the surface, and even with my relative inexperience, I could feel the simmering sexual tension that surrounded us whenever we were together.

It was super-hot, as was the burning attraction that I felt for him. As corny as it sounded, he made me feel things that I'd only thought existed in romance films or novels. When I was with Oliver I felt sexy, desired, and so alive that my body was constantly alight with newly discovered sensations.

We hadn't swapped numbers, or addresses yet, though; a deliberate move on my part to try to slow down the growing relationship that was developing between us, because I suspected things might move rather quickly once I finally gave in to it. And I was now pretty sure I was going to give in to it.

Mr Oliver Wolfe and his Spanish charm had managed to firmly weave themselves into my heart, and regardless of the fact that he was the owner of a sex club, and a self-confessed kinky bastard, I was starting to think that I wanted to move things to the next level with him.

I was just pondering this last thought, with a secret smile and a heated blush, when the man in question joined me at the bar. Glancing at my watch, I smiled – I'd only arrived one minute and forty-four seconds ago, yet he was already by my side. This was his quickest appearance yet.

'Good evening, Robyn.' Oliver waited for me to stand and accept a brief kiss from him on my cheek – as he did every time we met now – but even though he approached our encounters in a cool, calm way, I still flushed every time I recalled how I'd climaxed so easily for him the other week.

His kiss lingered, and my eyelids fluttered shut as I spent a second absorbing the lovely tingles that skittered across my skin from the contact. When I opened my eyes, I found that he'd moved back, a sly smile curling his lips and giving away the fact that he'd seen my blissed-out response to his attention. Not that I cared any more. He knew I was attracted to him, we'd both confessed as much, and even with this knowledge he'd been the perfect gentleman and respected my need for some time to get to know him.

Settling himself on the chair next to me, he propped his foot on the rung on my stool and tilted his head to the side. 'How's your week been?'

I glanced down at the position of his foot and had to supress a grin – he always sat like this, *always*, and I couldn't help but wonder if he were somehow laying a claim on me by placing his foot there. A subtle warning to anyone else within our space that I was not available. Even though I technically was. Or perhaps that was just my infatuated brain being ridiculous.

'Not too bad. I normally like to take my laptop and head outside to do some writing, but with the rain we've had I've ended up stuck indoors. It's good to be out

125

tonight; I was starting to feel like I had cabin fever. How about you?'

Oliver gave a small shrug, then nodded. 'Busy, but fine. I'm glad it's Friday.'

I was glad it was Friday, too, but that was because I now looked forward to these meetings with Oliver so much that my entire week revolved around them. With his gentle flirting, care for me, and general loveliness I was getting more and more attached to him, and his proposition was never far from my mind.

Submitting to him. Exploring, sexually. It had become a rather tantalizing idea.

'It's funny you should mention the weather, because I have a proposition for you …' Oliver wore that irritatingly indecipherable expression he used so frequently.

A proposition? Was he referring to *the* proposition? Or a different one? 'Um, OK, what is it?'

Oliver straightened slightly in his seat and crossed his arms, something I'd come to realise he did when he was feeling determined. 'I'm going to Barcelona next week and I want you to come with me.'

What? He wanted me to go on holiday with him? So far, our times together had been within Club Twist, and all had been as just friends – albeit friends who flirted and seemed to be constantly surrounded by a haze of sexual tension. We hadn't even been on a date, but now he wanted me to go away with him?

'You work from home, and you did just say how depressing the weather is. It's lovely and warm in Barcelona at the moment.'

My face must have showed my confusion, because Oliver straightened his back, as if he was feeling defensive. 'I have some work to attend to during the day, and there's another club there, owned by a friend of mine. I thought it might be good for your research to visit it.'

Oh. So not so much a holiday with me, then, but an opportunity for him to have some company while he worked away. Oh yes, and to show me a sex club in a different country, let's not forget that little nugget. That description sounded far less romantic, but it didn't stop me from being tempted. Barcelona was one of my favourite cities, but I hadn't visited in ages, and he was right, the British weather at the moment was horrible.

'I promise to behave, if that's what's worrying you,' he added, taking a sip of his drink and watching me carefully over the rim of his glass as he did so.

Even if Oliver was busy during the day and only wanted to see me in the evenings, I could see the sights on my own during the day; soak up some culture, not to mention some much needed sunshine.

'You're hesitant, Robyn, which I find mildly insulting. I thought we'd grown closer these past weeks? I'm not that bad, am I?' His words shocked me, or more precisely his hurt tone, and a spear of guilt poked at my chest. Surely he couldn't think I was hesitating because I didn't trust him? It wasn't that at all, but I was just so stunned by the offer that I couldn't seem to form words.

Sighing, Oliver continued. 'If it's cost concerning you, then put it aside, I'm paying.'

My eyes widened further, but I was still speechless, and we both sat in silence for several more seconds, locked in a gaze that was making me feel breathless.

Finally, I managed to reconnect my tongue. 'We have grown closer, and it's been lovely, that wasn't why I hesitated, Oliver. I was just a little speechless. In a good way,' I added, to clarify myself.

'I'm glad.' His expression softened, and he nodded. 'Do you trust me, Robyn?' His low tone almost made it into a demand.

'Yes.' My reply was instant. He was right, we had got to know each other really well over these last few weeks; he made me feel safe, and I definitely trusted him.

My immediate answer seemed to be all he needed to hear, and he pulled in a breath as if calming himself. 'I don't want you to think I'm trying to pressurise you into anything by offering this trip, but I enjoy your company. There is no one else I would rather share my favourite city with.'

Wow. That was quite some statement.

'We'll have separate hotel rooms, of course, and I can provide contact numbers and hotel details to Sasha, too, so she'll know where you are at all times.'

I nodded, but if I were brutally honest with myself, I wasn't sure I wanted a separate room. I was becoming desperate to have a glimpse of the real Oliver Wolfe, the man behind the controlled image he always portrayed in public. I'd love to see what he was like when he first woke up with messy hair, brewed himself a coffee, or was having a shave, but seeing as he'd offered separate rooms perhaps it was him who wanted the distance between us.

Drawing in a breath, I considered his proposal briefly. I didn't have any commitments I couldn't leave for a week; it might do me a good to have a break from my book for a few days, and I didn't have any impending deadlines for the newspaper, so really there was nothing holding me back.

Chomping on my lower lip, I decided to embrace my inner confidence and throw caution to the wind. Sod it. I loved Barcelona, and I was growing increasingly attached to Oliver, so why not take the offer of a holiday with him? 'OK. Thank you, Oliver, that sounds amazing.'

Oliver's mouth dropped open and he gawked at me for a second, before recovering his composed expression and raising his eyebrows. 'Yes?'

'Yup,' I reiterated with an excited grin.

'You'll come with me?' He was always so controlled, and hardly ever let his guard down like this, so seeing him look so openly shocked made me giggle.

'Yes. I'd love to, thank you. I'll pay for my own flights, though.'

Clearing his throat, he nodded. 'Excellent. We fly Monday morning, and you're not paying for a thing.' He pulled his phone from his pocket, opened up a new contact in his address book, and handed it to me with a sly smile. 'I'll need your address so I can pick you up. Better add your phone number, too.'

I was going on holiday with a man who didn't even know my phone number, or where I lived. I must be mad. Or madly falling for him. One or the other. I had a distinct feeling I knew exactly which it was, but I chose to ignore it for now.

# Chapter Nineteen

## Robyn

Monday morning seemed to come around in a blur. I'd spent the best part of Saturday working my way through my wardrobe, trying to decide what to take with me to Barcelona, and most of Sunday being engulfed by Sasha as she tried to impart a lifetime of sexual experience onto me in a matter of hours. Not that I'd asked for her advice, but she had decided I needed to be "prepared" anyway. Thank God for the bottle of wine I had discovered in the cupboard. It was the only thing that had stopped me from throttling her.

Instead of making him come all the way up to our apartment to collect me, I had chosen to wait just inside the main entrance to our apartment block. Sasha, and her barely controlled eagerness, was also with me. Spot on ten a.m., there was a knock on the door which made my stomach flip with excitement.

Sasha squealed, hugged me tight, then gripped my shoulders and held me at arm's length. 'Have an amazing time, Rob. I want you to relax and enjoy yourself. No pressure. What will be, will be! And hopefully that involves you, The Big Bad Wolfe, and lots of hot, hot sex!' And having imparted that pearl of wisdom she landed a sloppy kiss on my cheek and dashed back towards the stairs.

Rolling my eyes at her retreating back, I took a calming breath, smoothed down my clothes, and pulled open the front door, only to freeze with my mouth hanging open.

I had never, ever, seen Oliver Wolfe dressed in anything other than a three-piece suit, but today he was gracing my eyes with a complete change; his feet were clad in black biker boots, worn grey jeans hung from his trim hips, and a white polo shirt clung to every muscle in his chest like it had been made to measure. Holy smokes. He was holding an umbrella up for me, too, and grinning with apparent delight, looking the most relaxed I'd ever seen him. He was so hot I couldn't get my brain to reengage so I could say hello.

'Good morning, Robyn.' Leaning in, he performed his usual kiss to my cheek, but this time it felt different; his lips paused on my skin as they often did, but then they drifted lower, almost but not quite skirting the edge of my mouth. I could have sworn I heard him take a breath, too, as if breathing me in.

Well, this was certainly a nice welcome.

Stepping back, I ran my gaze over him and then kick-started my tongue into use. 'Good morning. Wow.' Damn, I hadn't meant to say the "wow" out loud, but Oliver's smile only seemed to increase, so I shrugged it off and continued. 'You look …' *Hot. Relaxed. Sexy as hell. Completely and utterly fuckable* … 'So different.'

'And you look very beautiful. As always.'

OK. This was all starting off in a vastly different way to how I had been expecting. Not that I was complaining, I'd take compliments from Oliver all day long, but seeing as he'd said it was a business trip I'd sort of expected him to be suited and serious. I'd been wrong, and I'd never been happier with that fact.

'Let John take your bag,' Oliver murmured, just as a bald man in a suit appeared beside him. After giving me a brief smile and nod, John took my case and disappeared off down the steps, leaving Oliver and me to follow.

It was tipping it down with rain, but with Oliver sheltering me under the umbrella and the car just by the curb, I barely even got wet, and within seconds we were sliding into the back seats.

'I must apologise. I should have given you a little more idea of the direction we would take on this trip.' Clipping his seat belt in place, he turned more fully to face me, and

I used the moment to absorb his transformation into the casual man now sitting beside me. 'I have a little business in the city, but apart from that I was hoping we could just use the trip to get to know each other more. Keep things relaxed? Just enjoy yourself. If you wish to go to Fantasia one night, we can, but if not, that's fine too. Sound OK?'

'Sounds perfect.' I was so excited I practically gushed my reply. Relaxed sounded great to me, especially if it meant Oliver being as lovely as he currently was. 'What's Fantasia?'

He smiled, nodding his head. 'Sorry, yes, it's the club in Barcelona I mentioned, run by my childhood friend Matías. Its full name is Fantasias Traviesas, but everyone shortens it.' The way the Spanish rolled from his tongue almost made me quiver with delight.

'What does it mean?'

Oliver smirked, his smile darkening into something far more wicked, and then leaned in close to my ear. 'Naughty Fantasies.' His breath fluttered across my skin, causing a skittering of goose pimples to pop up along my neck. I flared my nostrils as I drew in a deep breath. Naughty Fantasies. How very appropriate. Since I'd met him, I'd had so many naughty fantasies about Oliver I could hardly keep track any more, and judging from the gleam in his eye, Oliver had guessed as much.

'We may need to act a little differently in the club, if we attend,' added Oliver, his tone dipping slightly.

'I'd quite like to see it,' I admitted, 'but what do you mean about acting differently?'

'It's not quite as restrained as Club Twist. Sometimes the Spaniards – well, they can be quite passionate, quite ardent in their advances ... I should know, I'm one of them.' He chuckled. 'If they see a pretty new girl in the club, you will be surrounded in seconds. I know we're just friends at present, but it will be better for you if you say you are with me. No one will bother you then.'

'Oh … OK.' Two things rang in my mind as we were driven to the airport – the fact that I would be his for the week, in the eyes of the other club goers at least, and the way he'd said we were just friends, but then added the "at present" bit, which had sounded decidedly like he considered it a temporary title.

Would we be more than friends by this time next week?

The drive to the airport was swift, as was check-in, and after a mere two-hour flight we were pushing our way through a crowded arrivals lounge at Barcelona's El Prat airport.

Crowds of men in maroon and blue Barcelona football shirts were singing and messing around as they collected their bags, and they were being so boisterous that at one point I got shoved sideways by them. In a flash, Oliver was facing off against one of them, his shoulders bristling with tension as he snapped something in Spanish. Then he took my hand to pull me away from them. My eyes widened at his display, but I couldn't deny that his protective behaviour was actually quite thrilling.

Over the following five minutes I became more and more alert with each passing second. Oliver seemed completely unaware, but since the run-in with the football fans at baggage claim, he still hadn't let go of my hand. I was trying to copy his cool, calm demeanour and appear nonchalant about this new progression to walking hand-in-hand status, but all I could focus on was the heat coursing around my system from his touch. My body was buzzing blissfully, and the feeling was starting to make me a bit unsteady on my feet.

As we paused to flag down a taxi, I stared down at our joined hands, then lifted my gaze to find Oliver watching me carefully. His eyes also flicked to our entwined fingers, then back at me. He gave a small squeeze of his hand, but did not let go. 'My apologies. I enjoy having contact with you, and I forgot myself. Is this OK?'

Was it? What did it mean when a guy who wanted me to submit to him suddenly started holding my hand? Talk about confusing messages. I couldn't deny that I liked the way it felt and was enjoying his touch, though, so I shrugged and gave a small smile. 'Um, yeah. Sure.'

Oliver grinned at my agreement, and gave my hand another squeeze before opening the door to a cab and helping me inside. As soon as we were belted up and on our way, he took hold of my hand again, leaving me sitting in stunned silence to marvel at the compete change in him since we'd begun this trip.

As Oliver had promised, we had separate rooms in the hotel – the very plush hotel, the cost of which he point blank refused to let me contribute to – although I did note that there was an adjoining door between our suites. Upon checking, this was unlocked. After discovering this, I spent a moment with my hand on the doorknob, wondering what that meant. Was it just a slip by the hotel? Or had Oliver had requested it be left open? And if he had, what did that mean?

After spending a minute getting myself worked up, I forced myself to dismiss it, and decided to try to do as Sasha had instructed and see how the week played out.

On the drive to the hotel we had agreed that we would take a trip to Fantasia tonight, which, I had to admit, was already getting me quite excited, but before that we were sightseeing, an equally tantalizing prospect.

After quickly freshening up, we set off, and it was immediately obvious just how at home Oliver was in the city. It was like getting a glimpse at some alter ego that he had kept hidden up until now; he was completely relaxed and smiling almost non-stop. His posture was perfect, as always, but it was more fluid, somehow, and he had a visible spring in his step. He was also still in his dressed-down state of jeans and a T-shirt, this time paired with a blazer, which was a sight I could certainly become rather fond of, if given the opportunity. On top of all of this, he held my hand at every available opportunity.

As we paused at an outdoor café opposite the cathedral Sagrada Família for our second coffee of the day, I discreetly watched Oliver as he chatted in Spanish with the café owner about something, and realised that I'd had a strange tightness in my chest for the best part of the morning. I'd been attracted to him from day one, but now, spending time with him like this, seeing this more relaxed side to him, and being the almost complete focus of his attention, I had a distinct feeling that I'd been right in my suspicions the other day – I was well on the way to falling for him.

As I took a sip of my coffee, I chewed nervously on my lip and tried to quell my panic. The big question was, if I did indeed fall for him, would Oliver catch me, or walk away?

## Chapter Twenty

### Robyn

Later that evening, after a delicious tapas dinner and a change of clothes – I was in a low-cut black dress and heels, and Oliver was now back to his standard killer three-piece suit – he guided me through the warm evening past various restaurants and bars until we came to a cobbled square. We were surrounded by stunning architecture on all sides, but on the opposite side to us was the most dramatic of all – a huge Gothic stone building, complete with turrets, and decorated with flags and bright banners proclaiming the name Fantasias Traviesas. Barcelona's very own version of Club Twist, and our destination for the night. If it was half as impressive inside as it was out here, then this was set to be a pretty phenomenal evening.

'People travel from all over for this place. Let's see what you think of it compared to Club Twist,' Oliver said with a grin as he approached the frontage, which was painted in bright scarlet paint.

Visually, it was bolder than Club Twist. The London club was discreetly hidden behind its façade of a disused theatre, but this place was screaming its identity loud and proud for all to see.

The main doors were open, and people were milling about at the entrance, all dressed to impress and clearly already enjoying their evenings. Before we reached the crowd, Oliver paused and looked down at me intently. 'Remember what I said about the clientele here, yes?'

How could I forget? Passionate, and likely to make a move on me if I didn't make it obvious that I was with him. Nodding, I swallowed down a ball of nerves and made the first move this time, by taking hold of his hand in mine.

Oliver's gaze dipped to where my fingers were now intertwined with his. He shared a heated glance with me and nodded his approval before leading me to the entrance. He had a brief conversation in Spanish with the suited man on the door, and after an obviously warm welcome and hefty handshake, the internal doors were opened for us as we were granted access.

Immediately I was swamped by similar sensations to the ones I had when entering Club Twist; dimness enfolded us into the comfortable sense of anonymity, and the heavy beat of the music flooded my veins like an infectious substance, making me feel I could throw my body around the dance floor, safe in the knowledge that no one knew me, or cared who I was.

I didn't, though. I gripped Oliver's hand, and allowed him to lead the way to the bar, which was illuminated by red neon bulbs, and clung to the entirety of the right-hand wall. There must have been at least six bartenders on duty, but they were all busy, so it obviously wasn't overkill.

Glancing around, I realised for the first time that this place was substantially larger than Club Twist. There was a dance floor dominating the ground floor that would rival a basketball court in its size, but as well as that, there were balconies running around the edge of the room on at least two further levels above us, all packed with dancers, indicating that this place occupied at least three floors.

As Oliver was finishing with our drinks order, he handed me my wine and grinned at a man approaching us. Turning, I watched as he embraced the tall, dark-headed stranger, giving the local greeting of a kiss to each cheek, before also exchanging a handshake and speaking some rapid-fire Spanish which I couldn't keep up with. I may not have understood the words, but the easy familiarity these two shared made it obvious they were good friends.

As soon as Oliver was back at my side he retook hold of my hand, a move which wasn't missed by his acquaintance, who gave our entwined hands a long look then raised an eyebrow in an amused glance towards Oliver.

'Well, well, I don't believe this has ever occurred before, my friend. I think introductions are in order, no?' His English was good, but spoken with a thick undertone of Spanish to it, and with his accompanying tan I could only assume he was a local. He was handsome, too, with dark green eyes, a square jaw, and long hair that curled at the nape of his neck.

'Matías, this is Robyn, my guest,' Oliver said, giving a wave of his free hand between us. 'Robyn, this is Matías. He's the owner of this place, one of my best friends, and a complete rogue. Watch yourself around him.' The warning was spoken in jest, but as I looked again at Matías and took in just how confident he seemed in his own skin, I decided that "rogue" wasn't far wrong. He was no doubt well aware of his good looks, and probably made full use of the fact that he owned a sex club by seducing countless women who walked through his doors.

The fact that the exact same comparison could be made with Oliver suddenly occurred to me, and I felt vaguely sick. He'd said he didn't play with the customers at Club Twist, but was that true? And if it was, then was he getting some action elsewhere, because I got the sense that he was an incredibly sexual man, and he certainly wasn't getting anything from me.

A sour tang of jealousy slicked across my tongue but, luckily, I was distracted from dwelling on the unpleasant thoughts by the feel of warm fingers taking hold of my free hand and lifting it. Barely a second later, Matías had my knuckles pressed to his lips as he gave my hand a very thorough kiss, his lips lingering for far longer than was necessary as they trailed along every bump and ridge of my knuckles. 'Beautiful Robyn, it is a pleasure to meet you.'

Blimey. Talk about over the top.

Oliver stepped forwards, and pushed his friend away from me with a low grumble. 'Matías, enough,' he growled, his warning clear in the lowering of his tone, and backed up by the squaring of his shoulders.

Matías seemed completely unfazed by Oliver's bristling tension, remaining relaxed and tucking his hands into his trouser pockets as he ran his gaze down my body and back up again. It was as if I was being inspected for sale, and I didn't like it one bit. If this was what Oliver had meant about the locals being forward, then I would definitely be gluing myself to his side for the remainder of the night.

'Relax, my friend.' Matías chuckled, giving Oliver a sturdy pat on the shoulder. 'I was just checking if sharing might be an option. But I see from your face that perhaps it is not.'

'No, it definitely is not,' Oliver confirmed shortly, dropping my hand and sliding his arm around waist and pulling me firmly into the loop of his arm.

Sharing? My eyes widened at the implications of his words, and I briefly wondered if he and Oliver had "shared" women in the past. It wasn't an image I wanted to dwell on for too long.

Laughing, Matías crossed his arms. He looked well and truly amused by something as his gaze moved from Oliver to mine. 'I am laughing, because my dear friend Oliver is never like this.' He pronounced his name as "Olive-ee-air", his tongue rolling around the name and making it sound so much more exotic. He leaned in conspiratorially. 'The word I need, it is …' He paused for a second, a frown briefly crossing his brows as he thought, then he grinned. 'Possessive. It is both surprising, and quite refreshing to see him acting in this manner.'

Possessive. Over me. And I was supposedly just his "friend".

'Although with a young beauty like you by his side, I

can understand why. If you were on my arm, I would no doubt feel the same.' Matías crooked his arm and offered it to me with a grin, and even though I could tell he was joking, I felt Oliver's arm around my waist tighten considerably.

'Don't push your luck, Matías.' Oliver warned again, his tone light, but holding an undercurrent of steel.

Well, this was very interesting. It also made what I was thinking of suggesting during this trip a little less embarrassing to contemplate, because if Oliver was acting this possessively over me, then surely he saw me as more than just a friend? Or was he simply doing as he promised, and protecting me from the advances of others?

Glancing up at Oliver, I saw him giving his friend an amused glance, then a slight shake of his head. 'Good to see you, too, Matías, even if you are as irritating as ever.'

Matías grinned, told the bar staff to make sure our drinks were on the house all evening, then left us to it, promising to see us again later in the evening.

Oliver gave me a quick tour of the club, seeming to have access behind the scenes, too, then got us some seats in the VIP area overlooking the dance floor.

It was very much like Club Twist; people were dancing below us, just like a normal nightclub, but if I leant to the side slightly, I could see two small stages containing sex shows. On one was a woman performing a simple striptease, and on the other a man was receiving a rather competent blow job from a blonde-haired woman as another girl writhed about on his face, seeking her own pleasure. I watched in aroused interest for a moment or two, before sitting back and laughing at how this type of sight no longer shocked me.

Luckily, Oliver had been distracted ordering drinks from a waiter, and so hadn't seen my interest in the sex shows, otherwise I would no doubt be subject to a flurry of teasing and suggestive comments. Once our drinks arrived, we sat back, sipping the cool white wine and both watching what was going on around us. Just as I found myself relaxing into his company, Oliver turned in his seat and landed me with one of his penetrating stares. I still had no idea quite how he managed to pour so much intensity into these looks, but God, he really did. Even his posture managed to show how focused he was on me, and I found myself holding my breath as I waited for whatever statement or question he was about to throw at me.

'So, I know you're single, but tell me about your past lovers.'

My eyes widened, and a lump of nerves formed in my throat that felt like I'd swallowed a tennis ball. My past lovers? Really? God. This was not a subject I was comfortable discussing. I struggled to talk about this type of thing with Chloe and Sasha, let alone Oliver.

Tilting his head, Oliver observed me with a small smile. 'Have I been too blunt again?' He didn't look at all embarrassed at all about his line of questioning.

'Uh, yeah, a little. I'm British, we're kinda reserved when it comes to subjects like this.'

Oliver indicated around us with a sweep of his arm and then smiled at me. 'Ah, but we're in Spain now, Robyn, and we have no such issues. What's the cause for embarrassment? It's just sex. Yes?'

Just sex.

Sex, which I had always found unsatisfying and fumbled. 'Um. Yeah, I guess.'

Oliver didn't say anything further, but from the gaze he was giving me, he definitely expected an answer. Pulling in a long sigh, I fiddled with the hem of my dress and gave a casual shrug. 'I've dated a few guys over the years, but, you know, nothing serious.'

'A few?' Oliver queried, clearly wanting a precise number. I suspected mine would be way smaller than his but, luckily, I wasn't going to be asking how many lovers he'd had – we were still at the "just friends" phase, so it didn't really seem appropriate. Not for me, anyway, but clearly Oliver had no such issues with his personal questions.

'Five,' I blurted out, immediately taking a giant swig of my drink to cover my self-consciousness.

'Just five?' he murmured, sounding surprised.

I nodded, my eyes darting around as I did everything within my power to try to avoid his curious gaze.

'And all vanilla?'

How could he be so casual discussing this? This was mortifying. 'Hmm. Yes.'

He absorbed this information with a small nod and a marginal narrowing of his eyes, as if he were slightly irritated by the thought of my past boyfriends, but I must have misread it, because that surely couldn't be the case.

I finally plucked up the courage to meet his eyes, and as I strayed over his handsome features I wondered again how many lovers he'd had during his life. My stomach churned at the thought. It would make me way too jealous, not to mention self-conscious, to try to compare myself to them.

Seeing as he had broached such personal subjects, I might however, find out a little more about why he didn't date.

'So, um, you said before that you don't date, does that mean you never have?'

Oliver raised an eyebrow at me in apparent amusement, then nodded. 'A fair question. I used to date, yes.' Was that all he was going to give me? I'd disclosed the number of people I'd slept with; I thought it was only fair that he gave me a bit more than that!

'But not any more?' I pushed.

Oliver sighed, but relented. 'No. When I was a teenager I dated a little. I had a fairly serious relationship with a girl called Abi when I was eighteen, but we had certain ...

issues … and spilt up. I haven't dated since.'

'Issues?' I asked, curious now as to what could have occurred between them to put him off dating for life.

'Yes.' The intensity of his stare, combined with the sharp tone, made it crystal clear that I wasn't going to be getting any more information from him on that particular subject. We didn't know each other well enough yet for me to feel comfortable with prying any further, so I left it, and luckily Oliver chose to fill the tense silence buy continuing his history. 'I met Alex at a party about a year later.'

He said the name as if I knew who he was talking about, but I didn't. 'Alex?'

Oliver raised an eyebrow and gave a thin smile. 'Alexandra. You met her briefly when we were in the bar next to Club Twist. One of the part-owners.'

Oh – *that* Alex. The blonde ice queen who had given me such a vicious glare. I had a sudden suspicion that I wasn't going to like the words that came from his lips next.

'I hadn't dated since the breakup with Abi, but I'd slept around a bit in between, like all guys that age do if they get the chance. Alex was older than me, and rather persistent. I ended up going home with her.'

Boom. He'd slept with her. I bloody well knew it!

A sickening feeling landed in my stomach like a lead weight, and I struggled not to let the jealousy show on my face as I drew in several shallow breaths through my teeth.

'I didn't realise it at the time, but it turned out she and I had a common need for control in the bedroom. I was just discovering my love of domination and control, so we still messed about that night, but I knew immediately that we weren't compatible and that nothing could come of it.' Oliver ran a hand through his hair, completely oblivious to just how much the idea of him "messing around" with the beautiful Alex was upsetting me.

'She had other plans, however. When I said no to

seeing her again she suggested that I join Club Twist. I did, and she's made various moves on me over the years. Since I was young and single, I used the club to meet partners, much to Alex's irritation.' He chuckled. 'It allowed me a freedom I hadn't experienced before, so I continued with the no-dating thing. But when David asked me to take over the accounts and join the ownership team I stopped mixing with the clients.'

*She's made various moves on him? Does that mean he still sleeps with her when it's convenient? Or does he turn her down?*

'I thought she had a partner? Joshua? How come she still tries it on with you?'

Oliver seemed amused by my interest, and as much as it might be giving away my jealousy, I still wanted to know. 'She is with Joshua, but their relationship is what you might term as "very open". They both sleep with other people.'

Oh. My face must have fallen at that news, because Oliver threw his head back and openly laughed at me, then leaned across to give my hand a brief squeeze.

'Don't look so horrified, Robyn. If it concerns you, you should know that it was a one-time thing, I have never slept with her again.' Oliver tilted his head to the side as if considering something and drew in a long breath. 'I know you are still undecided about how our future will play out, but it may interest you to know that you are the first woman I have spent time with like this since Abi.'

Wow. As simple as his words were, I felt ridiculously pleased by them.

I might not know much about Abi and his past with her, but all in all, it had been quite an enlightening night.

# Chapter Twenty-one

## Robyn

Today had been another beautiful day. We'd lounged around the hotel garden eating breakfast, wandered the paths of **Park Güell** – the public park that contained the brightly coloured creations of the famous Spanish artist, Antoni Gaudí – and were now showered and changed after the heat of the day, and once again sitting within Fantasia with a drink in our hands.

I hadn't slept that well last night, but with Oliver as company I wasn't feeling tired at all. The reason for my sleepless night was also linked to him – I'd lain awake for an absolute age wondering if I might get a visit from him through the door connecting our suites. The unlocked door. The idea of Oliver entering my room, perhaps gloriously naked, and slipping into my bed had upped my arousal to the point where I'd tossed and turned. But no visit had occurred, and eventually I'd fallen into a restless asleep.

Even with less sleep than usual, today had been an idyllic day. Oliver was the perfect guide – attentive, chatty, flirtatious, and knowledgeable – and I couldn't deny that I was absolutely loving this time with him.

Oliver's admission last night that I was the first woman he'd actually spent proper time with since his teenage romance had solidified my intent to pursue something with him, but my problem now was building the confidence to actually tell him that.

After two glasses of champagne to dull my inhibitions, I turned to Oliver, and decided to drop my bombshell. 'So, I – uh, I've been thinking, and I want to try.'

A second or two passed between us, then Oliver placed his glass down and turned to me, his movements precise and controlled, even though I could see a hint of excitement flickering in his eyes. 'Try?'

145

I was pretty sure he knew exactly what I was referring to, but my cheeks heated and I averted my eyes as I replied. 'Yeah, us … and the … submission thing.'

One of his eyebrows rose, and he drew in a breath so deep that his nostrils flared as he sat back and observed me for a second or two. He looked excited, but as usual, held his emotions mostly in check.

'You want to submit to me?'

I licked my lips and nodded. 'Yes.'

He pouted in apparent amusement. 'You're not playing me at my own games and teasing me, are you?' he asked with a cautious smile.

He thought I was joking? Didn't he have any idea how long it had taken me to build up the courage to say this to him? 'No, I'm serious.'

His eyes flared, and he nodded in appreciation. 'This makes me a very happy man, Robyn.'

Leaning towards me, he gave me his all-consuming intent stare; the one that sucked me in and somehow left me breathless all at once. 'You need to understand, that however I appear or sound, your welfare, pleasure, and safety will always be my paramount concern. You're safe with me.'

He looked and sounded completely genuine with those words, and I relaxed my shoulders. 'OK. I'm not sure I'll be very good at it all, though. I can be stubborn, does that mean I won't be a very good submissive?' I questioned cautiously.

'Only time will tell, but I've seen significant hints of a submissive side within you, and you react to me so beautifully, so I think perhaps we'll be a rather compatible combination,' Oliver said lightly, but his words made me frown.

'What hints?' I asked, slightly affronted by his statement.

Oliver laughed at my tone, and shook his head mildly.

Then, as if he couldn't resist, he lifted his hand and began to absently play with a strand of my hair. The feeling of his fingers twirling and gently stimulating my scalp was distracting, and I very nearly lost my train of thought completely.

'You say you're stubborn, but I see it more as a quiet determination, an understated strength, which is a perfect trait in a submissive. You apologise even when something isn't your fault; you lower your eyes when you get aroused; you do things that put others before yourself, and you like to please other people. You seem to rather like pleasing me, too.'

Wow. He was quite the list keeper, wasn't he?

With a casual shrug, he continued. 'These are all indications of a submissive nature, and before you get offended, I also find them very attractive qualities.'

We shared a heavy stare for a second or so, then Oliver steepled his fingers before himself, narrowing his eyes slightly. 'Before we start, I need to check that this is more than just a research mission for your book?' His tone was light, but his intense expression far from it.

Nodding, I mimicked his body positioning and turned towards him. 'Yes.' I pursed my lips in a deliberate attempt at slowing my runaway mouth down. 'This is for me … us. I won't write about it.'

'I will still help you with your research, Robyn, of course, but I'm glad to hear that your book is not your motivation for this,' he confessed, using his hand to indicate between the two of us. Oliver took a sip of his drink, then moved his right hand and gently ran his fingertips across my exposed shoulder, sending a shiver running down my spine. 'Now we have that cleared up, let's start with the basics, shall we?' He rubbed at his jaw thoughtfully. I didn't know how he could act so casually; my body was so alive with sensations from his touch and proximity that I was struggling to focus on what he was saying. 'I appreciate this will all be new and somewhat confusing at first, but I promise to guide you to the best of my ability.'

'Thank you. I trust you, Oliver, and I'm definitely curious about it. Curious about you,' I added, hoping not to give away quite how fond of him I was becoming.

He flashed me a wink and leaned closer. 'Excellent. Physical compatibility is an obvious must in a situation such as this. I think I know the answer to this question, but I shall ask it, nonetheless. Are you attracted to me physically, Robyn?' he asked, resting his knee up onto the seat between us so his body was turned and fully facing me. 'Aroused by me?'

'God, yes.' I winced as soon I heard the desperate words that had poured unrestrained from my lips. Damn it! I cleared my throat, embarrassed by my overly keen admission, but Oliver's lips quirked into a dark smile, as if thrilled by my runaway words.

'Perfect. I can assure you the feeling is completely mutual. You have sparked feelings within me that I thought had been lost forever. I've been drawn to you from the first time I saw you. To say I am attracted to you is an understatement ...' he admitted in a low raspy tone.

Wow. Yet another deep declaration. But the relief I felt at his words was immense, because in my more self-conscious moments this week I had wondered if I was merely a business transaction to him, another notch on his bedpost or something like that.

'Me, too,' I replied, which sounded so inadequate compared to his statement that I felt a need to say more. 'When you're near me it's like the air around me thickens and stops me being able to breathe ...' I stopped myself and snapped my teeth together. God, I sounded pathetic. If I wasn't careful I'd scare him off with my blabbing before we even got started.

Instead of mocking me, or looking horrified by my

honesty Oliver simply nodded and leaned forwards. 'Same,' he murmured, before leaning closer still, until his lips brushed my earlobe. 'And you're turned on by it? The idea of giving yourself to me?' I gulped at his blatant words, and he was so close that it must have been loud enough for him hear. Who was I kidding? It was probably loud enough for half the frigging customers to hear.

'Yes,' I admitted softly, causing his eyes to flash with desire.

Clearing my throat, I tried to push aside my lust and get the answers I needed, before I ended up throwing myself into something I didn't fully understand, and perhaps regretting it later. 'Will you explain a little more about what it would involve? What you would expect from me?'

'Of course, but first, just out of interest, what do you think it involves?' Oliver asked, turning my own question back around to me.

Pausing, I considered this for a moment, and thought about all the various things I'd seen on the internet when doing my research. 'I'm not sure, really. I suppose you want me to be subservient to you ...' A frown creased my brow as I thought more deeply about what that might actually mean. I'd only thought about potentially having some hot sex with Oliver; it hadn't really occurred to me until now what else might be included. The thought of being his little slave wasn't an appealing one.

My troubled expression was mirrored in Oliver's when I turned back to him. 'No. I have no wish to demean you. That's not how I get my kick,' he said with a shake of his head. 'Although the thought of you on your knees does hold quite an appeal,' he confessed, his eyes darkening. 'All dominants will be different, but for me it's about control over a shared experience. I want you to totally submit control to me. I have to know you trust me and respect me enough to do whatever I want, whenever I want.'

I nodded, somewhat relieved by his answer. I could kneel for him as long as I wasn't going to be some sort of sex slave.

'Think of it as a game with a few rules you have to follow,' he said simply.

'I'm not sure getting on my knees sounds much like a game,' I muttered, my nerves briefly overwhelming my ability to control my tongue.

It was immediately apparent that Oliver didn't appreciate my tone, because in response he merely narrowed his eyes, a wicked smile lingering on his lips as he chastised me for my petulance without even using one word. It was quite incredible just how powerful his expression was, and I quivered in my seat as I felt the full force of his stare travel through me.

'Sorry,' I mumbled, quite taken aback by the authority he managed to place in a simple glance. 'Please continue.'

He flashed me a pleased wink, then loosened off his neck and nodded. 'As I was saying, it's like a game with rules that you follow. I am in control of you and your safety, so you don't need to worry about making any decisions, you simply trust me and do as I ask without hesitation.'

'OK … that sounds all right, are there any other rules?'

'I don't tolerate lies, so honesty between us at all times is another rule.' He sipped his drink as he continued to think and nodded. 'As I mentioned last time we spoke about this, I would very much like it if you called me Sir when we are playing. I appreciate that you are new to all this, and might find that a little awkward in public places like here, or back in Club Twist, but I would expect it when we were together in a scene. Or together sexually.'

I blushed furiously at his mention of sex but nodded. 'Umm, OK …but surely calling you Sir, that's about degrading me, isn't it? Making me inferior to you?'

Oliver actually looked horrified by my statement,

recoiling in his seat and swiftly shaking his head. '*Dios*. No! Not at all. Not the way I see it, anyway. For me the title is all about power and dominance. I get a thrill from being an authority figure.' He took another sip and smiled. 'I thought women loved a man in charge, firemen, policemen, uniforms and all that?'

This was true; I had always had a thing for firemen. His words reassured me, but I got momentarily distracted by visions of just how good Oliver would look in a fireman's uniform, with his biceps bulging and a trace of ash mixing with the sweat on his forehead … yum.

Blinking away my fantasy, I nodded at him. As long as he respected me, seeing him as an authority figure wouldn't be a problem. Surprisingly, the idea of calling him Sir didn't really seem that peculiar to me now that he had explained it. He'd always had an air of authority about him, a calm confidence that somehow made me trust and respect him, and as such the title of "Sir" seemed to fit him rather well.

'I should warn you that if you hesitate to follow my commands or go against my requests, there will be consequences.'

Consequences… this must be what Samuel had been referring to when he told Sasha that Oliver had a reputation for being strict. 'That doesn't sound like a game either,' I whispered nervously.

Oliver absorbed my trembling voice and reached across and took my hand into his. 'Perhaps not, but it is important to me. I promise you will always be safe with me, Robyn. If you trust me and submit to me fully you shouldn't be questioning me or hesitating anyway, so it shouldn't be a problem.'

Curling my trembling fingers tighter around his I immediately felt the strength of his grip seep into me, and I sat taller and more confidently from his simple touch.

'Now. We need to discuss limits. Do you have any hard

limits?'

Hard limits? In my research I'd seen a few paragraphs about safe words, and I was fairly sure I could recall something about hard limits in some of the fiction I'd read, but that was a while ago, and I wasn't sure I knew the correct interpretation of the phrase.

Not wanting to get it wrong, I raised my eyebrows and hoped my confusion showed, which it obviously did, because Oliver nodded and placed his drink down. 'Hard limits are things you wouldn't want to do,' he explained gently.

*Oh. Of course.* 'I don't do tequila,' I joked lamely, but Oliver merely angled his head and gave me an intense stare that made it very clear he wasn't going to let me wriggle out of answering.

'Things you won't do sexually,' he added, even though I knew full well what he'd been referring to.

Pulling in a flustered breath, I hesitated in answering. My sex life up until now had been so limited and dull that I was quite keen to explore and see if sex lived up to the fuss that Sasha always made about it. I was quite up for trying new things, and as such, I had no clue if there were things I wouldn't want to do.

My pause obviously concerned Oliver, because a deep crease folded his forehead and he leaned in closer to me. 'You weren't untruthful to me yesterday when you told me about your previous lovers, were you? You have had sex before, haven't you?'

A startled giggle broke in my throat, and I nodded as my cheeks burned with embarrassment at this line of conversation. 'I have. But I've never done anything that required a conversation about limits before.'

Oliver considered me intently for several seconds and nodded. 'I understand that, but with me, things would be different. You can still walk away, if this is all too much.' He reached out and trailed a path from my knee to my upper thigh, then he bit down on his lower lip and gave me another of those panty-soaking stares through his lowered eyelashes. 'Although I really hope you won't.'

After bolstering my courage, I shook my head. 'I won't.'

A low, approving hum left Oliver's throat. 'Good. So, limits?'

I still had no idea what to say to that. 'Umm … I don't really know. I'm quite keen to explore new things.'

His grip on my hand increased, and Oliver's face tightened with desire at the same time. 'We shall certainly be doing that, Robyn. So, nothing springs to mind that you wouldn't do?' His tone gave away just how excited he was by my apparent open invitation to do whatever the hell he wanted to me.

'I guess nothing humiliating,' I pondered with a shrug, remembering images of women crawling on a leash that I'd seen. That held no interest to me at all.

'Of course. Perhaps it would be easier if I told you what I like, and then you can inform me if any of it is not to your liking?' Oliver suggested, his voice lowering to a heated whisper. I nodded my response and shifted closer in my curiosity so I could listen above the music of the club.

'I get my thrills from the bond between us, the trust, and the fact that you will comply with my requests without hesitation. The thought of you bending to my will has me harder than you can possibly imagine.' It was getting me pretty aroused too, and I felt my skin tingling with excited anticipation. 'And just to clarify, humiliation, degradation and extreme pain hold no interest for me whatsoever.'

OK, that was certainly good to know.

'I like bondage, predominantly using ropes or cuffs. I'm very much looking forward to tying you up and teasing you until you beg me to stop. If you give me your consent, of course.' My eyes widened. God. That sounded really hot. 'And I won't lie to you, there will be some pain,

153

but it will be relatively mild. I use it to sustain your pleasure, and I'm rather good at it, if I do say so myself. That may sound peculiar to you at the moment, Robyn, but once you have experienced how good it can be, you'll understand.'

My stomach clenched with nerves. Pain that sustained my pleasure? I wasn't sure how I felt about that, but I loved the wicked look twinkling in his eye and didn't feel half as scared as I perhaps should.

'Does that all sound OK so far?'

From the way my knickers were now soaked, I think it was fair to say that it all sounded more than OK. 'Y-y ...' I was so aroused that my voice had dried up. Laughing nervously, I took a quick sip of my drink and nodded. 'Yes, that sounds ... good.'

And it did. The idea of him "bending me to his will" sent desire shooting through my system like a potent drug.

He raised his glass and downed the remaining contents then hit me with a full-on mega-watt stare. 'Excellent. Final chance to walk away ... Do you definitely want to be with someone like me?' He shook his head as if somehow struggling to comprehend the idea. 'You're younger than me, and so much more ... innocent.'

I might be less inexperienced than him but I was no virgin, and as for the age thing, I didn't actually know how old he was. 'How old are you?'

'Would it matter?' he countered, immediately.

'Not at all, I was just curious.'

Smiling, he shifted on his seat and gave my hand a squeeze. 'Let's just say that I'm old enough to know better.'

What a peculiar reply. 'Know better than what?'

His right eyebrow arched high in his brow. 'Old enough to know better than to get involved with a determined sprite like you.'

Determined sprite? What did that even mean? 'Excuse

me?' Feeling slightly insulted, I tried to tug my hand away, but as he saw my stunned expression, Oliver laughed and squeezed my hand. 'Don't look so outraged, it was meant as a compliment. I merely wanted to convey that I feel a great deal for you, Robyn. You seem so innocent and shy, but you have this quiet determination burning within you that I suspect will challenge many of the ways I used to live my life. No doubt changing me for the better.'

I had absolutely no idea what he was talking about.

'So, knowing I am considerably older, you still want to be with me?'

Considerably older. He had me intrigued by his age now, but it wouldn't matter. He couldn't be that much older than me, late thirties, perhaps? If I had to guess an exact age, I'd put him at thirty-eight. Staring into his beautiful blue eyes, I threw myself right in at the deep end by nodding firmly. 'I want to be with you, Oliver,' I whispered.

Oliver drew in a long, satisfied breath, as if savouring the moment of his victory, and nodded. 'In that case, let us go somewhere a little quieter to continue this conversation.'

# Chapter Twenty-two

## Robyn

The "somewhere quieter" turned out to be Matías's office, a plush suite of rooms, complete with floor-to-ceiling windows that overlooked the mass of tangled bodies gyrating to the music on the dance floor below.

'Trust is paramount in a relationship like this. I mentioned before about training to develop it, which is something we may need to do. I have to know you trust me implicitly.'

'I do,' I replied, confident in my feelings for him.

Oliver bowed his head in appreciation and nodded. 'Good. Let's test it, then.'

He placed a hand on my lower back and guided me to the right of the room where there was a window area almost like a giant fishbowl. The floor was also glass, and as we stepped out it felt just like we were standing on a cloud above the revellers below.

Oliver positioned me to face him, then nodded once and walked away from me, leaving me in the glass area as he went right back inside the office and took a seat at the desk. He was still in my line of sight, but now sat a good ten metres away.

'Turn and face the crowd, Robyn.'

I did. Turning my back on him, I looked again at the dance floor, just about able to pick up the faint strains of the beat the dancers were throwing themselves around to.

'Remove your top.'

What? And show everyone my bra? Was he insane?

As I hesitated, I stared down at the people dancing below me, feeling as if I caught the eye of several as my gaze passed over them. They'd all be able to see me. Every single one of them would see me in my underwear. Except Oliver, of course, because he was behind me.

Swallowing hard, I was about to tell Oliver that I couldn't do it, when his words came back to me. "You have to trust me implicitly, Robyn."

I did trust him, but if I questioned this then I would be proving the exact opposite. Suddenly I found myself not caring if the club goers saw me. I was in a different country, and they were all strangers anyway, so what did it really matter? He'd said that submission was about giving up my worries and following his commands, so he must have a good reason for asking me to do this.

Gripping the hem of my top, I pulled it up over my head and let it hang loosely from my fingers for a second before dropping it to the floor.

I heard him hum behind me, and smiled that I had pleased him. 'And your bra, please.' God. Well, that was certainly another level. But once again, I trusted in why he was asking me to do this and removed it without question.

Oliver was too far away to see anything but my back, and the people below didn't appear to be paying any attention to the fact that I now stood topless in the walkway above them, so it actually felt quite liberating.

'Lean forwards and press your breasts to the glass. Let them see how beautiful you are.' Oliver's voice was gruffer this time, as if he was desperate to come across the room and take a look himself, but I didn't dare turn to him.

As embarrassed as this demand made me feel, Oliver had requested it, so I dropped my inhibitions and followed his request. The cool glass made me shudder as I draped my weight into it, and my nipples peaked to hard bullets as I splayed my palms against the surface to steady myself.

I'd only been in the position for a few seconds when I felt the heat of Oliver approaching behind me. The air fizzled with his closeness, then he cocooned me within his suit jacket, wrapping it around me and covering my bare breasts before pulling me into his arms so I could snuggle against his chest. The weight of the jacket, and the scent of him on the fabric, combined with the adrenaline rushing in my system and made me feel giddy.

'So brave, thank you.' He placed a hot kiss on the top of my head. 'In case you were wondering, no one could see you,' Oliver murmured against my ear. Guiding me sideways, he pointed to a small panel on the wall, which simply said "Mist". Making sure I was fully covered by his jacket, Oliver pressed the button and as a red light came on I saw a minor change in the colour of the glass before us.

'The glass has a mist function. It's barely visible from inside, because we can always see out, but when the green light below that button is illuminated it means the glass is misted. Now that I have switched it off, the people outside can see in.'

Looking over the crowd, I saw there was some sort of sex show happening on the main stage in the distance, but I pulled my eyes away, watching instead the writhing bodies lost in the music. As my gaze drifted over the dancers I saw Matías just below us, talking with two women. As if he felt my gaze, he glanced up at us. His eyes skimmed my strange state of dress and I blushed at being caught wrapped in Oliver's jacket. It could have been worse, though: if the button had been pressed earlier he'd have seen me with my breasts pressed against the glass. A knowing smirk crossed his lips, before he winked and turned away.

'Why did you make me do it, if no one could see?'

'I knew that intrinsically your mind would question the idea of being naked before other people, perhaps even rebel against it. I was curious to see how you would respond. Would you follow my commands, or not?' He leaned down and picked up my clothes for me, briefly caressing the lace of my bra before holding them out for me. 'You were perfect, Robyn. Thank you.' He pressed the button again, misting the glass, and smiled down at me. 'You can dress again.'

My fingers brushed his as I took my top, and tingles flared at the contact, making me suck in a small breath. My eyes flicked to his to see if he'd noticed, and the answering smirk on his lip told me that he had. Of course he had. This man missed nothing. What was I getting myself into? My reactions to him were going to devour me alive and leave nothing but overwrought emotions and a bundle of arousal at this rate.

Oliver gave me some privacy while I put my bra and top back on, then approached me with a look of intent purpose on his face. 'Now we have that out of the way, I can't wait a minute longer for us to begin properly, if you are still happy to?'

The adrenaline from my strip tease was still flowing around my system, boosting my confidence, and I found myself nodding without even considering it. 'I am.'

He gifted me with a broad smile, and the small lapses of his usual control showed me just how excited he was about this as well. 'Very good. Come with me, Robyn, we'll find a better space than this office,' he commanded softly, stretching out a hand towards me.

*Here we go, then.*

Looking at his hand, I noticed that, once again, I was left to walk to him. He was rarely the one to make the first move these days, which I could only assume was a dominant thing; asserting his control by making me go to him.

As I stepped forward, I saw a brief softening in his features, one that almost looked like relief, and he cleared his throat. 'This isn't me enforcing my control,' he murmured, once again having read my exact thoughts. 'Not at all. In a relationship such as ours, the submissive holds all the power.'

Frowning, I paused, halfway to him. I was submitting, giving myself over to him, how could I be the one with the power?

'If you say no, nothing happens. This –' he waggled his hand in the gap between us '– is my way of giving you the choice. If you choose to come to me, I know you are willing. If I hold my hand out and you don't accept it, I know you aren't.

'Before tonight you may have believed that it is me as the Dominant who holds the authority, but you'd be wrong. I'm handing you ultimate control over whether we continue or not.'

Wow. When he put it that way it made it incredibly simple to go to him. I might be submitting, but I still had control. Taking a deep breath, I took the last two steps and accepted his hand without hesitation, a move that made Oliver dip his head in an appreciative nod.

We left the room, and I followed Oliver back down to the main dance floor, then through a door at the side of the club. We entered a darkened corridor, and as my eyes adjusted to the light, I saw that it was actually rather plush; thick carpets, inlaid wooden doors and discreet uplights that made it feel like the corridor of a posh hotel. It was similar to the long corridor in Club Twist, so presumably these were the private rooms that people could hire out.

Oliver paused briefly at a computer console that was labelled as "staff only", but after pressing a few buttons he examined the screen, nodded, then continued down the corridor. He obviously knew his way around, because he led me past several more closed doors until finally stopping by one and pushing it open.

The room was dominated by a huge four-poster bed made up with pristine white sheets, which I immediately found to be an odd colour choice, seeing what the sheets here must be frequently subjected to. *Ugh,* what a thought. The walls were neutral, just like the corridor, but there was a large wooden shelving unit in one corner holding all sorts of objects that most people would never lay eyes on in real life; whips, canes, floggers, and various other things

I recognised from my research.

My breath caught as I looked at the top shelf. It held lots of spiky metal cuffs, knives, and chains, and was far more daunting than the rest, instantly making me feel sick.

Distracting myself from the torture shelf, I looked back at the room and bed and saw that actually both were far from normal. The ceiling contained several rows of bolts and hooks, as did each post of the bed frame, which were presumably for attaching things too. Or attaching people to … *Oh God*.

Fear swamped me like a surge of freezing water pouring down on me. I suddenly wasn't sure I was ready for this.

My hand limply fell from Oliver's, and I drew to a halt just inside the door while he progressed into the room with an easy familiarity. It was clean and neat, but a sleazy, uncomfortable feeling slid across my skin as my gaze passed around my surroundings again. 'How many people have used this room?' I blurted out suddenly, causing Oliver to turn and raise an eyebrow.

'Tonight, or in total?' he replied calmly. 'If you are concerned about hygiene I can assure you Fantasia maintains exceptionally high standards.' It must do, if it were brave enough to use white sheets in a room like this. Once again – *ugh*.

I suddenly felt rather like an unwitting prostitute, which wasn't a pleasant feeling at all. Perhaps this wasn't such a good idea. Seeing how familiar he'd been with this club since we arrived, I changed my approach as I spoke again, but this time my voice was a hoarse whisper. 'How many times have *you* used this room?'

For a few seconds, Oliver seemed to move in slow motion, so that each and every one of his movements and expressions was open and clear to me, something at complete odds to his usual carefully composed exterior. His eyes narrowed, he tensed his shoulders, and clenched his hands to fists at his sides, and he turned away from me and dropped his head down. I remained unmoving, watching the rise and fall of his broad shoulders for what felt like an eternity.

Just as I was wondering if I should say something to clarify what I was feeling, Oliver straightened up, rolled his shoulders back, and, after pulling in an audible breath, pivoted around towards me.

His gaze was so intense that I shivered from the force of it and froze, really not sure how I would react if he asked me to kneel, or tried anything with me now. My earlier arousal had been completely wiped out by the sight of this room, and the thoughts of all that must have occurred here.

To my surprise, instead of looking intent on something sexual, Oliver's expression completely shifted; gone was his frown, and in its place, was something that looked a lot like tenderness.

Blinking lazily, he drew in a deep breath and approached me. He took my hand, not speaking a word as he pulled me from the room and negotiated the dark corridors before coming to a fire escape. Slamming a hand into it, he pushed the door open and strode with purpose back out onto the busy evening street, leaving the club behind, and making me wonder if my reluctance in that room had just ruined any potential future between us.

## Chapter Twenty-Three

### Robyn

I clung to Oliver's hand, my mind in overdrive, and my feet struggling to keep up with his long-legged stride, but he didn't pause or speak until we were back inside the hotel and standing outside the doors to our adjoining rooms.

Should I just go back to my own room? Was he done with me now?

Answering my question, Oliver retained the grip on my hand and unlocked the door to his room, guiding me in with him. We entered, still in silence, and I paused just inside the door, feeling edgy and unsure where this was going. Briefly glancing around, I saw that Oliver's suite was just as luxurious as mine, containing this lounge area and a bedroom beyond, but it was far tidier than mine, and contained a lingering scent of his aftershave in the air.

He dropped my hand, walked over to the desk, and switched on a lamp, then crossed the room to switch off the main light, leaving us cast in a soft orange glow.

Coming to stand before me, he crossed his arms over his broad chest and sighed. 'You know I have a past, Robyn, I've never made a secret of that,' he murmured, his face still so infuriatingly difficult to read. He was right, he'd been totally upfront about the fact that while he didn't do relationships, he *did* do sex. I wasn't naive; even if he hadn't told me, I knew a man like him would have slept with plenty of other women before me, no doubt more than I would ever want to count, but even knowing that, there was no way I wanted to be sharing a bed that they'd used together, too, and I remained resilient in my earlier reaction.

'This can be our space. Just us. New to both you and me. I've never stayed in this hotel before ... never brought a woman here,' he added softly, and some of the tension left me. Not only had he picked up on my discomfort in Fantasia, he'd somehow managed to correctly identify the exact cause of it, too.

I still hadn't spoken, and Oliver's brow lowered with worry. 'Please don't be concerned. I don't want you to be afraid of me. Do you need some space? Do you want to go back to your own room?' There was a trace of desperation in his voice as he ran a hand through his hair in an agitated gesture, and although I had considered going back to my room, I found myself shaking my head.

'No.' It was the first word I'd spoken since we'd fled the club, and my voice came out dry and hoarse.

Oliver's eyes fluttered shut in apparent relief, then he nodded. 'Thank you. I need to apologise, I should never have taken you to that other room,' he murmured with a frown. 'You're new to all this, and things are different with you … *with us*.' He paused again, letting his words hang in the air. 'I've known it from the start. As soon as I met you I knew that things would be different between us.

'When I saw how you panicked just now, how much it disgusted you, I felt sick with myself. I never want you to feel like that around me. I'm not going to rush you or force you, Robyn, I never will. I want you to trust me, I *need* you to trust me.'

My throat was dry from the enormity of his confessions, but I managed a whisper. 'I do.' And it was true, I did. The fact that he hadn't pushed it in that other room had just acted to enforce that trust. My tiny words caused his eyes to close in relief and Oliver lowered his forehead to rest on mine.

'There are so many things I want to do with you, but for now I just have to hold you. I've wanted to for so long, ever since that first night when you walked in the bar and I laid eyes on you. I need to feel you close to me,' he admitted in a rough voice.

164

Opening his arms, he smiled, letting me make the move again; silently asking me to go to him, but giving me the choice. My body trembled with anticipation of his touch, so I stepped into him and wrapped my arms around his waist, snuggling my face into his shirt and absorbing how warm and strong he felt as he encased me in his arms.

He let out a small moan of pleasure, and his lips brushed across the side of my head as he placed a kiss on my temple and held me close.

'We're a perfect fit,' he mused softly, tucking me closer into his embrace. He was right, too: our bodies fitted together perfectly. It made me wonder if we'd fit together just as perfectly when we were naked. I suspected we might.

Tipping my head back, I watched as his eyes darkened.

'I'm very much looking forward to you submitting to me,' he added. 'You're so strong, but I think that you will enjoy handing over your power to me in the bedroom.'

I *was* strong, and I *was* independent, but Oliver was spot on with his observation, because the thought of him taking control of me was a huge turn-on. If doing so made Oliver happy, then that would be even better.

Shifting me in his arms, Oliver guided us towards the bedroom then stepped away from me. Remaining silent, he took off his suit jacket and hung it over the back of a chair then kicked off his shoes before starting to roll up his sleeves. I'd seen him do this several times now, and although I couldn't quite pinpoint why, it really turned me on. My heart rate rocketed as I watched him, and a flush travelled from my face down my neck.

Once his sleeves were rolled to his satisfaction, he walked over to the bed, lowered himself to sit on the edge, and looked up at me. 'Lay with me.' It wasn't a question, but even though it was said as a command something in his tone made me think that Oliver was almost desperate for me to comply.

He relaxed back onto the pillows, still mostly dressed, and stretched out his long legs while he watched to see what my reaction would be. I was still nervous, as I would be with any new boyfriend when things progressed to the bedroom stage, but his complete calm soothed me.

Being here in this private space with Oliver in all his masculine prowess, I found my arousal reigniting, and was suddenly keen to join him. I stepped out of my heels, then, with a shy smile, I moved towards him and crawled into position on the bed beside him.

To my surprise, Oliver didn't attempt to initiate a kiss, or anything more sexual. All he did was pull me against him with a groan and settle me on his body so my head was in the crook of his neck and my hand was lying on his chest.

Relaxing into the position, I sighed contentedly, and with every strong beat of his heart I felt my tensions drift away. Being near him had always filled me with ease, but lying with Oliver so intimately like this, surrounded by his warmth and scent, was just amazing.

Oliver's arm was wrapped around me, with his hand gently running back and forth along my arm in an apparently relaxed gesture, but under my hand I felt his pulse accelerating, until it was drumming in his chest frantically and betraying his excited state. As I gazed around us, I realised that his pulse wasn't the only indication of his mood. There was a bulge in the front of his trousers that made my eyes widen. There was no mistaking that as anything other than what it was – Oliver's very obvious, and very large, erection – and it was pulsing away against the fabric of his suit trousers, making me almost wild with the need to touch it.

As I lay there, I wondered what would happen next. Oliver was a self-confessed dominant, so I had no idea what to expect from our first time in a bed together, but I had thought he might have pushed things forwards a little quicker than this. He hadn't even kissed me yet; in fact, he hadn't even moved since we'd laid down.

As the minutes passed, I found myself growing increasingly agitated. I was aroused, very aroused, and the only way I could handle the ache between my legs was to shift my position every few seconds to try to quell the sensation. I squeezed my thighs together, but it wasn't helping, so in the end I pushed up onto my elbow and looked down at Oliver.

The tightly strung look of control on his face shocked me. He'd seemed so relaxed – apart from his erection and fast heartbeat – but one look at his expression and I saw just how hard he was trying to maintain control of himself.

'Hi,' I murmured softly, smiling shyly at him.

'Hi yourself,' he replied in a gruff voice. 'Are you OK?'

*No, I'm ridiculously horny and need relief,* I thought with a blush, but I didn't vocalise that out loud. 'I am. Aren't we going to … you know …?' I floundered, not sure what to say. 'I thought you might do your dominant thing …'

Oliver's eyes flashed with desire at my clumsy words, but then he smiled and shifted himself slightly so that he was also leaning up on one elbow facing me, our faces practically touching.

'No,' he replied softly. Then, seeing my confused expression, he smiled at me so tenderly that I felt a small piece of my heart crack off and liquefy for him.

'This is not how I would usually progress things, but I nearly messed up earlier by taking you to that room in the club. I'm not prepared to risk losing you, Robyn, so we're going to do things differently, take it slowly.' Cupping my face, he soothed his thumb over my cheek. I leaned into the touch, absorbing how good it felt, my eyes closing and a small moan escaping my throat.

'I won't rush this, no matter how much I want to kiss

you, or how tempting that might be. I just want to hold you tonight.' The soft, sweet intent in his words melted my heart and I smiled goofily.

As much as I loved his good intentions, though, I needed more from him tonight. My nerves about his lifestyle had made me hold back for so long, all the while craving his touch, so now that I was finally in his arms I wanted, *needed*, some physical reassurance that he felt this all as crazily as I did.

'Kiss me?' I asked huskily. 'Please, Oliver.' I tilted my head forward, about to initiate the kiss myself, but Oliver leaned slightly away.

'*Dios*, Robyn. You're killing me here,' he growled, and in response I sagged in relief, thrilled that he seemed just as affected by all this as I was. 'If you are to be making a request you should at least add "*Sir*".' His tone dropped lower, suddenly sounding so much darker than before. 'But that's not how this works. You don't give the orders.'

I pulled in a short breath at how commanding his voice now was, and quickly licked my lips. 'I'm sorry, Sir.'

Oliver sucked in a sharp breath and nodded. After flashing the briefest of winks, his expression returned to the intense one I'd noticed on the day we'd done the ready position training. The day he'd made me come in his arms. The wink seemed to be his way of trying to calm me, and I had to say, it worked a treat.

'You're learning, so I'll allow leniency. If you make the same slip and forget my title again, however, I will remind you with a punishment.'

Punishment. I really wasn't keen on that word, and my body tensed up. As if sensing the sudden change in my mood Oliver slid a hand to the base of my neck, rubbed away some of my tension, and brushed his lips over mine in the just the briefest of touches.

I wanted more. I wanted a real kiss from him, but as I tried to deepen the kiss he moved away again, causing a moan of protest to slip from my lips. I opened my eyes, expecting to find a castrating gaze levelled on me, but instead I found his pupils dilated with desire. 'I'll let you in on a little secret, Robyn; I find it incredibly hot how much you want this.'

He gazed at me, his eyes dropping to my lips and gradually lifting until our gazes locked. 'I can't simply kiss you and not want more. So you have a decision to make. We can continue as we are, simply lying together and enjoying the contact, or we can begin things properly. It's your choice, but be warned, if you say yes, I won't hold back. Are you really sure you want to start down this path tonight?'

I did. Oh, I really did. I wanted him on so many levels that I could hardly comprehend it, and without any hesitation, I answered him. 'Yes, Sir.'

# Chapter Twenty-four

## Robyn

As soon as my agreement left my lips, Oliver groaned long and low, then his lips were on me, avoiding my mouth, and instead trailing to my temple then my ear, nibbling on the sensitive lobe until I shivered with desire. 'As you wish. You have some safe words, please remember them; if you are fine, you say green. If you want to discuss something you say amber, and if you want to stop at any point you say red. I will always, *always*, stop if you say red, no matter what we are doing. Understand?'

'Yes, Sir.'

He nodded, and leaned back so he could look into my eyes. 'Please repeat the safe words, Robyn, so we have no misunderstandings.'

'Green for good, amber if I want to ask you something, Sir, and red if I want to stop.'

'Good girl.' He nodded in satisfaction. 'Now get on your knees and assume ready position one.'

I gasped at the sudden sharpness in his tone, but something inside me had my body instantly reacting to his words and I hastily scrambled to get myself up and into a kneeling position. The feel of his hand gripping my forearm stopped me. 'Your enthusiasm is hot, believe me, but relax. Try not to rush. Enjoy yourself. Make it like a show.'

I nodded, and raised my eyes to his. His pupils were so large now that his eyes looked black. They suited his dominant self perfectly. Dark eyes, just like his dark desires.

'Sorry, Sir, I just know that you said there would be punishments if I didn't follow your commands.'

He nodded, understanding dawning on his features. 'That's true, but as long as you are reacting to what I've asked of you, you won't ever be disciplined for taking your time.'

Ah, OK then. That sounded far better. Pulling in a calming breath, I tried to relax my trembling limbs and took my time to position myself in the centre of the bed on my knees. He hadn't asked me to undress, so I kept my clothes on, but followed his instructions, trying to do as he'd asked and make it more of a show. First, I slowly licked my lips, then gently flicked my hair over my shoulders. Straightening my back, I made my breasts stick out, then finally I placed my palms on my thighs and lowered my gaze.

Oliver made a noise of appreciation, but it was so strained that I risked a quick glance up to see if I was doing everything right. His nostrils flared, and a low growl rumbled from his chest. A second later, he shifted on the bed, his hand rising up to tangle in my hair as he gripped the back of my head and dragged my lips to his as if there was no way he could possibly resist me.

Considering the way he'd tugged me forwards, his lips were surprisingly gentle as they brushed back and forth over mine, taking his time as if breathing me in, teasing me, and coaxing me to open up for him.

I was desperate for a real kiss with him, so didn't need any coaxing at all. My lips parted on a groan and he wasted no time in pushing his tongue in to taste me for the first time. His tongue explored, twining with mine, urging me to give him more. I did. I might not have been an expert kisser, but I gave him everything I could, leaning forwards into him when he kissed me harder.

My lips would be bruised tomorrow, and probably my chin, from where his other hand was now gripping me with his thumb, but it felt so good, so right, that I found myself moaning again. I'd never been so vocal with a partner, and we'd barely even started.

His head shifted, changing the angle of his kiss, and as

171

his intensity kicked up yet another notch I found myself matching his strokes with my own, and sighing with contentment as he dug his fingers into the hair at the back of my scalp. He was just as skilled at kissing as I had imagined.

'Feel good?' he asked, giving a slight tug on my hair to tilt my head back for him. There was a tinge of pain, but I couldn't deny that I liked it.

'Yes.' The tug was sharper the second time around, instantly reminding me that I had forgotten my place again, and I quickly tried to soothe him. 'Yes, Sir, it feels amazing.'

He hummed his pleasure, and kissed me again, his hand still gripped in my hair and tipping my head back. My neck felt completely exposed like this, and as his lips trailed down the fragile skin, leaving a hot, wet trail in their wake, I shivered with desire.

I needed him, right now, and I couldn't help raising my hands to tug at the buttons of his shirt.

As soon as I pulled the first button open, Oliver shifted back, removing himself completely from the bed in one swift move as he shook his head.

'Uh-uh. There you go again, trying to lead. When you submit to me, you do things my way, and in my time. I think I'll have to help you remember my rules.' His eyes briefly flicked down my body and back up again. 'Stand and strip down to your underwear.'

Strip? My stomach lurched with nerves. Apart from the jacket he'd removed earlier he was still fully dressed, but now he wanted me starkers?

'You're hesitating, Robyn. Don't overthink it. Use a safe word, or follow my instructions. Those are your two choices.'

Once he'd made it that plain for me, I was off the bed before I'd even had chance to consider it. I didn't want this to stop, and I had no questions to ask, so really all I had to do was follow his lead. Simple. As I stood by the foot of the bed, I remembered his words from earlier and slowed things down instead of rushing.

Taking my time, I gripped the hem of my top and slowly began to drag it up my body and over my head, before tossing it aside. I snuck a quick glance at Oliver, and saw that he was now standing with his arms folded and a barely contained look of lust smouldering on his face. His expression gave me all the encouragement I needed to continue, and so I lowered my shaky fingers to the button of my jeans, popping it open and pulling the zip down.

Sliding my thumbs inside the waistband, I shimmed the tight denim down my legs and kicked them off, then straightened up so I stood before him in nothing but my matching black underwear. Thank goodness that Sasha had persuaded me to buy a few new sets for this trip.

Recalling the night that he had shown me the ready positions, I assumed position two; widening my legs, straightening my spine but lowering my eyes, and placing my palms on the outside of my thighs.

'*Dios*. You are just stunning, Robyn.' From the corner of my eye I watched as Oliver slowly stalked around me like someone might if they were examining a new car.

'Bra next. As it is your first experience with this type of play I shall allow you to keep your knickers on for the time being, if that makes you feel more comfortable.'

I bent my arms behind my back, but as I gripped the clasp of my bra, I paused and raised my eyes to his. 'Amber … I have a question, Sir.'

Immediately Oliver's demeanour changed, his prowling ceased, and a look of tender concern flooded his face. 'Good girl. That is exactly what the safe words are for. Ask away.'

'Are … are you staying fully dressed, Sir? Is that how this works?'

I saw a hint of a smile curve Oliver's lips, then he uncrossed his arms and pushed his hands into his trouser pockets.

'It depends on the scene. Why, would you feel more at ease if I undressed?'

I had thought I would, but suddenly my imagination created visions of him naked in my mind, and I wasn't so sure. I had a feeling that he would be quite an impressive sight minus his clothes. Would that help relax me, or just wind me up further? I couldn't be sure, but I knew one thing, being undressed while he was still fully clothed made me feel vulnerable somehow, even though I trusted him, so I nodded. 'I would, Sir.'

Oliver smiled, as if something was highly amusing to him, then lowered his head to chuckle. The chuckle turned into a full-on laugh, and he ran a hand through his hair, still snickering to himself.

'I'm sorry, Sir, was that the wrong thing to say?'

Raising his eyes, he locked our gazes and shook his head. 'Not at all. I gave you the option, and you answered.' Licking his lips, he grinned again. 'I was laughing at myself, not you. I've never been so lenient in my life. It's just quite amusing, not to mention surprising.'

Raising his hands, he removed his waistcoat and began deftly undoing the buttons on his shirt, revealing inch after inch of perfectly tanned skin covered in a smattering of short, dark hair. Pulling the shirt from his waistband he slid it off, folded it, and placed it carefully on a dresser before returning to me and slipping his hands back into the pockets of his trousers. 'That is all I shall remove for the moment.'

My heart rate was now so frantic, that it was probably just as well he wasn't taking his trousers off. I might well have had a cardiac arrest if I had to deal with the vision of him fully naked. What a sight he was. After feeling his firm chest during our cuddle earlier I had expected him to

174

be quite toned, and boy was he. Defined, but not overly so; with curved biceps, broad forearms, flat pecs, and a set of abs that made me glad I did my weekly workouts.

'Now, before that short interruption, I believe I was about to remind you who is in control.'

He walked across to his suitcase and began to sort through the contents. I held my breath, wondering what he had in mind for me. Finally, he turned back, holding something small in one fist.

Standing before me, Oliver opened his hand, and I watched as a double-ended chain dropped from his fingers. It wasn't much thicker than a necklace, but each end was tipped with what looked like tiny bulldog clips.

'Nipple clamps. Have a look.' He held them out for me, and I took them, noticing that my hand now had a slight tremble.

My eyebrows rose as I examined the chain in greater detail. It was delicate, quite pretty, really, and each clip was silver and padded with black rubber. There was a small screw on one side, and a tiny white button on the other. They looked quite harmless. But from the name "clamp" I could only assume that they wouldn't be.

Taking them back from me, Oliver pinched one between his forefinger and thumb, making a show of opening the clamp then letting it click shut. 'They increase the blood flow to the nipple, intensifying sensation and adding to the overall impact of the scene. Hold out your little finger.'

I did so immediately, surprised at how easily I followed his commands without thinking. He opened the clamp, and placed it on the tip of my finger. 'This screw here tightens them.' He twisted the screw and it made a small click that sounded like a watch being wound, and I felt the clip tighten just a little. It didn't hurt at all, just squeezed my finger slightly.

'Are you happy to experiment with them?' Oliver

asked, watching my reactions closely.

'Um, OK.'

'OK, *Sir*. If you forget again I shall spank you to aid your memory,' he reminded me briskly, and I winced at the idea of a spanking. 'I think you'll like them, but let's see how sensitive you are first.' His eyes briefly dropped to my chest, then rose again. 'I recall asking you to remove your bra.'

He was right, I'd got so carried away watching him take off his shirt that I had completely forgotten about my bra. Reaching behind me, I unclasped it and shrugged out of it, dropping it to the floor. Straightening my shoulders, I tried to ignore the embarrassed blush that was flooding my face, but seeing as I felt like I was on fire, it was a difficult task.

I heard Oliver take in a short breath. 'Beautiful.' The word was murmured, as if he'd meant to think it, but had spoken it aloud by mistake. 'And there's that blush that I am so very fond of.' Reaching up, Oliver ran the tips of his fingers across my cheek and briefly brushed his thumb across my lips. 'You didn't blush in the office earlier when you took your top off and thought you were showing your breasts to the crowd, so why blush now?'

I gave a small shrug, but seeing his probing look I gave in and told the truth. 'I didn't care what they thought ... but I care about your opinion, Sir.'

Oliver stepped closer and gently trailed his hand down my neck, his fingers exploring my collar bone and shoulder before carefully moving to one breast. His touch was so light it was almost as if he was worried he was going to scare me off. 'Your body is beautiful, Robyn, even more perfect for me than I had anticipated.'

Lowering his head, Oliver kissed me again, this time skipping his gentle introductions and plunging his tongue straight into my mouth. As he kissed me, his fingers began to circle my nipples, then he caught them between one finger and thumb, giving a squeeze that sent a rush of desire straight between my legs and had me rolling onto my tiptoes.

Gasping, I ripped my mouth from his to draw in air, and arched my back, thrusting my breasts closer to his touch, a move which he rewarded me for by lowering his head and licking one nipple, before drawing it into his mouth and sucking hard.

I clutched at his shoulders, my eyes closing as my head swum from the delicious sensations in my body. Every touch to my breasts sent liquid heat streaming through my body, and I was having to squeeze my thighs together to stop myself squirming on the spot.

Suddenly, there was a cool tightness on my right nipple, and I opened my eyes to see that Oliver had applied the first clip and was now moving to my other breast to repeat the action. It didn't hurt, but I immediately felt what he meant about increasing the blood flow, because the whole area felt warmer and tighter.

'OK, so far?'

Nodding, I licked my lips. 'Yes, Sir.'

'Good. Try tightening them to another level.'

'No, it's OK, you do it, Sir.'

Oliver shook his head slowly, watching me through his lowered lashes. 'It wasn't a request, Robyn. That's not how this game works. Part of the pleasure I gain from this is seeing you do it yourself, knowing that you will tighten them just because I have asked you to.'

Oh. OK then. This must be what he was talking about earlier when he said that having me bend to his will turned him on.

I swallowed hard, but did as he had asked, using the small screw to click them one level tighter and gasping at the little pinch of pain that followed.

A low rumble of appreciation rose from his throat and I saw that Oliver's eyes had become heavy lidded. 'How does that feel?'

'It's OK. Not too painful. It actually feels kinda good,' I admitted. What was surprising to me was the way the little tweaks of pain sent shivers of pleasure running straight to my groin like they were on a hot wire.

'Good. It appears that you have forgotten my name again.'

No, I hadn't. But then seeing the intense look in his eyes I realised what he meant. *Sir*. I'd missed off his title again. Why did I keep forgetting?

'Bend over the end of the bed,' he requested crisply, and even though I suspected I knew what was coming – a spanking – I did it immediately, bending over and resting my elbows and forehead onto the covers. 'Good, but don't lean on the mattress.' He helped me adjust so that I was bent over the bed, but not touching it at all, then stroked my back gently. 'I am going to spank you to help you remember our roles, but I want your breasts to hang down. With the clips on it'll make it more intense, help remind you.'

'I'm sorry, *Sir*, I haven't forgotten your name, I'm just nervous.'

'I know, *cariño*.' His voice was soft, and his hand continued to soothe over my back.

'What does that word mean, Sir?' I asked curiously, knowing that it shouldn't be my main concern at the moment, but it had sound distinctly affectionate.

'*Cariño*? It means I care a great deal for you, Robyn. Its closest English equivalent would be... sweetheart, I suppose.'

Sweetheart. Just knowing he had called me something so lovely, and had openly admitted to caring for me a great deal, helped me to relax into the situation and I nodded.

'Unfortunately, I said I would discipline you if you forgot again, and you need to understand right from the outset that I am a man of my word.'

He was now stroking his hand over the lace of my knickers, round and around in an almost hypnotising pattern. 'I may be being lenient with you, but I'm not soft, and I did warn you this would be full-on.'

He had, so I really couldn't complain, but wow, this was seriously intense stuff. I could barely think straight.

'Have you ever been spanked before?' he asked, his hand still distracting me with the soothing massage I was receiving.

'Um, no, Sir.'

'In that case, I am honoured to be providing you with this first. We'll start light, and with a low number. Just four, I think. The appropriate response after each one is to count it, and thank me.'

God. This was all so overwhelming that I wasn't sure I'd be able to speak, but as the warmth of his hand disappeared and he landed the first sharp spank to my bum, I yelped, my breasts swinging with the contact and distracting me. But I managed to count it, and add his title. 'One. Thank you, Sir.' My voice was a breathy wheeze. He was right about the position, too. With my clamped boobs hanging down, I felt the spank radiate in both my breasts and my bum.

'Perfect, Robyn,' he murmured. 'You are just perfect.'

The next three were of a similar level of power, not really hard, but certainly enough to leave my bottom feeling warm. In fact, my whole body felt warm. As surprising as it was, the spanking had just added to my arousal.

His hand trailed across my bottom again, before briefly following the lace down between my legs, where he could no doubt feel just how wet I was. He let out a low appreciative hum as his fingers briefly massaged me through the lace, then his hands moved, landing on my shoulders and helping me to stand upright. With the thrumming desire flooding around my system I could barely stand on my own two feet and I staggered slightly until he supported my shoulders.

'OK, Robyn?'

I nodded, my head feeling disjointed from my body, and upon seeing my slightly dazed expression, Oliver looked into my eyes in concern. 'Do you need to discuss anything? What is your colour, please?'

It took me a second to work out what he meant, but then I remembered the safe words and nodded. 'No, I'm green, Sir, I'm good. Just a little overwhelmed with how good it all feels.' Oliver nodded at my honesty, then, lowering his head, he kissed me, touched me, and stroked me until I felt completely relaxed and boneless in his arms.

His hands played with my breasts, stroking my trapped nipples and causing me to gasp into his mouth as he suddenly tightened each clamp by another click that caused me to grip his shoulders in surprise. I thought I was supposed to be the one tightening them?

They weren't painful as such, just tight, and the sensation was … different, which was probably what made it slightly uncomfortable, but when he was kissing me, it made the sensations so much more intense. It must be what he meant about pain being used to prolong my pleasure.

'Who gives the commands, *cariño*?'

His use of *sweetheart* made my heart melt. 'You, Sir,' I gasped, my voice so breathy that it could have come straight from a porn film.

'That's right. Now that we have that established, let us continue. Would you like to tighten them one more notch?'

Did I? They were somewhat uncomfortable now, although I had to say that when he touched me at the same time the edge of pain definitely softened towards an all-consuming pleasure. But as I looked at Oliver's face flushed with desire, desire for me, I remembered back to some of the things I'd learned when watching in Club Twist and formed an answer in my mind.

'I would like to do whatever pleases you, Sir.' I whispered, my eyes never leaving his. Quite apparently, I had done well in my reply because Oliver murmured his approval and closed his eyes for several seconds.

'A very good answer, Robyn. Very pleasing.' I was rewarded with another blistering kiss which knocked any remaining air from my lungs. 'In which case I would like you to tighten them both one more notch, while I stroke your clit. You must not come.'

I didn't see that coming would be too much of an issue. The clamps were getting pretty painful now and would surely dull any arousal that his touch on my clit would cause, but I didn't dare say that out loud.

I raised my fingers to the tiny screw on the first clamp and trembled as Oliver lowered his hand to my belly and dipped inside my panties. He traced the edge of my landing strip, then pushed his hand lower on a groan.

As I clicked the clamp, his finger ran along my slit to my clit, and a zap of pure pleasure rushed from my tightened nipple straight to my core. Wow. That was surprisingly powerful and so much more pleasurable than when he'd merely been touching my skin. My free hand jerked out, and I gripped his forearm to steady myself.

I was so wet that Oliver's fingers were sliding over me with ease, and I could even feel dampness on my thighs. I repeated the action with the other clip, and he touched me the whole time, upping my desire to the point where I felt my internal muscles clench.

God, I was going to come, but he'd told me I wasn't allowed.

'Oliver, stop ... *Sir* ... I'm close ... stop ...' I stuttered desperately, gripping at his arm and frantic not to go against his command.

Oliver grinned, which I hadn't expected, but then instead of stopping he slowed his fingers just enough to allow me to fall back from the cusp of orgasm. I gasped my relief, my fingers still clutching his arm as I sank forwards against his chest, panting. 'Good girl, Robyn. I wanted to see if you would try and sneak a climax or not, but everything you have done so far has just been perfect.'

His gaze was still locked with mine. Biting down on his lower lip, Oliver slowly began to press first one, then two fingers inside me.

He groaned at the same time as I moaned, our sounds so primitively erotic that it sent shivers across my skin.

'*Dios*, Robyn. You feel so good.'

'Oh God…' It felt so incredible that I was struggling to remain standing, my fingers clawing at his chest and my head rolling uselessly upon my shoulders.

Looking down, Oliver jerked his chin at the clamps. 'The small white buttons are how you release the clips,' he informed me softly. 'You might be surprised by the sensations you get as you release them. The blood will rush back, and it will be more intense than the feeling of the tightness you are currently experiencing. If done at the correct time it can create a huge boost to your orgasm. You are allowed to come at any point now, but you must only press the buttons when I tell you too, do you understand?'

'Yes, sir.'

Oliver gently removed his fingers. Then, to my shock, he lifted them to his mouth and sucked on them, all the while staring directly into my eyes. 'You taste so good, Robyn,' he muttered, as I stood there gawking at his deliciously dirty actions. His eyes closed as he licked his fingers clean, and a low groan left his throat before he scooped me into his arms to carry me to the bed.

Laying me down, he set about kissing me, his fingers dipping back inside my knickers and once again beginning to move inside me. It felt like he was touching me everywhere on my overheated body, and as a result my arousal had spiked to almost volcanic levels. All the while my trembling fingers were settled on the clamps on my nipples as I writhed around below him, waiting for his command. I simply wasn't used to being the sole focus of someone's attention like this when in bed. It was incredible, and utterly overwhelming.

As his fingers upped the speed inside me, I knew it wasn't going to be long until I came, and a desperate moan broke in my throat as I threw my head back.

Oliver pressed his thumb onto my clit and began to circle, and just as I felt the first spasm of my climax grip around his fingers, he raised his head and stared down at me.

'Do it now,' he urged me harshly. 'Release the clips and come for me, Robyn.' With that, I pressed the clips and was immediately swamped by sensations; pain and throbbing came first, briefly flitting through my mind, but these were quickly forgotten as my mind, body, and soul were swamped by the most all-consuming orgasm of my entire life.

My body bucked wildly beneath him as my orgasm continued to rip through me in such powerful bursts that my leg muscles actually ached from the spasms. With his free hand, Oliver pushed my limp fingers away from my breast and his lips found my throbbing nipple, roughly pulling it into his mouth and sucking. Amazingly, his attention to my already sore peak somehow spiked a second wave of climax to sweep through me, and I began to clench violently, my hips thrusting against his hand in a series of uncoordinated jerks as I yelled out incomprehensible words.

Crazily, I then started to sob. The level of pleasure he was giving me was just so intense it was almost unbearable. I was now so over-sensitised that if he didn't remove his hand immediately, I was sure I would actually burst into flames.

I continued to groan, cry, and writhe below him as Oliver skilfully worked me down, then gently removed his fingers from my throbbing core and dragged me into his arms so I was cradled against his chest.

Even though that had been the best orgasm of my life, I continued to cry in great wracking sobs against his shoulder, sucking in ragged breaths and shuddering from the outpouring of emotion I was experiencing.

'Did I hurt you?' he asked softly, stroking damp hair back from my wet cheeks and tilting my head so he could look down at me. The concern on his face set off another wave of tears and my throat felt so thick that I couldn't speak, but I did at least manage to shake my head to tell him "no".

'Good.' He rocked me in his arms, seeming to completely understand my confused state, and the need to calm down for a few minutes.

He held me as if I weighed nothing, soothing my arms with gentle caresses, his solid strength so comforting to me. 'Shhh, it's OK, *cariño*. Cry if you need to.'

As Oliver held me and gently stroked my hair, reality began to come back to me and I was gripped with horrendous embarrassment – Oliver had just given me one of the most erotic moments of my life, not to mention the best orgasm *ever*, and what was my response? I break down and cry on him before he's even had a chance to climax himself. I bit my lip and winced when I realised I could still feel him hard and pulsing against the curve of my thigh.

My tears had subsided now, so I drew in a shaky breath, finally plucking up the courage to lean back and look at Oliver.

'You don't need to call me Sir anymore, not now the scene has finished. Tell me, do you know why you're crying?' He sounded genuinely concerned.

'Not really … I feel like an idiot. I think it was all just a little bit overwhelming, that's all.'

Nodding in agreement, Oliver lifted one hand and

184

soothed the back of his hand down my cheek before leaning forwards and placing a brief kiss on my lips. 'It's a perfectly normal reaction, and completely understandable. You've never done anything like that before, and I didn't exactly hold back, so your body will have been on sensory overload.' He could say that again; I could still barely think straight after the spanking, nipple clamps, orders, and seismic orgasm.

'Sometimes when the pressure is released in the form of an orgasm it allows all the other pent-up emotions to flow freely as well. Tears included.'

I guess that made sense.

Once again remembering that he still hadn't climaxed, I began to try to shift in his arms so I could reach a hand down between us and continue things for him, but before I managed it, he gripped my wandering hand and brought it to his lips, placing a kiss on my knuckles.

'Thank you for the thought, Robyn, but no, we can do that at some later point. At the moment the most important thing for me is to make sure you're OK, and talk about what you're feeling. This first session together is where I learn all about your reactions, responses and needs.'

Oh. I didn't know how to respond to that, so I just nodded and let him cradle me against him. We sat in silence for what felt like an age until I started to shiver from the chill of the air con. Oliver dragged a blanket up around us and continued to stroke my back, and I simply lay crumpled on him, too exhausted to move, apart from one hand, which was lightly trailing up and down his chest, enjoying exploring the bumps and ridges there.

'So, did you enjoy it?' he finally asked.

I snorted out a laugh and nodded. 'I was nervous at first, but yes, it was incredible, Oliver. The pain and pleasure mix that you told me about beforehand, it was so ... intense. That was the best sexual experience of my life, not to mention the best orgasm.'

'Good, I'm glad.' Oliver seemed content with my reply, but didn't look half as smug as I'd expected. He just looked … happy. Replete.

'You're pretty intense, too, you know? As is the connection between us,' I admitted, still amazed by just how potent it was to be within touching distance of this amazing man.

'It is. That's why I knew we'd be so good together.' He smiled. 'You were so perfect, Robyn. I suspected you would enjoy submitting, but I never expected you to take to it so immediately. How are you feeling now that you've come down from it?'

'Emotionally drained,' I mumbled, my body feeling so heavy I could hardly bear the thought of moving. 'It was just so incredibly consuming. I feel exhausted now; it's like I've run a marathon.'

'Yes, this type of sex can require good stamina levels,' Oliver commented lightly.

*This type of sex.* I blushed at his words and lowered my face away from his.

He didn't let me hide for long, though, and used his thumb to gently tip my face up again just seconds later so that he could stare into my eyes. 'You need to shake off this shame that you seem to be feeling. What we have just done together was done as two consenting adults. You said yourself that it was the best sexual experience of your life, so why should you feel ashamed by it? Just because it might not be considered the norm to use things like nipple clamps doesn't mean it's wrong.'

'I know. I think it'll just take a bit of getting used to, that's all.' Something disturbing suddenly occurred to me. 'We hadn't decided to progress things before this trip, so why were those clamps in your case?'

Oliver paused for several seconds, and from the twitching at the corners of his lips, it looked decidedly like he was trying to suppress a smile. 'Are you asking if I was planning a trip to Fantasia without you?'

Shocked, I sat up straighter and tried to drag the blanket up to cover myself. I hadn't been thinking that, but I was now. 'Were you?' I blurted, knowing that my outraged tone wouldn't have been tolerated a few minutes ago during our scene.

Instead of replying, he merely raised his arm and propped it behind his head, reclining lazily on the bed and showing off his bloody gorgeous chest to perfection, before asking a question of his own. 'Would you have been jealous?'

'No.' I practically spat my response.

I barely even saw Oliver move, but suddenly I found myself being flipped over onto my stomach with apparent ease, before the sheet was thrown back and a stinging spank landed on my bottom.

'Don't lie to me. Never lie to me. Remember it's one of the rules. I won't tolerate it being broken.'

One hand was gently pressing me into the bed to stop me moving, while his other was now soothing my bum over the thin layer of my panties. It tickled, and I squirmed below his touch, quite surprised by how much I had enjoyed both of the spankings tonight. 'Well, stop teasing me then!'

Another spank landed, this time on the opposite buttock, and just a little firmer than the previous one. 'And lose the cheek, little one. It doesn't suit you. Not in the bedroom, anyway. I enjoy the way you challenge me, Robyn, you constantly make me rethink myself. I wouldn't ever want that to stop, but in the bedroom, I'm in control.'

I couldn't deny the fact that I had very much enjoyed how he had taken control in here, so, pulling in a slow breath, I pushed away my sarcasm, and turned my head towards him.

'Yes,' I whispered.

His eyes flicked around my face, then he frowned.

'Yes?'

Nodding, I gave a small shrug, deciding to admit my feelings. 'Yes, I would have been jealous if you'd gone to the club without me.'

His nostrils flared as he drew in a small, sharp breath, but then he gave one small nod and leaned down to place a kiss on the top of my head. 'I had no intentions of using those clamps with anyone but you. In fact, they are brand new, purchased specifically for you in the hope that you would one day decide to explore with me. I simply packed them because I'm an optimist. I'd been hoping that spending some time together would help you decide, and it seems that it did.'

They were brand new? And just for me? Well, that made me feel quite a bit better. Relaxing, I wiggled my bum under his hand, hoping for some more of his touch.

Oliver chuckled, and gave my bottom another squeeze, accompanied by an appreciative hum, before laying a kiss on my shoulder blade and pulling me back below the covers. 'As tempting as that is, you're tired. Save that thought for tomorrow. Let's sleep.'

And sleep I did. Almost as soon as he'd said the words I felt my eyelids drooping as if as if they, too, were obediently following his every command.

## Chapter Twenty-five

### Robyn

As soon as I woke up, I knew that I was alone. Oliver's body heat last night had been intense and blanketing as I'd slipped into my slumber, but now I was cold, and definitely not being cradled by his strong arms any more.

I extended my hand to my side, just to check, but feeling the cool sheets beside me, I sat up and glanced across to see if Oliver was in the room. He wasn't, and confusingly, as I looked around, I saw my belongings on the dresser, and my coat hanging on the hook.

I was in my own suite?

I had definitely fallen asleep in his arms last night, in his room, but running my hands over the soft cotton I found my sheets crumped and warm, indicating that I'd spent a fair while in them. The pillow next to mine, however, was untouched, seeming to indicate that Oliver hadn't joined me. Somehow, at some point, he had moved me back into my own bed and left me here, but when, and more importantly, why?

Could it be that sleeping alone was one of his rules, too, and he'd forgotten to mention it to me?

As I sat there pondering this, there was a knock at the door to my suite, shortly followed by a muffled voice calling out that it was room service.

I quickly pulled on the robe provided by the hotel, opened the door, and found a smartly dressed waiter holding a large tray. '*Buenos días, señora*. Breakfast, compliments of Señor Wolfe. He also asked me to give you this note.' I accepted the envelope he was holding out to me, then waited for him to place down the breakfast tray and leave. Frowning, I looked down at the note and slid my finger under the tab of the envelope to open it.

*Robyn,*

*My apologies that I am not with you this morning, I have some business to attend to in the city. Have a lazy morning, or perhaps sightsee, and I shall meet you in the hotel foyer at 1 p.m.*

*Yours, Oliver*

Scanning the note again, I relaxed, my earlier anxiety at his absence now quelled by his explanation. I ran my fingertip across the neat, slanting script, and smiled at his sign-off before placing it down on the table.

*Yours.* I wondered if he meant that in the way I was hoping.

## Oliver

Sipping my coffee, I adjusted my sunglasses and tried to focus on watching the world go by for a few minutes. After just a few seconds, however, my mind predictably returned once again to Robyn, and I sighed, before removing my glasses and rubbing at my face.

She'd been the entire focus of my thoughts since I'd moved her back to her room at a little past two o'clock this morning. I'd had to move her, because after she'd fallen asleep all I'd been able to do was stare at her and absorb every tiny detail of her face, and I'd been at risk of having a completely sleepless night. Even with her safely back in her own bed, I'd barely slept, and although it was true that I'd had some business to attend to, I could have easily rearranged it. I hadn't, though, because after the events of last night I'd needed a few hours to myself to try to get my head straight.

I'd had a few hours now, though, and I still couldn't quite process how I felt. But what scared me more, was *how much* I was feeling. I'd known Robyn was special to me, more so that any woman that had come before, but *dios*, it was overwhelming just what feelings she had sparked in me.

Drawing in a breath, I tried to re-establish my usual calm and control. Given that last night had been one of the most incredible of my life, it was quite a difficult task.

Perhaps instead of focusing on my feelings, I should concentrate on the physical side of things. That might help distract me and get me back on track. Sex. It was one of my favourite pastimes, and perfect to lose myself in as a distraction. I still had the best part of a week to enjoy with Robyn; five nights where we could explore her submission to me.

A wicked smile curled on my lips. Yes, that was exactly what I'd concentrate on. Standing up, I drained my coffee cup, put my shades back on, and strode with purpose back in the direction of the hotel.

## Chapter Twenty-six

### Oliver

Robyn had recently showered after another day spent sightseeing, but it had been a pointless act, seeing as I fully intended to have her warm and sweating again within a matter of minutes.

A trickle of water ran down her chest, slowing as it reached the peak of one nipple, then curving sideways into the valley between her naked breasts. I watched avidly as she shuddered, a soft moan escaping her lips, and her back arching further as I trailed the melting ice cube across her collar bones. It was the most erotic of sights, and I absorbed every tiny detail of it. Every tiny detail of *her*.

Robyn let out another small whimper, and I smirked at her response, my cock giving another leap in my trousers and reminding me that I was well overdue for some release – but that could wait. I was enjoying the scene before me far too much to rush it.

Robyn knelt on the foot of the bed, naked, legs spread, blindfolded, and demonstrating a perfect example of her ready position. I hadn't allowed her the privacy of her knickers tonight as I had last night, and as anticipated, her pussy was just as beautiful as the rest of her; with a neatly trimmed strip of hair and pretty pink lips which were already shining with her arousal and begging for me to touch them, or perhaps taste.

I'd decided to introduce a little light bondage tonight, too, and had borrowed a metal spreader bar and a long length of velvet from Fantasia to assist me. I'd used the bar between her knees, attaching the leather cuffs so that even though she was kneeling, she could no longer close her legs if she tried.

I loved the way she was now so open to me, but what had surprised me more, was just how much Robyn had seemed to like it when I attached the bar. My little Robyn was taking to this lifestyle in great leaps and bounds, and her enthusiasm for it all thrilled me no end.

As for the velvet, I had tied her arms behind her back. Her wrists were bound together tightly and attached to the lower half of the bedpost. It presented her beautiful breasts to perfection. She looked utterly gorgeous, and I very much doubted that I would be able to maintain my control of last night and keep my cock in my trousers.

I was desperate for release. So much so, that I'd been hard on and off for the best part of the day. I'd denied myself, though, and so the temptation to remove my trousers was almost overwhelming. I kept the thin barrier in place, however, as a reminder that I needed to maintain my control, even if only for a short while longer. I wanted to get off almost as much as I wanted my next breath, but I would ensure that Robyn climaxed first.

Having placed the ice cube back into the glass, I circled her nipples with my chilled fingers, delighting in her breathy moan, and the way she bit down on her lower lip to try and keep control of herself.

I drew a fresh ice cube from the glass, dropped to my knees, and lowered my face between her legs, inhaling her delicious musky arousal, before leaning back slightly and running my tongue from the cuff at her knee all the way up the inside of her thigh. As soon as I had lapped my way to the apex of her legs, I sat back and followed the trail with the ice cube, shocking her heated body with the cold ice, and causing goose pimples to pop on her skin.

As I repeated this over and over again, I got closer and closer to her core on each trip, but deliberately avoided the area that she must be desperate for me to touch. At the start of our session tonight I had asked her to remain quiet and still, and I had then deliberately tested her with my actions, but true to form, Robyn had maintained her submissive role superbly. I had expected her to break down and beg, but she didn't. Apart from briefly writhing under my touch she maintained a still and mostly silent position.

Finally, I rewarded her by nuzzling into her warmth and sucking her clit into my mouth. At the same time, I teased Robyn's opening with the ice cube, and the shock of so much sensation caused her to jerk against my mouth and yelp.

'Oliver! Sir! Please!' She gasped, making her first breach of my rules, and begging as I'd hoped she might. I smiled against her heated flesh, thrilled by the play between us, and how perfect her responses were.

Seeing as her wrists were bound to the bedpost, and her knees were spread wide, she couldn't escape my advances. Over the next few minutes, I upped her pleasure by focusing on her clit but alternating the use of my hot tongue and the cold ice, until the cube was nothing but water trickling down my wrist and Robyn was gasping for air and so close to her climax that I could taste it on my tongue.

Pressing two fingers into her channel, I felt her clench around me, and so crooked them to work her G-spot, easily finding the patch of rougher skin and beginning a massage with my fingertips that I knew would have her coming apart in my arms within seconds.

'You may come,' I murmured against her skin, and then, using my teeth, I began to work her clit again, tugging and nibbling in time with my fingers until she whimpered, then arched her back as she began to climax across my tongue and around my fingers. I grinned at how responsive she was to my touch, then worked her down, until she was almost boneless in her pleasure, her cheeks flushed, and beads of sweat building on her skin.

Almost as soon as she had recovered her breath, Robyn licked her lips, and tilted her head up. Even though her eyes were blindfolded, she instinctively seemed to know where I was standing. 'Please ... Sir, let me finish it for you, too?'

These first few days were supposed to be about settling Robyn into this new relationship, focusing on her; her pleasure, her comfort, and her feelings. But I was only human, and the way she was making me feel had me accepting her offer and practically ripping my trousers open and guiding my raging hard-on towards her mouth.

I didn't untie her hands, or remove the spreader, or blindfold, but Robyn seemed to automatically know what I wanted, because before I'd even touched the tip of my cock to her lips she had opened her mouth for me. I drew in a satisfied breath – she was so, so perfect, it almost defied belief.

Shifting myself forwards, I pressed into her mouth, and as she eagerly wrapped her lips around my cock I groaned loudly, giving away far more about how I was feeling than I usually would. Throwing my head back, I thrust forwards more, then slid a hand to the back of her head, steadying her movements as she took me to the back of her mouth greedily.

*Dios*. Pleasure seared through my body, weakening my knees to the point where I had to clasp at the bedpost to stop myself from buckling over. Thank God Robyn was blindfolded, because I would never usually allow myself to show a weakness like that.

Thinking of her blindfold, I realised that I was perhaps overstepping myself. She certainly seemed keen to continue, but as a Dom I prided myself on always checking a sub's comfort levels when indulging in new experiences. Not only was this the first blow job she'd given me, but she was also bound, spread, and blindfolded, which could easily add up and overwhelm her.

Glancing down at her, I used my grip on her hair to reluctantly pull myself from her mouth. She groaned her annoyance at my move, which gave me a good indication that she was fine and enjoying herself, but I would still check. Using my hand to continue a slow stroke on my cock, I cleared my throat and spoke. 'What colour are you, *cariño*?'

'Colour? Oh ... green, Sir. Definitely green,' she murmured, giving her lips a lick and smiling shyly. 'And if you're wondering, I'm also green with swallowing ...'

*Dios*. I hadn't been intending on going that far with her tonight, not with all the additional bondage and sight deprivation, but if she was offering it up on a plate like that, I was hardly going to turn her down.

A groan rumbled in my chest, and I bit my lip, thrusting forwards again and holding myself deeply inside her mouth for a second, before releasing my hold on her and allowing her to continue at her own pace.

It felt so amazing that it was blinding me, and I couldn't think of anything but the rush of desire that was pulsating around my system and fast bubbling to the surface.

Robyn hollowed her cheeks out, sucking me in and out with hard, short jerks of her head, while also working my tip with swirls of her tongue. It was a potent combination, better than even I could have guided her to do, and, in no time, I felt my balls lifting as my orgasm rushed upon me.

As my climax began to coat the inside of her mouth, I kept one hand cradling her head as she continued to work me, and let my head drop back from the dizzying pleasure spiralling through me.

One thing was sure – focusing on the physical bond between us was certainly working out pretty well for me at the moment, because I wasn't thinking of anything but the feel of her lips and the heaven of finding my release in her mouth.

### Robyn

Oliver didn't allow himself much time to recover from his

climax, but instead, almost as soon as he had come he carefully slipped from my mouth, and after a brief sound of rustling, he began undoing my hands and releasing the bar from my knees. I hadn't been too sure about the spreader when he'd first shown it to me, but once it was on I'd found the sensation to be incredibly overwhelming, in a good way. A very good way. Knowing that he could touch me at any point, with or without my consent, had for some reason turned me on immensely.

The bar clattered to the floor and, the next moment, I found myself being scooped into his arms and cradled against his warm, naked chest. Resting into his strength, I instinctively wrapped my arms around his neck as he carried me, then I felt us lowering as he sunk onto the bed, before shifting us backwards.

As our bodies moulded together it became obvious that Oliver was now completely naked below me. The heat of his groin was almost burning my bottom, and the hairs on his thighs felt wiry and ticklish, rubbing at my sensitive skin deliciously.

He was quite the tease, wasn't he? I was yet to see him completely naked, and yet now that I was blindfolded he'd decided to strip off. Damn it. Now my hands were itching to rip off my blindfold so I could give him a thorough look over, but I resisted, just … opting to leave him in control of if, or hopefully when, I would get to see him.

Despite his very recent orgasm, Oliver's groin didn't seem to be softening at all below me, but I had to say, I was feeling similarly aroused, even though I, too, had just climaxed. This man had ignited something within me that I just didn't know I had in me, and the feel of him so intimately wrapped around me made my core clench with enthusiasm at the possibility of round two.

This all felt quite different from last night, because I'd only seen him topless yesterday, and even when we went to bed, he'd chosen to keep his boxer shorts on when he had curled up behind me.

Once we were settled, I felt his hands at the back of my head as he began to undo the blindfold for me, and my heart rate accelerated with excitement. I'd begun to wonder if he was just teasing me with his nakedness, and wasn't going to let me see him tonight, but it seemed my fears were misplaced.

The knot slipped free, and he pulled the blindfold gently from my eyes. Even though Oliver had switched off the main light, and swapped it for a single small lamp, I had to scrunch my eyes shut as the light felt almost blinding after so long of being locked in the darkness.

As I blinked to try to clear my vision, I suddenly felt warmth on my eyelids and realised that Oliver had leaned forwards and was fluttering gentle kisses on both of my closed eyes. That was almost a romantic gesture, and I had to try really hard not to get carried away with the feelings that it caused to swirl in my belly.

'Hey, *cariño*. Welcome back,' he whispered. Brushing some hairs back from my face, he then looked deeply into my eyes and laid a stunning, affectionate smile on me.

'Hi.' My cheeks heated, and I felt oddly shy after the intimacy of what we had just shared.

Cupping my jaw, he brought my lips to his for a reverently soft kiss and I realised I could still taste a trace of my own musk there.

'So, how was that for you?'

Ah yes. Oliver and his post-sex questions. I was starting to get used to this part of things now, but I still took my time to think through my answer, because I knew he wouldn't like it if I just came out with a generic "it was amazing" kind of reply.

He'd certainly been right when he'd warned me that the blindfold would make it all more intense, because it really had. Every touch, sound, and feeling had been amplified, each sensation identifiable and incredible in its own right.

I was certainly keen to experiment with that type of thing again.

'The blindfold was a lot of fun. You were right, it made everything far more sensitive.' I paused, looking down at my wrists and knees, my flush deepening as I recalled how Oliver had fucked my mouth while my hands had been tied behind my back. If someone like Sasha had described it to me before I'd done it, I would never have thought I would like being so vulnerable, but it had been H.O.T.

'And the, um … the … bar, and you know, how you tied my wrists?' Oliver's eyes flashed with heat, but he stayed silent, allowing me time to expel all of my feelings. 'That was really fun too. I wasn't quite as sure about the bar at the start – it looked like a medieval torture implement – and losing the use of my arms made me feel a bit exposed at first, but in the end, I enjoyed what we did. Really enjoyed it.' I licked my lips, remembering how they'd felt stretched as I'd tried my best to pleasure him, and I saw his eyes dip and watch the journey of my tongue.

'I trust you, Oliver, I really do, so it was actually quite liberating to just give up my concerns and enjoy what you did.'

'And you definitely liked it? I wasn't too rough?' he enquired, a touch of concern colouring his tone.

Taking in a deep breath, I finally gave up on trying to be coy, and grinned. It was probably the filthiest smile I'd ever smiled in my life, but seeing the amazing things I'd just experienced with this man, I think it was justified. 'I did, Oliver. Very much so.'

Oliver's nostrils flared at my declaration, and he lowered his forehead to rest upon mine, drawing in a deep, ragged breath as he did so. '*Dios*, Robyn. How did I survive before we met? We are so perfectly matched.'

He placed a lingering kiss on my lips, then began softly massaging my wrists where I had been tied to the bedframe.

Once again, I decided it was safest not to overthink his seemingly romantic declarations, and instead looked down to watch him as he took care of me. The skin of my wrists was a little reddened, but wasn't sore at all. I wouldn't turn down his attention, though, because the feel of his gentle, caring touch was lovely, and actually making me feel a little sleepy.

We sat in silence like that for several minutes, our naked bodies pressed together and heads resting just a few inches apart as we came down from the experiences we had shared.

'I've been pretty full-on with you, Robyn, when really I should have been gently introducing you to submission, so I feel the need to apologise.'

The rueful, apologetic expression on his face made me smile, and I immediately shook my head. 'Oliver, I've loved every minute so far,' I confessed, hoping to reassure him, while simultaneously hoping there would be many, many more minutes spent together with him in my future.

He drew in a long breath, and nodded, relief spreading on his features. 'You're taking to it so beautifully that I kept forgetting myself.' He placed a brief kiss on my lips and shook his head in apparent wonder. 'The strength of the bond between us ... it has somewhat taken me by surprise. We feel so perfect together, so right.' Oliver suddenly brought himself up short, as if perhaps he was worried that he'd said too much, but secretly his words thrilled me.

Clearing his throat, he straightened back and leaned his head on the headboard. 'So, overall tonight was good?' Oliver murmured, as he busied himself by extending the wrist massage to where the cuffs on the spreader had restrained my knees.

His gentle caresses were making me feel boneless, but remembering how he'd said he needed my reassurances in the first few sessions, I pulled my drowsy mind together to reply. 'Honestly, Oliver, it was really good.'

He gave a small cough, then dipped his head so he could look in my eyes. 'And the blow job … you were OK with how that played out? It wasn't too much?'

He sounded regretful, so I could only assume that he was referring to the way he had used my mouth towards the end. Mostly he'd let me lead, but there had been a couple of times where he had taken over and really thrust into my mouth with abandon. It had taken me by surprise at first, and made me gag slightly on one occasion, but I couldn't deny that it had been amazing to make him lose control like that. Hot. Really hot.

'No.' I shook my head sharply, to try to dispel his worries. 'I'd never really thought that I'd like it rough, but … but that was amazing, Oliver. I know you wouldn't ever push me too far.' Brushing aside my embarrassment, I decided to confess something to him. 'And the swallowing thing? I've never done that with anyone before.' Oliver's eyes widened, then a pleased blush spread on his cheeks. 'I just felt the urge with you.'

He briefly closed his eyes, then he placed a short, hard kiss on my lips. 'Thank you. I very much enjoyed it.' With a contented sigh, Oliver shifted us both below the blankets and I snuggled closer to his chest, enjoying the feel of his strength strong body wrapped around me as I started to slip towards a sated sleep. This was going to be a night I remembered for quite some time to come, that was for sure.

## Chapter Twenty-seven

## Robyn

We'd been in Barcelona for three nights now, and I'd spent the last two with Oliver in his suite. We'd explored submission, experimented with toys and bondage, and while we'd not had full sex yet, we'd now both achieved climaxes – me multiple, him one. Both nights I'd fallen asleep in his arms, and in his bed, but yet again this morning as I woke up, I found myself alone.

I was sure I hadn't imagined it – Oliver's warmth had definitely been my companion as I fell asleep last night, but as I became aware of the daylight across my face, I felt cooler, knowing that he was no longer in the bed with me.

Sitting up, I frowned. To add to it, I was in my own suite again. I wasn't sure I liked this part of it all. The two nights I'd spent with Oliver had been incredible, but waking up by myself, having been moved to a different room, brought me back down to earth with a gigantic bump. I'd been satisfied with yesterday's explanation that he had business to attend to, but what was the reason today?

Maybe this was his way of keeping us from getting too involved with each other, and I was just being overly sensitive because I was falling for him. The thought made me feel wretched, and I slipped from the bed and trudged towards the bathroom, hoping to shower away some of my disappointment at waking up on my own.

The warm water helped clear my head, and as I stood under the jets a smile slipped to my lips as I thought back over all that had occurred between us since we'd been in Barcelona. I'd been so nervous the first night, but so far everything between us had been incredible – except the waking up alone bit.

I genuinely hadn't known what to expect from this type

of relationship, but although Oliver had stuck to his word and been strict, he also made me feel completely at ease. With him to guide me, letting go of my inhibitions had been far easier than I'd expected, but I suspected that had a lot to do with the way we connected, and wasn't a general reflection of my sudden bravery. He had me under such a spell that I couldn't help but respond to him.

Grabbing a towel, I gave my hair a rough dry and then wrapped it around my body. I ran a brush through my damp hair, flicked it over my shoulder, and looked at myself in the mirror long and hard. There was a slight tension in my expression, and I knew why. Waking up alone was still bugging me. It almost felt like a rejection of sorts. I'd never been needy in past relationships, but with Oliver I could already feel myself wanting more, which was a dangerous emotion to even contemplate where Mr Wolfe was concerned.

The things he did to me were phenomenal, but was that level of pleasure worth risking my heart for? Because I had a feeling that if I continued things with Oliver that was exactly what I would be doing.

I still had no clue when he'd moved me to my room, either. When the sun came up? Or as soon as I had fallen asleep?

He didn't seem to mind snuggling, though, because both nights I'd fallen asleep cradled against his chest. I couldn't deny that I'd been hoping that I'd wake up there today, too, but so far this was my reality – my own room and cold sheets beside me.

I was still contemplating this as I wandered back into my room wrapped in the towel. There was a noise at the door to the adjoining bedroom and I jumped, turning towards the sound with a startled yelp. There was no knock, but the door opened, and Oliver strode in with a tray in his hands.

God, he was in jeans again. I couldn't decide which outfit he looked better in, jeans or a suit. Both had merits of their own. These jeans were pale blue, and paired with a black, round-neck T-shirt that wasn't exactly tight, but was snug enough to define the trim muscles underneath. He looked breath-taking, and it made something inside my chest constrict almost painfully.

'Good morning,' he said softly, his eyes sweeping over my damp post-shower state and lighting with a playful twinkle. 'I brought breakfast. Well, brunch really, seeing as it's so late.'

So he was happy to eat with me, just not sleep a full night with me? God, I was so confused. I glanced absently at the clock, seeing that it was already half past eleven, but then dropped my eyes to the bed, unable to shake off the niggle of frustration in my belly.

'Haven't you heard of knocking?' I muttered, still feeling slightly off kilter and defensive after my earlier thoughts about needing to protect my heart from this dangerously alluring man.

Oliver stilled, his eyebrows rising in surprise at my tone, but then his challenging smirk returned. 'Why? Would you have turned me away if I had knocked?'

Damn. That wasn't what I'd meant at all. Blinking, I shrugged, and pulled the towel tighter around my body. 'No ... but I could have been naked.'

Oliver placed the tray on the table. He turned and stared at me, and began stalking towards me. He didn't walk, or stride like a normal man might. Oh no, his steps were predatory. He was coming to get me, like I was his chosen prey for the day, I was sure of it.

My heart rate accelerated, and my skin heated as I absorbed just how intently focused on me he was Confidence oozed from his every pore. He really was so good at the hot, brooding man thing.

'I didn't hear any complaints when I saw you naked last night,' he murmured, reaching my side and folding his arms across his chest. 'Or the night before.'

I felt well and truly flustered by his intensity as I struggled for what to say. 'N ... no ... but that was d-d-different.'

He leaned close to me, and I got a waft of his delicious scent. His normal clean scent was mixed with the citrus of the hotel shower gel today, and smelled so good that it seemed to make my brain foggy.

'D-d-different?' he asked, deliberately stuttering to tease me about my fumbled sentence. Then, before I'd even realised what he was doing, he'd gripped the edge of the towel and ripped it clean from my body. He scooped me up and threw me unceremoniously onto the bed so I was spread-eagled, naked, and shocked in the centre of the gigantic mattress.

I tried to sit up, but Oliver pounced on me like a tiger taking down his prey, sprawling his big, hot body over mine as he smoothly pinned my hands above my head in one large palm and leaned down to lick and kiss a hot trail across my breasts with his tongue. 'I don't see how this is any different to our last two nights together,' he murmured around one nipple, his words vibrating across my skin and hardening it into a needy peak. 'You're still naked, still just as rebellious, still just as gorgeous ...' He bit down gently on the tight bud, causing me to arch my back and let out a breathy moan as my earlier mood was erased, just like that. I was so easy where this man was concerned. 'And still just as responsive,' he finished smugly, leaning up to place a brief kiss on my lips.

'And I'm still just as tempted, and still just as hard,' he admitted with a lazy grin as he thrust his arousal against my thigh, 'but that will have to wait for later, because you need to eat.' With that, Oliver gracefully rose from the bed, taking one of my hands and pulling me up with him.

205

He let go of my hand, went to the wardrobe and pulled out one of the robes that the hotel provided, and helped me into the soft cotton gown.

Frowning, I pouted, not an expression I adopted very frequently, but after getting a brief taste of his supreme sexing I had been left wanting more. Much more. Including his company in between my sheets when I first woke up.

'Why don't you let me sleep in your bed?' I blurted, taking myself by surprise as the words escaped my mouth. 'Is that one of your rules, too?'

Oliver was halfway through lifting one of the silver lids on the breakfast tray, but paused at my words, allowing the scent of bacon to waft into the room. Tilting his head, he observed me for several seconds, and I held my breath for each and every one of them. I could practically hear the cogs in his mind working, as if he were trying to deduce where my sudden statement had come from, but was drawing a blank.

He placed the lid back on the breakfast, and turned to give me his full attention. 'Is that why you were tetchy just now?'

I stayed silent, simply maintaining his gaze, and watching him as he sighed and stepped closer to me again.

He cupped my cheek and soothed his thumb over the warm skin. 'I haven't shared a bed with a woman for an entire night for a very, very long time,' he confessed with a shrug, 'because quite frankly, I haven't wanted to prolong things in that way.'

Prolong things? So I was fine for him to mess about with sexually for a few hours, but I wasn't worth his time for a whole night? I suddenly felt like a complete slut, and the air rushed from my lungs in a hurt gasp. I don't think he couldn't have wounded me more if he'd actually punched me in the stomach.

Appalled at both myself, and him, I tried to step away, thinking that perhaps I'd grab a taxi to the airport and pay for a flight home, but Oliver stopped me by sliding his hand to the back of my neck and gripping hard, refusing to let me get away.

'Let go of me,' I demanded, my voice nowhere near as loud and defiant as I would have liked as I twisted uselessly in his grasp. Instead of letting go, Oliver gripped tighter, his fingers fisting his fingers in the hair at my nape as his body moved even closer to mine.

'In a second, but you didn't let me finish. Listen to the rest of what I have to say.' Oliver's words were a demand, but he softened his hold on me, releasing my hair but keeping me captured by looping his arms around my shoulders, trapping me within his personal space.

'What I was going to say, was that with other women I haven't wanted to prolong things, but with you, and this is a very important "but", *cariño* ... but with you, that is not the reason why you and I haven't spent the full night together. Can I explain, or do you still want me to let you go?'

He let his words hang in the air for a few seconds, and when I obediently stayed still and quiet, he nodded and placed a single kiss on my forehead. 'I wanted you in my bed all night more than you can imagine, more than even I could understand,' he admitted quietly, 'but I was attempting to be a gentleman.' He gently brushed back some hair from my face and smiled softly.

'Submission is an overwhelming thing, and it's new for you. I was trying to give you space to come to terms with it all. I thought I could achieve that by moving you back to your room so when you woke you could process everything that had gone on between us.'

Oh. That hadn't even crossed my mind.

'Now that I know you want company through the night, I shall happily oblige next time.' His hands continued to soothe me, touching across my cheeks and for some reason I felt the need to apologise for jumping to conclusions.

'Sorry, Oliver. That was very thoughtful of you. Thank you.'

He grinned and gave a wiggle of his eyebrows. 'I do try. I might enjoy the sight of you on your knees for me, but I'm not a complete monster.' His eyes flashed with something dark and devious, and in response my core clenched. I had enjoyed being on my knees for him far more than I had expected, too.

Suddenly I became aware that the robe wasn't tied yet, and was hanging open, revealing a sliver of my naked body. Oliver also seemed to realise this, because he stopped his gentle, reassuring touches and slid his hands down to my waist, inside the fabric, and gave a more purposeful caress.

'Are you OK, now?' he enquired, his voice low and silky.

'Yes.' I nodded, just as my tummy grumbled loudly.

'And hungry, apparently,' he commented with a smile, dropping his hands from my body with a reluctant chuckle, and tying the robe for me. 'Come, the food will be getting cold.'

'We could always eat later?' I suggested, taking his hand and giving a hopeful squeeze.

Oliver grinned, apparently pleased by my response, but then he shook his head, his expression turning thoughtful. 'As much as I'd like to give in to that look in your eye, I won't, because I have somewhere I'd like to take you today.'

This was news, because our plans for the day had been to relax by the pool then venture out for some tapas. 'I thought today was a pool day?'

'It was, but there's been a change of plan,' he informed me as he led me to the table, and helped me into my seat, before taking the chair opposite me.

'Cool. Where are we going?'

After draping a napkin across his lap, Oliver raised his head and gave me a long, hard stare. The look was certainly intriguing, because it seemed to be a mix of excitement and nerves. 'It's a surprise, but I think you'll like it.' Saying no more, he pulled the lid off the tray revealing a Spanish omelette, bacon, orange juice, and a pot of coffee. 'I hope you will, anyway,' he added, his tone low and thoughtful again.

This was a new side to Oliver that I was seeing. Nervousness was not a trait I had witnessed in him before, but he definitely seemed to be a little edgy, and deep in thought about something, so now my curiosity was well and truly piqued.

Where on earth was he planning on taking me?

# Chapter Twenty-eight

## Robyn

After a thirty-minute drive from the busy centre of Barcelona, we had descended into lush green countryside, and hadn't seen a soul, apart from the occasional farmer working in the sun-drenched fields.

A smattering of pale umber houses on the top of the next hill were the first buildings I'd seen for over ten minutes, and turned out to be our destination. After navigating the narrow streets of the small village, past a bar and cobbled marketplace, Oliver pulled into the driveway of a larger house on the far edge of the town.

Following Oliver's lead, I climbed from the hire car and turned to look at the house before me. It was large and typically Spanish in style. Built from rough bricks which had been painted white, it had a terracotta tiled roof, and pale blue shutters lined every window; all of which were thrown open to let in the blissfully warm afternoon.

It was certainly a beautiful property, but why were we here? Confused, I turned to Oliver and saw him gazing at the house with an affectionate smile on his face. 'Where are we?'

Taking my hand, he led me to the huge wooden front door and knocked sharply with his knuckles. 'You'll see shortly.'

The door opened, then, seconds later, Oliver was being dragged from my grasp, and pulled into a hug by an older lady who was speaking Spanish at him so quickly that the only word I recognised was his name; which was once again pronounced "Olive-ee-air". His reply was equally as rapid. My language skills were rusty, but I made out one word: *mamá*.

My God, was this his mother? He'd taken me to his house? His family?

Just as my shock was sinking in, Oliver and the woman separated, and both turned to me. Taking my hand again, Oliver pulled me closer, saying something to the woman, then smiling down at me, but still looking just a little bit nervous. 'Robyn, this is my *mamá*, Sofia.'

Sofia didn't wait for any further introductions. She simply pulled me into a huge hug and proceeded to kiss me in greeting, first on my left cheek then my right, all the while gushing away in rapid-fire Spanish which I couldn't understand.

'English, *Mamá*, Robyn doesn't speak too much Spanish.'

Leaning back, she grinned at me, her blue eyes twinkling in her tanned face as she lifted her hands and gave my shoulders an affectionate rub. 'Of course, I'm sorry. It is a good excuse for me to practice my English, no? Welcome, beautiful Robyn, it is a pleasure to meet you. Come on in! Come meet Richard, Oliver's father, he's around here somewhere.' Her expression was so open and welcoming that I instantly relaxed and found myself returning her smile.

'I'll get us some drinks.' She threw her arms towards the door and bustled inside, calling out something in Spanish, presumably to someone else within the house.

So, his secret plan for the day was for me to meet his folks. Well, this was certainly a turn-up for the books.

'I hope you don't mind me bringing you here?' Oliver looked uncertain, as if perhaps he'd taken a step too far, and to be honest, I was a little confused by his actions; Oliver and I were supposedly just sharing a temporary sexual relationship – that was what he had wanted, what he'd said he was capable of – so I wasn't entirely sure why he would want to introduce me to his family. But he certainly seemed keen for me to do just that, so I smiled back at him and nodded, intent on following Sasha's words of advice and just enjoying myself. 'Not at all.'

211

'You'll like my father, he's a tease like me, and some of my sisters are home, too, so my mother is cooking a traditional Spanish buffet for our visit. I think you'll enjoy it.'

And enjoy it I did. Over the next several hours, I was introduced to Oliver's father – who was English, and the reason Sofia was so fluent in the language – three of Oliver's five sisters, Isabella, Mary, and Rowena, all of whom were lovely, if somewhat feisty, and such a huge group of nieces and nephews that I could barely believe they all belonged to just the three sisters. Apparently, his other two sisters were away at university, but also came home on frequent visits. After initially feeling nervous thanks to the crowd that had met me in the garden, I was made to feel so incredibly welcome by all of them.

Red wine flowed freely, and Sofia had indeed prepared a feast of delicious delicacies which we all tucked into with gusto. Paella, mussels in garlic and white wine, a rabbit casserole, a whole baked cod infused with Spanish spices ... The list was almost endless, and it was all delicious.

Before the meal Oliver spent some time entertaining his nieces and nephews – which he did effortlessly and with obvious pleasure – but apart from that he barely let go of me all night. If he didn't have his arm wrapped firmly around my shoulders, then he was gripping my hand, or rubbing my thigh, and on several occasions, I spotted his family watching us, and our close physical contact, with open curiosity. With all the attention he was lavishing upon me, I was pretty curious, too. The evening had been lovely, but talk about confusing!

Oliver was supposed to be my temporary Dom, yet here I was, sharing dinner with practically his whole family. I couldn't quite get my head around what that might mean. If indeed it meant anything at all.

A warm breath fluttered on my neck as Oliver shifted himself even closer to me, and placed a kiss on my shoulder, obviously not caring if his family noticed his open affection. This all felt very relationship-like, and if I wasn't careful my heart might just get a bit carried away with it all. 'Have you enjoyed yourself, Robyn?'

Instinctively I moved my body into his, my free hand resting on his thigh, and my head leaning against his as if it were the most natural thing in the world. I smiled goofily, and nodded.

Goofily? Oh dear. I think I had *already* got carried away with it all. 'I've had the best night, Oliver. Thank you.'

'Good, I'm glad.' Leaning back slightly, he gazed at me with a soft smile on his face, then gently dragged a few stray wisps of hair from my face and tucked them behind my ear, a sweet gesture that did nothing to calm the swirl of emotions in my chest. 'It's getting late, but I've drunk too much to drive. Are you OK with staying here? My mother has the spare bed made up for us.'

Did he mean that? Bed, as in one? Not separate rooms like we had so far? Blinking in surprise, I nodded, my smile widening. I'd been dreaming about what it might be like to wake up beside Oliver, and now it looked like I might get my chance to find out.

'The spare room is in there,' he informed me, pointing to a building across the courtyard, which was separate from the main house. 'Nice and private,' he added, winking at me, a gesture that made my stomach quiver with some unnamed emotion as we stood and began to bid goodnight to everyone.

Once Sofia had pulled me into a tight hug, she leaned back then frowned. 'You've come with no bags, let me get you some toiletries.' I was about to tell her not to worry, but she hurried into the house before I could stop her. Returning with some towels, she also handed me a small basket that contained two toothbrushes, toothpaste, soap and shampoo.

'Thank you so much, Sofia, and thank you for your hospitality tonight, I've had a wonderful evening.'

Sofia beamed at me and gave my arm an affectionate rub. As her eyes briefly flicked between Oliver and me, her smile softened. 'You are welcome here anytime. We have loved having Oliver and his *dulce pequeño petirrojo* home with us tonight.'

'*Mamá*,' Oliver chided, his voice holding a note of warning as he gave his mum a rueful look and rolled his eyes.

As we walked towards the guest room I looked up at him curiously. 'What did your mum just call me? She said something in Spanish, but I didn't understand it.'

We had arrived at our door. He pushed it open then paused, turning to look down at me with a slight blush rising on his cheeks. 'She called you a sweet little robin. Like the bird.'

My eyebrows rose in surprise, partly at the phrase, and partly at the affectionate expression that crossed his features as he said it. 'If she's giving you a nickname it means she really likes you.' Cupping my cheek, he smiled softly. '*Mi dulce pequeño petirrojo.*' My Spanish was good enough that I knew he'd just added the word "my" on the front of the nickname. *My sweet little Robin.* His. Wow. Hearing it in his low, gravelly tone made it sound even better than it had the first time, and it sent a shudder of desire straight to my core.

'You go on in and get ready, t. The pipes out here aren't from the mains, so I just want to grab us some bottles of water.'

'OK.' Oliver returned to the main house and I placed down the towels and basket before briefly exploring the room. It was lovely. Simple, yet cosy. As I wondered what the evening would hold, I replayed his words in my mind and brought myself up short. *Get yourself ready.* Had he meant my ready position? Everything tonight so far had been a million miles away from our previous nights as Dom and sub, but perhaps it had all been for show somehow? Was he expecting me to submit now?

I wasn't sure but, erring on the side of caution, I quickly undressed and knelt on the rug in the centre of the floor in my ready position.

Oliver wasn't long, his footsteps striding swiftly across the stone steps outside before he came to an abrupt halt in the doorway when he saw me on the floor. I heard the noise of water bottles being placed on the side, then he shut the door behind him, and I watched his feet as he stood just inside the threshold, presumably still looking at me.

I felt like I'd knelt there for an eternity, but finally he shifted his feet and cleared his throat. 'Stand up, Robyn.'

Wondering if I had done something wrong, I accepted his offered hand as he helped me to my feet, then watched as he peeled off his short-sleeved white shirt to expose his gorgeous tanned, toned chest. To my surprise, instead of initiating something sexual, he draped it around my shoulders to cover me up.

What on earth was going on?

'We need to talk,' he murmured, the odd lilt to his voice sending shivers of worry through my chest.

# Chapter Twenty-nine

## Robyn

Talk? I was naked, and offering myself up to him, but he wanted to talk? That didn't sound good, at all. Oliver remained silent for a second, not meeting my eyes and continuing to fiddle with the collar of the shirt at my neck before letting out a low sigh. None of which helped to settle my jittery nerves.

Unsure about what exactly was occurring, I gripped the shirt front and pulled it around myself in a defensive gesture, keeping silent and watching warily as he gazed down at me for several seconds. Whatever it was going on inside his head, he looked almost torn by it, which didn't reassure me at all.

Drawing in a deep breath, Oliver dragged me into his arms and buried his head into the hair at the side of the neck. He inhaled deeply, then scooped me into his arms and carried me to the head of the bed.

After shifting to get us both back against the head rest he cradled me on his bare chest and let out a deep breath as he looked down at me intently. 'Listen ...' He paused awkwardly, 'My initial offer was to introduce you to submission to aid your research and allow us to explore a little ... but, I want to change my proposition.'

I frowned. He was changing his mind about me? If he was thinking about finishing things, then it didn't seem to match the fact that he was currently holding me so closely.

'We've grown to know each other these last few weeks, and while I was thrilled on Tuesday night when you said you wanted to submit to me, I ... I've come to realise that I also want other things with you.'

'Other things?' This was all so surprising that my voice sounded dry, and feather-light.

'Indeed. I want more, Robyn. It's not something I ever

thought I'd say, but there you go. I said you would change me, and it looks like I was correct,' he mused, raising a hand to tuck some stray wisps of hair behind my ear. I tilted my head into his palm as if it were custom made to fit there, and a thrill ran through me from the warmth of his skin.

'These last two nights together have made it abundantly clear to me that, with you, it needs to be everything, or nothing. I can't do this any other way, not with you.'

Wow. This was a very rapid direction change from his original intentions.

'Wh ...' My voice was so thick I had to clear my throat three times before I could speak. 'What do you mean, exactly?'

'You will submit to only me. Sleep with only me. No one else,' Oliver demanded, lowering his voice until each word seemed to vibrate right through my body. Seeing my shocked expression, he nodded once, his earlier nervousness now gone, replaced by an intent determination. 'I want us to be exclusive, Robyn,' he stated. I barely had time to get my head around his words before he continued. 'I'm not looking for a full-time submissive, but I'd like to continue our play sessions, if you're happy with that. Outside of those times we'd simply be together. A couple. In a relationship, I suppose you'd call it.'

*A couple!* Seeing where I'd met Oliver, and what our time together had started out as, being in a proper couple with him was just a crazy thought.

'And you, would you only sleep with me?' I asked, wondering if he intended his rules to apply to both of us, and hoping desperately that he did.

'Of course.' He made a face as if my question was ridiculous, and I felt immediately reassured.

I'd come to Barcelona knowing that I was going to submit to Oliver, and thinking that we might have sex at some point, but now he'd laid this on me. He wanted sex, submission, and *everything*.

But what did I want? Did I want a relationship with him? A man of an age I still didn't know, who seemed beyond my level in terms of sexual experience, sophistication, social standing ... everything really. He was what I might term as "way out of my league", and yet he wanted me. As soon as the question crossed my mind I had to struggle not to laugh out loud – of course I wanted a relationship with him! I'd started to fall for him weeks ago, so what he was now offering was perfect.

Without realising that I was doing it, I felt myself nodding keenly, my head bobbing about like one of those annoying car toys. 'Yes.'

'Yes?' His whole body seemed to bristle with anticipation below mine. 'Yes to what?'

'Yes, to it all,' I whispered.

'You'll be with me? And submit to me?' He sounded disbelieving, but in response I grinned. *Be with me.* It seemed such a funny phrase, so juvenile, almost like playground talk of "will you be my girlfriend?" and so funny to hear from Oliver's sophisticated lips.

'Yes, Oliver, I'll be with you,' I answered, still grinning. Oliver's face softened into an equally broad smile that made him look young, reckless and even more ridiculously handsome than usual. I knew I shouldn't be questioning this, but I couldn't help myself. 'I thought you didn't date, though?'

Oliver gave a wry smile, and nodded. 'I didn't.' He cupped my jaw and gently rubbed the pad of his thumb across my cheek, his gaze roaming about my face as if absorbing every detail of my features. 'And then you came along. My Robyn with a y,' he murmured thoughtfully, 'I think I've unknowingly been waiting a very long time for you.'

Talk about deep. He looked completely sincere, so

much so that my eyes were burning slightly with happy tears. He liked me, and wanted to progress things with me, and somehow, I just knew that his words hadn't been said on a whim. He'd meant every single one of them.

'So, what now?' I asked in a whisper.

Oliver shifted me slightly in his grasp, and gently trailed one finger down the side of my jaw and along the column of my neck until it dipped beneath the open collar of the shirt I still had draped around me.

'Well, if it's agreeable with you, now I would like to take my time exploring your body. No Sir, or sub, just you and me, and what I've been dying to do to you for weeks.'

I swallowed so loudly that it gurgled in the air between us, causing Oliver to chuckle, and lower his mouth to kiss along my jaw. 'Was that a noise of agreement?'

Licking my parched lips, I nodded, then joined him in a shy smile. 'Yes.'

No sooner had the word slipped from my mouth than his lips were upon mine, sealing the deal with a scorching kiss that had me gasping for air, and clutching at the warm skin of his shoulders to steady myself. I was so committed to the kiss that I barely felt us moving, but as a cooler breeze shifted across my skin I realised that I was once again naked, the shirt now tossed to the side.

Oliver must have moved me with considerable stealth, because I was no longer in his arms either, but lying on the bed beside him as he knelt over me and smiled down at me with a look so adoring that it made my heart race with the implications of what was occurring between us.

This was really happening. Oliver. Me. No titles, no commands, just us. *Everything*.

'You are so beautiful, Robyn,' he murmured, shaking his head in awe and moving his hands to the belt at his waist. What I'd seen of him so far was all pretty bloody impressive, too, but the adrenaline rushing around my system seemed to have rendered me incapable of returning his compliment.

The scraping sound of his zipper made my breath catch, as I realised that I was about to get my first proper view of him fully naked. With him kneeling like this beside me, I had a perfect close-up view of his gorgeous chest, and toned arms, and took the opportunity to openly gawk at him.

His muscles fascinated me. Previous boyfriends had been OK to look at, but Oliver was something else entirely. His body was lean, with defined pecs, a flat stomach with a hint of a six-pack, and that delicious V of muscle at his waist that disappeared down into his trousers and promised so much below. He wasn't ripped like a body builder, but he didn't have an ounce of fat on him, either.

'I rather like it when you stare at me like that,' Oliver commented, as he made quick work of his belt buckle. 'You look like you want to eat me alive.'

I grinned, and swallowed hard to try to kick-start my saliva glands so I might be able to speak again. 'That's exactly what I want to do.'

His eyes darkened at my bold claim, and a smile pulled at his lips as he ripped the belt from his trousers and threw it aside before leaping gracefully from the bed and removing the rest of his clothes.

When he was finally naked, my eyes dipped lower and I couldn't help the needy moan that grew in my throat. Seeing him in all his glory had been well worth the wait. He was gorgeous, and rather impressively aroused, with his long, hard cock curving up towards his navel and tempting me to reach out for it. He climbed back onto the bed and crawled towards me, the look of utter possessive determination on his face enough to make my core clench with need. He was such an innately sexual man, his every move, heated look, and touch all seemed to come so easily to him, and turned me on until I could barely keep still.

It had only been a matter of a minute or so since we'd kissed, but it felt like an eternity, and so I greedily reached for him and dragged him towards me so we could kiss again. Our lips met clumsily at first, because of my desperation, but Oliver seamlessly took over, slowing my movements so we could enjoy the moment and really appreciate how good we felt together like this. And it was so good I could hardly cope with the feelings flowing around my body.

But cope I did. I planned to take full advantage of this night with this gorgeous man, and so, following his lead, I forced my hands to slow, too. As we continued to kiss, I began to explore the flat planes of his back, the bumps and dips of his spine, and the firm fullness of his bum – which was definitely the nicest arse I'd ever had the pleasure of fondling.

He was supporting his weight on one arm as he leaned above me, but Oliver's free hand was also moving across my skin, teasing and pulling at my nipples, trailing down over my quivering stomach, and circling across the ticklish spots at my hipbones until I was writhing below him, my hips jerking and bucking with each contact and desperate for his touch to move just a fraction lower to where I needed it the most.

He didn't leave me waiting long, but as soon as he trailed his fingers down and felt the slickness between my legs, he let out a rough groan and ripped his lips from mine. 'I have to taste you,' he rasped, his eyes wide and wild with his apparent desperation.

Instead of crawling down between my legs, Oliver took the shortest route, simply turning himself on the spot and leaning down over my belly to bury his head between my legs. He was on all fours, so his knees were now next to my head, and his cock hanging there, tempting me to touch

221

it as it throbbed and jerked in the air. Reaching up with my right hand, I gripped his erection and gave a slow drag of my hand from balls to tip, which gained me the reward of a hard suck to my clit.

A yelp tore its way up my throat, and my hips jerked upwards into his face, causing Oliver to chuckle against my skin and up his efforts even more. I let out another breathy moan, again causing Oliver to laugh, but then he removed his lips briefly from his task and glanced back at me in amusement.

'Hush, *cariño,* the windows are open and some of my family are still on the terrace outside.'

Shit. He was right. I had been so focused on the moment that I had blocked out everything else, but if I listened hard I could hear the quiet murmur of voices up on the patio. They were quite a way away, but still, I didn't want them to overhear me while I shagged their son.

Feeling carefree and wild, I maintained his gaze and gave his cock a squeeze before slowly trailing my tongue across my lips. 'Perhaps you should put something in my mouth to quieten me, then.'

Oliver's eyebrows jumped in surprise, but he didn't take long to follow my suggestion. Grabbing some pillows, he propped my head up a bit, and retook his kneeling position so one leg was either side of my head. Oliver's beautiful cock was now swaying like a pole just above my face. He slid his knees down the bed, lowering his hips until the tip of his erection bumped against my lips. I opened immediately, licking the broad head and humming my approval when I tasted the saltiness of pre-come already coating the tip.

Oliver growled, but dropped his head and resumed licking and teasing at my slick flesh. He nibbled on my lower lips, tugged and teased my clit with his teeth and tongue, and dipped his tongue in and out of my opening in a series of moves that quickly drove me wild.

Reaching up, I slid both of my hands around to rest on his buttocks, using my grip there to help me lift my head up and down so I could take more of him into my mouth with each movement.

We might not be playing as Dom and sub tonight, but there was no getting away from the fact that this was an extremely dominant position. If he chose to, Oliver could easily thrust right in my mouth and make me gag, but he didn't. He continued to lick and suck at me, all the while giving small, shallow thrusts into my mouth, showing an amazing amount of self-control in such an intense situation.

Taking my clit into his mouth, he began to suck on it in a rhythmic motion; hard, soft, hard, soft, hard, soft, and after the rest of his build-up, it was enough to cause a climax to come rushing up on me. Planting my feet on the mattress, I bent my knees and squeezed my thighs around his head as Oliver held my hips down and wouldn't let me escape the pleasure of his mouth as he worked me through my orgasm.

I muffled my pleasured cries on his cock, jerking my head up to take even more of his length into my mouth, and having to fight the urge to clench my teeth and bite when the peak of my pleasure crested and my body was reduced to a jellified state below him.

As my body floated on the receding waves of my pleasure, I tried to up my moves so Oliver could achieve his climax, too. I bobbed my head up so frantically that he bumped against the back of my throat and I gagged on almost every move, but I didn't care. If the noises he was now making were any indication, then Oliver seemed to be loving this, and from the jerking of his hips it seemed that he was close to losing control. Just as I thought I was about to make him come, he bolted upright, ripping his cock from my mouth and spinning on the bed to drop down beside me and kiss me hard on the lips.

Our tastes mingled, the saltiness of his pre-come on my tongue and the musk of my arousal that was spread across his lips and nose, but it didn't bother me. If anything, it just seemed to heighten how erotic this all felt.

His hot body pressed against mine, he ground his jutting arousal against my hip, until he finally lifted his head and shifted his body so he was nestled between my legs, his cock lying heavy and hard on my belly.

'*Dios*, you are so incredible, Robyn.' He trailed his lips across my jaw, before coming back to my mouth. 'That felt amazing, but if it is OK with you, I really want to be buried inside of you tonight.'

I wiggled my hips to show just how much I liked that idea, but also backed it up with a frantic nod and audible reply. 'God, yes.'

'Condom,' he muttered, moving as if to lift off me, but I linked my legs around his waist and held him close. 'I'm on the pill,' I whispered, 'and clean.'

Oliver's eyes flashed with lust, and he nodded. 'I'm also clean, and so desperate to feel you wrapped around me that I can't wait another second.' Jerking his hips back, he lined up the tip of his cock with my entrance and stared into my eyes as he slowly began to press forwards.

I sucked in a gasp at the feel of his hot, hard shaft rubbing across my sensitive flesh then pushing inside. He was stretching me, and while it felt really bloody good, he was also broad, bigger than any of my exes had been, and I had to grip his biceps to make him slow down so I could accommodate him. 'Yes ... like that ... slowly ... let me get used to you.'

Oliver nodded, seeming to understand my need for a second or two to adjust to his size, even though his self-control did seem to be taking a toll on his composure; there was now a visible tension in his jaw, and a sheen of sweat on his forehead. Like a true gentleman, though, he took care of me, easing himself in and out of me inch by inch, allowing me to stretch around him until finally he was buried to the hilt.

We both let out shuddered groans of approval, and Oliver placed another heated kiss on my lips as he slowly ground his hips in a circle to help me adjust to the feel of him moving inside me.

'OK, *cariño*?' he asked softly, the complete adoration and concern in his tone almost undoing me. As I gazed into his intent blue eyes I got a warm, tight feeling in my chest, which was comforting, but simultaneously almost overwhelming. It was all too clear to me what it was – I had fallen for him. Fallen so fast and so hard that it would be terrifying if I let myself dwell upon it.

So I didn't.

Instead, I focused on the here and now, and the incredible feeling of being full to the brim with Oliver Wolfe. 'Yes ... Oh God, yes. It feels amazing.'

'*You* feel amazing,' he corrected me. 'Or perhaps I should say *we* feel amazing.'

He was right there; we really did feel amazing together. We fitted like two pieces of a jigsaw. Oliver withdrew to the tip, then oh-so-slowly pressed forward again, his shaft managing to rub against every sweet spot and sensitised nerve along the way. Pleasure spiralled through me, and I threw my head back and clenched my eyes shut to try to avoid yelling out my enjoyment.

We kept at the slow, smooth, rhythm for several minutes until our bodies were slick against each other and the scent of sex filled the air around us. We also continued to up the arousal levels by exploring, teasing and tweaking with our hands as our lips met and breaths combined within a deep, sensual kiss.

Oliver's moves were almost tender, but even though I knew he was still trying to go slow to let me fully stretch for him, I had a feeling that he was enjoying this slow intimacy just as much as I was.

No matter which way I looked at it, this felt a lot like lovemaking to me.

After a beautiful age of his careful attention, my body began to grow greedy for more, and I slid my hands down to grip his buttocks and encourage him to increase the speed and power of his strokes. He didn't need telling twice, and immediately lifted his body up slightly so he could thrust with more depth. The new angle was perfect. He hit my G-spot with such precision it was like we'd been made to fit together, and I couldn't help it; a pleasured cry flew from my lips, shattering the otherwise quiet night.

Oliver murmured his approval of the new position, too, and helped me muffle my cries by kissing them away for me. His tongue worked my mouth, relaxing and teasing me with slow rolls of his tongue, while his hips drove me wild with increasingly harder and harder thrusts until I felt my channel clench around him.

'You're close,' he murmured against my lips. 'So am I. Try and wait for me.' Wait? I really wasn't sure I had that type of control over my body, but if Oliver had requested it, then I'd certainly try.

He gave up on the kissing, and instead just stared down at me as he continued to drive into me with smooth, deep jerks of his hips, hitting my clitoris and G-spot with each one until I felt sure that I was going to fail on my waiting mission.

'I'm so close now, Robyn, come ... now,' he murmured through gritted teeth, his hip movements becoming less well timed as he sunk in and out at a rapid speed. I would never have thought it possible, but his words, his permission, did indeed trigger my climax, and suddenly the pleasure that had been coiled low in my belly exploded, causing my channel to clench and hips to jerk upwards as I clutched to him and hid my cries in the firm muscle of his shoulder.

Oliver cradled me to him, my body still gripping his in my orgasm as his hips continued to work on his climax. Then he reared back and hammered forwards hard enough that I shifted up the bed a little. He paused when he was buried deep, and groaned as he began to come. He ground his hips a few more times, working himself down, and I could feel him twitching and jerking deep within me, his warmth mixing with my own.

He rested his damp forehead upon mine, our eyes locked together, and a satisfied, gorgeous grin on his face which must have surely matched the broad smile on my own lips.

'That was ... just ... *wow*,' I murmured, knowing my description was hugely inadequate considering I'd just had the best sex of my entire life.

He dropped a kiss on my lips and nodded, letting out a contended sigh. 'It really was. Right from the start I suspected we'd be incredible together, Robyn, and we definitely just proved that I was right.'

'I ... I ...' There was something I wanted to tell him, but as soon as I tried to speak, embarrassment had me stopping and looking away.

A small frown flitted on his dark brows, and he tipped my chin up so he could look deep into my eyes. 'What is it, *cariño*?'

'It's nothing bad, Oliver, relax. I just wanted to say that ...' I paused again and decided to just confess. 'I've never had an orgasm through full sex before, and that one was incredible. Thank you.'

His face froze for a second, then he blinked in surprise several times. 'Never?'

I shook my head and decided I'd had enough of his intense stare so buried my face in his neck. 'No.'

A moment of silence passed between us, then Oliver swore quietly under his breath in Spanish. 'Five lovers, and none of them bothered to satisfy you ...?'

'Nope.'

Turning his head, he nuzzled his lips into the hair by my temple and placed a hot, open-mouthed kiss there. 'It's just as well you came into my club then, hmm?'

I giggled, snuggling closer, but Oliver growled and dragged me under the sheets with him, manoeuvring me so I was between his legs and trapped underneath his weight, and his fully erect cock. 'I think perhaps you need to experience it again …'

# Chapter Thirty

## Oliver

Shifting my position to alleviate the stiffness in my shoulder, I continued to watch Robyn as she slept beside me. I'd been gazing down at her for the best part of an hour now, but it would never be long enough. She was so beautiful, and so perfect. Perfect for me.

And *dios*, tonight had exceeded all my expectations. I was so glad I had finally made the choice to proceed things with her. It had been a close call for me, though. The last three days had totally thrown my usual composure, because I had discovered myself in a very unusual position – I had found myself growing attached to her. More than attached, which was not something I would usually have allowed. If she had been any other girl, I would have separated myself from the problem, broken things off with her, and moved on.

I'd even tried exactly that, by moving her back to her room each night to put a divide between us. But it had been useless, because she wasn't any other girl, she was my Robyn.

*Mi dulce pequeño petirrojo*. My sweet little Robin. The Spanish translation might have a spelling difference to her name, but there was no denying that I loved the way it rolled from my tongue.

So this morning, after realising that I couldn't beat the connection between us, I'd had to sit down and make some huge decisions. Monumental, really. Force myself to withdraw from her, or move things forwards.

After considering it long and hard, it had been blatantly obvious to me that walking away wasn't an option. And so here I was. Lying next to this incredible girl who had turned my world upside down.

We'd had full sex for the first time – twice – and it had been the best, most intimate experience of my life, and I now fully intended to spend the entire night with her wrapped in my arms.

Truthfully, the idea of a future with Robyn thrilled me far more than anything else had in years.

## Chapter Thirty-one

## Robyn

The rest of the week in Barcelona had flown by in a whirl of passionate sex, beautiful sunsets, and delicious dinners. I'd been well and truly spoilt rotten, but before I could believe it, it was over, we had boarded our flight, and within two hours had arrived back at my apartment building.

Maintaining his role as the perfect gentleman, Oliver insisted on carrying my luggage inside for me, even though I only had one small case. The gesture was sweet, so I didn't complain. Besides, it meant I got to spend a few more minutes with him before we parted, so I clung to his hand and absorbed the delicious tingles that his touch caused in my body.

He placed the case down outside my door, and I began to search for my keys at the same time as wondering what would happen next between us.

Had he meant all those impassioned declarations about us being exclusive? Or had they just been well spun lines, effectively delivered to help secure my place in his bed for the week? I was usually pretty good at judging people's intentions, but Oliver was still such an enigma to me that I really couldn't tell.

Finally, I dragged my key from my bag. I pushed it into the lock, but then hesitated, dug up my courage, and turned to him. If I didn't ask him now, I'd definitely be stewing over it later.

'So, now we're back, what happens?'

There must have been something telling in my tone, because Oliver lost his smile and stared at me for a few seconds, his face completely unreadable, before he drew in a long breath through his nose, and frowned. 'What do you mean, Robyn?' His voice was low, almost the tone he'd used when he was in his Dom role, and it sent an instant shiver of lust slithering through my system.

'I just wondered, you know … Before we left you didn't really want anything beyond helping me with my book research, and Barcelona was amazing, but … I wondered if maybe you might have changed your mind about it now that we're back home.' I was rambling dreadfully, and snapped my teeth shut, hoping I'd at least managed to make some sense.

Oliver's shoulders expanded on a breath, then he took a step towards me, causing me to step back and bump into the door as his body entered my space, seeming impossibly tall as he leaned down over me. 'I'm a little thrown by this line of conversation. We agreed to exclusivity, Robyn. A relationship. You must recall our talk? Or are *you* the one changing your mind?'

His words would have relaxed me, but with his close proximity and heated stare all I felt was extreme arousal as it flooded my system like a tidal wave. 'No, I'm not. And I do remember … but I wasn't sure if it was just a line to get me into your bed for the week.'

Oliver exhaled a dry laugh, and slid his hands around my waist, lowering his lips to my neck. 'If I had simply wanted to get you in bed, I'm fairly confident that I could have achieved that without using any "lines". But that is not all I want.' He trailed his lips up my neck, and across my jaw until they reached my mouth, where they brushed back and forth several times over my lips. 'Not at all.'

I gripped at his suit lapels, scrunching up handfuls of the expensive material as my legs grew wobbly from the intensity that always surrounded us when he was feeling purposeful like this.

'You, me, together. Exclusive. I meant every word.' He rubbed the tip of his nose across mine, then he dipped his head so our eyes were level and locked. 'I trust that is still agreeable with you?'

Thrilled, I nodded jerkily, a smile skipping to my lips. 'Yes. Most definitely, yes.' As soon as he had my agreement, Oliver cupped the back of my head and dragged us together, his tongue thrusting into my mouth, and my lips surrendering immediately as a breathy gasp rose in my throat.

Behind my back, the door suddenly gave way, but Oliver's arm encased me. He pulled me firmly against him, preventing me from falling.

'I heard a key, are you struggling with the ...? Oh!' I was vaguely aware of Sasha now standing behind us, but Oliver's kiss was so all-consuming that I didn't even bother to acknowledge my flatmate.

Oliver continued to grip me, turning us sideways and backing me into the adjacent wall, hard. If his arm hadn't been around my back and the other cupping my head, I think his move would have knocked some wind from my lungs, but as it was, he protected me, all the while kissing me deeply and thoroughly.

Sasha was still loitering like the complete perv that she was, and although I could have stopped Oliver and spoken to her, I didn't, because he felt too bloody good pressed against me. He was now grinding his hips against mine, tongue searching and exploring deep in my mouth, and my hands were sliding across his back and gripping his arse to pull his hard groin closer to mine. If we'd been naked, we would have practically been having sex right in front of her.

'I'll just ... um ... leave you guys to it ...' There was a quiet click of the apartment door closing as Sasha left, then the only sounds in the small hallway were our raised breaths and some low, sexual groans.

Oliver continued to practically hump me in the hallway for another minute or so, before dragging his mouth away on a growl. '*Dios*, what are you doing to me? I never lose control of myself like this, but with you ...' He left his

233

sentence unfinished, as if mulling it over in his mind, and stepped back slightly. I noticed that his hands still lingered on my hips, as if he were physically unable to fully tear himself away from me yet, and that idea thrilled me.

'Can I see you tomorrow?' he asked, his face softening into the gorgeous relaxed smile that had been commonplace during our trip. Before Barcelona, he'd been so careful with his facial expressions that, apart from the occasional slip, all I'd really seen was his carefully constructed mask of control and authority that he wore at Club Twist.

Now, though, I felt like I'd started to see the real Oliver Wolfe; excited grins, sweet smiles, affectionate softening of his features as he spoke with his family, not to mention the blissed-out look that swept over his face as he reached an orgasmic peak while I was wrapped around him.

I couldn't help but reach up to stroke my thumb across the curve of his lips. This was my favourite of his looks. Mind you, the intense, dominant expression he used when telling me to get down on my knees was definitely on my favourites list, too.

'I'd love that. Maybe we should go to your place, though. That way we can avoid Sasha and her untimely interruptions.'

Instead of laughing, as I had expected, Oliver frowned, and shook his head. 'Maybe, but my house is a complete tip. Let's meet at the club and decide on our plans from there.'

I couldn't imagine him as a messy person, but I shrugged and nodded. As long as I was with him, I didn't really care where we spent the night. 'OK, I'll come down with Sasha. I suspect she'll want to use up all of her free entry vouchers.'

'Perfect. How many vouchers do you have left?'

I played with the lapels of his jacket, smoothing them across his chest and trying to straighten out the scrunched-up damage I had done earlier. 'I don't know, a few.'

'Are you going to join?' he asked tentatively. 'I can get you permanent entry, if you'd like. I'd happily pay for your membership?'

I'd need to decide fairly soon if I was going to join or not, because once our guest vouchers were gone that would be it, no more entry. I didn't like the idea of him paying for me, though, it would almost be like he was paying me for sex.

Forcing a smile to my lips, I loosened off my tension, but shook my head. 'Thank you, but if I join I'll pay for it myself. You've already treated me to far too many things over the last week.'

He raised an eyebrow as if about to challenge me, but then conceded with a nod. 'Very well, as you wish. Now, as much as I'd like to stay, I really must go to work.'

That had been far easier than I'd expected. From the look that had crossed his features I'd thought he would be more stubborn about paying for my membership, so it was quite a relief that I didn't have an argument about money to contend with.

I rolled onto my tiptoes and placed a brief kiss on his lips, already knowing that I was going to miss him dreadfully the minute he left. 'OK, I'll see you tomorrow night.'

Nodding, Oliver raised a hand and stroked my cheek, looking just as reluctant to leave. 'Thank you for an amazing week,' he murmured, before dragging his thumb over my lips and turning to walk away.

Licking my lips, I watched Oliver's retreating back and couldn't help but bite down on my lower lip, still able to taste the remains of his kiss there. That man, *my man*, really was something else.

'Ho-ly fuck a duck!' Sasha exclaimed behind me, as I heard the apartment door flying open.

'Hmmm. Yes, quite,' was the only reply I could manage.

As he turned into the stairwell at the far end of the corridor, he glanced back in my direction and caught me staring at him. My cheeks heated, but Oliver grinned, winked at me, and was gone. There was no way my body, heart, and soul were going to survive him.

Once he had disappeared, I winced in preparation for the onslaught I knew I was about to receive from my bestie, and reluctantly turned to face her. As expected, Sasha stood behind me with flushed cheeks and her mouth hanging wide open.

'You went away, adamant that you were "just friends getting to know each other,"' she shrieked, making quotation marks with her fingers. Then she grabbed my hand and dragged me inside the apartment.

'I don't have any friends who kiss me like that!' she giggled, clearly loving the gossip that was playing out before her eyes. 'Come, sit, I need details. So, things have obviously developed while you were relaxing in the Spanish sun?'

Dumping my case down inside the door, I nodded. 'Yeah, they have,' I confessed, grinning like an idiot.

'I knew they would! The chemistry between you two is scorching! So, did you shag him?'

'Yup.' I had tried to be nonchalant, but Sasha made an excited gurgling noise, all the while clapping her hands joyfully like a performing seal.

'Yesss! And was I right?' she asked eagerly, leaning forwards in her desperation for details.

'About what?' I asked, confused, and barely able to keep up with her quick fire-questions.

She opened a bottle of water, took a swig, then waved her arms around as if it should be obvious what she was talking about, but with Sasha's jumbled way of thinking, nothing was ever obvious. 'About him being an older man and shit-hot in the sack?'

'Oh, that.' I gave a shrug which was meant to be carefree, but probably ended up looking awkward and uncomfortable. 'No and yes.'

Sasha spat out a mouthful of her drink and slammed the bottle down on the coffee table. 'He wasn't good in bed? Seriously? From the way he just kissed you out there I would definitely have put him in the nine out of ten bracket, skills-wise, possibly even an elusive ten.'

I grinned, keen to set her straight. 'You're right there, he is *amazing* in bed,' I corrected her. 'I said no, because I still don't know how old he is.'

'Oh.' She looked perturbed by this nugget of information and moved back slightly. 'You didn't ask?'

'Oh, I asked all right, he just wouldn't tell me.'

'Really?'

'Mm-hmm, just said he was "old enough to know better".'

'Better than what?' she asked, repeating the exact words I had said to Oliver.

'Better than to get involved with a "determined sprite" like me. Apparently, it was a compliment.'

'Sprite? Like an imp?'

I shrugged, still not entirely sure what he'd meant, either.

'Wow. Intriguing. But he was hot in the sack, yeah?'

Grinning, I nodded, embracing the flush on my cheeks for once, instead of feeling betrayed by it. 'Oh yeah. A definite ten. Fuck, Sash, he was out of this world good!'

Sasha did a little gleeful jig on the spot, then collapsed on the sofa. 'Oh man! This is so awesome!' She fanned her face, her grin now matching mine. 'The way he just threw you against the wall and kissed you like you were the air he needed to live? Fuck me, Robyn, that was

237

seriously hot. Is he always that intense?' she squeaked, grabbing my hand.

'Yeah…' was all I said, but internally I was agreeing with her wholeheartedly. That kiss had been volcanic in its levels of heat, and yes, Oliver was always that intense.

'So…' Sasha leaned in even closer, her voice lowering as a wicked twinkle lit in her eyes. 'Did you do any kinky stuff?'

'Um, yeah. Some.' I was happy to talk about my relationship with Oliver, but giving Sasha full-on details of the most intimate parts of it was still a level too far for me.

'Really? Did he whip you?'

'What? No!' I screeched, appalled at the idea. 'Oh my God, is that even a thing people do for pleasure?'

She shrugged, sipping her water again. 'Apparently. I quite like the idea of it.'

'Jesus. I don't. No. No, he didn't do anything like that.' But I think I now had something to add to my hard limits list that Oliver had talked about. *Whips? I don't think so.*

And so it carried on, Sasha firing questions at me so rapidly that I could barely keep up, and me answering most of them, while still trying to come to terms with the fact that I now had a boyfriend. A kinky-arsed, absolutely gorgeous, slightly OCD boyfriend. But a boyfriend nonetheless.

## Chapter Thirty-two

### Robyn

I can't deny that in the six weeks since returning from Barcelona I'd landed back in my old life with a bit of a bump. I was no longer spending every day and evening with Oliver, and as ridiculous as it seemed after our relatively short relationship, I often found myself missing him immensely.

Apart from my occasional pining sessions, things with him were going far better than I could ever have imagined. Due to his current work schedule we only saw each other properly at weekends, but we also squeezed in a brief lunch on Wednesdays, because, apparently, he couldn't go a full week without seeing me. A sentiment that had made me blush furiously when he'd first expressed it, but absolutely thrilled me.

Three dates a week was nowhere near as much contact and time together as we'd had in Barcelona, but seeing as I was desperately trying to finish my manuscript, it was working out well for both of us. Besides, it was only temporary; my book would be completed soon, and Oliver was only this busy because his work in finance meant that this time of year was particularly hectic.

The old saying of "absence makes the heart grow fonder" certainly seemed to the case for us, or at least "absence make the lust grow stronger" might be more appropriate, because we'd always leap on one another when we first met up, laying X-rated kisses on each other regardless of where we were or how many people might be watching.

We'd fallen into quite a nice routine; we tended to meet at Club Twist on a Friday, where I was now brave enough to do a little bit of play on occasions. The spanking in Barcelona had triggered this further exploration, because I had enjoyed it far more than I'd expected to. I still couldn't get over my aversion to using the beds at the club, but so far we'd used the St. Andrew's cross in one room for a very enlightening flogging session – God, he was skilled with those little leather strands – and a bench for paddling in another. The paddling had been like a more intense spanking, and while I had enjoyed it, Oliver's use of a flogger was still my preferred toy.

Afterwards, he would always come back to our apartment and stay the night, often ending up staying Saturday night, too.

Today, as I'd eaten my dinner alone, I'd decided that I was enjoying the club far more than I'd ever expected to, and had finally decided that it might be the time to look into membership.

I grabbed my bag and wandered towards the front door, before pausing and backtracking to Chloe's bedroom door. Poking my head around the doorframe, I saw Chloe sorting through her washing pile. 'Hey, Chloe. I'm popping to Club Twist, you want to come with me?'

Folding the T-shirt in her hands, she frowned as she looked at her clock, then across at me. 'It's seven o'clock, and it's Thursday,' she stated, as if that explained why she looked so confused. I suppose it was understandable; we never went to the club mid-week, and certainly never this early. 'Are you going to see Oliver or something?'

'Nah, I need to finish a chapter for my editor, but I thought I'd take a break and go over there to enquire about membership. Just see how much it costs, you know, in case I decide to join.'

She raised her eyebrows and a small smile curled her lips. 'My God. You're seriously considering it, aren't you?'

I shrugged, embarrassed by the fact that I was indeed considering joining London's most exclusive sex club. 'I haven't decided yet, but our guest vouchers won't last forever, and seeing as Oliver is there so frequently, it kinda makes sense.'

Biting on her lower lip, she put down the washing and gave me a cautious glance. 'Did you ever ask him about the blonde woman I saw him with?'

I had no doubts about Oliver's commitment to me, but I still found myself crossing my arms defensively as I nodded. 'Yes. He told me he's not married and doesn't have a girlfriend. Satisfied?'

Chloe didn't look entirely convinced, but she nodded anyway. 'So, you're going to join the club, then?'

'I think so. Would you join?'

She scrunched up her face. 'If you'd asked me that a few weeks ago I'd have point-blank said no, but now … I dunno …' She shrugged. 'It's a great bar, the music is awesome, and I've actually found some of the things there quite intriguing.' Giving me an amused look, she grinned. 'I know, I know. I didn't expect to be saying that, either, but hey, there you go. I guess it depends how expensive it is.'

'Come with me, then, we can ask. Then maybe grab a quick dinner somewhere on the way home.'

'Dinner? Now you've tempted me.' Chloe gave her hair a quick brush and glanced down at her clothes. 'I'm in my scruffs. Let me just change my clothes and we can go.'

It felt weird arriving at the club before the sun had even fully set, but as I glanced around the now familiar interior, I smiled. As much as it had shocked me at first, I had embraced the fact that this place embodied all of my deepest desires. The taboo thoughts that sometimes crept into my dreams, the fantasies I had never dared utter out loud, and the longing for something *more* from my life, something different.

Something a lot like Oliver Wolfe.

Just thinking about him caused a smile to pull at my

lips, and I strode up to the guy manning the door and boldly expressed our interest in joining.

Apparently, the club liked to maintain its exclusive status, so only took on a maximum of ten new members every month, and only gave out a limited number of the guest voucher booklets that we had been using up to now. This month's quota for membership wasn't full, so Chloe and I were taken into separate rooms to go through our various options. Once the prices had been made clear to me I sat back, genuinely surprised by how reasonable it was.

I pulled out my wallet, slipped my Visa card out, then paused. Was I really doing this? Joining Club Twist? What the hell would my parents say if I told them? They'd be horrified! Rolling my eyes, I tried to dismiss what went on within these walls and considered it on a practical level. Meeting up with Oliver would be far easier if I could just walk in here whenever I pleased, so, dismissing my embarrassment, I signed up and paid the balance.

I left the office with my shiny new membership card safely stowed in my wallet, and found Chloe out on the street waiting for me. As I got closer, she shook her head and made a disgusted expression. 'Can you believe those prices? Jesus, you'd think the place was coated in solid fucking gold or something!'

Confused, I stopped in my tracks and frowned at her back as she stomped off down the road. Chloe spun around when she noticed my absence, and shrugged her shoulders. 'What?'

'You didn't join, then?'

Her mouth dropped open. 'For three hundred and fifty quid a month? Fuck no!'

'Three hundred and fifty?' I squealed, wondering how the hell the fees we'd been quoted could be so vastly different.

'Yeah. Why, what did they quote you?' Chloe asked,

looking perplexed.

'Twenty quid a month if I got a year's membership up front. I already signed up.'

Her jaw dropped open in shock. 'Twenty?'

I dragged my purse from my bag, pulled the receipt from within it, and took a closer look for a second before Chloe whipped it from my hand and examined it.

After a minute, she frowned. 'Who was your sponsor?' she asked, her expression just as baffled as I felt.

'Sponsor? What do you mean?'

'It says here in the small print that your membership was "sponsored to reduce fee".'

Leaning over her shoulder, I squinted at the small print, because it really was bloody tiny, but when I saw the words she had been referring to I immediately felt shock settle in my system. There was only one person who would have done that, wasn't there?

Oliver.

I grabbed the receipt from her hand and charged back in the direction of the club, determined to find out once and for all.

Behind me there was the unmistakable slapping sound of Chloe's Converse as she tried to keep up with me, then the feel of her hand gripping my elbow as she took hold of my arm and dragged me to a stop just outside the doors. 'You think Oliver paid it?'

'Who else would?' I breathed in exasperation. 'But I told him very firmly that I didn't want him to.'

'Why? I'd be thrilled if a guy had just spent over four grand on me,' she whispered, sounding slightly awed by the idea. I wasn't awed, though, I was pissed off. I wouldn't be reliant on anyone for money, let alone my brand-new boyfriend.

And four grand? Was that right? Quickly calculating it, I almost gagged when I added it all up. Was that what I was worth to him? A year's worth of fun in the sack for the grand total of four thousand two hundred pounds?

I could see from her face that Chloe had more to say, but for some reason I couldn't quell the furious anger inside me, and I shook my head vehemently to silence her. I couldn't quite put my finger on why it had annoyed me so much, but I knew that I felt cheap, dirty, and more than anything, irritated that he had paid for it even though I'd told him not to.

Slamming my hand on the front door, it practically bounced against the wall as I charged back in and faced off with the woman on reception who had just sorted out my membership for me.

'My membership was subsidised. Was it Oliver Wolfe who did it?' I demanded, banging my fist down on the counter.

Her eyes widened, and she glanced between Chloe and me before shifting uncomfortably on the spot. 'Uh ... that's private information, I'm afraid.'

'For fuck's sakes,' I breathed, 'I want to cancel it, then.'

My tirade was causing the woman to visibly squirm on the spot. 'Umm ... I'm afraid all payments are non-refundable ...'

'Perfect,' I muttered, pulling my phone out to call Oliver while I was still wound up about it.

'Uh ... Mr Wolfe is in the bar, if you'd like to discuss it with him? He's in a meeting with Mr Halton.'

He was here? My eyebrows jumped to my hairline, but after glaring at the poor quivering woman, I turned to Chloe. 'I'm going to speak to him, but this won't be pretty. You may as well go home, I'll be back soon.'

She looked distinctly uncomfortable. 'Are you sure you'll be OK? I can stay.'

'Nope, I'm fine, thanks.' Dismissing her concerns, I spun on my heel, and charged through the entry doors, scanning the bar in search of Oliver.

It was early, but the club still had quite a few people

enjoying a post-work drink, so the task wasn't quite as easy as I'd thought it would be at this hour.

Oliver wasn't on his usual stool, but as my gaze travelled over the other people at the bar, and the dancers on the floor, I finally saw his familiar broad figure on a sofa at the far side with David.

My shoulders set back, I defiantly charged across and skidded to a halt before him. Oliver glanced up, a smile breaking on his face as he realised it was me, before melting into a frown when he took in my furious expression.

'I can't believe you! I told you I didn't want your money, and yet you still paid for my membership! What part of no didn't you understand?'

Oliver watched my tirade, and his expression barely altered the entire time. It was almost as if he couldn't hear my words, but, just as I paused to drag in some air he drew in a breath through his nose, and raised one eyebrow high. 'I advise you to think very carefully about your volume, words, and location, Robyn.'

There was a low, dangerous edge to his voice, one I recognised immediately as the dominant side of his personality that I now had an intimate knowledge of, and it brought me up short. It either meant I was about to get well and truly sexed to within an inch of my life, or I was about to be punished.

Seeing as I'd just yelled at him, I could only assume it was going to be the latter.

As I ran his words through my mind, I had a flashback to one of my first times at Club Twist, when I'd watched a Domme punish her sub because he'd been slightly sarcastic to her. At the time Oliver had said it was the etiquette of the club, and that if someone agrees to be a Dom or sub, they must act like one while within the walls of the club.

Shit.

I might not kneel at his feet when we were here, but for all intents and purposes I was his sub, wasn't I? And I'd just yelled at him like a toddler having a tantrum. As panic swirled in my belly I started to wonder what the heck had prompted me to be quite so hasty and loud in my rant. I might be angry, but I was an adult, supposedly in a relationship with this man before me. I should have spoken to him in private about my irritations, not yelled at him.

David stood up, and, after flashing me a wary glance, sidled off, leaving us to it, and making a run from whatever fallout was about to occur.

Blinking several times, I looked at Oliver and saw his gaze sweep briefly around the room before returning to mine. There was a muscle jumping at the corner of his jaw, and his eyes were dangerously dark. He looked really frigging pissed off.

'I don't know what gave you the impression that I had paid your fees, but I didn't.'

What? Now that really did surprise me. Surely it had been him? If not, who else would? 'You must have done.' I had intended to state my claim with some confidence, but the unwavering look on his face had completely stumped me, and I ended up almost whispering it.

Oliver gave one swift shake of his head. 'You may believe that, but are mistaken, Robyn. You asked me not to, and I respected your wishes.'

Staring at his unchanging expression, I could only see honesty there, and I rapidly came to the horrible conclusion that while someone had paid for my membership, it hadn't been Oliver. I may just have caused quite a scene for absolutely no reason.

Drawing in another breath, I glanced around and realised that every single person in here was now staring at us, and that even the music had stopped. Shit. He was one of the bosses, a Dom respected by every single member here, and I had just come in yelling my arse off like a petulant kid.

*Incorrectly* yelling at him, too. Fuck.

In the normal world, it would be like standing up in front of a packed board meeting and screaming rubbish at the CEO of the company where you worked. In other words, completely inappropriate behaviour and not to be tolerated.

Shit, shit, shit. Things between us were new, still fragile, and I was well on the way to ruining them. How could I turn it around?

Swallowing hard, I swivelled my head back and found Oliver still sitting on the sofa in apparent relaxation, but the tension in his muscles, and the tick in his clenched jaw were obvious to me. The almost bland expression on his face was the most terrifying thing, though, because rather than being angry, the glint in his eyes seemed to be reflecting complete and utter disappointment, which was so much worse. Fuck. He'd been right when he said I had submissive traits, because suddenly I felt well and truly like a piece of shit. I *did* like to please him, and, realising how monumentally I had messed up, I suddenly felt sick to my core.

'Oliver ...' I began, but his nostrils flared at my use of his name, and not his title. His eyes sparked with disapproval, and my knees weakened. I'd witnessed Dominants verbally chastising their subs, but Oliver's ability to express himself through a facial expression was incredibly powerful, meaning that no words were needed. As I looked at his glare I realised that I was going to have to work way harder than a flimsy apology if I wanted to make this right.

Stumbling towards him, I did the only thing I could think of that might vaguely appease for my outburst – I stopped just before him, and, after giving him a weak, apologetic smile, I folded down to my knees and laid my palms on my thighs. Keeping my shoulders back, I dropped my eyes down.

I was wearing a skirt today, so the floor felt rough beneath my knees, but I dismissed it and focused on my apology. 'I'm so sorry, Sir.' I spoke each word loudly and clearly, so that he would hear them, and hopefully a few of the people around us, too, which might make up for the embarrassment I had no doubt caused him.

To my dismay, he didn't say a word, and didn't make any move to touch me either. Shit. I didn't want to risk looking up, but as panicked tears started to leak from my eyes, I decided to lift a hand and place it on the unrelenting muscle of his thigh. 'Please forgive me, Sir.'

Even with my repeated apology, he didn't move at all, and every second ticked by as if it was stuck in thick treacle.

Finally, I felt him shift slightly, then my hand was covered by the warmth of his palm as he laid it over mine, but still he didn't speak.

Keeping my eyes tilted down reverently, I waited in pained silence, where the only thing to break the quiet around us was a deep, sarcastic laugh to my right. 'Seriously? You're going to let her get away with that, Oliver? She needs punishing.'

Within a split second, Oliver had leaped to his feet and darted around me. I heard a small scuffle then Oliver's furious tone. 'Do I tell you how to treat your trainees, Dominic?'

Dominic. The huge guy I'd met on my very first night here. I'd seen him several times since then, and he always made my skin crawl. I knew that things between him and Oliver were already strained, and now I'd just added to it with my stupid outburst. Damn. I was the first girl Oliver had let close for years, "his trainee", as he'd just called me, and I'd let him down in the worst way. If possible, I felt even guiltier, and had to really fight not to let my shoulders hunch with mortification.

'Well?' Oliver demanded, his tone the lowest and deadliest I'd ever heard.

'No.'

'Then mind your own fucking business!' These words were roared out in total opposition to Oliver's usual cool, calm demeanour, and it didn't pass my notice that he'd sworn in English, which he never did, but I didn't dare look up, instead forcing myself to remain rigidly in the correct submissive position.

'Don't you all have better things to stare at?' he snapped, and around us I heard people start to shift and talk again, before music once again filled the club.

Through my lowered eyes, I saw Oliver's black boots and dark jeans enter my vision as he moved back to the sofa and took his seat. He didn't speak or touch me at first, and as much as I wanted to look up at him, I didn't. Instead, I stared at the seam on his jeans, trying to retain my position and focusing on counting the small stitches to ground me.

It felt like an age had passed, but it was probably no more than a second or two, when he gently laid a hand on the top of my head and caressed down to my cheek, which he cupped gently. 'Stand up, Robyn, and assume the standing ready position.'

My ready position. Oh God. His gentle touch had tricked me into thinking that I had got away with my slip, but was he actually about to punish me right here?

I didn't want to further upset him, so I didn't question it or hesitate, and instead stood and took up my position. Feet spread, hands on my thighs, back straight and eyes averted.

My gaze might have been turned towards the floor, but I could still see Oliver as he also stood, and slowly rolled up the sleeves of his pale grey shirt.

Oh God. In our time together, I had learned that this was sort of his "thing". If we were doing a scene where he wasn't undressing, then he always, *always*, rolled up his shirt sleeves. He took his time until the cotton was folded meticulously just below his elbows, then walked around me in a painfully slow circle, as if trying to decide exactly what he should do with me.

My heart was beating so hard and fast that I could feel it drumming against my ribs, and roaring in my ears, but I centred my entire focus on Oliver to stop me from completely freaking out.

Oliver leaned in close beside me; he trailed his nose through my hair, and his breath warmed my skin until I actually shivered from the anticipation of what might occur.

'Good girl. I accept your apology, *cariño*.' He murmured the words in a tone so low that only I would be able to hear them. A choked sob broke in my throat, which I swallowed down before speaking. 'Thank you, Sir,' I whispered, my voice thick with the tears now flowing readily from my eyes.

'Look up at me, Robyn.'

Sniffing hard to try to make sure I didn't have a runny nose, I raised my head and locked my gaze with his. As soon as he took in my pathetic look, his expression softened, and he looped a hand behind my neck and gently cradled my head against the firmness of his chest.

'Hey, sshhh. It's OK,' he murmured softly beside my ear, running his warm hands up and down my arms to soothe me.

Around us, I was vaguely aware of the noises from the club; the clinking of glasses, murmur of interested voices as they watched our scene unfold, and the low beat of the music, but I blocked it all out. None of it mattered; all I cared about was the man standing before me.

Oliver lowered his lips into my hair and placed a kiss on the top of my head. 'You're trembling, *cariño*, are you OK?'

'I'm so sorry, Sir, I really wasn't thinking ...' I mumbled again.

'And I already accepted your apology. You don't need to repeat it.' His voice was soft, but firm, reminding me that repetitions irritated him. 'Now. What am I going to do with you, hmm?' Oliver murmured, tilting my head back so he could look into my eyes. His expression was intent and fastened on me so securely that I didn't dare to even blink, even though my mind was racing through possibilities of what he might do next. 'This isn't because of Dominic's comments. I will not have others dictate how we run our relationship,' he stated in a low tone. 'I have never, and will never punish you because I'm feeling irritated. That's not how our relationship works. We might not have been together long, but we're more than just this club and the life it represents, you know that.'

A small smile tugged my lips upwards at his sweet words, but I was intensely aware that curious eyes were still watching us as we stood together by the sofa. 'But you hold a senior position, Sir, and you need to set an example.'

He nodded, seemingly pleased by my understanding of the situation. 'Indeed. I have a certain status within these walls, and as such I cannot allow your actions to go unaccounted for.'

'I understand. You ... you *should* punish me, Sir,' I mumbled, replaying just how hideous my outburst must have looked to anyone here who lived this lifestyle and knew of Oliver's position within the club. 'It's what I deserve, and it's what would be expected of you here.' And as insane as the words sounded, I meant every single one of them. I'd become accustomed to this lifestyle and what would be expected of me if I chose to enter it, and enter it I had. My eyes were wide open, and I had a full understanding of the path I had chosen.

'Indeed. The members will be outraged if I allow you

to get away with your outburst.'

My cheeks heated again at his reminder of my foolishness, my blush deepening when I tried to imagine what he was planning on doing to me. Would he flog me? Paddle me? Strip me naked and spank me right here, for everyone to watch?

As if reading my mind, Oliver barked out a short, low laugh. 'There's zero chance that I'm letting anyone else get a look at your gorgeous body, Robyn, but perhaps we can put on a little show with your clothes on.'

'Yes, Sir,' I agreed, surprised by how arousing the idea of doing a scene in public with Oliver was.

'Good girl. We're going to move to the small side stage. Follow me, and resume your standing ready posture when we get there.'

With that, Oliver stepped away from me and pointed to the spot directly behind him before starting a slow pace through the large room. I followed behind him, with my eyes lowered, and hands joined, and tried to look as sorry for myself as I could.

He walked directly to the side stage and pointed again, indicating where I should stand, then spent several moments fetching a wooden chair and sitting himself down onto it.

'Eyes on me, Robyn,' Oliver announced. His tone was loud enough that I knew people around me were now looking, but I kept my focus on him, and him alone. He made a show of patting his thighs and smiled wickedly. 'Across my lap.'

This was new. There was no bench like we'd used before, and he didn't appear to have any toys with him, so it seemed I was about to receive a traditional spanking. Whereas that might have put some people off, it did the complete opposite to me and I was aware just how wet I already was between my legs.

Oliver had only spanked me once before, back on our

first night together in Barcelona, and he'd gone light and only given me four repetitions. Since then he'd done a good deal of exploration with my limits, so I had a feeling he wouldn't be quite so forgiving this time.

A nervous swallow forced its way down my throat, and as I began to make my way towards him an excited murmur broke out across the crowd around me.

Remembering how he'd taught me to make these scenes like a show, I edged forwards and wondered how on earth I was going to manage to crawl across his lap and make it graceful. Thankfully, Oliver seemed pick up on my hesitation and raised his hands to assist me, handling my body as if I were light as a feather. Once I was settled, he flicked my skirt up to expose my knickers, and gave a satisfied hum of approval.

The strength of his legs was now below my stomach, my breasts were draped across his thigh and only just restrained within my bra, my palms and toes were on the floor and my arse must have been displayed to perfection for him, and all the club goers nearby. Thank God, I had chosen a nice pair of knickers today!

This was an incredibly vulnerable position to be in, and if I had been with anyone but Oliver I would probably have panicked at how helpless I was, but with him, I felt utterly safe. Almost protected, somehow, which, given what he was about to do to my bum, was probably stupid, but was most certainly the case.

A warm hand landed on my bottom and softly caressed over the lace. Oliver gently trailed the fingers of his other hand up my back, across my shoulders, and into my hair. 'I always like to see your beautiful face, but when we're exploring new positions it's even more important to me.' He encouraged me to turn my head so it was facing in his direction, then carefully brushed my hair back from my face so I could see him. 'I can judge your reactions better this way.'

Stroking my cheek, he smiled down at me. 'OK so far, *cariño?*'

*Cariño.* Sweetheart. My heart melted just a little every time I heard that nickname from his lips. He always sounded so loving when he said it, and I nodded, a small smile tugging at my lips, regardless of the peculiar position I was in. 'Yes, Sir.'

'Good girl. Please remind me of your safe words.'

'Green, amber, and red.'

He nodded and gave me an intent look. 'Use them if you need to. So, you understand why this is happening?'

Images of me yelling at him in the club swum in my mind, and my eyes fluttered shut in embarrassment. I still couldn't quite understand why I had overreacted in that way. Maybe I was due my period and was hormonal. 'Because I'm an idiot,' I mumbled. The hand at my bottom suddenly paused and gripped the flesh hard enough to make me wince.

'Robyn, look at me.' His tone was harsh, and I opened my eyes immediately to find him frowning down at me. 'Enough with the self-critique. You are far from being an idiot, but I wish to know that you understand why I am going to spank you.'

Swallowing hard, I tried again. 'When we're in the club I'm your sub, and I should act appropriately. I showed you up. It won't happen again, Sir.'

'Indeed. So, how many spanks do you think you should receive, Robyn?'

I knew from experience now exactly how this type of question was supposed to be answered, so I didn't hesitate in my response. 'As many as you wish, Sir.'

Oliver hummed his approval of my reply and nodded. 'Twenty it is, then.' The hand on my arse gripped tighter, his fingers biting into the flesh, and he bent forwards to speak near my ear. 'These will be harder than last time.'

I had expected him to go harder, but twenty? That was

certainly a big step up from the four I'd received in Barcelona. Trusting him completely, I simply nodded my head and relaxed my body across his lap. The close position of our bodies pressed his erection into my side, and the warmth of his hand continuously stroking across my bottom was making me shudder with desire.

He lifted his hand from my bum, cool air rushing in where his skin had been just a second before, but before I could really register the cold I heard a faint swish in the air then yelped as he landed his first spank. It was definitely harder, and I sucked in a deep breath, one of my hands leaving the floor and flailing briefly before I gripped at his firm calf muscle to ground myself.

The painful heat on my buttock quickly bloomed into pleasure, then I counted and expressed my thanks, making sure it was loud enough for everyone around to hear.

Absorbing the sting of the second blow, I arched my back and lifted my bottom, shamelessly indicating that I wanted more. Warmth tingled across my skin, and adrenaline flooded my system, mixing with desire so potently that I dropped my head and moaned in a low, needy tone.

'Eyes up, Robyn. Let me see your face,' Oliver reminded me crisply, and I quickly looked up and met his gaze. His pupils were dilated, and his eyes almost glowing with desire as he nodded and gave me a reassuring wink.

The next eighteen seemed to blur into one long succession of pleasurable pain. Before Oliver, I would never have dreamt that a little pain could heighten my desire like this, but the way he worked my body was like magic, prolonging and building my pleasure as he played my sensitive skin like a skilled musician.

The final spank landed, and as soon as I had drowsily murmured my thanks, the room tipped as Oliver lifted me with ease. He encouraged me to wrap my legs around his waist and drape my arms around my neck, then strode

# Chapter Thirty-three

## Robyn

With me safely enclosed in his arms, Oliver walked through the bar towards the corridor that led to the rooms which could be hired out. A relieved breath left my lungs as we left the scrutiny of the club goers, and I further relaxed as he skipped the private bedrooms that I disliked so much and carried me up a further flight of stairs towards his office.

Once he'd kicked the door shut behind us, Oliver crossed the room and lowered himself into his large leather office chair, with me still attached to him like a baby chimpanzee.

I made no attempt to separate us, and instead burrowed my face further into his neck. I hated that I felt so needy, it wasn't a usual emotion for me, but after my stupid outburst, and the intensity of that scene in the club, I did. I think I was still recovering from the guilt I felt, too, because it was quite clear to me just how massively I had overreacted and caused Oliver embarrassment. He could quite easily have just finished with me there and then.

As we sat quietly for a few seconds it occurred to me that I still didn't know who had paid for my membership, but before I could dwell on that, Oliver spoke.

'So, perhaps we should talk, hmm?'

Swallowing, I raised my head and met his eyes. He looked calmer now, but there was still something darker swirling in his denim blues. 'I came down tonight to join the club, and when I paid I found out that someone had subsidised my membership. I assumed it was you, and I … well, I freaked out. As you saw.'

Oliver frowned, but nodded. 'I can check the account later to see who paid it. What I don't understand is why the idea of me paying it upset you so much?'

257

Now that some time had passed and I'd cooled off, I had to admit that I wasn't entirely sure myself. Remembering back to my heated words with Chloe, I shrugged. 'It made me feel cheap.' I whispered. 'Like you were sort of paying me for sex, or something.'

'*Dios.*' Oliver cursed, his word hissed out angrily, and I shifted as he hastily sat himself up straighter and took hold of my chin between his forefinger and thumb so he could stare into my eyes. 'How could you even think that?' he demanded. 'Even if I had paid your subscription, it would be because I care about you and wanted to help you out, not for any other reason.'

With the closeness of our faces there was no way I could mistake the utter truth behind his words, and my shoulders sagged in relief.

I stroked his cheek, the slight stubble tickling my thumb. 'I'm so sor …' My words were cut off by Oliver as he closed the gap between our lips and placed a short, hard kiss on my lips.

'We've dealt with it, there's no need to keep repeating, Robyn,' he reminded me, and so I decided to show him how sorry I was in a different way, and closed the gap between our mouths again.

My kiss wasn't short and sharp like his had been. I still had lust burning in my system from the spanking, so I took my time, licking a path along his lower lip, dotting kisses onto his jaw, chin, and lip before opening my mouth and pressing my tongue against his lips, requesting entry. He complied on a groan, his warm mouth opening to me as he slid one hand up my back and cupped my head. Our tongues twined lazily, but there was a heated undertone to the kiss, one that promised naughtiness to come in the very near future.

Pulling back slightly, Oliver parted our lips. 'You were so perfect in your submission just now. You looked beautiful across my lap, and seeing you drop to your knees in the middle of the club made me so hard that my balls are still aching.'

He was still hard, too, because I could feel the solid heat of his erection below my bottom, and so I teased him by giving a wiggle before climbing from his lap and taking my time arranging myself into a perfect kneeling position by his feet. I didn't avert my gaze as I should have, because I wanted to watch his reaction, but I placed my hands on my thighs, spread my knees, and gave a flirtatious smile. 'You mean like this, Sir?'

Oliver sucked in a harsh breath, and leaned forwards to rest his elbows onto his knees as he observed my position. 'Tease,' he murmured. 'But I'll let you off, seeing as you look so fucking gorgeous.'

My smile widened at the obvious pleasure in his eyes, and I giggled at his lusty tone. It was the second time tonight that I'd heard him swear in English instead of Spanish, and I took the slip as a further compliment.

He leaned forwards to run his thumb across my lower lip, and I couldn't help but briefly suck it into my mouth and swirl my tongue around the tip.

Oliver's eyes blazed. Then, with a grin, he sat back in his chair and folded his arms over his chest. His jeans were bulging at the front, and with the way his legs were spread and he was grinning at me, he looked well and truly sinful.

'The only thing that would have improved our scene downstairs would have been if you were naked,' he commented softly. 'Perhaps we can rectify that now, hmmm?' My eyebrows rose, but I stood up and began to slowly remove my clothing, making it into a show, just as he liked. I might have looked calm and hopefully seductive, but the whole time I was overwhelmingly aware of just how aroused I was. My heart was pounding, I was damp between my legs, and my skin prickled as a delicious heat spread through my body.

I took up my standing ready position and waited in

expectation as Oliver's eyes roved over my naked form. I didn't have to wait long, because after just a few seconds he stood, dramatically swept the contents of his desk top onto the floor, and scooped me up to lay me out on the cool wood before him.

*Wow. That was quite a reaction!*

After briefly assessing my position with a wicked grin, he nudged his way between my spread legs and was on me instantly, acting like a crazed animal as he caressed my body and his lips descended to one nipple where they toyed with the needy peak so deliciously that I thought I was going to come right there and then.

I fumbled with his shirt, but I was too high on adrenaline to manage the little buttons with my trembling fingers. Suddenly Oliver stood up, growled some indecipherable Spanish phrase, and ripped his shirt open. Buttons went flying everywhere, and as he dragged the cotton from his arms I lay there staring up at this wild version of my man, and loving every second of his primal display.

His belt and jeans were tugged open with the same desperation, releasing his jutting erection. Then, without bothering to remove his trousers, he was falling back between my legs. I could instantly tell that this wasn't going to be tender and slow. As if reading my thoughts, Oliver guided the thick head of his cock to my entrance before jerking his hips forwards and thrusting into me in one hard push.

A garbled cry left my throat as his width stretched me, and I wrapped my legs around his hips as he began to thrust hard and fast. Gripping my thighs around him, I tugged him as close as I possibly could, and groaned again at the feeling of every single inch of him sliding firmly in and out of my channel.

It was so good that I wanted to scream out, but we were in his office, so instead I silenced my cries by latching my lips onto his neck, and half-kissing, half-sucking to muffle my moans.

He seemed to really like me chomping on his neck, because he leaned into the contact and his cock thickened inside me. 'Yes, harder, Robyn. Mark me.'

Mark him? I was so dizzy from pleasure that I didn't even hesitate to comply, and my teeth bit down harder as I continued to suck and lick on his neck.

Oliver groaned and upped the pace of his hips and it was almost too much. My body was already blazing from the sensations of the spanking, and to suddenly have him stimulating not only my clit with the grinding of his pelvic bone, but my G-spot with his cock on every hard thrust, was just overwhelming.

'Oliver … *Sir* … I'm going to come.' It was a warning of sorts, but more of a breathy plea, really. I needed to come so badly that it was all I could seem to focus on.

'No! Together. *Dios*, Robyn, I'm close, wait.'

Wait? He often said this, but I honestly don't think he had any idea what he was doing to me when we were together like this. Waiting was nearly impossible. Each slam of his hips was utterly perfect, and my climax was already swirling in the pit of my stomach just waiting to erupt.

Gritting my teeth, I tried my hardest to comply, focusing my mind on analysing every sensation in my body, rather than letting them overwhelm me, and, miraculously, it seemed to work.

Unfortunately, it only worked for about ten seconds, then the burning pleasure was back, my core clenching and clit throbbing as a monumental orgasm began to rear up on me. There was no way I could hold it back for much longer.

'Now!' Oliver roared, jabbing his hips forwards again, causing me to scream my relief. I relaxed my muscles all at once, and finally gave in to the climax that rushed at me and seemed to swallow me whole in a continual stream of clenching muscles, pleasured sobs, and bright lights as Oliver groaned his own release above me.

My head banged loudly on the desk as I relaxed the muscles in my neck, and my arms fell useless to my sides, hanging limply from the desk as I tried to recover my shattered breathing. I felt totally wrung out, but in the best possible way.

After several gentler thrusts to work himself down, Oliver collapsed on top of me. He didn't allow his weight to squash me for too long, and while his breathing was still ragged he carefully slid from within me, placed a brief kiss on my lips, and scooped me up into his arms.

My body felt tender from the roughness of our coupling, but it was a pleasant reminder of the explosiveness of what had occurred, and a soft smile spread on my lips as I linked my arms around his neck. Trailing my fingers across his exposed skin, I suddenly felt a damp patch, and leaned back before gasping in horror.

He had a bright red love bite on his neck. I knew I'd bitten and sucked quite hard, but I didn't think it had been *that* hard. Oops.

'Oliver, shit … I'm sorry, I've left a really red mark on your neck.'

Somehow, Oliver managed to walk us both across the room towards the mirror on the far wall. How he achieved this, I will never know, because my body felt like jelly, but he did. He tilted his head to examine the red circular mark and grinned. 'I approve.'

*OK, so he took that a lot better than I expected.*

He lowered himself to the leather couch beside us and arranged my boneless form on top of his, my naked skin warmed by the heat of his body as he continued to pant below me. I giggled at the rough feel of denim below my thighs, a reminder of how desperate he'd been to get inside me.

Oliver murmured several low Spanish words, his lips pressed into the hair on the top of my head and placing kisses there between each gasped word.

'What were you saying?' I whispered, feeling sleepy and so content with him that I very nearly found myself telling him I was falling in love him. I blinked, glad I hadn't made the slip, and shocked that my mind had jumped to that conclusion. Love. I knew I'd been falling for him since our week together in Barcelona, but were these overwhelming feelings I had love? Chewing on my lower lip, I decided that, yes, they probably were.

Before I could contemplate it any further, Oliver placed a kiss on my temple. 'I was just saying how incredible you are,' he breathed, pulling me higher in his arms so my head was now resting next to his on the arm of the sofa and our eyes were locked. 'Are you OK? Was I too rough?'

'No, it was perfect.' It was too early to tell him I loved him, but I could share some of my feelings, so, taking a bit of a risk, I gave a shy smile and rubbed his bare chest. '*You're* perfect.' It wasn't a declaration of love, but I had to say something to let him know how important he was to me.

'I'm far from perfect, but thank you.' Oliver blinked twice, his gaze trailing across my face, before he drew in a breath as if about to make some monumental confession. 'You don't know how special you are, Robyn.' He stroked my cheek, brushing some stray hairs back from my eyes. 'You have rather quickly become the most important thing in my life.'

Wow. It seemed like we were both in the mood for declarations tonight.

'Maybe I could come back to yours tonight? See where you live? Snuggle?'

I had thought my suggestion would make him smile and agree, but instead, Oliver seemed to briefly tense below me. 'Probably best to just wait until tomorrow night, I've got a really early start in the morning.'

Something about his tone felt off, but I couldn't put my finger on why that might be. Did he really have an early start, or was there some other reason he didn't want me seeing his house? He did seem to keep avoiding me visiting.

'I don't mind getting up early. I can get the train home,' I suggested, still hoping for a night in Oliver's arms.

'No. I won't have time to drive you home, and I'm not having you travelling on the Underground before the sun is even up. It's not safe.' The thumb at my chin gripped me slightly more firmly. He stared down at me and shook his head. 'I'll drop you home tonight, but I promise to stay over at yours tomorrow night.'

His tone indicated that was the end to the conversation, but something about it still felt slightly strained, so I reluctantly nodded and stayed silent.

We sat like that for quite some time, with me worrying about his slightly strange mood until a chill of nervous goose bumps ran across my skin. Oliver winked down at me, looking completely relaxed again, and helped me to sit my exhausted body upright. 'You're shivering, let's get you dressed.'

He collected my scattered clothes for me, and delivered them back to me with a scorching kiss to my lips that soon stopped my shivers. His strange mood had now vanished, and I could only assume that I had somehow been misreading his tone.

As I was pulling my clothes back on, a thought occurred to me. 'Oh yeah, is it possible for you to check who paid for my membership, or do I need to speak to David?'

Oliver had pulled a fresh shirt from his cupboard and was fastening the final button as he nodded to me, then walked over to his desk. The contents of the top were still scattered across the floor where he'd swept them off in his passion, including his other shirt and all the scattered buttons, and he smirked at me as he quickly gathered up the pens, paper and phone, before resetting them in neat order.

He withdrew a small laptop from the top drawer and flipped the lid open, logging on while I quickly finished dressing.

'OK, let's take a look,' Oliver murmured as his fingers flew over the keys at a rapid pace. 'You do know that if it's a man who's sponsored your membership, I'll have to kill him, hmm?'

I laughed, but when I glanced at Oliver's completely serious face the giggle quickly died in my throat. *My God, I think he's actually serious.* 'I … I don't know any other men at the club,' I stammered. 'You're the only one I've ever spoken to.'

Oliver leaned back in his chair and reached across to snag my wrist, easily pulling me across into his lap again. A startled yelp left my lips at my new position and I found myself under the close scrutiny of Oliver's dark gaze as his lips hovered just above mine. 'I should hope so,' he countered, before placing a hard, possessive kiss on my lips.

Where had this side to him come from? He was usually so laid back and relaxed. I wouldn't complain too much, though. Oliver getting possessive over me was actually a rather nice feeling.

Keeping me snuggled in his arms, Oliver leaned around me and opened up a programme on his laptop. The screen filled with numerous pale blue columns and boxes, none of which made any sense to me, then he scrolled through for a minute or two. After typing my name into a search box, he examined the screen, snickered, flicked the lid of the laptop closed and grinned at me.

'Sasha paid it.'

What?

'Sasha?' I repeated, a frown settling on my brows.

'Indeed. A Sasha Mortimer is listed as the owner of the bank account that paid for the subsidy on your membership. I assume that is her?'

Sasha had paid over four grand for my membership? This didn't make any sense. 'It is … but why would she pay it?'

Oliver eased me from his lap and stood up, shrugging on his jacket as he did so. 'I have no idea, you'll have to ask her that. I do hope you yell at her with as much ferocity as you did me, though,' he added as an afterthought.

My cheeks flooded with heat, and the urge to apologise again flew upon me. Knowing that Oliver had already brought me up on that twice already this evening, I held my tongue and instead gave him a contrite look.

'Hey, I know, *cariño,* I know. You're still learning how this lifestyle works. It's OK, it's all forgotten now,' he murmured softly, acknowledging what he had obviously read in my expression. Taking my hand, he flicked off the office light and led me from the room.

## Chapter Thirty-Four

## Robyn

Oliver dropped me home and, after promising to see me at the club the following night, disappeared off to get back to his meeting with David – the one that I had so rudely interrupted earlier.

Shaking off my residual guilt, I watched him go, then wandered into the flat. I was met by the delicious smell of one of Sasha's famous Thai creations, and my stomach instantly growled in hunger. Taking my coat off, I smirked – all the action with Oliver had worked up my appetite – and made my way to the kitchen, hoping there might be some food going spare.

'Yum, it smells delicious in here.'

Sasha was at the cooker, and turned to grin at me. 'Thanks! It's chicken Penang curry. Want some?'

'Yes, please.' It would save me cooking, and besides, this smelled way better than anything I could whip up.

'Chloe said you were mad with Oliver, but she rushed off to wash her hair before telling me why. Everything OK?'

Suddenly remembering that I was supposed to be in a mood with her, I planted my hands firmly on my hips, raised one eyebrow high, and fixed my best attempt at a glare on my face. It probably wasn't very convincing, because my anger had subsided now, and was partly distracted by hunger, but I had to at least try.

It took her several seconds to drag her eyes away from her stirring, but finally, Sasha glanced across at me and flinched. 'Woah. What's that look for?' she asked in alarm.

'You! Sasha! That's what this look is for!' I squawked, irritated, but nowhere near as venomous as I had been when I'd yelled at Oliver earlier. 'You paid for most of my Club Twist membership without telling me, and I blamed

Oliver for it and we had a blazing row! That's what!' I blurted.

Wincing, Sasha pulled a face. 'That's why you were mad at Oliver? Oops.' She put down the wooden spoon and gave me her full attention.

Seeing her contrite expression, I softened my posture and huffed out a breath. 'It was very generous of you, Sash, but you could have told me. I yelled at him like a complete lunatic.'

Sasha's face crumpled into an almost comical grimace as she bit down on her lower lip. 'Shit, really? What happened?'

With a sigh, I recounted my yelling match, and explained how I'd jumped to the conclusion that he was the mystery donor of my membership payment.

'And this was right in the middle of the club?' she squeaked. 'Was it busy?'

'Busy enough.' Running a hand through my hair, I frowned, my cheeks heating again as I recalled the way he had calmly sat there and watched me ranting at him. 'It was so embarrassing. You know how important he is there. I think everyone was just waiting for him to punish me there and then.'

'And did he?' From the rapt expression on her face, Sasha was well and truly into my tale now.

'Yes.' Sasha's eyes flew open at my reply, so I decided to give her the dirt she was obviously desperate for. 'He spanked me in front of everyone, which I am blaming you for.'

Sasha clutched at her cheeks in excitement and jigged up and down on the spot. 'Oh my God! That is so hot!'

I rolled my eyes at her excitement. Then, feeling reckless, I added some more juicy details that I knew my filth-loving friend would like. 'Then he took me to his office and fucked me on his desk so hard that I can still feel it now,' I admitted, shifting my thighs and feeling the pleasant ache deep inside me.

Sasha's eyes were practically bulging from her head at this nugget of information. 'Holy crap on a stick! I want a more detailed description than that,' she exclaimed, popping a lid on the pan before taking my hand and dragging me to the sofa.

She sat down and patted the cushion next to her in invitation. Flopping down, I gave her a cautious look, and decided to get my point across before giving in to her demands for naughty details. 'Before we start, I'm paying you back, Sash. Four frigging grand? Are you nuts? There's no way I can accept that much.'

Shaking her head adamantly, Sasha folded her arms. 'No way. I have all the inheritance from my parents just sitting in my bank account going mouldy. You know how loaded they were. I'll never spend it all. I knew you wouldn't join if you knew the price, but I like it there ... and I can't go on my own, can I? So I signed you up.'

'You didn't sign me up, though,' Chloe announced petulantly, as she joined us in the lounge and plonked herself into an armchair. Her hair was tied up in a towel after her shower, and she was struggling to get her feet into some gigantic pink slippers, but she still managed to give Sasha a very effective frown as she did so.

Sasha raised her eyebrows and flashed me an amused glance before looking back at Chloe. 'No, sorry, Chloe. I didn't think you'd want to join. I mean it's a sex club, and you're so ... so ...' Sasha struggled to describe our Goody Two-Shoes flat mate.

'Dull? Prudish? Boring?' Chloe provided, her tone high-pitched and mildly irritated.

'Nooooo!' Sasha countered, but unfortunately using a tone which seemed to scream "yeeessss".

Rolling her eyes, Chloe waved a hand dismissively in the air. 'It's fine. I know I'm not as brave as you two, but actually, I've enjoyed the times we've been to Club Twist. It's been quite ... enlightening.'

'Would this have anything to do with the cute ribbon-tying guy you've chatted to a few times?' Sasha speculated with a grin.

Chloe's cheeks turned as red as a tomato and she shrugged. 'Maybe. I haven't spoken to him recently because he's always doing a scene when we're there, but he caught my eye last week and he smiled at me. I might pluck up the courage to buy him a drink if I see him again.'

My eyebrows popped up in surprise, just as Sasha let out a startled splutter. 'Wow. Well, fair play. I'll sign you up too, then. I can do it tomorrow night when we go down.'

Chloe grinned and leaned forwards in her seat, apparently having none of the issues about cost that I was. 'Really?'

'Sure. It'll be fun. Our year of exploration.'

'Awesome! Thanks, Sash! I can't afford to pay you back yet, though. How about I do your share of the cleaning as a trade?' Chloe suggested hopefully.

Sasha nodded. 'You have a deal, my friend. I fucking hate scrubbing the toilet.'

Chloe looked at me, and the smile on her face became a little forced. 'Talking of the club, are you sure you're OK with Oliver?'

God, was this where she brought up the issue of him and the blonde woman, *again*? Or the fact that I still hadn't seen his house? I was convinced of his dedication to me, so I really didn't want to be discussing either of those topics. I frowned at her, and my tone probably came out a little harsher than I intended. 'Of course, why?'

Chloe bounced her leg nervously a few times and shrugged. She cleared her throat. 'I don't know, he just seems so intense all the time. I ... I followed you into the club earlier to check you were all right, and I saw the way he was looking at you when you were yelling at him.' She fixed me with a worried expression. 'He was so cold... so serious. So ... domineering.'

I forced aside the embarrassment I felt at the fact that Chloe had probably also seen me dropping to my knees for him, and smiled at her. 'Isn't that kind of the point? He is a dominant, after all.'

Reluctantly, Chloe smiled along with me. 'Yeah, I suppose so. I guess I was just worried about you. It all seems really full-on.' She paused and leaned across to touch my shoulder. 'You're definitely okay with it all? You like the stuff he does with you?' Her bottom lip was really taking a battering as she began chewing on it again. Bless her, she was obviously really worried about me.

'I am totally fine with it all, honestly, Chloe. Oliver is a perfect gentleman. He might be domineering, but he takes care of me. He'd never ever hurt me.'

She weighed this up for a second or two, then nodded, looking reassured. 'OK, great. You keep doing your thing with Oliver and I'll mind my own business.'

Sasha stood up and went to check on her culinary creation before spinning to us with a grin. 'I've got plenty of curry to go around. Let's eat.'

'Thanks, Sasha. That would be great.' Chloe started to set the table, and looked across at me with a grin. 'Robyn still needs to fill me in on the details of what happened after she dropped to her knees in the middle of the club earlier ...'

Great, so she had seen my little display then. Sitting back with my glass of wine, I swallowed my embarrassment and repeated the story, with Sasha helpfully jumping in every two minutes to add any details that I had forgotten.

# Chapter Thirty-five

## Robyn

Today was Friday, which meant I would be seeing Oliver at the club again in just an hour. I was nervous, though, because I would also have to see all the regulars and staff who witnessed my outburst yesterday – and my subsequent spanking.

Standing back, I looked in the mirror and gave my reflection a critical assessment. I had on a black skirt that fell to just above my knees, my high-heeled leather boots, which I still had a love-hate relationship with, and a pale grey sleeveless top which highlighted my cleavage without being explicit. After checking how cool it was outside, I'd also gone back and put on some pale black stockings so I wouldn't shiver on my way to the club.

After yesterday's fiasco, I was far more aware today as I dressed. Oliver was a big deal at Club Twist, and he'd picked me to be with him. Was this suitable attire for his chosen partner? I had no idea.

Just as I was finishing applying my mascara, the doorbell rang. Sasha and Chloe had popped out ten minutes ago to grab us a bottle of wine to have while we were getting ready, so I could only assume they had forgotten their keys.

Rolling my eyes, I dumped my mascara down and headed through the apartment to yank open the door. 'I swear if you were any more disorganised you would forget your head … oh!'

It wasn't Sasha behind the door, it was Oliver. Oliver, looking supremely hot; with freshly trimmed hair, clean-shaven jaw, and dressed in a navy three-piece suit, pale blue shirt, and maroon tie. He had a hand propped on the doorframe, and jacket undone, so with his arm raised it pulled his waistcoat tight across his stomach and chest and made him look supremely sexy.

'Wow.' I hadn't meant to say it out loud, but from the amused look Oliver gave me, I just had.

'I'll take that as a compliment, and then return it with one of my own. You look absolutely gorgeous, Robyn.' His words were accompanied by several steps forwards, and he placed a hand on my hip and slid it to the base of my back. 'This top is very sexy,' he murmured, lowering his head and placing a kiss on one of my exposed shoulders, then the other. Then, taking me by surprise, he dropped to his haunches and traced my leather boots from the toe to my knee, before looking up at me with a wicked glint in his eye. 'And these boots ... I've had fantasies about these boots, you know?'

Fantasies? My throat dried up as the heat level between us rose significantly. 'Really? What type of fantasies?'

'You, with your legs wrapped around my waist wearing those boots and nothing else while I fuck you against a wall. Hard.'

Woah. I think I liked these boots even more now.

'Perhaps we can make it a reality one day?' I suggested breathily, glad that my tone didn't give away how light-headed and wobbly I suddenly felt.

Oliver's eyes narrowed, and he nodded, slowly. 'Oh, I intend to.' With his promise hanging in the air, he leaned forwards and nuzzled his lips under the hem of my skirt to kiss my thigh, then looked up at me in surprise. 'Stockings, too?'

I bit on my lower lip and nodded, then watched as Oliver raised my skirt to give my stockings a more thorough examination. His eyes visibly widened as he traced the lacy garter tops with his fingers. Then he hissed out a heated breath before his fingers bit into my thigh as he dragged me forwards again and ran his lips and teeth up the exposed skin between the top of the garter and my black lace panties.

'*Dios*. You could not be any sexier,' he murmured, glancing up at me and still looking like he had filthy things on his mind. Filthy was good. Especially when on Oliver's face.

'Although perhaps I could buy you a suspender belt to go with these, hmm? Then I could enjoy undoing the clips with my teeth ...'

A vision of him doing just that sprung to my mind, and a shuddery, aroused breath escaped my throat, audibly whistling across my lips as it did so.

Oliver smirked at my response, but instead of initiating something further, he placed one final open-mouthed kiss on my thigh and righted my skirt for me, before standing up.

His face was still dark with desire, but there was a playful smile on his face as he adjusted his groin with a wince. 'If we're not careful, we won't make it out of the door.' He widened his stance and shook his head in amusement. 'I knew picking you up might lead to distractions.'

Oliver usually met me at the club, so this was definitely a change from the norm. 'So, how come you are here?'

Stepping back, he slid his hands into his trouser pockets and once again shifted what was apparently an uncomfortable arousal, before raising his eyebrows and grinning at me.

'I rather like the distractions you provide.' He smirked, then put on a playful look of offence. 'You aren't happy to see me?'

I gave a dry snort, returning his teasing smile. 'Of course I am! But I thought we were meeting at the club, that's all.'

He nodded, and the playful look morphed into the soft, affectionate expression that I so adored. 'We were, but when we spoke on the phone earlier you sounded nervous, so I thought I'd come across and surprise you, so we could go together.'

My shoulders sagged with relief, and I rolled onto my tiptoes to place a lingering kiss on his lips. 'After everything that happened yesterday, I *was* nervous, thank you.' As I moved back, I saw the love bite I had given him was really visible above his low-collared shirt, and I winced at how red it still was. Oops. I still couldn't believe that he'd demanded I mark him. More than that, I couldn't believe I'd complied. Must have been the heat of the moment making me do crazy things.

'I saw Sasha downstairs, by the way, and she said to tell you that she and Chloe would meet us at the club. I suspect she decided to leave us in private, in case I was here for a booty call.'

Well, that sounded promising. 'And are you?' I asked speculatively, my lips still hovering just over his.

'Well, it's always tempting with you, Robyn. But with you looking so gorgeous, I'd like to take you to the club and show you off instead.'

I pouted, but couldn't deny that his compliment made me feel all fuzzy inside.

Shifting forwards, he pulled me closer and nibbled a teasing trail up my neck towards my ear. 'Don't worry, I'll have my wicked way with you later. Preferably with your boots and stockings involved ...'

A shudder ran down my spine at his promise, and by the time he released me, and I stepped back, I was feeling overheated and lusty, and tempted to force him to skip the club and just take me to bed.

'I wanted to ask you something ...' His tone was speculative. 'I know that the whole submission thing is still relatively new to you, so feel free to say no, but I was wondering if you would wear this for me tonight?' Oliver dipped a hand into his pocket and pulled out what looked like a black leather string and held it up for me to examine.

275

'This is a collar. Dominants can present them to a submissive, if they wish to make the relationship more official.' He cleared his throat before continuing. 'It's a big deal to me, Robyn. I've never given one to anyone before.'

I was struck speechless by his final words, and so silently took the collar and looked at it more carefully. It wasn't just a leather string as I had first thought. It was actually a little thicker, probably about five millimetres in diameter, and so soft to touch. The ends were fitted with silver clasps for closing it and, in the centre, there was a circular silver pendant about the size of a five pence coin.

Looking closer at the pendant, I saw that it had a simple inscription: the letters *O.W.* Oliver's initials. 'It's to let people know you aren't available. If they look closely they'll see you belong with me,' he told me, seeming to carefully watch my reaction to the collar. As I turned it in my fingers I saw that there was something else inscribed on the other side. I brought it closer to read and sucked in a small breath. *Cariño*. His nickname for me was delicately engraved into the silver.

'You only have to wear it at the club, but it would mean a great deal to me if you did.'

It was basically a sexy choker, and I liked it a lot, so this wasn't a hard decision to make. 'Of course.' Nodding, I lifted it to my neck, and turned so he could do up the clasp for me. Once it was attached around my neck, I stroked at the small pendant which sat right in the hollow of my throat.

Oliver followed the path of my hand, and lowered his head to kiss the silver disk, his lips fluttering over the skin of my neck in the process. 'Mine,' he murmured softly, before kissing me on the lips.

'Thank you for accepting this.' From his tone I could tell how important this was to him, and so tried to show my appreciation back.

'Thank you for offering it.' Licking my lips, I added

one final word in a breathy whisper. 'Sir.'

Oliver's eyes shot to mine, wide and surprised, and he clutched me to him and pressed his tongue into my mouth, groaning and smothering me with his intoxicating passion. He was so sexy when he was desperate and intense like this.

Several minutes later, he dragged himself away from me, muttering something about staying in for the night, but then shrugged his shoulders and grinned at me. 'We should go now, otherwise we really won't be making it out of here tonight.'

Sharing his grin, I grabbed my bag and keys and followed him from the flat.

Half an hour later, we entered the club hand in hand, and headed to the bar, where Oliver shifted two stools closer together, before helping me up onto one of the red leather seats. Once we were settled and drinks had been ordered, he took hold of my hand again, turning in his stool so he could also place his free hand on my thigh, and one foot on the rung of my chair. Once again, his positioning was quite a possessive statement, and one that didn't go unnoticed by those around us.

Over the hour that followed, I was relieved that nobody commented on what had happened yesterday, but with the addition of my new collar and the fact that Oliver was notably more touchy-feely with me, I had found several sets of curious eyes looking at our close contact.

My new collar might look small, but it was clearly a big deal in here, because Marcus, Sasha's unrequited crush, had seen it, grinned, and slapped Oliver heartily on the back. The scarier guy, Nathan, had actually given a small smile, cracking his icy demeanour, before shaking hands with Oliver and placing a brief congratulatory kiss on my cheek.

Alexandra was in the club tonight, too, but although I

277

was sure she also saw the collar at my neck, she didn't comment on it when she approached us.

Now I knew that Oliver had slept with her in the past, the very sight of her perfect long legs and manicured eyebrows made me feel physically sick. I'd never experienced jealousy like this before, but every time I saw her it bubbled in my system, especially because she always went out of her way to touch him.

Tonight was no different, and even though I was sitting just beside him and holding his hand, she still laid her hand on his shoulder and started to run her fingernails up and down his arm.

Her gaze was focused solely on Oliver as if I didn't even exist, but Oliver flicked her hand away, a look of complete disinterest on his face.

She must have a thicker skin than me, because Alex ignored the way he dismissed her, and instead stared at Oliver's neck, zeroing in on the love bite there. Damn it, I shouldn't have got so carried away in the heat of the moment, or maybe he should have worn a higher collared shirt to hide it and not shown it off quite so bloody proudly.

Clicking her tongue, Alex flicked a snide smile at me before looking back to Oliver. 'Love bites, Oliver? Really? A little old for that aren't you?' As she reached out to trace the red mark, something inside of me snapped and I dipped forwards to grip her wrist. Hard. I didn't hold back at all, squeezing her bony arm hard enough that she sucked in a shocked breath.

Pulling her away from Oliver, I then leaned in and placed a long, wet kiss on the mark on his neck, which caused Oliver to lean into my touch, and hum his appreciation with a low chuckle.

'Old enough to know better, *Sir*,' I whispered softly, mentioning our little private joke while smiling against his neck as he slid a hand around my waist and pulled me closer.

Realising I still had hold of Alex's wrist, I dropped it as if it were a piece of slimy garbage, and allowed Oliver to sweep me into his arms. My smile widened to a broad grin a second later, as I saw the shocked look Alex gave us as she walked away, rubbing at her wrist.

Oliver tucked me between his thighs, nestling me about as close as he could get without actually being inside me. 'Hmm. I'm supposed to be the dominant one, but I rather like it when you get territorial,' he mumbled, kissing along my jaw and finishing up at my lips.

Just as I was about to suggest heading back to the flat to make his fantasy about me, my boots, and the hard fuck against a wall a reality, Oliver's phone vibrated on the bar beside us.

He picked it up, swiped the screen with his thumb, and read whatever alert he had just received. 'It's an email from David asking for some help in his office with a tax issue.' Checking his watch, he frowned. 'Cheeky bugger. He never usually asks me to work out of hours, but I promise I'll be quick. You'll be OK here on your own for a few minutes?'

Looked like the fantasy would have to wait a little while, then, but I smiled and nodded. 'Of course.'

Oliver strode straight towards David's office and I snagged the attention of the girl serving and ordered a glass of wine. Natalia worked regular shifts here, and was incredibly shy, but we were starting to build a nice friendship.

As Natalia placed my drink down I reached for it, but in the process managed to put my arm straight into a sticky patch of spilt beer on the bar. She looked embarrassed and quickly wiped the surface before offering me a tissue, but I'd need water to get the stain off, so I slid from my stool. 'I'll go and rinse it in the bathroom. Can you watch my drink, please?'

Natalia smiled and moved my drink to the side. 'Of course.'

I paid a trip to the toilets to freshen up, and had just locked the cubicle door when there was the sound of several pairs of high heels clip-clopping into the toilets.

'That lipstick is gorgeous! Can I borrow some?'

'Sure, it'll match your dress perfectly.'

I smiled at the normality of the conversation. We might be in a sex club, but the girls still worried about the same stuff as you'd hear in any nightclub toilet.

'So did you see that Mr Wolfe is here with that girl again?' I tensed at the mention of Oliver, trying to pee really quietly in the hopes that they wouldn't realise that anyone was in here with them.

'I did. It is strange, he's not had a sub for ages. Like years. Why now? And why her?'

It was said in a particularly bitchy tone, and my mouth dropped open in offence. *Why me?* Was that a valid question I needed to be asking myself? No. I might not have a big head, but I knew I was pretty, and Oliver had told on multiple occasions that I was special to him. The connection between us spoke for itself. Pushing the questions aside, I sorted myself out and smoothed down my skirt, but didn't flush the toilet, just so I could listen in for a while longer.

'But hey, look on the bright side, I see it as a sign that he's getting back in the game. I reckon he'll just fuck her at the club for a week or so then be ready to move on to us.'

My eyes widened, and my blood started to heat with irritation. I'd forgotten just how bitchy girls could be when they wanted.

'Oooh, I hadn't thought of it like that!' the second voice replied gleefully.

'I bet he can't even remember her name!' A third girl added with confidence. 'And a love bite on his neck? What are they, teenagers?'

That was it, I couldn't stay silent for a moment longer. I unlocked the cubicle and made my way to the mirror, enjoying the reflection of their shocked expressions as they watched me emerge.

'Gosh, you do have a lot of questions, don't you?' I asked, with a serious expression on my face as I rinsed off my hands and dried them with a paper towel. 'Let me help you out. We might play at the club, but Oliver prefers to make love to me at home, in *our* bed.' This was playing it up a little bit. We'd never referred to it as "making love", and we only went to my apartment, which couldn't exactly be described as our home, but hey, they'd been gossiping, so I think it was fair to play it up a little. I paused for drama and applied a flick of gloss to my lips.

'And I'm sure you'll be reassured to know that he definitely knows my name, because he screams it when I make him come.' I played briefly with the silver disk at my neck, a move that successfully drew the gazes of all three girls to my new collar. 'And sorry, but I don't think he'll be fucking me and moving on to you, either, girls, because he asked me to wear his collar today. Said he wanted everyone to know I belong to him.' The one whose face was a mask of Botox gasped at my blatancy as I popped my gloss away and zipped up my bag. The eyes of the three women were now as wide as saucers, so I twined the pendant, making sure they'd be able to get a good view of his initials on one side, and my name on the other. I let out a fake, girly giggle, and caressed the word he had engraved on it. 'This is his Spanish nickname for me.'

As the three of them hurried away, I decided to give them one final snippet of gossip. 'Oh, and just so you know, the mark on his neck isn't just a hickey ...' I deliberately made eye contact with all three of them in the mirror before finishing. 'It's a mark of ownership, he's mine, so keep your fucking hands off.' I flashed them all a fake saccharine-sweet smile and turned back to the mirrors with my head held high and my heart hammering in my chest.

What a run-in! First Alex, and now this. I couldn't believe I'd been so brazen, and a smile cracked on my face as I imagined Oliver's face when I told him about it later.

I tucked my handbag at the side of the sinks and gave the sticky patch on my arm a rinse – in my rush to set the girls straight I'd missed it earlier.

Hearing another cubicle open behind me, I tensed, and desperately hoped it wasn't a friend of the three women I had just dispatched, but sidestepped to give them room at the sinks. I was about to look up when a hand clamped around my mouth from behind and something rough fell over my eyes, plunging me into darkness.

*What the hell?*

Some kinky-arsed shit might go on within the walls of Club Twist, but being blindfolded in the bathroom? This was a whole other level. I struggled, and was just wondering if it was indeed a friend of the three women enacting out some peculiar revenge on me, when a brief hint of an unfamiliar scent hit my nose. It smelled distinctly masculine, like an aftershave or musky shower gel.

The scent wasn't Oliver's, so it wasn't him playing one of his tricks on me, and as the grip tightened instant panic flooded my system like a bucket of ice water being thrown over me.

I writhed against the grip holding me, and as I stamped my foot down and managed to make contact with something – a shin, I think – I managed to shift myself in the tight grasp. Hope flared in my system, but as I drew in a sharp, terrified breath my nostrils filled with a strong chemical scent and I realised with growing horror that it wasn't just a hand over my mouth, it was a cloth.

A cloth soaked in something so potent it rendered me

light-headed and overwhelmingly tired, and within seconds, my limbs felt leaden.

My body was no longer mine to control. I was vaguely aware of being carried, then dropped onto something cold and hard. As my eyes rolled back in my head I heard the slam of a car door followed shortly by an engine revving to life below me.

After that, there was only darkness.

## Chapter Thirty-six

### Oliver

Letting out an irritated breath, I gave one more knock on David's office door. Hearing nothing but silence from within I tried the handle. Finding it locked up tight, I growled my annoyance and spun on the spot to stride back towards the club.

I liked David, but summoning me to his office and not even being there was seriously pushing the boundaries of friendship. I hadn't seen him in the bar either, so where the hell was he?

Arriving back at the bar, I passed my glance over the crowd, but David was nowhere to be seen. I could do without this. It was Friday, my night with Robyn, and my irritation rose.

Leaning over the bar, I grabbed the attention of the closest server, a young girl called Natalia, and enquired after David. 'I haven't seen him, Sir, but I only came on my shift recently. Did you try his office?'

'Yes, he's not there.' I nodded curtly, deciding to return to Robyn and get our evening back on track. If David needed me so desperately he could come and find me.

I made my way through the busy bar and arrived at the stool where I'd left Robyn, but it was empty. Pulling out my phone, I called her, but even though her mobile rang, there was no reply.

It was quite boisterous in here tonight, and I knew that Robyn wasn't always comfortable with everything that went on inside the walls of Twist, so I made my way towards the entrance, wondering if she had popped out to get some air.

There was no sign of her outside, and Darren on the door didn't remember seeing her either, so I went back inside, assuming we had somehow crossed paths.

Once again at the bar, Natalia was busy serving someone, but Alex was nearby, so I caught her eye instead. 'Did you see where Robyn went?'

Alex raised an eyebrow and gave me a seductive smile. 'If you're looking for some company, Oliver, I'd be happy to help out.'

Drawing in an exasperated breath, I shook my head. 'Alex, I don't have time for your games. Have you seen her, or not?'

Alex's lips tightened, and her face turned sour at my tone. 'She must have wandered off. That's what happens when you can't control your trainees. I heard about yesterday. Apparently, your new subbie has quite the mouth on her.' *Dios*, she really was such a bitch. I couldn't believe I hadn't seen it before Robyn came into my life.

Overhearing us, Natalia frowned. She glanced behind her and retrieved a glass of wine. 'Robyn asked me to watch this while she nipped to the toilet, Sir, but she hasn't come back yet. She's been gone quite a while.'

Ignoring Alex, I tried Robyn's phone again, but as before I got a ringing tone, but no reply. I couldn't quite put my finger on why, but my stomach clenched uncomfortably, and I had the distinct feeling that something was wrong.

I spun from the bar and charged directly towards the ladies' toilets. As I reached the shiny silver door I didn't knock or hesitate. Instead, I slammed my palm on the surface and pushed it open. I practically knocked over the woman attempting to leave. She raised her arms in shock and I glowered down at her when I saw Robyn's distinctive red handbag clutched in her hands.

'Robyn?' I called out, while still blocking the door and trapping the trembling woman inside. There was no answer to my yell, but I leaned into the room and scanned for any sign of Robyn.

The cubicle doors were all open and there was no one

else inside, so I turned my attention to the woman. 'Why do you have that bag?' I couldn't help the growl to my voice, and she visibly wilted before me as she staggered backwards another step.

'It … it … it was left beside the sinks. I noticed it because a phone was ringing. I was just on my way to hand it in at the bar.'

'Did you see the girl who it belongs to? Brunette, about the same height as you?'

Her head shook so frantically that it made her eyes bulge, and she held the bag out towards me in shaking hands. 'No, no one else has been in here.'

Clutching Robyn's bag, I strode back towards the bar, bumping straight into Marcus and Nathan just inside the main room. 'Have either of you seen Robyn?' I demanded.

Nathan frowned, then raised an eyebrow and crossed his arms over his chest. 'Nice manners. No "would you like a drink?" or "come and join us for the evening".' I didn't have time for his sarcasm. Something was wrong, I just knew it.

Before they could answer, Dominic passed close beside us, his usual swagger in his step, and a petite blonde tucked under his arm. From the direction of his path, they were heading to one of the private rooms together. I might not like him, but perhaps his height could prove useful for me, so I reached across and indicated for him to come closer.

'What? I'm kind of in the middle of something here,' he sneered, smirking down at the blonde before looking back at me. God, I hated to ask for his help, but where Robyn was concerned, I would lay my pride on the line.

'Robyn's disappeared. I can't find her. She left her drink at the bar, and her handbag was in the bathroom. Can any of you see her?'

My blunt statement closed down any more comments from Nathan, and even Dominic's expression lost his usual cockiness as all three of them frowned in concern and began to glance around the club. 'Could she be sick and have gone home?' Dominic asked, stepping up onto a small stage behind him and passing his gaze around again.

'I doubt it. We hadn't been here that long, and I'm sure she would have told me if she was feeling unwell. Besides, she'd never leave her handbag.' I ran a hand through my hair, trying not to panic, and hating the utter loss of control that was burning in my system.

'*Mierda!* Where the fuck is David?' I spat, wondering if perhaps he and Robyn were together somewhere. It would make sense, seeing as I currently couldn't find either of them.

'David?' Marcus repeated with a frown. 'I saw him yesterday. His sister Ellen is visiting so they were heading out of town for a few days.'

That brought me up short. 'What? He's not here tonight?'

Marcus shook his head. 'Nope, said he'd be back Monday.'

My frown deepened, as did the sickening sensation of unease in my stomach. 'He emailed me fifteen minutes ago asking me if I could pop up to his office and do him a favour.'

'Maybe he changed his plans?' Marcus suggested weakly, but he, Dominic, and Nathan all frowned in unison, before the blonde with Dominic started to get impatient and tug on his hand. Glancing at his "date", Dominic looked back at me. 'Is there anything else I can do to help?'

I shook my head, thinking that my next port of call needed to be a phone call to David to find out what the hell was going on, then perhaps one to Sasha, if David didn't give me any leads.

'No. Carry on with your night, thank you.'

Dominic nodded, and jerked a thumb over his shoulder

towards the private rooms before giving the girl a wolfish grin. 'We'll be in room six if you need me.'

There was not a chance that I would be interrupting whatever kinky activities Dominic would be getting up to, but I grunted my thanks, then pulled out my phone. I was already searching for David's number, when Nathan placed a supportive hand on my shoulder. 'Is she here with her mates?'

'They are coming down tonight, but I haven't seen them yet.'

Nathan nodded. 'OK. You call David, and Marcus and I will have a scout around the club, just to check if we can see her, or her friends. She might be dancing, or chatting to someone in a corner.'

My gut was telling me it wasn't quite as simple as that, and I very much doubted that she was dancing, as Robyn always avoided the dance floor, but I appreciated their effort. Nodding to them as they stepped away, I moved towards the reception area to place my call to David. The call went through, and after seemingly endless rings, David finally answered.

'Oliver, what's up my man?'

'David, where are you?'

There was a pause down the line, presumably in reaction to my terse tone, but then I heard him clear his throat. 'I'm on my way back from the Lake District with Ellen, why?'

'Why did you email me asking me to come to the club if you knew you weren't going to be here?' I demanded, starting to suspect that it hadn't been David who had sent that email.

'What? I've been with El all day. I didn't email you.'

I knew it. What the hell was going on? 'I got an email from you just now.'

'Oliver, mate, I'm telling you I didn't email. I'm sorry there's been a mix up, but there's no need to sound so pissy with me.'

A vague thought passed through my mind that Robyn's disappearance could have something to do with David, but surely it couldn't? I considered him a true friend. Yet he was apparently away, and Robyn was now absent, too, and the email had come from his locked office. None of it made any sense.

Hoping my suspicions were incorrect, I forged on with my enquiry. 'Robyn's gone missing from the club.' Seeing as I hadn't checked with Sasha yet, I wasn't entirely sure that was an accurate statement, but the evidence was certainly leading that way.

'What the fuck?' David exclaimed. 'And you got an email from me? Are you sure it was my email address?'

'Definitely. It was your Club Twist address.'

'Fuck. That account is only set up for my work laptop. Someone must have got into my office. Look, I'm the only one with a key, and we're a couple of hours away at least. I'll be there as soon as I can.'

'Fine.' I had no intention of waiting. As soon as I hung up this phone I was going back upstairs and kicking his goddam door down, then I'd check the CCTV myself.

It turned out that David's office door was something akin to that of the safe in a top-notch casino. I kicked the thing for at least half an hour, until my foot ached and I was coated in sweat, and it hadn't even shifted slightly.

Even with the combined strength of Nathan and me kicking in unison, the innocent-looking door remained solid. It must have multiple bolt locks in the frame to strengthen it.

It was now hours since I'd received the email from "David", but there was still no sign of Robyn. I'd called the police, but they'd been next to useless, simply registering my concern and telling me to call back once she had been missing for more than twelve hours.

Marcus had tracked down Sasha and Chloe, who were dancing in the club, but neither of them had heard from her since they'd left the house earlier in the evening. After thoroughly searching the club, Marcus had driven Sasha back to the girls' flat to check, but as of yet he hadn't called or arrived back with any news.

It was all utterly infuriating. Much to my growing irritation, David was still on the road. The longer he took to arrive, the more my suspicions around his conveniently timed holiday with his sister rose.

Could he have taken Robyn?

Each time the thought arose in my mind, I immediately counteracted the idea with a simple statement. *Why would he ever do that?* He and I shared a genuine friendship, Robyn liked him, and he had seemed honestly thrilled when I'd told him how serious things were between Robyn and me. It just didn't make any sense.

While waiting for Marcus and David, I'd managed to piece together what I thought might have happened today. Someone had wanted to take Robyn – perhaps David, or maybe someone else – and knowing that I would be with her in the club on a Friday they had lured me away with the fake email from David, then taken their opportunity while I was out of the way.

That meant that practically every regular member of the club who had signed in tonight was a suspect. And all the staff members. I still couldn't get my head around it, but it would seem that someone here at Club Twist had a deep enough fascination with my girl that they had gone to extreme lengths to take her.

'*Dios!*' I slammed my hand against the door of David's office and threw my head back to release a loud roar of anger. I felt so useless, but with Marcus checking the flat, and the police unable to do anything, waiting here so I could check the CCTV cameras seemed like my only option.

Assuming it wasn't David who took her, I knew he had secret CCTV cameras installed in his office, so if someone had broken in and used his computer to send me an email we'd be able to find out who it was by looking back through the footage. As far as I was concerned, whoever sent that email now had my girl.

# Chapter Thirty-Seven

## Robyn

Breathe.

*Breathe.*

I was dizzy, hyperventilating and sobbing wildly, none of which was going to help me right now. Although the dizziness and unconsciousness that kept coming at me in waves was quite a relief, because it allowed me time away from the horrific enormity of what was happening to me.

I'd been kidnapped.

Breathe.

Air rushed into my lungs, and I felt lucid, for the moment, anyway.

Finally managing to calm myself a little, I licked my lips and tasted the salt of my own tears on my tongue. Drawing in another long, steady breath to clear my foggy head, I rested my forehead forwards onto my knees.

I'd completely lost track of time since I'd been taken. I might have been sitting here mere minutes, hours or perhaps a day, but the fact that I still had some feeling left in my bum seemed to indicate that it hadn't been as long as it felt.

I was still completely clueless as to where I was, why I was here, or who might have taken me, but now my initial panic and the heavy sleepiness was clearing, my mind began to regain some of its sharpness and I tried to take note of my surroundings to see if there was anything I could use to aid my escape.

The surface I sat on was hard, probably a floor, but I was blindfolded, so it made it difficult to tell. Whatever was beneath me was cold and damp and making me feel chilled to my bones.

I might be pretty clueless about what the fuck was happening to me, but one thing I was sure of. I was no longer at Club Twist. The car, or van, or whatever I had been driven in, had made several stops in our journey, and although I'd been drugged, each time the engine had rumbled and restarted below me I had been partially awoken from my foggy state.

Wriggling my body, I realised that my hands were tied behind my back with a scratchy rope, and my knee-high boots had been removed because I could feel rope around the bare skin of my ankles, too. From a brief exploration with my fingers I decided that the wall behind me was bare brick, or rock. This, combined with the dank-smelling air around me, led me to believe that I was probably in a garage, or perhaps cellar of some sort.

Maybe I could somehow shift myself across the floor and kick my way out of the door? If there was a door that I could access.

Rocking forwards, I let out my fury in an angry yell, but the sudden exhalation of breath made my head spin wildly, and just when I thought I heard the creak of a door nearby, darkness descended upon me again.

## Chapter Thirty-eight

## Oliver

This was madness. I was sure I was going insane. It felt like my call to David had been days ago, and in that time, I had gone over and over the evening's occurrences so many times that my skull throbbed. I was beside myself with worry, my body was fidgety, and I needed to hit out at something. Or someone, because as soon as I found out who had taken Robyn, there wouldn't be any stopping me.

Finally, after I'd practically worn a trench in the carpet from my pacing, I heard the door at the far end of the corridor open. David jogged towards me. 'Traffic on the motorway was a fucking nightmare. Have you found her yet?'

'No. I think someone's taken her, but I have no idea why.'

David frowned at me as he pulled out a large bunch of keys and unlocked his office. 'Are you sure? It sounds pretty extreme, Oliver.'

'I know, but she wouldn't leave without telling me, David, she just wouldn't.'

At that moment, Marcus hurried up towards us, with a worried-looking Sasha hot on his heels. 'We've checked the club, the flat, and local friends' places. No sign of her anywhere. Any luck here?'

David shook his head grimly and shoved open the door to his office. 'I've only just arrived. Let's check the camera footage and see what the hell has been going on around here.' Hearing how determined he sounded eased my concerns that he might be involved.

But if not him, who the hell had Robyn?

'When exactly was this?'

I checked my watch and my stomach dropped as I realised it was now over five and a half hours since I'd last seen Robyn. 'Around seven o'clock. She left a drink at the bar and her handbag was found in the toilets. But if someone emailed me pretending to be you, they must be involved somehow. Who else has access to this office?'

'No one.' David sat at the desk and cursed. 'The laptop is open. I never leave it open. Someone has definitely been in here.' After rapidly typing for several seconds he shook his head. 'Whoever they are, they must know a thing or two about hacking, because this laptop is password protected.'

I stepped behind him, and watched as David brought up the CCTV footage from his office, then, in a different box, the footage from the corridor outside. As the clock in the left-hand corner showed 18:50, the door at the end of the corridor opened and someone entered wearing a hooded jacket.

Only staff should have had access to that corridor, but David had a large staff here, and with the big baggy jacket and grainy images it was near impossible to tell who it was.

We watched as the figure glanced each way before unlocking the office door and entering. The entire time their face was obscured by the hood. 'Motherfucker!' David exclaimed angrily. 'Who the fuck is that, and how the hell did they get a copy of my key?'

'Check the footage from near the ladies' toilets. I want to see if we can see her being taken,' I demanded, barely holding back from leaning over him and taking control of the laptop.

Scrolling through some other footage, David then found the bar and I watched the scene from earlier in the evening, as Robyn and I first entered. We sat at the bar for some time before I could be seen checking my phone and reading the email from David. She kissed me on the cheek as I headed off to David's office, and took a seat at the bar. My heart clenched at the sight of her, and I ground my teeth together. She ordered a drink and chatted briefly with Natalia behind the bar, before disappearing in the direction of the toilets.

The camera from the toilet corridor showed her entering the ladies' at six minutes past seven. Then, thirty seconds later, a very familiar figure followed. My entire body clenched as I leaned closer to watch. The hood was down now, their face clearly visible, and after checking that no one was watching they slipped inside the women's toilets.

The sight of them carrying Robyn's limp body out just two minutes later was the final straw, and the chair that I was leaning on flew across the room as my arms jerked up in agitation and a roar left my lungs.

'I don't believe it ... but they were downstairs ...?' Marcus stuttered in disbelief.

*Mierda!* I didn't believe it either. I was usually such a good people reader, but tonight I had been well and truly played.

Kicking out at the door in frustration I watched as it bounced on its hinges, and spun on my heel to turn and face David as rage boiled up inside me.

He held up his hands, not needing any prompting from me. 'I know their home address. Let's go.'

## Chapter Thirty-nine

## Robyn

Wakefulness had come upon me again, but even though my eyes were open I was still swathed in darkness. This blindfold was so fucking frustrating! If I could see where I was I'd feel so much more settled.

Remembering the squeak of a door just before my last bout of unconsciousness, I strained my ears, trying to listen for any sounds around me. All seemed quiet, but the thick blindfold covering my eyes was tied so that the cloth also covered my ears, making everything sound muffled.

Not being able to see was making me panic even more than the sensation of being bound. I had to get this cloth off. I rubbed my forehead on my knees in the hope of dislodging the material that was keeping me blind, but a voice beside me froze me in place.

'I wouldn't bother, if I were you. I'm good with knots; it's tied tight.'

The deep voice was muffled, but close beside me, and I yelped and leaned away from where the sound had come from. I had thought I was alone, but clearly, I was not, and from the deep rumble of the voice, my companion was male.

Now I knew there was someone in this space with me I reverted into my original full freak-out mode; screaming and wriggling until sweat prickled on my neck and I was panting hard.

A hand landed on the top of my head and gripped, firmly enough to still me. 'Stop!'

'Fuck you! Let me go, you fucking freak!' My throat hurt from yelling, but there was no way I was stopping. Quitting simply wasn't a word in my vocabulary.

'Your manners need significant work.'

My manners? I'd been forcibly taken against my will,

and I was being told off for *my* manners?

What. The. Fuck?

The terrifying roar that emanated from my captor was enough to make my stomach clench with fear. 'Enough! Close that rude mouth, or I'll gag you!'

I snapped my lips shut, desperately trying at the same time to work out if the voice was someone familiar from the club, but it was too distorted from the cloth over my ears.

Large hands gripped me under my armpits and hauled me upright. With a chilling efficiency, my wrists were untied, then attached to some sort of chain above me and pulled up until they were fully extended and I was having to stand on my tiptoes.

'Now that you're awake, let's make a start.'

Make a start? I had no wish to start anything with this freak, except for my escape attempt, so I thrashed my legs around as much as I could. Even with all my effort, it wasn't enough, though, because my captor easily managed to still my kicking limbs and attach my ankles to some sort of clip on the floor. The only thing I felt any relief about was the fact that I was still fully dressed, and my legs were attached with the ankles together, making me feel slightly less vulnerable.

Once I was well and truly strung up and barely able to move, my blindfold was untied and pulled off, leaving me blinking against the bright lights of the room. It took me several long moments to recover my vision, but once I did, I let out a scream so blood-curdling that it wouldn't have been amiss in a slasher film, because the sight before me was completely and utterly terrifying.

Standing before me was a huge man dressed all in black, with his feet splayed and arms crossed over his chest. His hands were gloved, but the most chilling thing was his face, which I couldn't see at all because it was covered in a grotesque black plastic mask of a grimacing clown.

The scene around us didn't settle my nerves, either, because I'd been right about one thing. I was in a cellar, but this was a cellar like no other I'd ever seen. Every single wall was covered in hooks loaded with implements that seemed to be aimed at inflicting pain. Whips, spiked chains, clamps, knives. My mind could barely take it all in, and as I ran my terrified gaze around again a lump of terror blocked my throat and started to choke me.

'Finally, I have you here with me. We're going to have so much fun, Robyn.'

Robyn. He knew my name. But who the hell was this? Now that my ears weren't covered by the thick cloth I had thought I might be able to recognise his voice, but the latex mask he was wearing made his tone sound slurred and difficult to understand.

As I wracked my brain, trying to work out who it was holding me captive, he reached up and undid his mask.

I held my breath in terrified fascination as I watched him work the bindings at the back of the mask, and then a shocked gasp tore up my throat as he finally pulled it off with a dramatic flick.

Even though I instantly recognised the face of the dark-haired man before me, his eyes were vacant and unfamiliar, and my brain struggled to compute why on earth he'd taken me.

Dominic. It was Dominic behind the mask, and there was some vague reassurance in the fact that at least I knew him, but he'd still kidnapped me, so I was hardly feeling calm. I knew he and Oliver didn't get on, but this was beyond extreme. Why had he taken me, and what was he planning on doing to me?

'What the hell are doing, Dominic? Why am I here?'

'Don't refer to me as Dominic. I am your Master now and you shall call me as such.'

*Call him Master? I don't fucking think so.*

He must have seen my revolted expression, because he moved closer, close enough that I could see the darker blue flecks in his icy blue eyes, and he ran a finger underneath the leather of my collar. A sneer curled his lips. Then, with no warning, he curled his fingers into a fist and ripped the strip from my neck. My head jerked with the tug, and the leather burned the skin at the back of my neck as it gave way, causing me to cry out in shock and pain.

I watched in distress as he threw my collar away to the side. It was my last link to Oliver, and as the leather strip and tag skidded across the floor and disappeared under a cupboard, a sob rose in my throat.

Ignoring my anguish, Dominic continued as if we were simply discussing the morning's news. 'And as for why you are here? I'm teaching you a lesson, my pet, just as Oliver should have yesterday. Twenty lousy spanks for your petulant behaviour? You yelled at him like *you* were the one in charge, and he just sat there and took it like a sap. It was fucking pathetic.'

This was all to do with yesterday and my outburst when I thought Oliver had paid for my club membership? I vaguely recalled Dominic teasing Oliver about my behaviour and asking if he was "going to let me get away with it", but I'd thought it had been just that – teasing. Quite apparently for Dominic, it went quite a bit deeper.

'They're all fucking pathetic,' he spat, his face scrunching into an irritated grimace. 'None of them know about real discipline. Not like me.'

Dominic was pacing now. His expression was dark, but his posture seemed agitated, as if he wasn't entirely with it. 'He didn't even hit you hard,' he muttered with apparent distain.

Hit me that hard? Suddenly a cold chill ran through my already terrified body as Oliver's warnings about Dominic came rushing back to me; he'd said he was into some "extreme stuff", and liked to dish out "serious amounts of pain" while having sex. Briefly glancing around the room of torture implements again, I could well believe it.

Panic, terror, and fear swirled in my system, until all the lights seemed to be shining brighter, and the air felt thinner, as if I couldn't quite get enough to breathe. I felt like I might pass out, but with Dominic sneering at me from a few feet away I really needed to stay conscious.

Fucking hell. I really had been kidnapped by a sadist, and as that realisation hit me it sucked the remaining air from my lungs and turned my legs to jelly, leaving me hanging limply from my wrists for a few seconds.

'You're here because you need to learn to behave. I'll teach you better than Oliver ever could.'

I was breathing so frantically that my breaths were whistling from my nostrils, but the mention of Oliver brought hope rushing to my mind. 'O-Oliver was with me at the club, Dominic, he'll know I'm missing.'

'Call me Master!' he snarled, spit flying from his mouth. 'Christ, you're a fucking shit sub.'

Ignoring his outburst, I shook my head. 'He'll find me, I know he will,' I stated with as much certainty as I could, but my remark didn't even make Dominic pause. In fact, he threw his head back and cackled as if he had completely lost his mind.

'I don't think so. Loverboy won't have a clue that it was me, not after my stellar acting performance back at the bar.'

What? Panic flooded my system again, and I blinked several times, trying to work out what he meant. 'What do you mean?' As much as I had tried to put on a brave front, my voice was whisper-thin, showing every ounce of my fear.

Dominic swaggered over to the wall beside me and leaned on it with an arrogance that made me want to vomit. 'I played it fucking perfectly, Robyn. Once I had you drugged and locked in the van, I went back inside and picked up a random blonde so it would like I'd been there all night.' He ran a hand over his short hair and grinned wickedly, apparently completely at ease with his mention of drugging me and locking me in a van. 'I hung around near the bar so I was there when Oliver realised you were missing. You should have seen his face. I thought he was going to cry! He's such a fuckin pussy. I made sure he saw me, and then acted completely oblivious, and suitably concerned about your disappearance. It was fucking perfect, and he fell for it hook, line, and sinker.'

Holy shit. So Oliver knew I was missing, but would never suspect that it was Dominic who had taken me?

How the hell would he ever find me?

How the hell would anybody find me?

I was broken from that panicked thought as Dominic continued to speak. 'Behaviour like yours yesterday would never have been allowed in the children's home when I was growing up. Do you know what they did to us if we dared talk back or argue?'

I was slipping into shock now, and instead of answering, I just stared at him. While he waited for my answer, Dominic moved closer and took the hem of my T-shirt into his hands, rolling it all up and tucking it under the elastic of my bra strap so that my entire midsection and back were exposed to him. The feel of his fingers brushing my bare skin made me shudder, but with the way I was stretched out there was no room for me to flinch away from him.

'Well? Answer me, Pet.' The way he called me "Pet" sickened me to my stomach, but his voice held a lower, scarier tone than before, indicating that he definitely wanted an answer this time, and so I swallowed and tried to calm my skittering heartbeat. God, at this rate I might well have a full-on cardiac arrest.

'N … no.'

'No, *Master*,' he corrected crisply, but I would not give

him the satisfaction of calling him that.

'Let me give you a clue.' He grabbed his shirt and ripped it over his head before turning around so I could see the full expanse of his broad back. A horrified gasp left my lungs as I looked at the ugly criss-cross of long, puckered, red lines that littered every inch of his back. Holy shit. There had to be upwards of a hundred scars on his skin.

'They started when I was seven,' he murmured, apparently wanting to unburden himself on my unwilling ears. 'The counsellors at the children's home didn't like my attitude, so they used to hit me with belts, rulers, and even a cable from an old computer printer. Once they noticed how resilient I was to the pain they stopped holding back.'

He was being beaten at age seven? Jesus. No wonder he was messed up, but I didn't want to hear this. It didn't compensate for the fact that he had taken me against my will.

After standing still to give me time to look at his scars, Dominic walked to one wall and pulled down a vicious-looking bull whip before flicking it into the air until it cracked loudly. The noise made me whimper, and a trickle of cold sweat dribbled down my spine.

'I've found that this whip leaves a similar mark to the printer cable they used to use on me.'

*Oh fuck no.*

He repeated the wrist flick, and as I watched the whip blur in the air and crack in front of me I imagined it ripping through my skin. Goose pimples flooded my entire body, and I began to desperately shake my head.

'Pl-please … don't do this, Dominic …'

'My. Name. Is. *Master*!' he screamed, and as the final words left his lips he lurched his right arm up and flicked it forwards so that the whip stuck me across my stomach.

The bite of the pain was so intense it was almost indescribable, but as a best attempt I would say it was like a line of searing hot lava being thrown against my body. A garbled cry left my lips, and every fibre of my being fought to bend forwards and protect myself, but I couldn't; the chain on my wrists and cuffs on my ankles were holding me strung out too tightly.

The look in Dominic's eye was one I'll never, ever forget. It was almost like he had left the room and allowed a stranger to take over his body – a completely psychotic stranger. His eyes were dilated and black, but devoid of emotion, and as he raised his hand to flick the whip again, I could tell there was no point in trying to reason with him. He was no longer in control.

The second strike was even worse than the first, if that's possible. The curling tip of the leather was aimed to perfection so it wound around my side, cutting into my stomach, side, and back all in one go. It was like receiving three strikes for the price of one, and as the crippling pain hit my system I gave in and let my tears flow.

My cheeks were soaked in seconds, and as Dominic hit me again – this time on my other flank – I allowed my head to drop forwards. If I had to deal with this level of pain, then holding my head upright was the last thing I needed to be wasting energy on.

My eyesight was blurred with tears, and my head was dizzy from the pain, but just as I was wondering if I might pass out from the agony coursing through my system, there was a loud crashing noise close by, followed shortly by several bangs and voices shouting and swearing.

I thought for a second that Dominic was losing the plot and smashing the room up, but then something registered in my foggy mind that brought my head snapping up.

Spanish words …

*Oliver.*

Had I dreamed it? Conjured it up in my desperate imagination, or was Oliver really here?

Blinking desperately to clear my vision, I heard the

distinct sound of Spanish swear words again, mingled with English phrases, and hope soared in my heart. '*¡Hijo de puta!* Get away from her, you fucking son of a bitch!'

When my tears finally stopped enough for me to see clearly, I saw not only Oliver, but Marcus, David, and Nathan entering the room, all bristling with anger. While the other three stood inside the threshold, Oliver charged towards Dominic and tackled him around his centre like a rugby pro. The two of them briefly flew through the air, then Dominic grunted as they landed on the floor and the wind was knocked from his lungs. Oliver landed on top, quickly shifting so he sat astride him. Then, with an animalistic roar, he started to rain down punches on Dominic like a madman.

'Oliver, dude, calm the fuck down!' Marcus moved across the room, trying to pull Oliver back, but David wrapped a hand around his shoulder and stopped him.

'You see what this fucker has done to his girl? Let him have a few seconds of payback.'

Marcus's eyes flicked to mine and, after wincing at the sight of my abused body, he and David stood back while Oliver continued his tirade. David seemed to count off some mystery period in his head, before finally stepping in to stop Oliver. At first, he just shook off David's hand and carried on, but with the combined effort of David, Marcus, and Nathan, they finally managed to tear Oliver backwards.

Dominic raised his hands in surrender, but didn't try to stand up, which was probably just as well, seeing as there were four furious men glaring down at him and more than ready to kick him back to the dirt floor if necessary.

From the wild expression in Oliver's eyes, he was intent on going back and killing Dominic, but it was Nathan who stepped forwards and seemed to finally get through to him. 'This piece of shit isn't worth going to prison for. Leave him. Your girl needs you.' At his words,

Oliver's eyes sought me out, latching onto my gaze and seeming to draw us together.

He shot across the room in three huge strides, and cupped my face with such a gentle touch it was as if he thought I was made of glass.

'Robyn ... *Cariño* ... are you OK?' His eyes were searching mine, and as much as I wanted to be strong and say what he probably needed to hear, I couldn't. This had all been too much, and my emotions were in tatters, so I simply shook my head and started to cry again.

'*Dios*.' He briefly rested his forehead against mine, then tried to undo my wrists before expelling another low curse and turning towards his friends who were currently tying Dominic up in a corner. 'Somebody find me the keys to these fucking things!'

A second later there was a jingling sound of something metal being thrown across the room, then Oliver was frantically working his way through a small bunch of keys, trying each one in the locks at my wrists until I felt the cuffs release.

My arms had been above my head for so long that they felt like tree trunks, falling to my sides with such force that I keeled forwards. I was only stopped from hitting the floor because Oliver shifted and caught me over his shoulder, causing me to cry out in agony as the whip marks on my body made contact with the material of his shirt. Swearing loudly, he adjusted me to ease my pain, before shouting for someone to come and uncuff my feet.

I think it was Nathan who found the right key and released my feet so that I could fall into the safety of Oliver's arms, but I couldn't be sure. The emotion of the last hour had caught up with me and as well as my body feeling heavy, my eyelids did, too.

Now that I had Oliver clutching me to his chest, everything else could wait. Darkness began to overtake me again, and after initially fighting it, I decided I quite liked

306

the sensation. Slipping into unconsciousness meant that I couldn't feel the pain any more, and right now, that was just fine by me.

## Chapter Forty

### Oliver

Looking down at Robyn in my arms, I saw with alarm that her eyes were closed. I couldn't tell if she was asleep, or had passed out from the stress, and panic flew through my system for a second, before I noticed the regular intake of her breaths, and realised she must be OK.

Adjusting her in my arms, I winced at the deep ache in my knuckles from where I had laid into Dominic. Hitting the bastard's chin had felt like smashing my fist into a concrete block, but it had been worth it for the marginal sense of retribution it had given me.

A grunt from the corner had me turning, and I saw Nathan and David restraining Dominic and tying his hands to one of the hooks on the wall. He was bleeding heavily from his nose and a gash in his eyebrow. From the blank look in his eyes my beating didn't seem to have bothered him much, but it had sure as hell made me feel better.

Stepping closer, I could hear David trying to speak to him, but Dominic was just staring sightlessly ahead, muttering something about "beating some manners into him". I exchanged a concerned glance with David, who stood up and came to stand beside me.

David gently picked up Robyn's wrist and checked her pulse. After nodding his satisfaction, he glanced back at Dominic, who was now rocking back and forth on his haunches.

'He's not making any sense. I think he's had a breakdown of some sort.'

Back when David had first asked me if I wanted to invest into Club Twist he and I had sat down and discussed other possible business partners. Dominic had been a sticking point, because while we'd both agreed that his sexual preferences were far more extreme than we were comfortable with, David was in favour of letting him in, whereas I was not.

David had overruled me, though, arguing that Dominic had been a long-standing member of the club even before he'd become one of its owners, and had never caused any major issues, which I had to grudgingly admit was true. He liked to posture around in front of some of the other Doms in the club, which had always irritated me, but we'd just put that down to arrogance, and I had reluctantly given in.

David was the majority shareholder, so I'd had to stand back and let him lead, but I had always had a feeling about Dominic, something I couldn't quite place, but that just didn't sit right with me.

It would seem that after years of seeming just about stable, he had finally flipped, and I'd been proved right in my concerns.

I might feel a slither of sympathy for his horrendous upbringing and the abuse he'd suffered, but that didn't diminish the fact that he had kidnapped and whipped Robyn, and my whole body tensed as I turned to David.

'Please don't suggest letting him off with this,' I growled, my face so tense that my eyeballs were surely bulging from their sockets.

'Mate, seriously, as if I would' David replied, running a hand through his hair. 'Marcus has already called the police, and they're five minutes away, but with his current behaviour, I think it's likely that he's going to need psychiatric screening, too.'

That was agreeable to me, as long as justice was done. Nodding at David, I adjusted Robyn in my arms and lowered my lips to her hair, and even though she wouldn't be aware of it, I found myself kissing her over and over.

# Chapter Forty-one

## Robyn

As I started to wake, I felt like I had been sleeping on a cloud; soft fluffiness surrounded me, cocooning me in gentle safety and warmth, and I smiled contentedly.

Finally deciding to open my eyes, I blinked, and frowned. I was in my own bedroom, but I *was* sleeping in a cloud. Instead of my usual blankets, my body was surrounded by a pile of fluffy whiteness – what looked like a brand-new super-stuffed duvet, which certainly didn't belong to me.

I went to push myself upright, trying to work out what the heck was going on, but I was stopped in my tracks by a tight, searing pain around my stomach and back that caused a sharp gasp to leave my lungs. As I looked down and saw several large bruises across my midsection and a bandage covering one area, the mattress shifted next to me, and Oliver's concerned face came into view over the top of the white cotton mountain.

'Hey, you're awake. Take it easy, lay back down.'

With prickly pain still circling me, I didn't argue, and gingerly lay back as memories of yesterday started to flood back into my mind.

Dominic.

His basement of pain.

The whip.

So *that* explained the bruises and bandage, not to mention why I was in so much pain.

I vaguely recalled giving my statement to a policewoman, and I had blurry recollections of being attended to by a doctor, but I squeezed my eyes shut against the images, not keen on reliving any of it just at the moment.

A huge shudder ripped through my body. Seconds later,

Oliver was clambering over the mounds of white and gently arranging my naked, trembling body into the circle of his arms. As well as my torso, my wrists were also bruised from the bindings, and although I couldn't see my feet, I guessed my ankles were, too. Moving hurt almost more than I could bear, but I endured it, because once I was settled in his embrace I felt utterly safe and secure, and my pain somehow seemed dulled.

'What's with the new duvet?' I asked, my voice croaky from its first usage.

Oliver's chest rose and fell beneath me as he took in a long breath, then he placed a kiss on the top of my head before speaking. 'While you were sleeping you couldn't settle properly. You were ... you were crying in your sleep ...' He let out a shuddering breath. 'I thought it might be due to pain, so I went out and bought this extra-thick duvet to cushion you.

'How are you feeling?' he asked gently.

Drawing in a deep breath, I winced as agony sliced through my torso again. 'Sore. But I'm OK.' Which was true, because I was safe now, and in his arms, and I knew I would be OK in the long run.

Cupping my face, he tilted my jaw up so he could look into my eyes. 'Now you're awake, I need to ask. Do you need me to get you a doctor?'

I blinked and shook my head. 'I've already seen a doctor,' I mumbled, although perhaps I had dreamed that. 'Honestly, Oliver, I'll be fine. You arrived just after he had started, so he only managed to hit me a few times.' At my words, Oliver tensed below me, and his jaw tightened so much that his lips turned pure white with anger. Trying to reassure him, I stroked his forearm. 'I'm sure I'll heal in a few days.'

Drawing in a long breath as if calming himself, Oliver shook his head. 'That's not what I meant. I already had my private physician check your wounds this morning when

311

we arrived back here. I meant … do you need … a … gynaecologist? Did he … did he touch you?' Oliver paused, his eyes clenching shut as he cradled me against him looking distinctly pained, 'Robyn, did he rape you?'

Oh. Seeing how desperate Oliver looked, I shook my head immediately, trying to calm him. 'No. Oliver, no, he didn't.' Thinking about it, it didn't seem as if that was what Dominic had wanted from me. He'd certainly had ample opportunity.

'You can tell me the truth, Robyn. None of this is your fault, *cariño.*' Oliver's face was still taut with tension, so I ran my fingers over his cheek and jaw until his muscles slackened slightly.

'Honestly, Oliver, he didn't touch me sexually. He seemed more intent on punishing me. He said I was a shit sub and needed to learn. He… … he wanted me to call him master.' Despite the gravity of the situation, I found myself giving a dry, humourless laugh. 'I probably am a shit sub.'

Oliver clicked his tongue dismissively and leaned down to place a gentle kiss on my lips. 'You're fucking perfect, Robyn.' He rubbed his nose against the tip of mine, just like my mum used to do when I was younger, and I felt my heart melt.

'So … where is he now?' I asked, not sure I wanted to know the answer. If Dominic was still free to return to Club Twist, then there was no way I would ever be able to step foot inside that place again.

'In police custody in a secure hospital,' Oliver murmured.

'Hospital?' I mumbled, confused. I'd seen Oliver get in a few hits on him, but it hadn't seemed enough for hospital.

'A secure mental facility. We suspect he's had a breakdown of some sort, so he's being checked over by a team of physiatrists.'

Wow. That would explain his bizarre behaviour. He had definitely seemed very detached from reality. 'Will ... will he be let out?' I stammered, my heart rate rocketing.

'No, *cariño*, no. I spoke to my solicitor last night, and he got some advice from his friend who is a prosecution lawyer. For what he did to you – kidnapping with intent, and deliberate bodily harm – he'll be looking at ten years to life in a secure mental facility.

'You're safe, Robyn. You'll never see him again. Trust me.' I did trust Oliver. I trusted him with my life. That knowledge, plus the determination I could see on his face, helped me relax back into his embrace, but as I did, Oliver frowned, his eyes zeroing in on my neck. With the upmost care, he traced his thumb around the skin there.

'I didn't see this mark yesterday. It must have been hidden by your hair. Did he ... did he try and strangle you?' The barely concealed outrage in his voice showed me just how close Oliver was to losing control and I tried to work out what mark he was referring to.

'No. It's from the collar you gave me. Dominic ripped it off, and the leather cut into my skin a bit as he did.' Considering all that had happened in the last twenty-four hours, it was the last thing I should be thinking about, but I felt really sad at the loss of the small pendant.

With a growl, Oliver leaned to the side and picked up a tube of antiseptic cream from the bedside table. He squeezed a small amount onto the tip of his finger and wordlessly began to smooth it around the wound at my neck. 'It's OK, *cariño*. You don't have to wear one again.'

Sitting up, I frowned. 'What? Why?'

Oliver screwed the lid back on the cream and examined me intently. 'If it triggers bad memories for you, then you don't have to wear one again.'

313

My head began to shake of its own accord. 'No! It triggers good memories for me ... You gave it to me, and you said it was special. That you'd never given one before ...'

'All of which is true,' Oliver said quietly with a nod of his head.

'I loved it,' I admitted sadly, raising my hand and feeling the empty space where the leather had been.

'In which case, we shall replace it as soon as you are feeling better.' He placed a kiss on my temple and pulled me close again.

A noise at the door disturbed our quiet time, and a second later, Sasha's head popped in.

Letting out a curse, Oliver dragged a sheet up to cover my body, and once I was swathed to his satisfaction I threw Sasha a chastising look. 'You seriously need to learn to knock,'

'Oops. Sorry.' She didn't look repentant at all. 'I heard voices, so I just wanted to check in and see how you were doing.'

Allowing my head to flop back onto Oliver's chest, I gave a small shrug. 'Not bad, all things considered.'

'Thank God. I was so bloody worried.' She took a step closer and winced as she looked at the bruising on my wrists. 'Do you need anything?'

'Coffee would be amazing.' It was the first thing that popped into my head.

At my words, Sasha grinned and nodded. 'You must be feeling OK, then. You always have been a coffee monster. I'll bring some in.' With that, Sasha left us alone again and closed the door behind her.

'She'll be in here every five minutes. You should have taken me back to your place so we could have had some peace. Which I've still not seen, by the way,' I added teasingly, hoping to try to lighten Oliver's mood and distract him from worrying about me.

It wasn't entirely successful, because Oliver rolled his eyes. 'This again,' he mumbled. 'I didn't take you back to my place because we've not been together that long, and seeing as yesterday must have been really traumatic for you I thought you would feel safer on familiar territory.'

Oh. When he put it like that, it was actually rather sweet of him.

'You can see my place once you're healed.' With that, he pulled me into his chest and effectively ended the conversation by kissing me until I relaxed into his arms and forgot about everything except the man wrapped around me.

# Chapter Forty-two

## Oliver

'How's Robyn getting on now?' Marcus asked carefully, as he unzipped his squash racquet and rolled his shoulders in warm-up. He was right to be careful, too, because in the week since Dominic had abducted her I had been so overly protective that even my closest friends had commented that being around me was like treading on broken glass.

'She's doing really well, all things considered.'

'You still camped out at her place?'

'Yeah. Well, I've been there all week, but I'm going back to mine tonight.' Being away from Robyn hadn't been an option for me in the initial days after I'd got her back, so I'd been practically living at her flat and conducting work from her sofa on my laptop. I wasn't thrilled by the idea of leaving her tonight, but this morning she'd told me she needed a night alone to prove to us both that she really was OK now. I was feeling so possessive over her at the moment that I might have put up a bigger fight about it, if she lived on her own. But knowing that Sasha and Chloe would be with her had allowed me to just about get over my worry.

So, today was the first time I was leaving Robyn for any significant length of time; first to go to work, and now to play squash with Marcus, and I couldn't deny that I'd felt a little fidgety and anxious all day.

'You'll be asking her to move in with you next,' Marcus teased, seemingly trying to lighten the air, but I stayed silent. He had no idea how many times I had considered doing just that over this last week, but seeing as taking Robyn to mine still posed certain problems of its own, I'd held back.

I'd really been looking forward to our weekly squash game. We'd skipped last week as I hadn't wanted to leave

Robyn, but a good tiring game should help to relive some of my tension.

I began my own warm-up, circling my neck, rolling my shoulders and briefly jogging on the spot, but the whole time my mind dwelled on various images of Robyn, and how brave she had been in the last week. It turned out that my little bird was quite the fighter.

'She's incredible, Marcus. She's taken it all in her stride. To be honest, I think I've struggled with it more than she has. I've been a little prickly, as I'm sure you and Nathan might have noticed. Sorry about that.'

'No apology required,' Marcus stated, with a shake of his head. 'It's a completely understandable reaction, mate. She's your girl, of course you feel protective. But Dominic's locked away now and she's safe, so you guys can get back to just enjoying being together.'

I let out a long, relieved breath as his words washed over me. It was true, she was safe.

'With the exception of the Dominic situation, it's a long while since I've seen you this happy with a girl, Oliver, a very long time. I'm stoked for you.'

I nodded my agreement with a small smile and my cheeks heated slightly. 'Thanks.'

We took turns lightly hitting the ball against the back wall to warm it up, and I decided it was about time to shift the focus away from myself for a while. I'd been rather self-absorbed since the kidnapping, but I knew that Marcus also had issues he was dealing with.

'So how about you? How are you doing? We haven't really had time to sit down and talk about how you feel since splitting with Celia.' Celia – the ex who had chosen America over Marcus, and a woman I had never been fond of.

Marcus looked at me with a raised eyebrow and sighed. 'You always hated her. I should have listened to you from the start.'

317

'She wasn't my favourite person, no,' I admitted. Something had always seemed off about her, but I'd never been able to put my finger on it. 'What caused you two to break up? You said you'd tell me once you got back to the UK, but we've never really got around to it.' Marcus and I had always been open in our conversations about sex and relationships, so I was slightly surprised about how quiet he'd been on the subject of his recent split.

Marcus didn't reply, but as the ball bounced before him he stepped into his next shot and smashed it so hard that the ball rebounded off the back wall and hit the ceiling before falling to the court floor. 'Fuck. Sorry.'

Glancing across, I saw his shoulders were tense, cheeks red, and his eyes were averted away from me. He looked pissed off, or perhaps even furious, and I began to wonder if perhaps I wasn't the only one struggling with some deeper personal issues at the moment.

From the grimace he flashed me, I'd guess there was a little more to the breakup than he'd originally let on. Perhaps she'd cheated on him and bruised his pride?

'You want to talk about it?' I offered, already suspecting from his violent reaction that this was going to be a closed subject for Marcus.

'No.' His reply was immediate, and sharp, causing me to pause and rest my hands on my hips in curiosity. Marcus was usually the most laidback guy I knew, and it was so rare for him to lose his temper that I was genuinely shocked. He retrieved the ball, let out a long, heavy breath, and gave me a tight, apologetic smile.

'Sorry, mate. Thank you, but no, I don't want to talk about it.' He chucked the ball to me and lowered himself into a crouch, ready to receive a serve. 'Let's start a proper game. Less talking, more hitting. You serve first.'

The conversation ended there, but I made a note not to be so self-centred and to keep a closer eye on him in the coming weeks to check he was definitely OK.

Marcus had mentioned that he'd stopped playing squash while he'd been in the US, and it was showing a little in his game, because he was nowhere near as quick as he used to be which was probably the only reason I managed to well and truly beat him again. He won a couple of games, though, so as we made our way back towards the changing rooms we were both tired and in better spirits than earlier.

Feeling lighter in spirits than I had in weeks, I chuckled, remembering something I'd been meaning to tell him for a while now. 'By the way, did you know Robyn's friend Sasha has the hots for you?'

Marcus opened his locker and laughed. 'Sasha? I didn't know that, no.'

'Yep. She's your type, no?'

Marcus nodded, then pulled his towel out. 'Looks-wise, yes. She's undeniably pretty. She did sort of try it on with me the first night they came to the club, but I'm not really up for something casual right now.'

This was news. Before he'd got together with Celia, Marcus had *always* been up for something casual. It was one of the things that we'd had in common. Casual meant no strings, which meant no hassle. It had been perfect for me back then, but funnily enough, that type of relationship held zero appeal for me now.

'You and she looked pretty cosy when you were working together to help me look for Robyn.' It had been a hellish night, but even I hadn't missed the way he and Sasha had been looking at each other. There had been some pretty heavy chemistry hanging in the air.

'We may have exchanged a few flirtatious glances, but I think that's just her style. She seems to have her tongue stuck down the throat of a different guy every time I see her.'

I couldn't deny that he had a point there. I'd also seen Sasha with numerous different men at the club, and Robyn had all but confirmed that her friend was rather casual in her approach to dating.

'Perhaps she's just acting like that to get your attention,' I speculated, because even though Sasha messed around with other guys, I'd noticed just how frequently her eyes were focused on Marcus.

'Maybe.'

Marcus seemed to be responding with a little too much nonchalance, leading me to believe that perhaps he was more interested than he was letting on. 'You're not even up for a bit of fun? I would have thought that now you're single again you would jump at the chance of a hot girl throwing herself at you?'

'Nah. To be honest I'm kinda avoiding the whole dating scene for a while, casual or otherwise.'

I could understand that. It was exactly how I'd felt when everything had gone wrong with Abi all those years ago. 'Fair enough.' I decided to let the subject drop, and grabbed my towel and shower bag before following Marcus in the direction of the showers.

The showers here were private, with each cubicle having its own door, but we often stripped off outside and hung our clothes on the hooks to avoid them getting wet on the floor. As Marcus pulled his T-shirt off, a flash of red caught in my peripheral vision and I looked across at his torso and sucked in a shocked breath. He had several vivid red scars lacing across his side – not entirely dissimilar to the colour of those marking Dominic's body. Upon hearing my intake of breath, he quickly covered himself with a towel.

'Marcus, what the hell?' Those scars looked vicious, and definitely hadn't been there before he'd left for the US. I hadn't noticed them since his return, but they would certainly explain why he was so much stiffer in his movements around the squash court.

'Accident in the US. And before you ask, no, I don't

want to talk about that either.'

Accident? Car accident? Or work accident? But before I could push him any further Marcus hung his damp sports clothes up and shut himself away in his cubicle, effectively ending the conversation.

That was twice he'd been short with me today, which was so out of character, I couldn't help but suspect that there was something he wasn't telling me. I knew Marcus well enough to know that he was a stubborn guy, though, so forcing him wouldn't get me any answers.

I'd have to wait and hope he'd tell me in his own time.

# Chapter Forty-three

## Robyn

Sasha had been like my shadow today, following me around the house, eating when I ate, and even offering to dry my hair for me after I'd had a shower. If she'd been bearing gifts of chocolate or wine I might have tolerated it for a bit longer, but by just gone lunchtime her constant closeness was starting to grate on my nerves.

'I'm not going to break, you know? What's with the constant supervision?'

Sasha attempted an innocent, unaware expression, as if she had no idea what I was talking about, but after I propped my hands on my hips and gave her a firm look she relented and held her hands up in defeat.

'OK, OK, so Oliver may have asked me to keep an eye on you today.'

'May have?' I demanded, wondering why everyone around me seemed to think I needed wrapping in bubble wrap since the stuff with Dominic had occurred. Yes, it had been fucking terrifying at the time, but I'd dealt with it. A couple of trips to a therapist this week hadn't hurt, but I was fine now. Genuinely fine.

'OK. He *did* ask me to keep an eye on you. You know, coz it's his first day properly back at work, and your first day being here on your own.'

Oliver's concern was very sweet, and I'd absolutely loved having him here pretty much non-stop for the past week, but he was going to exhaust himself if he tried to keep up this level of protectiveness.

'I'm fine, Sash, honestly.'

She grinned at me, and knocked her shoulder against mine in that way she had. 'I know you are, chick. But you know Oliver, he's very difficult to say no to when he asks you to do something.'

Ha! Wasn't that just the truth?

'What about you, though? Shouldn't you be at work?'

'Nah, it's cool. I was owed a couple of days off in lieu. It was about time I took them.'

The sound of the doorbell ringing made both Sasha and I jump, but wanting to prove that I really was fine now, I rolled my eyes and went to see who it was.

I checked the spyhole. A man in a delivery uniform held a huge bunch of flowers, so I pulled it open.

'Hey. I have a delivery for Sasha Mortimer.'

It was actually two separate bunches of flowers, so after signing the receipt, I cradled them into my arms and went back inside, closing the door behind me.

'You have some flowers,' I remarked, inhaling the beautiful scent.

Sasha skipped over gleefully. 'For me? Makes a change!' she remarked. She had a point, because the flat was already swathed in several bunches of flowers that Oliver had bought for me – one each day this week.

She took the card from the first bunch and read it. Her nose crinkled up and she held it out to me. 'Boo. These are for you.'

Juggling the other bunch across to her, I took the arrangement that was for me, and read the card.

*Robyn, I'm glad to hear you are feeling recovered. Marcus.*

Well, it was straight to the point, I supposed, but very sweet of him to send them.

'They're from Marcus. What does the other card say?' I asked, placing mine down on a table and glancing across just in time to see a blush creeping its way up Sasha's neck. Wow. This was new – she hardly ever blushed.

'It says, "Sasha, sorry I scared the crap out of you. I'll work on not being an insensitive arse. Marcus." Then

323

there's a little winky face.'

A laugh burst from my throat at the expression on Sasha's face, and I moved closer to have a look. 'What does it mean?'

Sasha was still looking a bit of a funny colour, but then she seemed to shake herself out of it and put the flowers down. 'Well, on the night you ... well, you know ... the night that all the shit happened, Marcus was searching for you, but he found me on the dance floor. Chloe was in the loo, and instead of calmly asking if I'd seen you, he strode up and declared that you'd been fucking kidnapped.' Her description came to a dead halt as she slapped a hand over her mouth and cringed. 'Which obviously you had ... but at the time it sounded crazy, and as his note says, he scared the absolutely crap out of me.' She let out a dry chuckle and reread the card. 'Later on, I told him he was a shit messenger, and an insensitive arse, hence the second comment.'

'Maybe next time we see him you should ask him to buy you a drink by way of apology,' I ventured, fairly sure that Sasha still liked Marcus way more than she was letting on.

'Hmm. Maybe...' was all the answer I got before Chloe wandered into the lounge and came up short.

'*More* flowers from Oliver?' She gawked in bewilderment, taking in the two new bunches on the table.

'Nope, these are from Marcus,' Sasha informed her, tucking the card into the pocket of her jeans.

Chloe made a face, as if she wished that she were the one being bought flowers, then glanced around the room. 'So where is Oliver?'

'At work. Then I think he was playing squash with Marcus and then he's heading home for the night.'

'He's not staying here again?' she asked in surprise. The idea of not having him here after seeing him near constantly for the last week caused my stomach to clench, but I gave what I hoped was a nonchalant shrug and shook my head. 'Nope. I told him to go home. He can't exactly stay here forever, can he?'

'Not really. But you could stay at his. Have you even seen his house yet?' she asked. To my ears, there was something slightly off about her tone and I stiffened. Not this topic again.

'Not yet, but he lives miles away in Holland Park. It's easier for him to drive here.'

'Easier, is it?' Chloe mimicked, crossing her arms and frowning.

'You work near there, Chloe, you know how difficult the trains are to get there,' Sasha intervened.

I studied Chloe's expression intently, feeling my hackles rising at her interest in my relationship. 'If you have something to say, Chloe, just spit it out.'

She let out a huffed breath and nervously chewed on a fingernail. 'I just keep thinking about that woman he was with in my office, Robyn. They looked really close … and he still hasn't shown you his house.'

'What exactly are you implying?' I demanded, slamming my hands onto my hips.

Chloe looked uncomfortable with this inquisition, but seeing as she was the one to start it, it was tough luck. 'Like maybe he's hiding something? I dunno, something just doesn't sit right with me.'

Just as I was about to step up and defend Oliver, Sasha, my trusty sidekick, did it for me, bless her. 'Fuck off with your pessimism, Chloe. You've seen how protective of Robyn Oliver has been since the shit with Dominic. He's got the feels, big time. There's no way he's playing around.'

Chloe took in a breath as if she was planning on saying more, but then snapped her teeth shut and nodded. 'That's true …' Running a hand through her hair, she offered me an apologetic smile. 'Sorry, Rob. I'm probably just being paranoid because of my shitty relationship history. Forgive me?'

Stepping forwards, she held her hands out in the offer of a hug. After rolling my eyes, I stepped forwards and accepted her apology cuddle.

'Well, after causing all that trouble, I'm off to the gym. See you guys in a bit.'

Once Chloe had gone, Sasha approached me from the side, holding out two bottles of beer and the television remote. 'Ignore her, babes. Oliver is a total dude. It's been obvious from the get-go just how into you he is. So, how does beer and a movie sound?'

Grinning at my bestie, I nodded. It sounded pretty awesome to me.

## Chapter Forty-four

### Robyn

'Oh Rob-yyyyn! Come out here for a second.' Frowning at the sing-song quality to Sasha's voice as it floated through to my bedroom, I glanced at the clock. My frown deepened. It was ten past eleven. We'd watched movies all afternoon, accompanied by several beers, and so now I was in bed feeling sleepy and just a little bit tipsy. What on earth could she need me for?

I slid reluctantly from my lovely warm covers and wandered out in my pyjamas, curious to see what was so important.

It turned out to be a "who", not a "what," because as I entered our living room I found Oliver lounging against the doorframe, looking gorgeous in one of his trademark suits, with his hands shoved in his pockets and a lazy grin splitting his unfairly handsome face.

'Look who's back again!' Sasha stood beside him, and made a "ta-da" noise, and after grinning at me she disappeared from the room, leaving me gawking at Oliver with my mouth hanging open.

I'd actually told him to stay at his place tonight, because I wanted to prove to him that I was fine now – strong, and fully recovered from the Dominic thing – but God he was a welcome sight in our doorway. It had only been twelve hours since I'd last seen him, but I wanted to jump into his arms and devour him.

So I did. Without even hesitating, I advanced towards him. I slid my arms around his middle and buried my face into his collar. Yum. Even at the end of the day he still smelled so good. 'Hey! This is a nice surprise!'

He pulled his hands from his pockets, wrapped them around me, and tugged me even closer. 'I missed you. I

327

ended up sorting something for David at the club, so as I was local-ish I decided to drop by and say goodnight.'

Local-ish. The club wasn't that close to our flat, so the fact that he had popped in anyway made me ridiculously pleased. 'Come in.'

'I have a gift for you,' Oliver announced, picking up a large bag to his right and handing it to me.

'Wow. Thank you.' I recognised the name on the bag as a top London shoemaker, and quickly pulled open the long box inside to discover a beautiful pair of black leather knee-high boots nestling inside tissue paper within.

'To replace the ones you lost,' he murmured quietly, reminding me that my last pair had ended up being left in Dominic's dungeon of terror.

Reaching in, I ran my fingers over the leather and it practically melted under my fingers. Woah. These looked, and felt, way more expensive than my old pair. 'Wow, thank you.'

'You are most welcome.' Oliver's eyes twinkled with something that made me blush as I remembered his fantasy about me in knee-highs against a wall ... Hmm. We still needed to make that one a reality.

'I also got you this ...' he added, pulling out a small black velvet box and popping it open to reveal a new collar. My breath caught as a flash of Dominic ripping my last one from my throat flicked in my mind. Pushing the unwelcome memory away, I reached up to gently touch my replacement, and glanced up to find Oliver watching me carefully.

'You seemed disappointed by the loss of the last one, but you don't have to wear it if it triggers any bad memories.'

'No. I love it.' The small silver disc had the same engravings on it – Oliver's initials on one side, and *cariño* on the other – but instead of a circular silver disk, this one was a delicate heart shape. The collar was a little more intricate than the last one, too, containing not only a leather strip, but what appeared to be a platinum necklace plaited together with the leather. It made it look more like a necklace, as opposed to a collar, and something I could wear on a day-to-day basis.

'Thank you, Oliver, it's gorgeous!' I exclaimed in a hushed whisper, much to Oliver's apparent pleasure. Winking at me, he clicked the box shut again, popped it in the bag with the boots, and set both of my gifts onto the hall table beside us.

Looking down at the tiny vest top and shorts I was wearing, I grinned. 'Come through to the lounge. Let me just go and put a few more clothes on.'

Before I'd managed to turn away fully, Oliver caught my wrist and lowered his head beside my ear. 'I believe you're braless at the moment, am I correct?' he murmured in a low tone. Seeing as my nipples were standing to attention in his presence it was a fairly needless question.

'Mmm-hum.' I hummed my answer, my voice now paralysed by the sheer intensity of his gaze.

'Stay that way,' he instructed me, trailing a finger across the underside of one breast.

I was immensely glad that Sasha had chosen to leave us alone and wasn't eagerly watching every second of this play out, because knowing my nosey bestie, she totally would be.

Where exactly was he going with this line of conversation? Maybe he was here for a much-needed booty call? Even though he'd slept here every night this week, we hadn't had sex. We'd snuggled, kissed and touched, but in his head, he'd obviously decided that I was in recovery, and had held himself back from sex. He'd treated me like a fragile ornament, so some sexy time certainly wouldn't go amiss. Besides, I'd already warmed my bed up, so it wouldn't exactly be a hardship to be dragged back to it by Oliver.

His fingers retraced their path, brushing briefly along the side of my other breast. It was a fairly innocent touch, but my nipples peaked even further to attention and stuck out as if reaching for him. God, my body was positively shameless where this man was concerned. Oliver chuckled and released me, leaving me breathless and dizzy and cursing how little control I had over myself when I was around him.

'You can touch me, Oliver. I'm totally fine.'

He smiled and nodded, but made no move to restart his touch, so I decided to try and play him at his own game. Licking my lips, I slid a hand down to play with the waistband of my loose pyjama shorts.

'I'm knickerless, too,' I informed him softly, watching with enjoyment as his eyes widened and his gaze turned hungry.

There was a long pause, as if he were fighting with whether or not we should proceed. Then, finally, he tilted his head and narrowed his eyes wickedly.

'Is that so?'

Oh goodie, it looked like my plan was working.

'Mmm-hmm.'

Oliver groaned, and shoved his hands deep into his trouser pockets, adjusting himself then giving me a heated look as Sasha swanned back into the room, turned on the television, and threw herself down on the sofa.

*Damn it!* Ripping my hand from my shorts, I cleared my throat and grinned at Oliver, who was also beaming from ear to ear. 'It's late. I know I suggested you stay at your place tonight, but now you're here, you're welcome to sleep over again.' I dragged him to the kitchen end of the room in the hope that some distance from Sasha might help disguise my beaded nipples and Oliver's tenting hard-on.

'I'd love to, but I have an early meeting.' Which I suspected was his way of trying to give me the space in my recovery that I had requested. 'I'll have a coffee, though, if you're offering.'

'Of course.' I set about filling the kettle, while Oliver pulled out some mugs, looking at home and comfortable in our flat after his week of staying here.

I made a coffee for Oliver and Sasha, and a decaf tea for myself, and Sasha joined us at the breakfast bar to get her drink. Just as I was about to move towards the table, I felt Oliver trail his hand down my side before lifting the leg of my shorts and dipping inside to stroke my upper thigh.

What on earth was he playing at? He hadn't touched me sexually all week when we'd had the privacy of my bedroom surrounding us, but now that Sasha was just a few feet away, he wanted to play? Not wanting to draw her attention, I muffled my shocked gasp by pretending to take a sip of my tea, and managed not to flap my hands and try and swat him away.

'Thanks for the brew,' Sasha sounded distracted, presumably by the magazine in her hand, or perhaps the game show on the television. She took her coffee back to the sofa, all the while Oliver was exploring inside my shorts, and letting out his own low growl upon discovering my bare bottom.

Cupping my right bum cheek, he gave a squeeze that had me briefly rolling to my tiptoes. 'You were telling the truth. Well, well, you are being naughty tonight.'

I wanted to say that I wasn't deliberately being naughty, I had just been getting ready for bed as I had every night this week, but he seemed rather thrilled by my lack of underwear so I kept quiet.

Gripping my mug to try and ground myself, I stood there frozen in shock as Oliver lowered himself to the kitchen stool beside me. He looked me directly in the eye, then made a show of wiping a drip of coffee from his mug, before sucking his finger to clean it. This all seemed a little over the top to me, until a second later when he adjusted his position on the stool and trailed his hand up my leg and into my loose pyjama shorts.

Just as I thought he was only teasing me like usual, the finger that he had licked suddenly zeroed in on my damp channel and began to press inside.

So we'd gone from treating me like glass, to fingering me in public?

My gaze darted to Sasha across the other side of the room. She was still intently focused on her magazine and didn't seem to be aware of what was going on just meters away, but still, he couldn't finger me with her right there!

Quite apparently, he could, and would, because Oliver didn't stop. With his eyes blazing, he buried the finger deeper within my now soaked channel. The noise of the television covered my gasp, but I rapidly tried to grip Oliver's wrist to stop him. He placed his coffee down and stopped me with his free hand, then leaned in closer to me. 'Remember the rules, Robyn. I lead. You said you were fine. Are you really fine? Or shall I stop?'

His fingers paused while he waited for my answer, and I was so desperate for him to treat me like he had before the Dominic stuff, that I nodded. 'I am fine.'

'Then we continue but this is my game. You don't get to lead.' His warm breath fluttered across my cheek, making me dizzy with the sensations flooding my body, and as he spoke he pressed his finger gently in and out of me again.

'Oliver...' My gaze flashed to Sasha again, and back to my man, who was still staring at me with a determined expression on his face. Fuck. I let out a soft, desperate moan, but in response Oliver gave a minute shake of his head to silence me and added his thumb into the action as it started to circle on my clit.

'Remember the role of a sub. You don't have to worry about a thing, just follow my lead, understand?' he

332

whispered hotly against my cheek.

This was wrong on so many levels, but God it felt so right. 'B ... but ...'

Oliver raised an eyebrow at my slightly hesitant reply. Upon seeing his chastising look, I felt the inner submissive part of me melt into compliance. 'Yes, Sir.'

Leaning close to my ear, he brushed his lips over my neck and whispered hotly against my skin. 'Good girl.' Normally I had no issues following his lead, but this was a whole other level of kink. My best friend was in the same room as me while my boyfriend was happily fingering me; I could barely think straight. There was one saving grace to this whole crazy situation – the breakfast bar was between us and Sasha, so at least we had some privacy from her.

'How's your tea?' Oliver asked me out of the blue, causing my eyes to shoot to his in confusion. His decision to play with me in the kitchen had well and truly distracted me from my tea and he bloody well knew it.

How he expected me to answer when his finger was knuckle deep inside me I had no idea, but judging from his expectant expression he definitely wanted me to play along with his little game, and that meant I had to find my voice. 'Fine, thank you.'

His right eyebrow quirked, and with a subtle shift of his position he worked a second finger inside me, deep and high. 'Just fine?'

It was so much better than fine, it felt flipping incredible, but he was such an utter bastard for doing this to me here. But oh God, it felt soooo good.

Leaning my head closer to his, I gave in and lolled it onto his shoulder. 'It's amazing, *Sir*.' I added his title in a whispered breath so only we would hear, but he gave me an appreciative nod in response. 'Best "tea" I've ever had,' I added breathily.

Using our closeness, he nuzzled in by my ear again and

333

placed a kiss on the sensitive skin of my neck. 'Hmm, that's a much better description. Now, stay silent and grip the counter, Robyn, because I'm going to make you come.'

Oh jeez-us. I'd wondered if he'd take it this far. Secretly I'd been hoping that he would tease me, maybe take me close to the edge, but then sweep me into his arms and dash off to my room to finish the job with some privacy. But no. Apparently Oliver had no such morals, and this was happening right here and now.

His fingers kept up their perfect strokes, and his thumb continued to deliciously tease my clit, but I honestly think it was the burning intensity in his stare that finally sent me over the edge, because Oliver was looking at me as if I were the only woman on this entire planet, like I was the sole focus of his existence and his very reason for being.

He was looking at me as if he loved me.

The sight of such emotion flowing from his denim blue eyes was enough to break me down, and as I gripped the counter for dear life as my body jerked with release, I kept my eyes locked with his and silently rode out the overwhelming orgasm that swept through my body.

'So beautiful,' Oliver murmured. I wasn't sure if he was referring to me, or the sight of me climaxing for him, but either way didn't really matter, because he looked just as blissed out as I felt, even though he hadn't achieved his own release.

He hadn't said the "love" words that had seemed to be pouring from his expression, but then again, neither had I, and I knew for sure now that I definitely was in love with him. Perhaps that declaration would be better saved for when we were in private somewhere, perhaps before a sweet, romantic interlude, and not here, with Sasha just a few feet away, and my kinky man touching me up regardless of the company.

Pulling in a breath to recover, I released my tight hold on the counter and glanced down at his groin, smiling at the predictably large bulge there. 'Perhaps you should reconsider staying over?' I murmured, before lowering my voice even more, and taking a gentle hold of his cock through his trousers. 'Then I could sort this out for you.'

A hissed breath escaped his lips, and Oliver briefly closed his eyes as if considering my offer. With a small moan, he blinked his eyes open and removed my hand from his crotch. 'I'd love to, but I really can't, *cariño.*' Glancing at his watch, he frowned and stood from the stool. 'In fact, I should get going.'

Sasha was still reading in the lounge, so I dragged up every last shred of my self-control and forced my wobbly, post-orgasmic legs to walk with him to the door.

Considering he'd just made me come right there in the same room as Sasha, I would have thought that Oliver had had his fun for the night, but no. He proceeded to press me up against the wall right in her direct line of vision, and kiss the living hell out of me until I was panting and utterly desperate for him to change his mind and stay the night.

'Are you sure you don't want to stay?' I whispered, my voice sounding just as needy as my body felt.

'You know I'd love to, but you wanted the night alone. You can do this,' he reassured me, and I knew he was right. As much as I was proving to him that I was fine, I was also proving it to myself.

'But I'll see you on Friday and I'll definitely stay over then.'

Seeing an opportunity to prove Chloe wrong about her earlier concerns over Oliver, I raised my eyebrows expectantly. 'Or maybe I could stay at yours?'

His reply was immediate, and not what I wanted to hear. 'That might be problematic,' he paused, rubbing at his chin as if thinking. 'I have some decorators in at the moment. My house is a like a building site.'

His apparent attempt at avoidance made panic curl in

my stomach for a second, before I swallowed it down. No! I would not let Chloe and her stupid comments wheedle their way into my head and ruin what I had with this incredible man.

Glancing briefly at Sasha, I saw her giving me a "keep going" motion with her hands, so I shrugged and gave him a playful smile. 'I don't mind a bit of mess.' Leaning closer, I placed a hand on his thigh – the one furthest from Sasha so she couldn't see – then dug my fingernails in and dragged my touch higher towards his groin.

'We could have some fun christening the rooms inside your house ...' I leaned back and gave him a flirtatious grin, and was thrilled to see that his pupils had dilated with desire as he flicked a look towards Sasha – who was apparently once again fascinated by the magazine in her hands – and back at me.

'Determined to see my house, aren't you?' he asked in a tone that I simply couldn't decipher, so I just shrugged and nodded.

Just when I thought he was going to try and deter me again, he drew in a breath, and nodded. 'It's a deal then. Friday we'll skip the club and I'll cook for you at mine.'

Oh! Dinner, too? Well, that was an even better outcome than I had anticipated!

He turned to leave, but suddenly spun on his heel and dragged me into his arms. 'If you need me tonight just call, OK?' It seemed as though he was torn between giving in and staying, and abiding by my request.

I nodded. Then with one more thorough kiss to seal his statement, he was gone.

Turning away from the door with a goofy smile on my face, I found my expression mirrored in Sasha's face as she jumped up and jigged from foot to foot and clapped. 'You're going to his place!' she exclaimed gleefully.

I knew she'd been listening in, but felt a sizzling blush rush to my cheeks at the realisation that my savvy mate had probably been just as observant of what had gone on between Oliver and me behind the kitchen counter.

## Chapter Forty-five

### Robyn

As much as I was telling everyone that I was fine and dandy now, I couldn't deny the fact that I was immensely relieved not to be going to Club Twist when Friday finally came around. Even knowing that Dominic wouldn't be there, the idea of walking through the front doors gave me goose bumps. I *would* go back there, eventually, but for tonight I was very happy with the prospect of seeing where Oliver lived.

At six-thirty that night, I found myself on a very fancy street in Holland Park being helped from Oliver's car by the man himself. Wow. This area was posh. After I'd had a quick glance around and gawked at the beautiful three-storey townhouses that surrounded us, he ushered me towards a midnight blue front door and into a warmly lit hallway.

'Come on in.'

Now we had some light above us I could properly see Oliver for the first time since he'd picked me up outside my flat half an hour ago. My man looked good … He was dressed in faded blue jeans which were snug in all the right places, a white polo shirt that made his tan even more obvious, and a black blazer. I rarely saw him so dressed down; he was usually fully suited and booted, so I'd named this style his Barcelona look, because he'd worn similar outfits all week over there, often without the jacket, due to the heat.

His hair was damp, presumably from a recent shower, and as we entered his house I noticed that he immediately kicked off his shoes and socks. Hmm. All in all, it was a rather pleasant view to start the weekend off in style.

Glancing at my legs, he gave a wolfish grin. 'Keep your boots on, if you like,' he murmured, but from the tone of his voice it sounded more like a demand than an offer, and I smiled shyly and glanced down at my legs. I'd decided to wear the new boots he had bought me, and had paired them with a short skirt, stockings, and a newly purchased suspender belt; which I was hoping he might rather like when he discovered it later. I was also wearing my new collar, but that was currently hidden behind a thin lacy scarf, so he wouldn't see it until I chose to remove the scarf and make my big reveal.

As my eyes skimmed his space for the first time, practically all that filled it were paint pots, ladders and dust sheets. Seeing me looking at the mess that surrounded us he grinned and shrugged. 'This is one of the reasons I haven't invited you over. I'm having the whole place redone and the work is taking a little longer than anticipated.' He seemed completely relaxed, and the slight lingering concern I'd had from Chloe's words about the blonde she'd seen him with at her office vanished as I slid out of my light summer jacket, choosing to keep my scarf on for now.

'The hall is the worst,' Oliver commented, breaking me from my curious assessment and drawing my attention back to him. 'Once I knew you were coming, I moved all the paint out here so at least the other rooms are usable, even if not particularly pretty.'

Given all that we had now done together, it was silly to be nervous, but being here in his private space for the first time had given me butterflies. Taking a breath to try to settle my nerves, I noticed a delicious smell in the air. 'Something smells good.'

'Thank you. I've got Spanish chicken cooking in the slow cooker. My mother's recipe. Come through to the kitchen with me and I'll get us some drinks.'

## Oliver

Things with Robyn had been so easy. Right from the start, being with her had always just felt ... right, somehow. But tonight was different. She was different. Interestingly enough, Robyn actually seemed nervous, which was not something I'd seen in her since we'd settled into our more stable relationship. Perhaps it was the newness of our surroundings that was unsettling her, so I opted to try to get things back onto our usual, comfortable companionship by turning to the tried and tested method of relaxation – alcohol.

'Wine? Soft drink, or gin and tonic?'

'Gin, please.' Robyn's gaze darted around my kitchen with curiosity.

'Coming up. Make yourself at home,' I offered, as I lifted two glasses from a cupboard.

After I had poured the gin, I glanced across at Robyn, who was now at the far end of my kitchen diner, poking around and doing exactly as I had requested – making herself at home.

I was hoping that, one day soon, this *would* be her home. Not that I'd brought that subject up yet, but since the situation with Dominic I had been going out of my mind with worry every time that she and I were apart. It might be viewed as too soon by some people, but I was old enough to know that a connection like ours didn't come around often.

If we lived together my mind would certainly be at ease, but there was still one rather large hurdle that I needed to sort out before that could ever happen. Hopefully I could resolve it in the morning.

Brushing off my thoughts, I went to the fridge to get the tonic water. As I put the finishing touches to our drinks, Robyn left the far corner and worked her way around the kitchen, oohing and ahhing at various gadgets I owned and seeming to like the space as much as I did.

We were having Bombay Sapphire, my preferred gin, so I was serving it long over ice, with a slice of cucumber and a thin strip of lemon peel. Having prepared the garnishes, I pulled the ice tray from the fridge, jerked it to free up the cubes, and popped two into each drink.

The crack of the ice as I broke it from the tray caused Robyn to abruptly turn in my direction, and we both paused, staring at the tray of ice for a second. One of our most memorable times together had included ice cubes; back in Barcelona, when I had teased her entire body with them until she'd come apart in my arms. My groin hardened at the memory, and I bit my lower lip as erotic images from that night flooded my mind.

Glancing up at Robyn, I found her frozen to the spot, halfway across the kitchen towards me and also staring at the ice tray in my hand.

Her cheeks flushed, and I watched with pleasure as she raised a hand and gently rubbed at her lips – the exact same spot where I had first touched the ice cube against her body all those weeks ago.

Robyn let out a small gasp, then shifted her legs, squeezing her thighs together and squirming briefly on the spot as if suddenly aroused. Very aroused, if the deepening colour in her cheeks and ever-expanding pupils were anything to go by.

There she was.

This was the beautiful, expressive girl I had come to know since we'd been together. Finally, she was back in the present with me, and her nerves from earlier seemed to have passed.

I'd been relatively gentle with her since the Dominic situation, but perhaps tonight was the night to get things back on track properly, as she had requested. She had gone to all the trouble of wearing stockings and those new knee-high boots, after all.

I'd already put some cubes into the drinks, but I decided to tease my girl anyway. 'Ice?' I asked, my tone dropping to a low husk.

She was well aware that I'd already iced the drinks, and her eyes darted to mine. I watched in pleasure as she licked her lips and performed a slow, sensual nod.

'Yes, please. *Sir.*' As she spoke, she casually removed the scarf at her neck, drawing my eyes down so I saw her new collar nestled around her neck. I actually felt my breath catch in my throat at the significance of the moment. *Mine.*

I'd thought that sight was breath-taking, but then Robyn upped it, by dropping a hand to her skirt and inching the fabric up at one side. It looked an innocent enough move at first, like she was scratching an itch or something, until I caught a glimpse of a suspender belt at the top of her thigh.

*Dios.* Her collar was a hot enough sight, but to combine it with stockings, suspenders, and those boots? It seemed my little Robyn had gone to some lengths to prepare a special treat for me. And what a treat it was.

I felt like the luckiest man on earth as I looked at her. She was so amazing. So perfect. My nostrils flared as I drew in a long, deep breath to try to calm myself. I believe the English phrase is "bring it on", and as I left the drinks untouched on the counter and advanced on her, that was exactly what I intended to do.

# Chapter Forty-six

## Robyn

A bang woke me, and I sat up in bed and rubbed at my sleepy eyes trying to work out what the noise had been. It was dark, so presumably we'd ended up accidentally falling asleep after our deliciously tiring sexy time. Thoughts of what Oliver had done to me had me grinning, and glancing at my discarded boots and suspender belt – from the response they'd created in Oliver, those items would be getting a *lot* more use in future – but the further sounds of shuffling and movements from downstairs made my ears perk up again.

Thinking it might be an intruder, I quickly looked towards Oliver to see if he was awake.

His eyes were indeed open, but he didn't look nearly as startled as I felt. In fact, he seemed to be resigned to something as he sat up and grimaced, before drawing in a long, deep breath and closing his eyes in apparent frustration. 'This is just great.'

I was about to ask what he meant, when a woman's voice floated up the stairs. 'Oliver? Darling? I'm home, are you in?'

*Darling?*

Who the fuck was that? And she'd definitely said *I'm home,* indicating that she lived here. Suddenly Chloe's words of warning were ringing in my mind again – how she'd seen him looking very cosy with a blonde, and how he'd had his arm around her – and I had a sudden feeling that I may have been well and truly tricked.

He *did* have a girlfriend, or wife! Why else would there be a woman downstairs proclaiming she was home, and calling him darling?

After all his talk about not tolerating lies he had outright lied to me. The hypocritical fuck!

I was such a gullible idiot. Chloe had told me what she'd seen, but I had blindly ignored it, choosing to trust my gut and believe that Oliver was being honest with me.

Leaping from under the covers, I had to stifle a yelp at the faint twinge of pain from my healing wounds. I turned my most affronted glare to Oliver while also pointing an accusing finger at him. 'You fucking liar! You live with someone!' I dragged the sheet from the bed, wrapped it tightly around myself, and glared at him as the first sting of tears hit the backs of my eyes. 'I asked you outright when we first met, and you lied to my face!'

Ignoring my outburst, Oliver shook his head in irritation. 'Typical, this is the night she chooses to come home early,' he muttered under his breath, but it was loud enough for me to hear, and only acted to further heighten my fury.

Oliver at least had the grace to look a little awkward as he climbed from the bed and checked his watch, but he didn't try to deny anything, which just sent my anger sky-rocketing. 'Fucking hell! You utter bastard! You're married, aren't you?'

His expression suddenly changed to that of his dominant persona. He stood there, stark naked, with his legs splayed wide, and arms crossed over his bare chest as he stared at me intently. Even under these horrific circumstances it was a bloody impressive sight. 'No, and watch your language, Robyn.'

'Fuck off!' I screamed, really close to either crying my eyes out, or smacking him around the head. 'Does she know about me?' I demanded, not sure why it was important, but somehow finding the words leaving my mouth anyway.

Oliver's shoulders slumped. 'No.'

'Fucking arsehole.' Acting purely on impulse, I tore the sheet from the bed and spun on my heel, wrenching the bedroom door open as I decided to set his wife, girlfriend,

344

or whatever she might be, straight about his low-life cheating ways, then get the hell out of here.

'Stop swearing! Robyn, come back. Let me explain. You don't want to go down there yet, believe me.'

Ignoring his call, I hiked the sheet up around my knees and charged down the stairs towards the kitchen and the noise of clanking crockery. My bare feet slapped across the tiled hallway as I barrelled towards the door. With my palm outstretched, I hit the door at full pelt, bursting into the brightly lit space only to skid to a very sudden, and rather shocked halt.

*Oh. My. God.*

Instead of finding Oliver's wronged woman as I had envisioned, I had instead come face to face with four, no wait, five smartly dressed women. All of whom appeared to be around their mid-sixties, and all of whom were staring at me with rapt fascination.

'Oh ...! Hello, and who might you be?' asked the woman currently holding a coffee pot mid-pour as she looked at me with a mix of open curiosity and shock.

'I ... uhhh ... sorry ...' I tried to reverse out of the room, but suddenly my back bumped into something warm and unrelenting as I realised that Oliver had joined me downstairs.

'Good evening, Val. You're home early,' Oliver remarked dryly from just behind me.

Val? Who the hell was Val? Leaning close behind me, Oliver gave a wry chuckle. 'I see you've made quite an impact on my aunt and her friends.'

Aunt? This was his aunt? Looking again at the woman in the centre I realised that if I ignored the dyed blonde bob, I could see a definite family resemblance. Facially, she looked a lot like his sisters that I had met in Spain, except considerably older. *Oh fuck! It really is his fucking aunt!*

'Ladies. You're all looking rather smart this evening,'

345

Oliver continued smoothly, nodding politely to the gathered crowd with his usual impeccable manners.

'Shame I can't say the same about you, eh, Oliver?' his aunt murmured, as a wicked glint twinkled in her eye and a grin threatened to crack on her lips.

'Oh, I don't know, Val, I rather like the view,' the woman next to her said, elbowing Oliver's aunt in the ribs and grinning at something beside me.

Noticing that all the eyes had left me, and were now focused just to my right, I glanced across and saw to my horror that Oliver had obviously hightailed it down the stairs after me, because he was dressed in just a pair of black boxer shorts. As well as being practically naked, he was sporting his tousled post-sex hair, which, combined with his muscular physique, made him look well and truly sinful. Holy smokes! He was going to give one of them a heart attack swanning around like that.

Clearing his throat, he ignored his aunt's pointed remark and slung an arm around my bare shoulders, pulling me firmly into his side and leaning causally onto the doorframe. 'How was bridge club, did any of you win?'

God, this was bloody surreal. I was dressed in nothing but a sheet, Oliver was in his boxers, and yet he was calmly greeting these women and discussing bridge! He sounded completely unaffected by the entire situation.

He might not be acknowledging my fidgeting verbally, but as I shuffled yet again on the cold marble floor, he gently stilled me by gripping my shoulder tighter and giving a small squeeze.

His contact went some way to reassuring me, but glancing at the clock I saw that it was only nine-thirty in the evening, so it really couldn't be more obvious what we'd just been up to. My cheeks were absolutely burning by this point, and the only thing stopping me from turning and dashing back upstairs was the fact that my feet were tangled in the bloody sheet and I'd probably end up dropping it and flashing them all my naked arse as I ran away.

'Forget bridge, Oliver! Aren't you going to introduce us to your ... um ... friend?'

He slid his arm down so it now rested around my waist, positioned himself slightly behind me, and settled his palm on my stomach, pulling me flush against his body. 'This is Robyn,' he said simply, his voice soft with an affection that he then backed up by placing just the smallest, briefest kiss on my temple.

I saw his aunt's eyebrows rise at the gesture, before Oliver indicated to the room with his free hand.

'And this is not a phantom wife or girlfriend as you assumed, but my father's sister, Valarie, or Val for short. And these are her bridge friends, Edith, Margaret, Caroline, and Joan.' He hadn't introduced me as his girlfriend, but his obvious display of affection was rather pleasing, even if it was in front of an audience.

Several of the ladies murmured a polite "hello" while still openly gawking at us, but I was frozen to the spot in shock. I mean, as far as first times meeting a family member of your new man can go, this surely would go down in history as one of the most disastrous.

'What do you mean "wife or girlfriend"?' Valarie asked with a comical frown.

'Robyn heard you come in and assumed I hadn't been entirely truthful with her. She jumped to the conclusion that perhaps I was married.'

Valarie chuckled, and rolled her eyes. 'The chance would be a fine thing. He's so absorbed with work he doesn't even date!' Pouring the final coffee, she looked up at us again with an inquisitive tilt to her head. 'Although perhaps our boy is finally changing his ways?'

Beside me, Oliver made a small agreeing hum in the back of his throat. 'Yes, it would certainly appear so.

Perhaps Robyn and I will go and get dressed.'

'Oh! Don't go yet!' Valarie seemed exceptionally keen to keep us in the room, whereas I couldn't wait to get out of there. God this was just so mortifying.

'Don't panic, *Tía*, we'll return once we are ... more appropriately attired.'

*Tía*? I thought he said her name was Valarie? Seeing my confused look, he grinned. '*Tía* is the term for aunt in Spanish. In my family we also use it as an affectionate title. Much like you might say auntie.' Looking across at his aunt again, Oliver bowed his head slightly. 'We will be back shortly.'

'Oh good! I'll make another pot of coffee.'

Forget coffee. I was going to need a quadruple rum to recover from the shock of this encounter.

With some difficulty, Oliver steered my frozen body back out of the kitchen. He guided me towards the stairs with a chuckle as I grabbed the handrail and let out a horrified groan.

'I can't believe that just happened!'

'I did warn you not to go downstairs straight away.'

Finally finding my tongue, I licked my dry lips and stabbed my finger into his solid chest. 'You said you didn't live with anyone!'

Shaking his head in amusement, he crossed his arms over his bare chest and leaned back against the wall, looking like the picture of calm. 'No. If I recall correctly, you asked if I was married, or had a girlfriend, which I am not, and do not, so I replied honestly with a simple "no". You never actually asked if I lived with anyone.'

As he ran a hand through his hair, his shoulders sagged a little and he shrugged, seeing my need for further explanation. 'When you said Chloe had seen me with a blonde in her office, I knew exactly what you were referring to, but at that point things hadn't developed between you and I, so I didn't feel the need to explain myself. Val is investing some of her savings, and I was with her that day as a guiding voice.'

'Oh my God, Oliver, why didn't you just tell me then that it was your aunt, and that you lived with her?' I grumbled, wondering how I was ever going to look the woman in the eye again.

He stopped abruptly and turned to me with a frown. 'I don't live with my aunt, she lives with me, and it's only temporary while the sale of her house goes through. My father's side of the family are mostly still based in England. Unfortunately, my uncle died a little over three years ago now. At first *Tía* didn't want to go back to their house, because it was too full of memories, but she didn't want to sell it, either, so she's been travelling and staying with various family members. She's been with me for the past six months and has finally decided to sell up and buy a small flat. The sale is taking longer than predicted to go through.' Scrubbing at the back of his neck, he gave me an embarrassed smile. 'And the reason I didn't tell you is obvious. I'm over forty; it's a little embarrassing to tell you I share a house with my aunt.'

He was over forty? Well, even if this did go down as a nightmare first encounter with his aunt, at least I was finally getting a clue about his real age.

'As embarrassing as having me run into a roomful of her and her friends wearing nothing but a flimsy sheet?' I blurted, mortification sweeping me as I relived the memory of his aunt and her friends staring at me as I charged into the kitchen.

Oliver snickered and pushed off from the wall to stalk towards me. 'Well, no, now you come to mention it, it wouldn't have been as embarrassing as that,' he replied with a deep chuckle, apparently loving my discomfort.

Rolling my eyes, I slumped forwards and rested my head onto his chest which was still shaking with his laughter. 'So you're over forty, huh?' I murmured teasingly, and in response I saw Oliver grin and roll his eyes.

'Hmm. I let that slip, didn't I?

'You did,' I agreed with a wiggle of my eyebrows.

'I said I was old enough to know better.'

'So do we have to keep playing this game, or are you just going to tell me how much over forty you are?'

'I'm fourteen years older than you. Happy?' I was twenty-seven, so that made him forty-one. I wasn't far off with my guess of thirty-eight, then.

'Sure it won't make you change your mind about me?' he enquired, his tone dropping and a flicker of concern crossed his brows.

'No. I've told you that before.'

We stood there like that for several seconds, then I groaned as the events of the kitchen flooded my mind again. 'God, I can't believe I just did that!'

Oliver eased me away from his body and slowly shook his head. 'No, neither can I.' Crossing his arms over his chest, he lowered his head slightly so he was looking at me through his lashes. As I took in his dominant expression, awareness zinged through my body. Woah. Where had this come from?

'I think perhaps you need a reminder about our bond of trust, hmm?'

Swallowing loudly, I pulled the sheet around me. 'What... what do you mean?'

'What do you mean, *Sir*,' he corrected me.

My eyes widened, and my mouth went dry as anticipation sizzled in my belly. God, I loved it when he was like this.

'I told you I wasn't married, but you still assumed the worst of me, *and* I asked you not to rush downstairs immediately when you heard Val, but you ignored me. Both of these errors require a correction.'

A correction? He hadn't used that term with me before,

350

and I frowned. 'What's a correction, Sir?' I asked in a nervous whisper, making sure to use his title this time.

'A correction is a punishment. It will remind you not to make the same mistake again.' He had a wicked glint in his eye as he took my hand and led me towards the stairs.

Well, this was unexpected, but undeniably a relief. I'd worried that the situation with Dominic might have affected the Dom/sub bond between Oliver and me, because we hadn't done a scene since the abduction, and he hadn't properly assumed that role with me, either. Even earlier, when he'd teased me with the ice, it had been mostly vanilla, but from his body language now, things certainly seemed to be looking up.

As we made our way back downstairs half an hour later, I winced at the remaining sting in my buttocks, then grinned broadly. The moment we had got back to his bedroom, Oliver had produced a flogger from within his wardrobe, and proceeded to demonstrate to me exactly how skilled he was with the toy. My shocked yelps had been smothered by the pillow below my face, and Oliver had somehow managed to make each flick of the leather tabs almost completely silent. It had been a rather pleasurable punishment, really, but when I'd laid there begging for him to make me come Oliver had grinned wickedly and then denied me. So, basically, I'd discovered that I was not a fan of orgasm denial, and Oliver had effectively made his point.

Knowing his aunt and her friends were downstairs had made the whole scene even more erotic, and I couldn't deny that I rather liked the feeling of naughtiness that surrounded me as we ventured back towards the kitchen, both still aroused.

Just as I was about to push the kitchen door open, Oliver gave my bum a gentle squeeze, causing a shot of pain to flash across my skin, and eliciting an aroused gasp of surprise from my lips.

He grinned, apparently loving me in this unsatisfied state, and jerked his chin towards the kitchen. 'Just so you know, I wasn't trying to hide you from Val, I was planning on introducing you to her in the morning over breakfast.' Suppressing a laugh, he rolled his eyes. 'I think your entrance trumped any introduction I could have made, though.'

I groaned, happy that he wanted me to meet his aunt, but absolutely mortified at how that meeting had occurred. 'Come on, let's go in, she's going to love you.'

'How can you be so sure?'

'Because I could see how excited she was. Valarie hasn't seen me with a woman for a very long time, so don't be surprised if she's a little over the top with you.'

As we entered the kitchen, I saw that Valarie's bridge friends had left, thankfully. From the keen smile on her face, and the half-full coffee cups scattered around the kitchen, I suspected she had chucked them out so she could focus on getting the gossip from Oliver and me, but I didn't say anything.

I was still too embarrassed to initiate conversation, but Valarie brushed it off, and pulled me into a tight hug, clearly very excited to meet me.

'Let's move to the lounge for our drinks, shall we?' Oliver and I followed behind her, choosing to sit in the end of the room where the sofas were clustered together within a sea of dust sheets. The painters had at least left the rooms usable, even if they didn't look particularly great yet.

Valarie clicked her tongue and looked to Oliver and me. 'I left the milk jug on the counter. Would one of you grab it while I pour, please?'

Keen to send Sasha and Chloe a text telling them that I had finally solved the mystery of the woman he'd been with at Chloe's work, I jumped up and went to get the milk.

I rushed out a text message telling the girls about Valarie, and that everything was fine, and also mentioning that his house was fricking incredible. I was just returning from the kitchen when I overheard Valarie's voice saying my name, so I paused outside the room to listen.

'Robyn. It's such a lovely name. So, where did you meet her?'

'At the club.' A shiver ran over my skin at his mention of the club, but I quickly contained the images of Dominic that flew to my mind, and pushed them away. Oliver's reply surprised me, because I wouldn't have expected his family to be aware of Club Twist, or what went on there. Perhaps he'd just told her it was a bar, or nightclub?

'Oh.' Valarie's voice audibly tightened. 'I see.' From her tone, I could only assume she was well aware of what type of club her nephew was part owner of. How weird. It was a sex club, for goodness' sakes. There was no way I'd tell my family something like that, let alone an aunt who I lived with.

I think my parents would faint if they knew where I now chose to spend my Friday nights, so it was definitely a secret best kept to myself.

Sneaking closer, I looked through the tiny gap in the door, fairly certain that I couldn't been seen from there.

Huffing out an impatient breath, Oliver shook his head. 'Don't look like that, *Tía*. It's not like you imagine at all. Besides, Robyn's a writer. She was in the club on a research visit and I agreed to answer some of her questions. We got to know each other, and things went from there.'

Which was all completely true, although I noticed that he didn't tell her I was now a fully paid up member, thanks to Sasha's generosity. There was a pause, then Valarie's face softened again. 'She's very pretty, Oliver.'

Oliver bowed his head for a second, then looked across at his aunt with an uncharacteristic blush on his cheeks.

'She is. She's also a perfect match for me.' A smile broke on his lips which warmed me to my core, and transformed him to his utterly handsome best.

There was another pause, and I was just about to re-enter when Oliver sighed heavily. 'I can see the look you're giving me. If you have something to say, *Tía*, just say it.'

A tingle of worry skittered across the hairs on the back of my neck as I craned closer to listen. 'I ... well, I was just going to say that you seem very happy. Don't let memories of Abi ruin it, will you?'

Abi? That was the ex he had mentioned when we'd spoken about our previous relationships. He'd said it was just lust, not love, but from the way his aunt was talking it was clear that the relationship had been important to him. My stomach did a nervous flip, because the tone of Val's voice was really strange. Had he loved Abi?

'Abi was a very long time ago.' The dismissive coldness to Oliver's tone when he replied shocked me, and made goose pimples appear on my arms.

'I know, but ...'

'No buts. This conversation is over.'

The mention of Abi was certainly sparking some serious reactions from Oliver, and I felt decidedly uneasy.

'I'm sorry, I didn't mean to bring a downer on your good mood. So, you and Robyn ... it's serious, then?' His aunt's tone was lighter now, as if trying to cajole him into a better frame of mind. I was aware of the fact that I had probably been away too long, but there was no way I could burst in without first hearing the answer to *that* question.

'I'm introducing her to you, what do you think?'

'There's no need for that tone, Oliver.' Valarie made a dismissive tutting sound with her tongue. 'I think you look happier than I've seen for a very long time.'

'I am,' Oliver agreed, his voice sounding warm and raspy again, and making me relax my stiff shoulders. 'And yes, it's serious.'

Hearing him tell his aunt it was serious gave me a warm feeling in my belly, and as I joined them in the room I placed the milk jug down, sat beside him again, and immediately picked up his hand and gave it a firm squeeze.

I still had unanswered questions about why Abi was such an intense subject for him, but for now at least, I was content. The mystery of the blonde had been solved, and my questions about Abi could wait.

## Chapter Forty-seven

## Robyn

'Hmmm. I could get used to waking up to this view.'

Oliver's murmured words fluttered into my mind, breaking me from my drowsy state and making me blink lazily.

I was warm, cosy, and wrapped in the scent of Oliver's aftershave which lingered on the duvet, and the man in question was currently rubbing his nose back and forth over the tip of mine.

I grinned, absorbing the lovely attention with a satisfied sigh. Blinking again, I realised there was one thing wrong with the scene – he wasn't in the bed with me, but standing beside it. I frowned when I noticed that not only was it still dark outside the curtains, but Oliver was almost fully dressed, too.

He smelled shower fresh, and looked perky and wide awake, which was a far cry from how I felt. Oliver stood back and continued to button up his shirt, but his eyes remained locked on mine.

'What time is it?' My voice was groggy, and as I cleared my throat I saw Oliver grinning at me.

'Five-thirty.'

*Five-thirty?* '*What?* It's Saturday! Are you crazy? It's still the middle of the night!' Flopping back onto my pillow, I tried to pull the duvet over my head only to have it ripped away from me again as Oliver chuckled loudly.

'Not so fast, *cariño.*'

My fists gripped the remaining sliver of the blanket in a desperate attempt to keep my warm cocoon, but Oliver was ruthless, tickling the soles of my feet until I was giggling so hard that I let go and allowed him to haul me into his arms. 'I have to pop to the office briefly this morning for a video meeting with a client in China. We're working on their time schedule, hence my early start.'

The feel of his warmth as he gripped me to his strong chest was all it took to get me to stop my wriggling, and I flopped against his crisp shirt with a sigh.

'You can stay in bed, if you wish, but I'm not sure how long I'll be, so I was going to give you a lift home to save you battling the trains. And facing a further grilling from Val,' he added with a grin. 'It's your choice.'

Hmm. Staying in bed was tempting, but Oliver had a point; as much as I liked his aunt, I'd only just met her, so I wouldn't feel comfortable chilling in his house while he wasn't there. Besides, he was right about the journey from his house to my flat – it took four different line changes on the Underground, and was a bit of a nightmare. Being in his bed alone wouldn't be nearly as much fun, either, so a lift would be easier, and I was awake now.

After pondering it for a second, I nodded. 'OK. I'll take the lift. Thanks.'

Oliver placed a kiss on my nose and nodded. 'Good. I'll come to your place as soon as I'm done at work.'

'Let's grab a quick breakfast first. Here, put this on just in case Val is up and about.' Seeing how bloody early it was, I highly doubted that she would be, but I accepted his offering of a plain black T-shirt for me, and as I slid it on, he looped a maroon tie around his neck and knotted it with swift perfection.

'I don't think I can eat yet. It's too early,' I grumbled, thinking longingly about the extra three hours' sleep I would have been getting if I'd slept at my own place last night. Mind you, I wouldn't have fallen asleep in Oliver's arms, so I think it was worth the sacrifice. Just.

'I also have coffee,' he offered helpfully as he held a hand out for me to take. 'Real coffee, from freshly ground beans.'

'Now you're talking my language.' Ignoring his outstretched arm, I jerked my thumb at the en suite. 'I need to pee, I'll meet you in the kitchen.'

After I'd done my business, brushed my teeth, and had a quick wash I joined Oliver in the kitchen and found him adding some jam to the top of several slices of toast.

He greeted me with another grin, and nodded towards one of the tall stools at the breakfast bar. 'Perfect timing.'

Placing down the plate, he didn't sit on the stool beside me as I'd thought he would, but instead remained standing and gently pushed his way between my legs.

He picked up a slice of toast and held it to my lips, and even though I hadn't thought I was hungry, the sugary-sweet smell had my mouth salivating in no time. I took a bite, then Oliver did the same, the two of us sharing the slice as he remained firmly planted between my legs.

We were just coming to the end of the second slice, when Oliver's free hand lowered and rested on my bare thigh. He was still feeding me toast, but as I took another bite, he began to trail his other hand up my leg and under the hem of the T-shirt.

Seeing as he'd dragged me out of bed, I wasn't wearing any knickers yet, and Oliver's eyes widened as he discovered this fact. 'You're going commando?'

I nodded my reply, and in response Oliver brushed his fingertips across my landing strip then briefly dipped lower to my core, and I couldn't help but suck in a shocked gasp.

'Did that hurt? Are you sore from yesterday, or are your bruises still painful?' he asked, concern flitting over his face as he discarded the toast on the plate and hunkered down so he could look directly in my eyes.

The bruises from Dominic's whip were still visible as yellowy stripes around my midsection, but had mostly healed now, apart from one where the whip had gone deeper and torn the skin. The scab on that one was itchy as hell.

But today's pain and sudden intake of breath had

nothing to do with them. Today's pain was a good kind; it was the lingering feeling of where Oliver had been buried deep and hard within me last night, and I couldn't help but bite my lip as I shook my head. 'My bruises are fine. And I'm not sore from yesterday's session, just a bit sensitive,' I replied with a blush, my core clenching as I remembered his games with the ice cubes, and just how hard he'd taken me against his kitchen wall and again in his bed.

'Let's see if I can make it better.' He was still gently exploring between my legs with his fingers. Then, before I could even register what he was doing, Oliver crouched down and ran a gentle lick of his tongue up my core.

'What about Valarie?' If his aunt walked in now, I'd die of embarrassment.

He dismissed my concerns with a silencing "shush" against my core, and my nerve endings exploded with pleasure. It only took a couple of desire-filled seconds for me to give up trying to reason with him. Instead, I clutched at his shoulder as a delighted gasp tore up my throat. I certainly hadn't expected this to be part of my breakfast.

Oliver's tongue massaged over my slightly sore flesh, soothing my opening, teasing my clit, and licking and sucking every single spot in between.

'Oliver ... more ... please ...' It was heavenly, and regardless of my tenderness, I wanted more. I lolled back on the kitchen surface, panting, and as he stood back up again I heard the sound of his zipper lowering.

Lifting my head, I watched him palm his erection as he nudged his way back between my thighs again. 'Let me know if it's too much,' he murmured as the broad head of his cock brushed against my needy opening.

It was always too much with Oliver; too much sensation, too many feelings, too much to comprehend, but that was what made it so overwhelmingly good.

The stool was almost the perfect height, but I tilted my hips to help him get the correct angle, and sat myself up again. Nodding his appreciation, Oliver began easing forwards just a little as he started to push inside.

Oliver took his time, giving me each inch in a painstakingly slow manoeuvre that had me clawing at his arms in desperation and trying to speed him up by wrapping my legs around his waist. He was having none of it, though, and simply pushed my legs wider and continued in his unhurried pace until he was buried within me to the hilt.

Instead of starting to thrust, Oliver leaned around me, picked up a piece of toast, and lifted it to my mouth again. I was hot, horny, and filled with his dick and he wanted me to eat? A shocked giggle broke in my throat, and I shook my head. 'No, thank you. Your cock has me a little too distracted to eat.'

Oliver barked out a laugh, then took a bite of the toast and gave a gentle roll of his hips which hit every sensitive spot perfectly and had me moaning and wrapping my arms around his neck.

'Well here's our conundrum, because I need to eat, but I also need to fuck you,' he explained in a completely serious tone. 'My meeting this morning is very important, I can't miss it, and I need to leave soon, so we'll have to multi-task.'

Seriously? Judging from the look in his eyes, he was deadly serious. The toast was still hanging in front of my lips, so I hesitantly took a small nibble and was immediately rewarded with a thrust of his hips. Taking another bite got me the same result, and I groaned as I swallowed.

That was how he was going to play this, was it?

Over the next few minutes it became blindingly obvious that yes, it was exactly how Oliver was going to play it, and every bite of food I took was rewarded with a thrust of his hips. It was far less vigorous than last night, but with his skilled rolls, thrusts, and grinds, I was soon approaching a climax.

Oliver popped the final bite of toast into his mouth. After swallowing it, he leaned forwards and licked my lower lip, removing a trace of jam then kissing me deeply.

He shifted his hands to my hips, and his moves became more urgent – still gentle, but just a little quicker – and it was all I needed to send me over the edge. I suppressed my cry of pleasure by kissing him deeper and gripping at his shirt until it was a crumpled mess in my fists. Pleasure exploded in my system, and my channel clamped around him, and in response Oliver growled into my mouth and began to circle his hips before suddenly pressing forwards and stilling as I felt his cock twitch and jerk with his own release.

He worked us both down with several slow rolls of his hips then lifted his head so he could join our gaze. 'Well, that certainly beats eating breakfast at my desk,' he commented, his eyes twinkling wickedly. He grabbed some kitchen roll, gently eased himself from within me, wiped us both clean and zipped up his trousers again.

'Perhaps we should move you in, then I could enjoy mornings like this every day.' The words were said so casually that, at first, I found myself agreeing and nodding happily. But then it hit me what he'd actually said.

*Move me in?*

*What*? Woah. He couldn't mean that, could he?

I must have looked shocked, because Oliver gave a small shrug and made an attempt at straightening out his scrunched shirt. 'Don't look so panicked. It was just an idea, but I'm a patient man, I can wait.' As easily as he'd said it, Oliver seemed to dismiss the idea, turning from me and pulling on his jacket before moving our plate to the dishwasher.

'We'll leave in about ten minutes, so you've got time for a shower if you're quick.'

He continued to tidy around, wiping the counter and

humming under his breath, but as I wobbled my way upstairs to the bathroom I couldn't quite dismiss his comment as easily.

Once I'd had a speedy shower and dressed, I returned downstairs to find Oliver by the front door, fiddling with his phone. He didn't mention the "maybe we should move you in" comment again, and so neither did I, although I couldn't deny that it certainly lingered in my mind.

The drive back was surprisingly quick at this time of the morning, and when we arrived back at my flat Oliver insisted on walking me up to my door because it was still quite dark outside. I'd like to think this was just because he was a gentleman, but I was pretty sure it had more to do with how overwhelmingly protective he was of me these days.

Not that I was going to complain. After the Dominic situation, it was kinda nice to have my very own drop-dead gorgeous guardian angel.

Once again, Oliver laid one of his stunning parting kisses on me. Then he set off, leaving me in a lusty, loved-up bubble and staring at him as he went.

Oliver was halfway down the corridor when he turned and glanced back at me, grinning when he caught me watching him. 'Hey, before I forget …' He dug into his trouser pocket and pulled something out before tossing it in my direction. 'Catch!'

I did catch it, just, lurching forwards and engaging all my long-buried rounders skills to wrap my fingers around the small bundle. Looking down, I saw a small, folded leather pouch of some kind, and frowned. 'What is it?'

'A key to my place. If you're brave enough to face Valarie's non-stop inquisitions, then you're welcome round anytime.'

A key to his house? My eyes widened, and I tried desperately to suppress my excited squeal. A key was a big deal, wasn't it? A really big deal.

Looking back at Oliver, I saw a soft, affectionate smile on his lips. 'I wouldn't want to terrify you by asking you to move in again, so this will do for now, hmm?' He winked at me, and pushed open the door to the stairwell. 'See you soon, *cariño.*' Then, before I could even say anything about his gesture, he was gone, and I was left with just the sound of his shoes trotting down the steps.

My fist was still gripped around the pouch, and so, looking down, I saw a small press stud and flicked it open. Just as he had said, it contained a shiny silver key. The leather was some sort of purpose-made key holder, with a loop sewn into the top that held the key safely nestled inside.

*Well I never.* Grinning like a complete idiot, I carefully closed the pouch again and clutched it to my chest as I stepped inside my flat and closed the door. Looking down at the soft brown leather again, I let out a squeal of excitement and couldn't help but jig on the spot.

'Well, someone's certainly in a good mood. Oliver's aunt must be quite the entertainer,' Sasha commented in amusement as she wandered into the kitchen, wrapped in her dressing gown and pouring herself a coffee.

Chloe entered, too, but she was dressed in her work clothes. She wrestled Sasha aside and grabbed a mug. 'So the mystery blonde from the office is just his aunt?'

I looked at my concerned friends and nodded. 'Yep. His dad's sister. She's been staying with him for a few months, but he was too embarrassed to tell me.'

Sasha took a sip of her coffee and groaned her appreciation. 'Why?'

'Because he's a grown man and thought it sounded lame to say he shared a house with his aunt. He knows it was stupid to hide it.'

'Fair play, I guess. Is she nice?' Chloe asked, picking up a bagel.

'Yes, she was lovely. Thank goodness.'

'I'm really glad it's all cleared up.' Chloe nodded happily and left in the direction of her room to finish getting ready.

As I slid off my handbag I once again felt the key pouch in my hand and smiled.

'Has Oliver fucked that smile onto your face?' Sasha asked with a wicked chuckle as she handed me a steaming cup of java from the jug.

'Sasha!' I chided, amazed that she still managed to shock me with her crudity from time to time.

'What? I'm just saying he's a keeper if he makes you grin like that.'

My shock softened, and I found a soppy smile spreading on my face again. 'Yeah. I think he's a keeper, too,' I admitted, opening up the pouch again and letting the key dangle down.

Sasha looked at it, then at me, with confusion growing on her face.

'It's a key to his house. He just gave it to me.'

'Wow, Rob, this is big news!' She grabbed the key from me and examined it, before frowning. 'Holy shit! You're not moving in with him, are you?'

'No!' I shook my head, but couldn't stop his earlier words repeating in my mind. Nor could I deny that the idea definitely held an appeal for me. To be with him all the time would be amazing. But it was way too soon for that.

Wasn't it?

Of course it was. His words had just been a joke. Hadn't they? Brushing aside my multitude of unanswered questions, I snatched the key back and tucked it safely inside my handbag. 'It's just so I can visit anytime I like, that's all.'

'Hmm. Sure it is. Why live in his gigantic London mansion when you can share this tiny flat with me and

Chlo, huh?'

'Oh shush. I'm not moving in with him.' I dumped my bag down on the armchair, kicked off my shoes, and watched Sasha as she poured a bowl of cereal and sat on the sofa.

'I've seen how protective he is of you now. I give you a month, max, before you move in with him.' Sasha shovelled in a mouthful of cornflakes.

'You're moving out?' Chloe squawked as she came dashing back into the lounge with an empty tampon box in her hand.

'No!' I repeated. 'Oliver just gave me a key to his place, that's all.'

Chloe nodded, a smile spreading on her lips. 'Exciting!' She waggled the box and grimaced. 'I'd love to stay and gossip, but some of us have to work on Saturdays, and I just came on. The bathroom box is empty. Either of you got a tampon?'

We all shared our toiletry supplies, so whoever was organised enough to spot when we were running low would normally buy some more. It was usually me, but I couldn't recall having bought any recently, which would serve as a lesson to these two that they should also take some responsibility for the shopping every now and then.

'If the box is empty then we're out,' Sasha chipped in, helpfully stating the obvious.

I grabbed my handbag, chucked Chloe the emergency tampon I kept in the side pocket, and made a mental note to replace it before my period was due.

'Thanks, you're a life saver!' She clutched it dramatically to her chest and grinned at me. 'OK, I'm off to work. You two can carry on discussing Oliver and all the pervy things you do together.'

Giggling, I settled myself on the sofa beside Sasha, a blush spreading on my cheeks as my mind flitted back to my kitchen encounter with Oliver this morning. With his aunt in the same house, that had been a seriously risky session.

'Ugh. Stop it,' Sasha warned, screwing up her face.

Genuinely confused, I turned to her. 'Stop what?'

'You get this really dopey look on your face when you think about having sex with Oliver,' she informed me, raising her eyebrows knowingly. 'It's not appropriate when I'm trying to eat.'

*Did I?* A flush spread across my cheeks, but then Sasha was hardly one to talk. How many times had I had to endure her gushed morning-after chats when one of her numerous men had left the apartment? Countless times, that's how many, and believe me when I say that she never held back on the details. *Ugh.*

'I obviously learned that look from you, then,' I replied snappily, a little put out that I was obviously so transparent to everyone in my life.

'Then you're learning from the best.' She grinned as we bumped shoulders affectionately, then she put her empty bowl down. 'So, seeing as I've finished breakfast now, and we're on the subject of sex, care to share your most recent encounter with me?' she asked, her eyes twinkling with wicked glee.

My cheeks were already burning from this whole conversation, so I decided to just indulge her. 'He shagged me on the kitchen counter this morning while feeding me breakfast.'

'*Ho-ly-fuck-a-duck!*' Sasha slapped her hands to her cheeks dramatically. 'God, your sex life at the moment sounds bloody brilliant. I'm so jealous! It's been at least two weeks since I got laid.'

Two measly weeks? Her weekend had probably only been "dry" because all the shit that happened to me probably distracted her from finding someone to shag. Throwing my head back, I laughed hard, but then had to concede that my sex life was pretty fricking awesome at

366

the moment, and nodded with a grin. Sex had never been this good, and Oliver was incredible.

Checking that the key he'd given me was still nestled in my bag, I smiled. 'He's quite a force of nature.' I agreed, sipping my coffee and letting out a satisfied sigh.

# Chapter Forty-eight

## Robyn

Tonight would be my first trip back to Club Twist since Dominic had abducted me from the ladies' room. I was nervous, and doing anything and everything to distract myself from dwelling on it.

One of the things on my to-do list was replacing all the bathroom supplies. After loaning Chloe my emergency tampon last week, I'd purchased another box and was now busy replacing the supplies in my handbag, and the bathroom. Staring at the box, I frowned and rubbed at my chin anxiously. I couldn't remember the last time I'd had my period. I was usually the week before Chloe, but I definitely hadn't had a period that recently.

I jogged to my room, grabbed my phone and quickly checked my dates. Finding the "P" in last month's calendar – my way of noting my period cycle so I could keep track – I counted forwards to today's date.

Then I counted again.

And again.

Still staring at my calendar, I started to feel sick. I was eleven days late. How could I be eleven days late? How had I not realised? I supposed with the stress of the abduction it had just passed me by.

I dropped my phone and my hands immediately went to my belly and stroked it. Holy shit ... That was nearly two weeks, which presumably meant I was pregnant? It still felt flat, well, as flat as usual, but then it was far too early to be showing anyway.

My hands left my belly, and instead dug into my hair, tugging in frustration. I didn't want a baby! Not yet, anyway, but my cycle was normally pretty regular, so I really couldn't see any other reason that I was so late.

With trembling limbs, I rushed back to the bathroom

before dropping onto my knees in front of the cabinet. Rummaging through the contents, I searched desperately for a pregnancy test, hoping that there might be a spare one floating about from Sasha's past scares.

There was no test, though, and with Oliver arriving to pick me up for the night in about ten minutes, I didn't have time to go out and get one. *Shit.*

Oliver picked me up at seven on the dot, and after arriving at the club and seeing how nervous I was, he'd scooted me straight upstairs to his office so I could relax into the idea of being here again.

Not that I could relax. Oliver thought I was nervous about being back at the Club for the first time since my abduction, but God, how very wrong he was. All I could think about was my diary and the eleven days that had passed since I should have got my period.

When Oliver opened the fridge in his office and pulled out a bottle of my favourite wine my stomach dropped. 'A drink will help you relax. You pour.' He placed the bottle and glass in front of me, looking gorgeously handsome and relaxed, but I just felt sick.

Looking at the wine, I chewed on my lower lip. Shit. How was I going to get around this? Maybe I could just avoid drinking tonight until I could get my hands on a pregnancy test tomorrow.

'Actually, I'm fine, thanks. I … uh … I … went for a run earlier, so I think I'll stick to water.' This was, of course, a complete lie, but as I stood up and walked towards the sink in the corner I prayed it sounded convincing.

Unfortunately, I didn't quite make it to the sink, because as I passed him, Oliver reached out and snagged my wrist, pulling me around to face him. He was frowning, and I immediately knew that he'd seen straight through my lie. Damn it, how did he always manage to do

369

this?

'Hey, I know you're a little nervous, but you're safe with me.'

I looked at his concerned face, and wanted to burst into tears. 'I know that.' I assured him, hoping I could pass off my turning down a drink without any further questions.

He gave me a long, searching look and frowned. 'It's not that, it is? What's wrong, Robyn?'

As I gazed up at his concerned stare I tried to work out what the hell I could say. I could lie and pretend that that it was just nerves about being back at the club, but Oliver had always been able to see through me so easily. Even as I considered lying, I knew I couldn't. I was eleven days late, so it seemed that there was really only one direction I could take. The truth.

'There's something I need to tell you.' I swallowed, dreading this conversation for so many reasons. Would he want the baby and offer to stay with me? Or would he see a child ruining his Dom lifestyle and break up with me? I really had no idea.

At my words, Oliver stood up and walked to the sink to get me the glass of water I'd mentioned. I decided to blurt it out while his back was turned and I wasn't making eye contact.

'I … I think I might be pregnant.'

At first, Oliver didn't outwardly respond. His body remained rigid, still facing away from me with his broad shoulders squared off, and neck tilted to one side like he was trying, but failing to absorb my words. I couldn't blame him for being shocked, because I was still struggling to come to terms with it myself.

Finally, he placed the glass down, and turned on the spot, his movement so tense he almost seemed to be moving in slow motion. Once his eyes met mine I felt my stomach drop to the floor, because there was no emotion in them whatsoever. Not shock, not happiness, not anger ... nothing. It was the closed-off expression I'd seen him use on other people throughout our time together, but I had hardly ever been on the receiving end of it. I was now, though, and it chilled me to the bone.

When he spoke, his voice was low and gruff, and the words were the last I could ever have imagined. 'Is it mine?'

My mouth dropped open in shock. Had I heard him correctly? *Was it his?* Had he really just asked that? I could barely compute his statement, and instead of saying anything, I stood there with my jaw slack and eyes wide. Did Oliver honestly believe that I would cheat on him? We might not have had a run of the mill start to our relationship, but since becoming exclusive we'd been so strong together.

I knew this wasn't exactly planned, so I'd expected him to be a bit shocked, but after seeing how great he'd been with his nieces and nephews in Barcelona I'd thought he might be happy, or at least not horrified.

Obviously, I was wrong.

I was so distracted by my thoughts that I barely registered the sound of movement behind me, but just as consternation rose in my system prompting me to give him a piece of my mind, I was silenced by Alexandra sputtering behind me.

'Pregnant? What a cunning little bitch! She's trying to trap you, Oliver. I told you she was no different to Abi.'

I had no idea what the hell this had to do with his ex, but it was obvious just how gleeful Alex was at our heated conversation. Not only was she speaking as if I wasn't even in the room, but the smug cow was only just managing to suppress her delighted grin.

'Get out, Alex!' Oliver spat. Alex fired back another snarky contribution before leaving the room, but my mind was numb and tuned out her words. I think I was slipping into shock. I needed to get away and try to clear my mind.

The rapid clicking of Alex's heels disappearing down the corridor was the only sound around us for several seconds as Oliver and I simply stared at each other, the weight of a thousand unsaid words seeming to settle on my shoulders. I was so astonished by his reaction that I couldn't speak. And even if I could, I wouldn't know what to say.

How could he doubt me like this?

I turned numbly on the spot and barely made it out of his office door before my tears started falling. When they came, they flooded down my cheeks and began dropping off my jaw and nose and rapidly soaking the front of my shirt.

I made it to the end of the corridor, but unfortunately as I reached the door that led to the club my fingers were trembling too badly to enter the damn code into the key pad, and I ended up pitifully resting my forehead against the door as I tried to bring my weeping under control.

I was too absorbed in my overwhelming emotions to hear the striding footsteps approaching, but suddenly I felt the air shift just behind me a second before hands landed on either side of me, effectively boxing me in.

'You didn't answer my question, Robyn. Is it mine?' Oliver's voice was as icy and unrecognisable as it had been earlier, and I still couldn't understand where this side of him was coming from. Where was his Spanish warmth now? Where was the passionate, caring man I'd fallen for?

I felt as if my life were falling apart chunk by hopeless chunk, and I couldn't for the life of me think what to do about it.

'Look at me, turn around,' he demanded in the low tone reserved for his dominant side when we were playing in a scene. This was turning into a scene all right, but a dramatic one, rather than a sexual one.

I raised my head from the doorframe and saw my sorry reflection in the central glass window; my nose was red

372

from crying, my cheeks tear-stained, and my eyes were unattractively bloodshot.

Letting out a long, slow breath, I followed his command, turning in the box of his arms, and reluctantly raised my eyes to his.

Oliver's face was still eerily blank, his eyes showing no emotion at all, but as he took in my pitiful expression, no doubt with dripping nose and running make-up, his brows flinched slightly. It was the first trace of emotion I'd seen since all this had begun. I still couldn't believe he'd asked me if it was his. Didn't he have any inclination how serious I was about him?

'Are you going to answer me?' he asked again.

I knew that by avoiding his request I probably made myself seem guilty, but I simply wasn't willing to give any credence to his appalling insinuations.

Looking him directly in the eye, I absorbed a final image of his beautiful features and shook my head. 'Actually, I think you've said quite enough for both of us. Goodbye, Oliver.'

I don't know what had prompted his lack of faith in me, but it seemed to have fired up my sudden bravery. My tears had stopped, and I tipped my jaw upwards in determination before finally succeeded in turning and typing in the code required to grant my escape.

The door opened with a gentle push, and I gave Oliver a final, fleeting look, seeing open shock on his expression as I took a deep breath and walked away from him.

My steps were a little wobbly. As I headed for the dance floor I heard a huge smashing sound and an almighty roar from behind me, and turned just in time to catch a glimpse of Oliver overturning a stack of chairs in the corridor then throwing his head back with the force of his scream.

Wow. I had no idea what had just happened in the last ten minutes, or why he seemed so infuriated, but with one more shuddered breath, I continued to walk away.

I was halfway towards the main entrance when I spotted Alex coming towards me from behind the bar. She had a bottle of Oliver's favoured whisky in one hand, and two glasses in the other. 'Goodbye, Robyn,' she sneered as she strutted past me in the direction I had just come from. I was amazed that she had refrained from adding the "good riddance" which had been so obvious in her tone.

I could do with a stiff drink myself, but seeing as I was almost certainly pregnant, it looked like that was off the cards for a fair few months. It was obviously Alex's intention, though; snuggle up to Oliver in his time of need with a dram or two of his favourite tipple. The bitch. I bet she'd just been waiting for something like this to happen so she could leap in and be his saviour.

Images of them sharing a drink together, and her touching him and comforting him, flooded my mind and I had to swallow hard and push the painful visions aside.

Part of me had desperately wanted Oliver to come after me; reach for me and pull me into his arms, or perhaps call out and apologise for his bizarre behaviour, but my hurt, shrinking heart was oddly glad that he didn't. If his reaction to my pregnancy was anything to go by, then I was better off on my own. Alex could have him.

## Chapter Forty-nine

### Robyn

I hadn't thought it was possible, but in the days that followed my disastrous confession to Oliver, things got even more screwed up.

On my way home from the club I got a double pack of pregnancy tests, the first of which was negative. So, with Sasha as my sidekick, I did the second test, which, confusingly, was also negative. We decided that perhaps they were a faulty batch, but I didn't see the point in getting more; I was pregnant, I had to be.

Chloe was away with work, and Sasha was supposed to be heading to see her brother for a few days that night, but was reluctant to leave me alone with all that was going on. Space could be good for me, though, so I shoved her out the door, and tried to distract myself from my problems by doing some writing.

About two hours later, my certainty on the fact that I was pregnant was suddenly shattered, as I was sat staring uselessly at my laptop and felt a tell-tale moisture between my legs, which indicated that my much-delayed period had just arrived.

A trip to the toilet confirmed this, and as I sat there shaking my head in disbelief I finally gave in to the tears that I'd been holding in since leaving Oliver at Club Twist. This type of late period had happened to me on one occasion in the past, when I was super-stressed. Perhaps the strain of trying to finish the book had caused the initial delay, and the abduction had been the cherry on the cake, affecting my cycle way more than I had realised.

I couldn't believe the timing. If I had got it just a few hours earlier, then none of this would have happened. I'd probably be sharing a drink with Oliver at the club now, or perhaps heading back here for a night of snuggling. I wasn't a huge fan of period sex, but in our time together Oliver had proven that he knew plenty of other fun ways we could fill a night in bed together when I was on my monthly cycle.

But that wasn't the case, it had happened, and over the next three days I well and truly wallowed in my upset in the oppressively silent flat by myself. I didn't hear from Oliver, and nor did I contact him. I felt completely strung out, which was partly hormonal, but mostly because of my shattered relationship with him. He'd come to mean so much to me over our time together, and I was really struggling to comprehend the fact that he was no longer going to be a part of my life.

When she returned the next evening, Sasha dumped her bag down on the living room floor and gave me an assessing gaze as if trying to work out if I was just as fragile as I had been when she had left.

I was, and from the consoling grimace on her face, she could clearly see it.

In the end she went for her trademark flippancy in an attempt at cheering me up, which was just as well, because sympathy would probably have made me cry.

'God, you look like shit, babe. Shame we can't cheer you up with wine, eh?' she grumbled, pouring herself a glass and flopping onto the sofa.

Silently getting up, I went to the kitchen to retrieve a glass then went to Sasha's side and held it out to her. 'I got my period.'

Her eyes popped out on stalks as she stared at me for a second, then hurriedly poured me a glass of red. 'Shit! You're not pregnant?'

I took a swig and jerkily shook my head. 'Nope. Never was. The tests were right. *Neg-a-tive*. I came on just after you left.'

'Wow.'

Yes, wow indeed. Talk about a shitty turn of circumstances. 'I'd been pretty worked up about finishing my book, and then with all the Dominic shit ... I guess stress just delayed it.'

Sasha took a healthy glug of her wine, and nodded solemnly. 'Yeah. That would make sense. That's happened to me before. When I was doing my dissertation, I was nearly three weeks late, and I'd been seeing four different guys at the time, so I was crapping myself!' she revealed in her typically over the top style. Sitting a little closer, she chewed on her lower lip. 'So this is pretty dramatic. What does it all mean?'

I took another large gulp of my wine, and shrugged. 'I guess it means I chucked away my relationship with Oliver over nothing, but that I got to see his true colours in the process.'

'Hmm. He must have had his reasons for his reaction ... Have you spoken to him? Has he called?' Sasha eyed me over the rim of her wine glass.

'I haven't called him.' I shrugged and fiddled with the sleeve of my jumper in an attempt to avoid eye contact with her. 'And I dunno if he's called me.'

Sighing heavily, she gave me a heavy stare. 'Can I take that to mean you still have your phone switched off?'

'So what if it is turned off?' I huffed. 'Even if he has been calling I don't want to speak to him.' Well, I sort of did. It might only be five days since I'd seen him, but I missed Oliver terribly. He'd become such a huge part of my life that the sudden departure of his all-consuming presence, his texts and phone calls, had been incredibly noticeable. "Noticeable" was such an understatement, though, because it was so much more than that – every time I allowed myself to think about Oliver it felt like I had a ragged, gaping hole in my heart.

Trying to push aside my pain, I shook my head. 'Just leave it, Sasha, I don't want to talk about him.' Then I gave up my pretence and chucked a pillow at her.

'Hey! Woah! Watch the vino!' she squawked, holding her wine aloft to avoid the cushion. She placed her glass on the coffee table, and, after giving me a shifty glance, she swooped forwards and scooped up my phone from the table.

'Oi! Give it back!' I lurched at her, scrabbling to get my phone back, but I was interrupted from my mission by the chiming of the doorbell behind me. 'Have the bloody thing, then. You don't know my PIN-code anyway,' I grumbled, walking to the door and checking the peephole to see a delivery guy outside, before I pulled it open.

'Package for Miss Scott?'

'Oh. That's me.' It seemed a strange time of night for a delivery, but I signed the electronic pad and took the packet before locking the door behind me and heading back to the sofa.

'You have twenty-six new text messages and sixty-three missed calls! Sixty-three!' Sasha informed me in shock, thrusting my phone at me and wiggling it in my face. 'I can't unlock it to see who they're from, but I reckon I can make an educated guess. I think Oliver wants to apologise.'

Sixty-three missed calls? Wow. It had been over five days since I'd seen him, but still, sixty-three calls was a hell of a lot.

'Maybe he should have thought of that before he went all ice-man on me,' I muttered, slipping a finger under the seal of the cardboard packet that had just been delivered.

I ripped it open with a flourish, taking out some of my pent-up frustration on the cardboard. The noise distracted Sasha from looking at my phone, and instead she looked at the package curiously. 'Ooh, what is it?'

Tipping the contents out, I found a small silver iPod, some pale pink headphones, and a folded piece of paper. Without even reading the note I intuitively knew who it was from, and my stomach clenched. My fingers were already trembling as I picked up the paper, but as soon as I saw Oliver's elegant handwriting on the note it turned to a full-on shake.

'It's from him,' I whispered, my voice quivering so badly that Sasha immediately shifted and sat next to me, placing a consoling hand on my arm.

Taking in a deep breath, I opened the note and read.

*Robyn,*

*I cannot express in words how sorry I am for my behaviour. Please believe me when I say I had my reasons for my words,* cariño, *which I wish to share with you. Please meet me so we can talk?*

*In the meantime, accept this iPod. I had been putting together a playlist for you of all the songs I found relevant to our relationship. I was planning on giving it to you on your birthday, but seeing as I screwed up so monumentally, I have finished it off so that I could give it to you now.*

*I hope it helps you understand the depth of what I feel for you, even if I can't vocalise it myself. The lyrics in these tracks express what I haven't been strong enough to.*

*Yours always, Oliver*

*P.S. It makes me very uncomfortable not being able to get in touch with you. Please turn your phone on.*

I stared at the note for a good few minutes, reading and rereading its contents. Unconsciously, I was also tracing the text with my finger, almost caressing it.

'Wow. Heavy stuff,' Sasha breathed, leaning over my shoulder to read the note. 'What does *cariño* mean?'

I swallowed hard. Even thinking about him saying the affectionate term made me want to cry. 'It's Spanish,' I croaked, having to clear my throat before continuing. 'It sort of translates to sweetheart. He calls me it all the time.' I carefully folded the paper and put it on the table before correcting myself. 'Or at least he did.'

Picking up the iPod, I stared down at it, stroking my finger gently over the small metallic square as I imagined Oliver holding it and packing it into the envelope. Sasha gave my shoulder a squeeze, and stood up. 'I'll give you some privacy.'

Giving her an appreciative nod, I popped the soft earbuds into my ears. With slightly trembling fingers I turned the device on and found just one single playlist listed in the memory, titled *Mi dulce pequeño petirrojo.*

Frowning, I wondered what it meant, then suddenly recalled our time in Barcelona and the name his mother had called me – *dulce pequeño petirrojo*, or "sweet little robin" – and Oliver's adaption, where he'd said, "my sweet little robin". My throat was instantly thick with emotion at the sweet title, but I tried to swallow it down and pressed play.

Oliver had mentioned the importance of the lyrics, so I closed my eyes and listened as various artists sung about passion, soulmates, and togetherness.

As the songs rolled from one to another, my chest felt tight, and tears built in my eyes, but when Jack Johnson started singing *Better Together* and saying how love was the answer, my tears finally started to fall. It was true, Oliver and I *had* been better together.

But could love be the answer?

I knew I loved him, but he'd never said it to me. Was that what he was trying to express to me with these songs?

*Better Together*. It hurt to listen to it, but it might be one of my favourite songs now. Without Oliver I didn't feel whole any more, but he was gone, and I just couldn't see how I could get over my hurt and take him back.

# Chapter Fifty

## Robyn

'Morning, babe,' Sasha cooed as she strolled past me, leafing through some post. 'I was just coming to get you. There's another delivery for you in the hall.'

Another delivery? 'From Oliver?' I croaked, my grip tightening on the iPod in my hand. I still had one earbud in now as I listened to the playlist again. In fact, I'd not taken it off as I'd slept last night, and had only briefly removed it when I'd showered five minutes ago. At this rate, it would need charging soon, but if I didn't relax my fist I was going to crush the poor thing before it had chance to run out of battery power.

'Yeah, I think so,' Sasha replied vaguely, seemingly absorbed in the letter she was examining.

God. I'd barely come to terms with the selection of songs on the iPod and what they represented. I wasn't sure I could deal with anything else yet. 'Didn't you bring it in?'

'Nah, it's big. Needs your signature.'

Normally the arrival of a large package would fill me with childlike excitement, but in the last week I'd really struggled to garner much enthusiasm for anything. What with the Dominic shite, then finishing with Oliver, it had been a hell of a rollercoaster. Sighing heavily, I walked over to the door.

Stepping out, I frowned when I found the hallway empty, but then nearly jumped out of my socks as I registered a dark shape in the periphery of my vision, down to my left-hand side.

My panicked imagination briefly conjured images of Dominic, here to finish what he had started, but no, as my dizzying panic passed, I registered that it was, in fact, Oliver, sitting against the wall, his knees bent, arms wrapped around his legs and head hanging forwards. At least it was, until he realised I stood there gawking at him, and he leaped to his feet in record speed.

'Robyn! Thank you so much for agreeing to see me.'

'I didn't,' I replied, all the while cursing Sasha. Delivery my arse. Shit. He was really here, right before me, and although I couldn't deny that his appearance was much more preferable than that of Dominic, I wasn't ready for this.

My wary eyes travelled up his frame, then up some more. Somehow, over our five-day absence, I'd forgotten how tall Oliver was. I began backing away into the flat to get me some space, but a sudden shove in my lower spine had me falling forwards into the hallway again. Spinning on the spot, I found Sasha, also known as the phantom pusher, who gave me a rueful look.

'Just give him two minutes, OK?' Sasha implored, before promptly closing the door on me.

'Hey!' I slammed my fist on it, but the catch had slipped into place, and the door wasn't budging an inch. She was supposed to be my best friend, the bloody traitor! I couldn't believe she'd done this.

'Robyn, please can we talk?' Oliver's pleading tone broke through my irritation at Sasha, and, after a calming breath, I reluctantly swivelled and faced him.

Oliver tried to step closer and touch me, so I sidestepped him and leaned on the opposite wall, crossing my arms defensively across my chest and shaking my head, hoping that I'd made my need for distance obvious.

He let out a heavy sigh, but nodded his understanding, then shoved his hands into his trouser pockets as if that was the only way he'd manage to keep his hands from reaching for me.

'I don't think we have anything to talk about, Oliver. You made it perfectly clear that you don't trust me, and as far as I'm concerned, without trust, a relationship is

382

worthless.'

Oliver ran a hand through his hair in agitation, leaving half of it tumbling across his brow and the other half in a messy mop on the top of his head. Narrowing my eyes, I realised that he looked far more unkempt than usual; scruffy stubble covered his chin, his shirt was partly untucked, and his suit was crumpled, as if he'd slept in it. Come to think of it, I was pretty sure that was the same navy pinstripe he'd been wearing days ago when we'd had our argument, so maybe he *had* been sleeping in it.

'I completely agree, but you need to know that I do trust you, Robyn, more so than you can know.'

A dismissive noise rose in my throat as I recalled his cold, hurtful words from the other day – *is it mine?* – and I shook my head as my eyes fluttered shut.

'I know I said some hideously hurtful things, but before you send me away, I at least want you to understand why. Please, just give me five minutes?'

The sudden appearance of Oliver on my doorstep finally caught up with me, and I found myself completely unable to reply. A dizzying amount of conflicting emotions were spinning in my brain, and I felt sick as I pressed a hand against the wall behind me to try to steady myself.

As I tried to sieve through all of the chaos in my scrambled mind, one thing leaped out at me as being important, so I quickly blurted it out. 'There's no baby, Oliver. I was wrong. I got my period on Friday night, so you don't have to pretend to be chivalrous and support me.'

He didn't flinch at my words. Instead, there seemed to be a shadow of disappointment on his features as he nodded slowly. 'I know, Sasha just told me, but that's not why I've come here today. I don't have to pretend with you, Robyn, not about anything.'

What could I say to that? I had no idea where all this was heading, but I tried to stay resolute, remembering how upset I'd been in his office when I'd walked away from him nearly a week ago.

Oliver lowered his dark eyes to my clenched fist, and I watched his gaze soften slightly as he realised it was the iPod that I was clutching.

'Does this mean you liked my gift?' he asked quietly, and as I became aware of the soft music still playing in one of my ears a small dry sob caught in my throat. 'That's the reason I haven't come around to see you sooner. I suspected you wouldn't agree to see me, so I wanted to finish off the playlist so at least you would have some understanding of how I feel about you.' He paused, taking a small step closer to me that made my breath catch in my throat. 'Did it work? Do you know how I feel, *cariño?*'

He cared for me a great deal, that much was clear from the deep, expressive lyrics, but that hardly compared to the all-consuming love I felt for him. In the end, I shrugged, but didn't reply.

Oliver placed one finger on my chin and gently tipped my face up so our gaze met. The denim blue of his eyes seemed to be swirling with emotion, and with the capturing intensity of his stare there was no way I could look away. 'Pregnant or not, I love you, Robyn.'

Oh God. Now he'd gone and said it. Just as his eyes were imploring me to believe him, my legs suddenly failed me, my knees buckling as I started to slide down the wall.

'Woah!' Oliver didn't let me get far, and smoothly scooped me into his arms to cradle me against his chest. It felt so reassuring to be back in his arms, so *right*, that it seemed pointless to struggle, so I didn't. I simply let my body go lax in his strong grip.

'Can I take you inside?' he whispered above me.

With a heavy sigh, I nodded my head once.

As if by magic, the door to the flat opened as we approached, and Sasha, my traitorous bestie, who had obviously been watching us through the spyhole, pulled it wide open with a flourish.

Slamming her hands on her hips, she raised her eyebrows and glared at Oliver. 'I've helped you out way more than you deserve, mister, so be warned, you hurt her again, and I'll kill you.' She jabbed him in the biceps with one pointed finger, and winked at me before disappearing towards the lounge.

'That's me told,' Oliver murmured as he adjusted me in his arms.

With Sasha now draped across a sofa, we didn't have many locations left for a private talk, and so, without saying a word, Oliver strode with purpose towards my bedroom. I suspected this had been Sasha's intention all along. I wasn't sure I was quite ready to be alone with him in such a personal space, but we did need privacy for this discussion.

I still couldn't quite face all that was happening here, so, instead of trying to deal with it yet, I shut my eyes and turned my face into his collar. Even if this turned out to be the last time I saw him, at least I'd be able to remember how he smelled, looked and felt.

'I wouldn't breathe too deeply. I haven't been home since I last saw you, so I haven't changed my clothes. They probably reek.'

My mind was suddenly filled with images of Alex sashaying towards Oliver's office as I left over five days ago, and for an awful second, I wondered if he'd been staying with her. 'Where have you been, then?'

Oliver kicked my bedroom door shut and gently placed me on the bed. He helped me remove the iPod which had got tangled between us, before standing back and raising an eyebrow at me in apparent amusement.

'From your tone, I take it you think I was with someone else, which I was not.' He undid his tie and threw it onto my dressing table before standing back and sliding his hands into his trouser pockets. 'I didn't want to go home and face a dressing down from *Tía* for screwing things up with you, so I've been sleeping at my office in the club,' he admitted. I almost laughed at his rueful expression and words, because the sight of a grown man worrying about what his aunt thought was really quite amusing. 'There are showers at the club, but unfortunately I didn't have any spare clothes in my office, so I've been wearing these all week. They're disgusting.

'I was on my own,' he added, apparently seeing something in my expression. 'Once you left, I debated chasing after you, but I knew I'd messed up badly and so decided to give you some time to cool off while I worked out how I could try and make amends.'

'I know Alex came to your office with your favourite whiskey,' I murmured, hating how needy I sounded, not to mention hypocritical – this whole issue was because I didn't think he trusted me, and now here I was doubting him. God, what a mess.

'She did,' he agreed with a nod. 'I kept the whiskey, but I sent her away.' He tilted his head to the side, observing me and giving me time to think. 'If you stop for a second to consider it, you know I'd never cheat on you, Robyn. Just as I know you would never cheat on me. It's instinctive, we're meant to be together. No one else can compare.'

I drew in a sharp breath at the complete conviction in his voice. He wasn't putting it out there as a possibility – he was stating facts.

Oliver lifted a hand to his chin and rubbed at the rough stubble there before giving me an imploring look. 'When I asked if the baby was mine, it was a knee-jerk reaction. I trust you implicitly, I do. I honestly wasn't thinking straight …'

I sat myself upright on the bed and wrapped my arms around my knees. 'But why? You say you trust me, but then why was that your initial reaction? I don't

386

understand.'

And I really didn't. Apparently, he not only trusted me, but loved me too. I still hadn't even begun to try and process that little nugget of information, but if that was the case, how could he have been so hurtful?

Oliver dropped his head for a second, took several deep breaths, and raised his eyes to mine again, but this time his deep blue pupils almost looked black. 'Because it's happened to me before.'

My eyebrows flew up in surprise, then I frowned, remembering Alex's words in his office, where she'd said I was a cunning bitch, just like Abi. Was that who he was talking about?

'You might recall I told you that I stopped dating after my relationship with Abi?' he murmured, sinking down onto the stool by my dressing table.

It looked like my suspicion was correct. This was about Abi. I nodded but, not knowing what else to say, I remained quiet.

'She was the first girl I'd developed real feelings for. In hindsight, I now know that it wasn't love, but at the time it felt quite potent.' He sat back, avoiding eye contact with me as if he were lost in a world of his own. 'We'd been together nearly a year when she told me she was pregnant. We'd always used contraception, so as you can imagine, it came as quite a surprise.' His eyes closed, and I saw his teeth clench and a muscle jump along his jaw. 'It wasn't ideal, we were both still quite young, but I told her I'd stand by her, support both her and the child.

'Abi suggested we got married, and seeing as I liked her and was already earning significantly more than her, it seemed a good solution.' Oliver drew in a long breath and raised his gaze to meet mine. 'We were engaged and had set up joint bank accounts by the time I found out that she'd been cheating on me all along and that the baby probably wasn't mine.' He let out a humourless bark of laughter, and shook his head in disgust. 'I'd never suspected a thing.'

Holy shit! My mouth dropped open in surprise, but I could see Oliver wasn't finished with his tale yet.

'Predictably, we argued. I confronted her about the other man, and she finally confessed that she was in love with him, and that they hadn't used protection, which was why she thought the baby was his.' He stopped to pull in a shuddering breath then continued. 'He was a dropout who wouldn't ever be able to provide for her and the child, so she'd decided to marry me instead. The safer option.' He shook his head again, presumably with the revulsion that I also felt. 'I threw her out, and about an hour later, she emptied out the joint bank accounts and has never been seen since.'

It was like a film script. It was so dramatic I could barely take it in. He'd lost his girlfriend, the potential of becoming a father, and all his money in one day?

Wow. No wonder he had given up on dating. And who the hell could simply see Oliver as "the safer option"? He was gorgeous, caring, confident and powerful ... He was everything I looked for in a man and more. There was no way he could be seen as a second choice.

'I got a letter a year later. It had a print-out of a DNA test in it that proved the baby wasn't mine. No apology, though, and no return of the thousands of pounds she'd stolen from me.' Oliver shrugged and let out a long breath as if finally letting go of his painful memories. 'So there you have it. I got royally fucked over by a woman and that's the real reason I haven't dated since.'

A tense silence hung between us, and as much as I knew I should probably say something to console him, I could hardly work out where to start. 'Oliver ... I ... I would never do that to you,' I stated with complete and utter conviction.

Oliver stood and moved across the room so swiftly that

I hardly saw him coming, but as soon as he reached the side of the bed he dropped to his knees and took hold of my hands. 'I know. Please, you don't need to say it, Robyn.'

'I could never cheat, you're too important to me,' I whispered, and as I spoke I realised I was talking as if we were still together, whereas in reality, I had no clue where things now stood between us.

He let out a low groan, and lowered his lips to kiss my knuckles. 'I can never apologise enough for my reaction when you said you were pregnant, I ... I wasn't thinking. It was a stupid response triggered by my weaknesses from the past, but believe me, I do trust you. I trust you with my life. I'm just hoping I can persuade you to let me back into yours?'

He'd hurt me with his words last week, but in reality, I now knew that his shock had been born from his own painful past. Could I let him back in? Try again?

As I was debating this, Oliver stood up. He still had hold of my hands, and after giving them a squeeze he gently laid them on my lap. 'I tell you what, why don't I give you some time to think this over?'

My reaction to his words was immediate, and I found myself sitting up abruptly. 'No! Don't go!' I had no clue how we were going to proceed, but I knew one thing; I didn't want him to go.

Oliver's face softened into a hopeful smile at my reaction, and he nodded once. 'I wasn't going. Now you've let me inside you'll need to prise me out of here with a crowbar,' he quipped. 'I just thought maybe I could jump in your shower to freshen up, give you a few minutes' quiet time.'

'Oh. OK.'

Bending forwards, he placed a brief kiss on the top of my head, then headed into the bathroom without looking back.

As soon as I heard the door click shut I collapsed backwards, the soft pillows engulfing me as if sensing the fact that I needed cocooning and comforting for a few moments, which I definitely did.

So what would happen now? Should we just carry on like we were before? Now that I knew the cause for his cold response and understood why he had reacted that way, I supposed there was nothing stopping us getting back together. He'd certainly been very remorseful about his behaviour. There was no baby to consider, I loved him, he'd said he loved me, and things between us had been incredible up until last week, so I'd have to be crazy to walk away from it.

Feeling my muscles relax for the first time in days, I enjoyed a moment of silence, then became very aware of the sound of running water coming from the shower. That meant Oliver was now naked in my bathroom.

Naked and wet.

Visions of his gorgeous body sprung to my mind: corded muscles; the smattering of hair on his chest; the infamous V that led from his belly down towards his deliciously perfect cock … A very loud swallow forced its way down my throat. I sat up, biting on my lower lip as I considered the option of going in there and joining him. After all, my period had finished now, and he hadn't locked the door, so he'd practically invited me.

Before I'd had time to climb from the bed, there was a soft noise at my door, followed by Sasha pushing her way in without any prior warning.

'Seriously, Sasha, you really need to knock before you barge in!' I exclaimed in exasperation with a roll of my eyes.

Sasha glanced around the room, then stepped in with a coffee pot in one hand and two mugs in the other. 'Nah. There's more possibility of seeing something juicy if I don't knock,' she replied cheerily, clearly not caring one bit. Looking towards the closed bathroom door, she placed the coffee down and turned to me. 'So, you guys haven't killed each other yet then?'

Shaking my head, I gave a wistful sigh and smiled. 'No. I don't think we will be, either.'

'Given that lusty look in your eye, I'd say you might be doing something else to each other in the not-so-distant future, though.' Sasha giggled. 'Probably just as well that I came in now and not in ten minutes, eh?'

My cheeks bloomed with heat, but I avoided too much embarrassment by standing up and shoving her back in the direction of the door. 'Yes, especially seeing as you never bloody knock!'

'I did the right thing getting you to talk with him though, didn't I?' she asked, her expression sobering for a second or two.

I nodded, a soft smile pulling at my lips. 'Yeah, you did. Thanks.'

She let out a relieved breath and smiled. 'OK, good. I'm glad you're working things out.'

'We are.'

'Don't go too easy on him, Rob. Make sure he knows what he did.' She had a point there. I'd been ready to leap in the shower and attack Oliver, but perhaps I should make him work for it just a little more.

Now that our touching moment was over, I began wrestling my bestie through the door again. As I succeeded in getting her into the corridor, she turned back to me with a grin. 'I'm off to my spinning class, so don't worry, there won't be any more interruptions from me, but I want full details later.'

'Yeah, yeah, just bugger off, would you!'

'I'm gone,' she replied with a wink before skipping off down the corridor giggling to herself.

Shutting the bedroom door behind her, I smiled to myself as I turned the lock, just in case she did decide to pop back, and turned back just as the bathroom door opened.

To my surprise, Oliver emerged with nothing more than a skimpy towel around his waist and a few droplets of water flowing over his skin.

'Jesus, Oliver. Where are your clothes?' His hair was damp and ruffled from a quick towel dry, and the light covering of hair on his chest was still flattened from the shower jets.

Oliver glanced down at his body, then slowly raised his head until he was looking up at me through his lowered brows with a wicked glint in his eye.

Oh, that was a dangerous expression.

It was also one of my favourites, which he knew, only too well. 'Am I distracting you?'

'Yes!' I spluttered, not sure where to look, but finding my eyes increasingly drawn to the flimsy bit of material covering his groin. Had he deliberately picked the smallest towel I owned?

Judging from the barely suppressed grin now gracing his face, yes, he had.

'My clothes are filthy. I couldn't face putting them back on,' he explained with a jerk of one shoulder. 'Besides, you've seen me naked plenty of times before.'

I huffed out a breath, well aware that I was close to losing this pointless battle and giving in to him. 'I know that. But I'm supposed to be angry with you.'

At my words, Oliver dropped his cocky expression, and stepped towards me with an expectant look on his bloody gorgeous face. 'You said "supposed to be angry with me". Does that mean you're not quite so angry any more?'

I pulled in a deep breath and looked into his beseeching eyes. I loved him so much it made my chest hurt. How could I stay mad at him?

'Not as much, no,' I conceded softly.

Oliver raised his hands and gently cupped my jaw, his

thumbs rubbing soothing circles on my cheeks. Hunkering down, he brought his face in line with mine, as if needing our eyes even closer so he could enforce the importance of this moment. 'I swear on my life I shall not let you down like that ever again, Robyn.' My eyes fluttered shut at the determination in his voice. 'Do you think perhaps you could forgive me?'

I nodded, then copied his action by stroking his cheek with my thumb, loving the feel of the rough stubble against my skin. 'Yes.'

With a groan that was suspiciously close to a growl, Oliver swept me into his arms and carried me to the bed, laying me across the sheets with the utmost care before lowering his lips to mine.

Given how careful he'd been with placing me down, I'd been expecting an equally soft kiss, so I sucked in a shocked breath when Oliver pinned my hands above my head and slammed his lips down upon mine in a kiss so hot, needy, and passionate that it had my heart rate soaring.

Wow. Perhaps this was his version of make-up sex. If it was, it was *hot*, because I loved feeling this needed by him.

Suddenly, he dragged his lips from mine and stared down at me. 'Do you still have your period? It doesn't bother me, but if you'd rather I delay this I will happily just hold you.'

'It's finished, don't stop,' I breathed, thankful that my four-day cycle hadn't lengthened just because I'd been so late.

His eyes flared with lust at my answer and he lowered his lips to mine again. His mouth moved against mine and our tongues tangled, and he adjusted his grip so that one of his hands held both of mine. He clawed at my clothes with his other. After trying and failing to remove my vest top, he ripped his mouth from mine with a growl, and stared down at me with eyes that were alight with desire and intent. Just one look at his blazing expression and I immediately knew that he was a man on a mission.

'Clothes off,' he growled, leaning above me so our noses were almost, but not quite touching. 'I'm just going to get something, but when I come back I want you naked on the bed with your legs spread.'

I gasped at his command, and in return Oliver grinned wickedly. 'I want the perfect view of your perfect pussy when I come back from the bathroom, I want to see exactly how much you want me. Understand?'

Holy fuck, this was hot. I loved it when he took charge like this, and his dirty words made my arousal soar to dizzying heights. I gulped in some much-needed air, and nodded. 'Yes, Sir.'

Oliver's nostrils flared at my use of his title, and he nodded once before glancing at his watch. 'You have one minute.' He strode into the bathroom and I scrabbled to my knees and tugged at my vest top. With his words still hanging heavy in the air I undressed at record speed before throwing aside my slight embarrassment and positioning myself exactly as he had requested.

# Chapter Fifty-one

## Oliver

I took several deep breaths and looked at my reflection in the bathroom mirror. My cheeks were flushed, eyes dilated, and hair a mess from my shower. I couldn't miss the smugness that rose on my features as I heard the faint sounds of Robyn scrabbling around in the bedroom, following my instructions, but then the arrogance dropped away as it properly dawned on me how lucky I was to be standing here.

After my cruel words last Friday, I was surprised that she was even speaking to me, let alone allowing me back into her life. I didn't deserve it, but my beautiful, sweet girl had given me a second chance. My head dropped forwards, chin touching my chest as I drew in several shallow breaths and tried to absorb how fortunate I was.

My earlier declaration of love hadn't been an attempt to console her, or cajole her into taking me back. It was God's honest truth. I loved her. I loved her so much my chest constricted at the thought that she might well have walked away from me because of my stupidity.

I loved her, body and soul, and I would spend the rest of my life proving it to her. I wanted her as my wife, and if we were lucky enough I wanted her to have my babies, too. That much had become crystal clear to me in our time apart, but there was no rush for those things. The most important thing was that we were together.

Lifting my head, I stared at myself in the mirror and reinforced the promise I had just made to Robyn – I would *never* let her down again. Then, feeling determined, I grabbed the thing I'd noticed in her bathroom cabinet earlier and turned to go and claim what was mine.

I was well aware of the instructions that I had given Robyn, but upon entering the bedroom, the sight that met me sucked the air from my lungs and made my dick as hard as concrete.

She was lain exactly as I had requested, but the vision was a thousand times better than I could have prepared myself for. She was propped on a pillow, her hair cascading around her head like a halo. Her arms were draped at her sides, hands lingering on her body, one on her thigh, and the other just below a breast.

I briefly tensed as I saw the faint marks across her torso left from Dominic's whip, but she had healed so well that even those wouldn't be visible soon.

The look on her face was so seductive that I only just managed to hold back my groan; her eyelids were half-closed with lust, so she was looking at me through her thick lashes, and her bottom lip had been drawn between her teeth as she waited expectantly for me to say or do something.

Finally, I trailed my gaze down her body to her legs, which were splayed wide open just as I had requested.

*Dios*, I was such a lucky bastard. Her perfect pink pussy was on full display, and glistening with her arousal, which also seemed to have slicked onto the tops of her thighs. My cock lurched its approval beneath my towel, the material feeling so rough against my sensitive skin that I ripped the cloth away as I growled and advanced towards her.

I couldn't wait to taste her, tease her, and bury myself inside her.

### Robyn

As Oliver stared down at me and took in my position on the bed he looked like his brain was about to explode. If I wasn't so distracted by my arousal, I probably would have laughed at his wide-eyed expression, but I was distracted, and by God I was *so* aroused.

396

So was he, because although he still had the ridiculously tiny towel around his waist, there was no mistaking the large bulge in the front. My eyes lingered on the sight, thrilled that I could affect him so badly. Seeing where my gaze was, he let out an animalistic growl and dragged the towel from his waist and threw it aside.

He was so hard his cock was bobbing up and down from the tension in his muscles, and the image made me bite down harder on my lower lip until I tasted a trace of copper in my mouth.

Just before he reached me, he brought something out from behind his back and chucked it on the bed beside me. Glancing down, I saw the purple shaft of my one and only vibrator, and my eyebrows rose at its appearance in our playtime.

I didn't have time to ask how he'd discovered it in my bathroom cabinet because, at that second, he dropped to his knees at the end of the bed and shoved his face between my legs. There was no warm-up, or gentle caresses; instead, his tongue instantly set about hard, short flicks to my clit which in my already aroused state had me groaning and writhing below him in seconds. His stubble was far longer than usual, the roughness merely adding to the erotic pleasure as he rubbed it mercilessly over my tender skin.

He gripped my thighs, forcing my legs even wider apart until the tips of his fingers went white from the strength of his grip and I could feel my hips complaining. I didn't notice the discomfort for long, though, because as he thrust two fingers inside me and ground them against my G-spot I exploded into a climax so sudden and shattering that I temporarily seemed to lose the feelings in my body.

All I could focus on was where his fingers were planted deep within me, rubbing over and over again as my body continued to jerk and clench in an orgasm so strong it was almost painful.

He'd been almost savage in his attack on me, but my God, it was a beautiful form of savagery, because this was the most erotic experience we'd ever shared.

Oliver licked and sucked at my arousal, cleaning my thighs with his tongue and working me down from my orgasm as I lay there, panting and dizzy. He didn't give me much reprieve, because as soon as my breathing started to settle he shifted onto the bed with me then picked up my vibrator and grinned down at me.

'Naughty, Robyn. Look what I found when I was looking for some shower gel.'

I smiled shyly, embarrassed that he'd found my only sex toy, but judging from the glint in his eye he was rather excited by his discovery.

The vibrator came to life in his hand, buzzing softly as he looked at it, then raised it to trail across my breasts. 'The batteries are strong, so either they're newly replaced, or you don't use this very often. Which is it?'

He circled the soft rubber around one breast and I gasped, my back arching as the vibrations hardened my nipple. 'The second one,' I breathed, my voice high and breathless.

'Have you used it since we've been together?'

'No.' I squirmed as he moved it to my other breast, but Oliver tutted at me and held me still by placing his free hand across my stomach. The inability to move intensified the feeling in my breast, and I had to bite down on my tender lower lip again as sensations started to overwhelm me.

'I'm glad. I rather like the idea of being the only thing to give you pleasure. Seeing as it's me in charge of this for the evening, though, perhaps I'll make an exception and let him join us in some teasing fun.'

He wasn't kidding about the teasing part, either. Oliver set about using the vibrator with ruthless efficiency, trailing over my clit, lips, and circling my core until I was a wet, trembling, writhing mess below his skilled hands. He must have used it on me for well over half an hour, or it could have been longer; my mind was so fogged up with lust and sexual frustration I lost track of time. He brought me to the edge of orgasm countless times, but not once did he let me come. No one touch with the vibrator at my clit was quite long enough, no dip inside against my G-spot quite firm enough.

As I felt my channel once again clenching and desperate to be filled, I gave in and begged. 'Oliver ...please ...'

'What it is, *cariño*?' he whispered, his lips and rough stubble trailing a hot path along the column of my neck and sending goose pimples scattering across my feverish skin.

'Please, Oliver. I can't wait any longer.'

'What is it you need? Tell me, and you may have it.'

'I need to ... to come ... please.'

Oliver hummed against my neck, as if considering my request, and I started to think that I might well cry with frustration if he didn't give me a release soon.

'Seeing as you've done so well, I think we can allow that.'

Oh, thank God!

Oliver knelt up beside me, then palmed his cock with his right hand, running slow, smooth strokes up and down his solid length. What a sight. All that muscle and strength towering over me made my mouth water. Oliver's eyes never left mine, and even though he was touching himself, I got the distinct impression that he was imagining my hands upon him. Or perhaps my lips.

It was such an erotic sight that my body felt even hotter than before, and anticipation coursed through my veins so rampantly that I could barely stay still.

'How would you like to achieve it? With this?' he asked, holding the vibrator out and running it along my quivering stomach. 'Or with this?' He dropped his gaze to his cock and gave another slow pull of his shaft, emphasising how good it felt by sucking in a slow, exaggerated breath between his teeth.

Holy fuck, that was so sexy. With my eyes fixed on his shaft, and the tight fist encompassing it, I swallowed loudly. That was what I wanted. All of it, inside me, right now. I pointed at his cock and licked my lips in anticipation of how it would feel inside me, how good it always felt inside me.

'Tell me properly, Robyn. What is it you want?'

'You …' Oliver raised an eyebrow at my breathy word, silently telling me that he wanted me to say more and describe it properly. 'Your cock … Oliver, please fuck me.'

A filthy grin burst to his face at my words. 'That's my girl.' No sooner were the words out of his mouth, Oliver threw the vibrator aside and pounced on me. Covering me with his hot, hard body, he pinned my hands above my head and stole my breath away with another deep kiss.

Lifting his lips just a fraction, he spoke against my mouth, each word a breathy tickle across my skin. 'You make me so hard, Robyn. You have no idea.'

Actually, I had a pretty good idea how hard I made him, because I could currently feel the steely length of his erection throbbing against my thigh.

'Enough teasing, now. When you next come I want it to be with me.' Then, not wasting another second, he positioned himself between my eager thighs and jerked his hips forwards to bury himself inside my slick entrance.

Even though I was supremely aroused I still cried out as he stretched me, and my noises of agonised pleasure somehow seemed to make him harder, if that was even possible, because he already felt as solid as stone. I felt him swell inside me, the heat from his cock almost burning me from the inside out.

Realising that he liked my mewls and moans, I upped the volume a little, and was rewarded with several even harder, deeper thrusts.

'Oliver … I'm already close.' I'd been so close for the last half an hour as he'd teased me with the vibrator, and my clit felt swollen and sensitive, so if he continued to pound into me like this there was no way I was going to last.

'Me too, *cariño*. Let it go.'

I did. As soon as he had given me permission I released my clenched muscles and, with one more thrust from Oliver that simultaneously hit my clit and my G-spot, I exploded into a climax so powerful that I screamed his name and clawed at his back in an effort to ground myself.

He came, too, roaring out a growl as I felt the first heat of his release inside me. The tightening spasms of my climax seemed to go on for an age, each one prolonged by a thrust of his cock, and shattering me with the strength of the pleasure he gave me.

Finally, we were spent, and he collapsed his weight on top of me. Holy shit. My body was soaked with sweat, muscles aching, and my channel was still clenching around him like a fist even long after my climax had ebbed. That had been some serious make-up sex.

As if wanting to trump his own performance, Oliver went and made it even more special by leaning up and looking down into my eyes and landing me with another heart-meltingly soft confession. 'I meant what I said in the corridor earlier, Robyn. I love you. You have me heart and soul, *cariño*.'

I had always thought it a bit cheesy in films or books where one person professes their love and the other immediately says it back, but seeing as I'd felt it for weeks but never voiced it, I decided to do so now, cheesy or not. I placed my hands over his where they were still cupping my face and gripped his wrists. 'I've never said these words to anyone before, but I love you, too, Oliver.'

And I really did. Our relationship might not have had the most conventional start, and we'd certainly had a few bumps along the way, but we were perfect for each other; he was the Dom to my sub, the hard to my soft, and the piece of me I'd never known was missing. I felt complete now, though, and I knew deep down in my soul that Oliver was right in what he'd said earlier. No one else could ever compete with what we had – we were simply meant to be together.

The End... *for now*.

If you would like to find out more about Oliver and Robyn's continuing relationship, and see if Sasha and Marcus ever take the leap and test out the chemistry between them, then keep your eye out for Book Two in the Club Twist series – A Price to Pay, due out in 2018.

Announcements about this series will also be made on my Facebook page: AliceRaineAuthor/

Or you could sign up to my mailing list: www.aliceraineauthor.com/contact

Thank you so much for reading – any reviews on Amazon or Goodreads are very much appreciated!

## The next books in the series...

Alice Raine is an internationally bestselling author of romance and erotica. Her passion is writing hot, intense stories that drag you in by your shirt cuffs and don't release you until the final page is done. Alice is a fan of a happy-ever-after ending, but be warned, she likes gritty storylines and loves to drop in unexpected twists and cliff-hangers too!

Located just outside of Oxford, Alice lives with her husband and two beloved rescue dogs. She spends her days wandering the countryside with her trusty hounds, or at her laptop lost in the vivid swirls of her wild imagination.

Alice loves chatting to readers, so if you'd like to get in touch, then find Alice at any of the links below:

Facebook: /AliceRaineAuthor/

Twitter: @AliceRaine1

Instagram: @alice_raine_author

Pintrest: alice3083/

Website: www.aliceraineauthor.com